Blind Fear

"Webb & Mann have done it again. *Blind Fear* has it all: great characters, an amazing plot, and an incredible setting. This novel moves like a hurricane!"

—Connor Sullivan,
acclaimed author of *Wolf Trap*

"*Blind Fear* takes off at a breakneck pace and never lets up—you won't be able to turn the pages fast enough!"

—Lisa Black,
New York Times bestselling author of
the Locard Institute series

Praise for previous books in
the Finn X series

"Sensationally good—an instant classic, maybe an instant legend."

—#1 *New York Times* bestselling author
Lee Child

"An absolutely amazing thriller! Exciting, action-packed, and twisty from stem to stern."

—#1 *New York Times* bestselling author
Brad Thor

"Deadly good, a five-star scorcher from first page to last . . . The enigmatic and mysterious Finn is the next big thriller superstar."

—#1 *New York Times* bestselling author
Robert Crais

"An edge-of-your-seat thriller with an original and engaging premise . . . Like speeding down a slalom course, once you get going there's no stopping. This one is not to be missed."

—*New York Times* bestselling author
STEVE BERRY

"Like Lee Child in his Jack Reacher novels, the authors can do more than power a pulse-racing narrative. . . . For readers who can't resist a bureaucracy-battling action hero, there's a new kid on the block."

—*Booklist* (starred review)

"A blockbuster . . . hands down, one of the best crime novels of the year."

—JEFFERY DEAVER,
New York Times bestselling author of
Hunting Time

"Propulsive action, a twisty and smart mystery, emotionally resonant characters, and top-notch writing that brings to life a rich, layered setting. Highly recommended."

—LOU BERNEY,
award-winning author of *November Road*

"A crucible of character, brought to life with a poetry of meticulous detail."

—DANIEL PYNE,
writer and showrunner of *Bosch*

By Brandon Webb & John David Mann

Nonfiction

The Red Circle

The Making of a Navy SEAL

Among Heroes

The Killing School

Total Focus

Mastering Fear

Fiction

Steel Fear

Cold Fear

Blind Fear

BLIND FEAR

Bantam | New York

BLIND FEAR

A Thriller

Brandon Webb & John David Mann

2024 Bantam Books Mass Market Edition

Published in the United States by Bantam Books, an imprint of Random House, a division of Penguin Random House LLC, New York.

Originally published in hardcover in the United States by Bantam Books, an imprint of Random House, a division of Penguin Random House LLC, in 2023.

ISBN 9780593599037
Ebook ISBN 9780593599020

Cover design: Carlos Beltrán
Cover images: Petar Belobrajdic/Getty Images (ocean), Cavan/Alamy Images (palm tree)

Map design by John David Mann

Cloud art: eyetronic/stock.adobe.com and JSirlin/stock.adobe.com

Printed in the United States of America

randomhousebooks.com

2 4 6 8 9 7 5 3 1

Bantam Books mass market edition: June 2024

For my mom, Lynn Merriam, always inspiring me to make the impossible possible. —B.T.W.

For my mom, Carolyn Mann, the best storyteller I've ever known. —J.D.M.

Contents

Puerto Rico

OLD SAN JUAN
LA PERLA
Castillo San Cristóbal
Plaza Colón
pier 9
SAN JUAN BAY

Arecibo
Aguadilla
SAN JUAN
Rincón
Lares
El Yunque
Fajardo
Mayagüez
Caguas
Humacao
VIEQUES
Ponce
Salinas

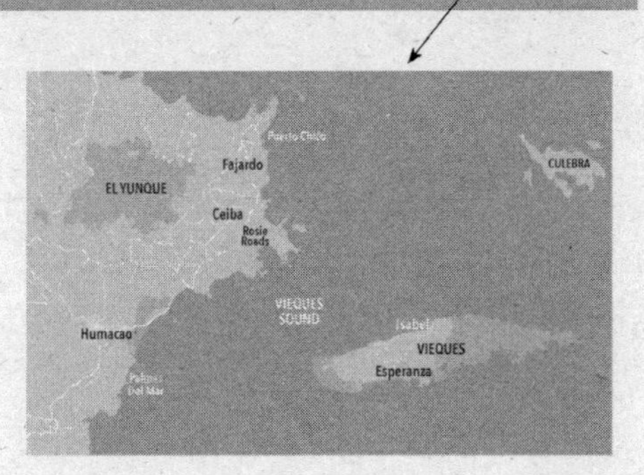
Fajardo
CULEBRA
EL YUNQUE
Ceiba
Rosie Roads
VIEQUES SOUND
Humacao
VIEQUES
Esperanza

BLIND FEAR

Prologue

They have been out there for hours, climbing the great rock cliffs overlooking Black Sand Beach, then down by the water, poking through the shells and driftwood left by the ebbing tide, cooling off in the sky-blue sea as they drift toward the western tip of their island home.

Playa Grande, Playa Vaca, Playa Vieja . . . they swim past beach after beach: robin's-egg sky, glass-clear aqua water, fish darting in a million colors, the soft crash of the surf, and not another soul in sight.

This is their heaven.

Viequesssss . . . even the name sounds like surf breaking over sand.

Half a mile off shore, just west of Playa Vieja, the boy sees his sister far ahead of him, laughing and making friends with an enormous sea turtle, her pink snorkel draped around her neck. He almost catches up with her, but she leaves her new reptilian friend and strikes out farther west, soon rounding the island's southwest corner and tracing the coast-line northward.

The boy follows wearily.

She might be three years younger than him, but man, she packs a ferocious kick.

"¡Oye! ¡No vayas tan rápido!" *Hey! Slow down!*

Is she ignoring him, or does she just not hear?

"¡Oye! ¡Regresa!" *Turn back!* "Papi dijo—"

"¡Papi dijo!" she echoes over her shoulder. *Papi said!* "¡Papi dijo, Papi dijo!" She flashes a grin back in his direction.

He sighs and swims on. His little sister can drive him crazy, but he can never stay mad at her for long.

They're coming up the far side now, toward Punta Boca Quebrada, a secluded little paradise. To the boy, this spot is pure magic. Such magnificent coral reefs, such an underwater explosion of color!—and still mostly untouched by the turistas, who are put off by the sting of sea urchins and persistent swarm of sand flies, especially nasty on still, hot days like this.

The flies don't bother the boy. They are old acquaintances.

The two are trespassing on restricted territory now, off limits to civilians, in part because of the danger of unexploded ordnance, left over from decades of constant bombardment when the US Navy still used the island for target practice. No place for little nenes and nenas.

A late-afternoon fog presses in around them.

Thirty feet away, just at the edge of visibility, the boy glimpses a fin moving slowly across his line of sight.

Shark.

The fog thickens.

Two more fins, then two more beyond those.

Circling them.

"Oye," he says softly.

The girl turns in the water and now she sees them, too.

She looks back at her brother.

He looks at her.

For a moment neither moves.

Then she grins and leans her head closer to the nearest fin.

"¡Bú!" she says softly.

The boy sighs and begins quietly sidestroking away from the shiver of sharks.

His sister follows suit. They both recognize the brownish, rounded fins. Nurse sharks can grow up to ten feet long and weigh as much as three hundred pounds, but they aren't really dangerous, not if you leave them alone.

Ignoring the little humans, the creatures move on up the coast, searching for shellfish to graze.

The two children turn south and head back the way they came.

The fog is already thinning. The setting sun spreads orange wings over the horizon, painting the sea in shades of crimson.

Soon it will be getting dark.

They swim on in silence, broken only by the *splish, splish* of their strokes.

After a few minutes a soft rain sweeps in from across the Caribbean, stippling the water's purple surface with pinpricks. A billion tiny pebbles hitting a billion little ponds, a rising whisper that turns to a roar.

The boy loves it when it rains.

"¡Mira!" the girl calls softly.

Look!

He glances back at his little sister, who is treading water as she peers out through the rain at something far off the coast. "Don't you see it?"

He swims back to her side and looks. He sees nothing.

"¡Una ballena!"

He sighs. He doesn't see any whale, and doesn't believe she does, either.

She wants to go inspect the thing, he can feel her intention. He puts out a hand and touches her arm.

We shouldn't.

She gently shrugs off his hand and throws a teasing little smile at him.

¡Papi dijo, Papi dijo!

She sets out.

He follows.

The location where she pointed has to be a mile off, a few degrees left of the sinking sun. Or maybe only half a mile. Impossible to say: Through the rain, in the fading light, visibility is poor.

He sees her pause in place, searching for the spot where she thinks the beast ought to be.

Nothing.

The boy finally reaches her just as she pulls on her snorkel and slips under the surface. He dives, too, trailing her by a few yards, and follows her in a wide lazy circle, finding nothing but more dark water and the usual swirls of sea life.

And then, just as he is about to surface, he catches a glimpse of it, maybe forty yards off, just below the water's surface: a long vague expanse of gray. The flank of a great beast.

There are humpbacks in these waters, sometimes sperm whales, and sei whales, too, but the boy thinks this might be bigger than any sei whale. Blue whales have been spotted in the Sound from time to time, the largest animal ever known. Although this one looks more gray than blue.

Whatever it was, it's gone now.

His sister turns back to look at him, her eyes wide, and points straight up.

They surface.

"Did you *see* it?" she gasps, and before he can reply she has clamped her lips back around her snorkel's pink mouthpiece and disappeared under the water again.

Once more, he follows, trailing behind her by eight or ten feet, knowing the whale is long gone and their search will be fruitless.

Suddenly she pulls short, as if startled.

He squints through the dark water, looking for what caused her to stop so abruptly. It takes a few seconds to register what he's seeing.

From out of the gloom a creature emerges, swimming closer in a long arc. A shark?

Turning in their direction now.

Not a shark.

And not one creature. Two. Swimming in tandem.

Two men, in wet suits, faces invisible behind their masks.

Swimming fast.

Straight for them.

Holding spearguns.

The boy grabs his sister's arm and turns blindly in the water, and they both swim the other direction as hard and fast as they can.

Swim as if their lives depend on it.

Monday

T minus 6

Monday morning, local weather services noted an unusual cloud cluster off the West African coast, moving rapidly over the Atlantic. The cluster was distinguished by coal-black clouds suffused with tiny flashes of iridescent light, and swarms of hot, dusty winds scooping down to sea level and up again, leaving a scatter of hail and hot drizzle in their wake. A sea captain off Cape Verde described it as "ominous."

Later in the day, the cluster was upgraded to an "investigative area" and given the designation "Invest 95L." The National Hurricane Center has begun collecting data.

1

Nico Santiago had a dream. He envisioned a thriving, dazzling Puerto Rico, envy of the States, jewel of the Caribbean, a transformation people would be talking about a hundred years from now, a metamorphosis that all started with his beloved city—San Juan, pride of the commonwealth.

Why not? Look what they'd done with New York City in the nineties. Clean up the street crime, purge the corruption. Lance the boil! Drain the infection!

Which meant taking down the Devil.

Yes, Nico was only one guy, a lowly homicide cop. But hey, every revolution started with some nobody who cared enough to act, right?

Which was why, at that moment, he was jumping over two toppled trash bins in the middle of the night, slipping on the grease-covered garbage that spilled over the cobblestones, and falling on his ass in an alley in La Perla, the sketchiest neighborhood in the city.

"¡Mierda!"

Nico swore under his breath as he scrabbled to his feet and kept running. Down a set of crumbling cement steps, across a narrow cobblestone street, hopping a chain-link fence, he ran on, straining to catch any scraps of sound beyond the slow pounding of the surf below and his own ragged breath.

There! A scuffle of footsteps, dead ahead.

Ha. The puta was heading for the shoreline—as if the rocks and seawater could save him! Just like he'd thought he could shake Nico in the first place by trying to disappear down here into the city's coastal underbelly.

La Perla: America's oldest shantytown. A shunned strip, third of a mile long, jammed outside the city walls down on the rocky Atlantic shore. Built over the ruins of a slaughterhouse, abutting the city's graveyard, original home of the homeless, the slaves, the non-white servants. La Perla was everything Nico loved and hated about his homeland. The uncrushable spirit of its people. The legacy of oppression, poverty, and crime.

The place where they shot "Despacito," the greatest music video ever made.

The one place in the city where, if you got into trouble at night, the police wouldn't come for you.

But I'm coming for you now, puta. And you are in one shit-pile of trouble, aren't you?

He heard the man's feet hit the cement boardwalk and go bolting off to the east. Nico followed, sprinting full-out . . . three hundred feet . . . five hundred feet . . .

He should have called his partner, shouldn't be out here on his own, shouldn't have been stalking this pendejo by himself. His superior officers had nixed the stakeout, nixed the whole investigation, in fact. Too hot, they said. Not worth the risk.

But it *was* worth the risk. Nico knew this in his gut. Nail this one guy and he could crack open the whole pineapple. Unmask the Devil himself and end this horrific reign of terror. He wouldn't risk his partner's badge, but he was fine with risking his own. So he'd laid the trap all by himself—and he'd caught a rat.

A thousand feet . . .

Only he'd gotten just a shave too close and spooked the mamabicho.

At the end of the strip, where it landed at the foot of the old stone castle that marked La Perla's eastern terminus, his quarry took a hard right, darting back into the tangle of shacks, a rabbit making a desperate dash for safety in the heart of his warren.

Nico didn't bother shouting *Stop!* or *Police!* or *You're under arrest!* Didn't waste his breath. Just took off after him.

And then everything went silent.

He skidded to a halt at the mouth of another narrow alleyway. Heard no fleeing footsteps, no scrambling over cobblestones. Only a dog barking and the distant curses of locals rousted from a hungover sleep.

The fine hairs on Nico's arms stood at attention.

He had to assume the man had a gun.

These days it seemed like everyone in Puerto Rico had a gun.

He couldn't see far enough into the alley to locate the man, was pretty sure the man couldn't see him, either. But they were both there, still and silent, each trying to get the drop on the other.

There was no nearby exit up through the city wall. The man was cornered.

But so, for all practical purposes, was Nico.

Suddenly Nico felt an irrational chill shiver through him.

Behind him, far above in the dark, stood an old

castle guard sentry-box. According to superstition, every guard who entered there would mysteriously vanish, never to be seen again. La Garita del Diablo, they called it. The Devil's Tower.

Focus, Nico.

He drew out his sidearm, took a few steadying breaths, and crouched down low to crawl his way into the alley, listening as hard as he could, straining to catch any telltale sounds of breath or movement from the other man, hearing nothing.

He began to crawl.

An endless minute ticked by. Then another.

A quarter of the way through.

Inch by agonizing inch.

Three minutes.

Halfway through.

And then a deep voice boomed out from the far end of the alley, shattering the silence.

"¡Quieto, cabrón!" *Freeze, asshole!*

Nico let out a harsh, ragged breath and felt his shoulders relax.

Caleb. His partner.

He almost laughed. No jodas . . . Caleb! That rum-smooth, James Earl Jones voice, the reason they called him "Calypso." Nico could pick that voice out of a crowd in the middle of a hurricane.

Gracias a Dios.

He took another hard breath and straightened from his crouch, letting the tension drain from his back muscles as the adrenaline flood receded, leaving behind its wreckage of ravaged nerve endings.

He had no idea how Cal had known he was here, why he was out here in the middle of the night when he ought to be home in bed or out drinking like any sane off-duty cop.

Didn't know, didn't care. He was just grateful his partner had showed. The chase was over. They were actually arresting this piece of shit, this stain of corruption—and with what this one guy knew, they could bring down the whole house of cards. His investigation was about to be vindicated. Puerto Rico, his homeland, would be cleansed of this plague, given a fresh start.

This night would change their lives, forever.

We did it, Lucy. We really did it.

He walked toward the end of the alley, where a shaft of moonlight revealed the enormous figure of Cal, feet spread apart, gun held out in a two-handed stance. The man Nico had been pursuing now knelt on the filthy alleyway floor, hands clasped behind his head.

Nico smiled.

"That's no ordinary asshole," he called out as he approached. "That particular asshole is deputy director of AP." Autoridad de los Puertos: Ports Authority. In charge of all seaports in Puerto Rico. "That particular asshole runs the docks. And also happens to work for the Devil. A direct report, Cal! Ave María purísma, a direct report!"

Cal threw him a quick glance, eyebrows raised.

"This puta can ID the son of a bitch!" Nico added, just to make the point abundantly clear. He'd been right all along. His stakeout had paid off. They were about to bring down the Devil.

Cal looked down at the kneeling man. "That true?"

The man said nothing.

Cal nodded, impressed. "Damn." He looked back at Nico. "Nice work. Stellar."

Nico grinned and put up his palm for a high five.

Cal raised his weapon and shot Nico point-blank in the face.

"¡Jesús!" The kneeling man nearly fell over. He stared up at Cal, his eyes wide as silver dollars. Then his face relaxed. He let out a rush of breath and broke into a grin.

"Gracias, compadre."

He got to his feet, shakily, brushing the filth off his knees. Grinned up at the big man.

"De nada," said Cal, and he plugged the man between the eyes.

The second pistol shot reverberated through the dark streets and died away in the surf.

Cal waited.

Listened.

Nobody came.

He holstered his 9mm. Reached into a back trouser pocket, withdrew a handkerchief, and wiped his face with it. Held it out and looked at it without expression. In the faint moonlight the smear of Nico's blood looked black.

He pocketed the cloth, then reached into an inside jacket pocket and slipped out a small leather case, the grain worn smooth. Zipped it open. A glint of moonlight flashed off the stainless steel.

One by one, he began removing his precision tools.

2

Finn awoke in a sweat, veins bulging on his neck.

He had trained himself to come out of sleep without a sound and lie silent on his bedroll, but in his dream he had been screaming—

He couldn't see. Where was he? He jerked his arms and felt the leather straps dig into his wrists. Why had they shackled him to this bed? He thrashed against the restraints—they couldn't do this! Why wouldn't they let his parents in to see him?

"Mama! Pop!" he screamed. "I'm in here!"

Out of nowhere a cluster of adults appeared, swarming over him, holding him down, chattering in words he couldn't understand, jabbing him with needles in a hundred places—

And now he lay on his mat, soundless, soaked in sweat, the echoing screams in his head gradually displaced by the steady pulse of his own heartbeat.

Trying to identify the feeling.

Terror . . . confusion . . . anger . . . desperation . . .

Nothing clicked.

He focused on the most vivid pieces of the memory—the leather straps, the cluster of grown-ups, the chattering, screaming for his parents—and ran the list again.

Terror . . . confusion . . . anger . . . desperation . . .

He took a breath and let it go.

The air hung over his tiny room like a canopy of wet netting. There was no AC; the place was cooled by ceiling fans. Only the fans weren't running.

Another blackout.

Benjamin Franklin had his "death and taxes." In Puerto Rico the two certainties were rain and power outages. Working electricity was a precious commodity these days. What power they could pull from their little generator, they put toward keeping the refrigeration running. Inventory before comfort.

He heard the old cook moving around in the kitchen out front.

The clock in his head said it was twelve fifteen.

Late for the old man to still be up and about.

In the dark, Finn stretched his arms above his head, heels pushing out in the opposite direction, drawing himself taut like a bow, stretching muscle and sinew, sending blood flow to peripheral nerves, then slowly released.

A muffled crash and soft curse. The old man had dropped a pot.

Which put Finn on alert.

Zacharias had been blind for nearly fifty years. His two grandchildren helped him keep his kitchen clean and perfectly organized, but he could make his way around his domain as well as any sighted cocinero. Better, in fact. His little seafood restaurant, Papi's, was one of the most popular spots on Vieques.

The old man ran the place himself, with Pedro and Miranda's help, and he did the lion's share of the cooking, too, though he relied on his one employee to help carry the load during peak hours. For the past eight months, that spot had been filled by an itinerant American. "Mimo," they called the newcomer, in part because he was silent when he walked.

Or nearly silent.

Unlike anyone else Finn had ever known, Zacharias could always hear him coming.

Watching the old man maneuver around the prep station and grill was a revelation. In his eight months on the island, Finn had learned a good deal from his employer. How to operate in the dark. How to execute even the most complex tasks by feel alone. The man was breathtaking with a French knife. Never missed a slice.

Let alone dropped a pot.

Something was wrong.

Finn sat up, felt around him, and fired up the Coleman. Stood and took it with him out front to enter the tiny kitchen.

When he parted the thin curtain and stepped through, the old man already stood facing him. Finn instantly read it on his friend's face, so when Zacharias spoke, he only confirmed what Finn had already sensed.

"They never came home."

3

Finn stood on the cliff, looking down at the black sand sparkling in the early-morning sun, at the wine-dark sea, flecked with streaks of liquid gold, stretching out to the silent horizon.

Nothing.

Nothing but the sighs of the wind, the soft thump of the surf, the lamentations of seagulls and shrill cries of terns.

The kids would have started out here, was his best guess. He could see them now, walking the beach, poking through the shells and driftwood left by the ebbing tide, and now out in the water, Miranda in the lead as usual, her pink snorkel sticking up above the ocean's speckled surface. He'd bought her that snorkel himself, and a matching blue one for Pedro, on a rare outing to "the big island," as the locals called Puerto Rico. A calculated risk, that little day trip. He'd paid in cash.

Los pollitos, Zacharias called them. My little chicks.

Finn made his way down to the beach and looked around.

Dove into the surf and explored the underwater perimeter.

Nothing.

June and July, these beaches had been teeming with people, most of them Puerto Rican residents come over to enjoy a little vacation time. Like New Yorkers summering on Nantucket.

Not now, at the tail end of August. Now they were in peak rainy season, peak mosquito season, peak hurricane season.

Right now the place was empty.

He thought again about the day he'd taken them over to the big island. Yes, he'd paid cash—but he still risked being spotted by a store CCTV. Why had he made that trip?

It puzzled him, the way these two had somehow insinuated themselves into his life. Or maybe it was he who'd insinuated himself into theirs. How and why that had happened was a mystery to him.

Finn was highly skilled at getting to know people, the way an anthropologist gets to know a tribe of aboriginals. A master of observation. But he didn't make "connections" the way others did.

Yet it was different with los pollitos and their papi. He didn't know why. It just was.

Finn spent the next few hours scouring the area, looking for anyone who might have been there the previous afternoon or evening. Who might have seen anything that mattered.

There were scattered residences dotting the land some way back from the beach. Finn would have gone door-to-door, but every one of them was currently empty of occupants. No intel to be gleaned there.

There was a gun club about a klick inland. Too early for clientele, not that there'd be any business likely the week before Labor Day, but Finn found the owner out walking the course and struck up a conversation. The gun club owner had sharp eyes and a good memory. He knew who Pedro and Miranda were, had often seen them out there. But not the day before. That was Sunday. He'd been home for the day.

Next, Finn checked out the radar station two and a half klicks to the west, a surveillance installation deployed by Uncle Sam, mainly for drug traffic interdiction purposes. The unmanned station was, no surprise there, deserted.

He came back down to the beach and started walking west.

Playa Grande . . . Playa Vaca . . . Playa Vieja . . .

Listening to the wind, which knew everything yet revealed none of its secrets.

At the end of Playa Vieja he turned inland again and hiked up through jungled terrain to the peak of Pirate Mountain, the highest point on Vieques. An old US Navy communications installation, now run by Homeland; closed to civilians, but the old hiking trail persisted.

At the summit he turned and looked down at the coast.

They'd shot the 1963 film *Lord of the Flies* here on Vieques, as Pedro had solemnly informed Finn.

"You know those great big rock formations overlooking Playa Grande? That's where the British choirboys murdered Simon and watched his body wash out to sea!"

Finn looked for bodies washed out to sea, but saw nothing.

He hiked back through the jungle, down to the beach, and walked on.

From here the shoreline gave way to rocks. It

would take a significant effort to keep going. Not a path for ordinary tourists.

Though of course, Pedro and Miranda were anything but ordinary tourists.

Finn started up and over the rocks. He'd hike clear around the island if it came to that. Then hike it again.

After another mile the shoreline angled north, rounding the western end of the island.

About halfway up the coast he stopped and looked out across the water toward Puerto Rico, some eight miles in the distance, too far to see from here over the curvature of the earth. Later in the day there would be a cumulus buildup over the Vieques Sound, feeding off the massive moisture of the big island's El Yunque Forest, a few miles in from the coast. But not now. Right now the morning air was clear as polished glass.

Ignoring the swarm of sand flies, he thought about Roosevelt Roads, the abandoned naval base just across the Sound from where he stood. A key strategic US sea and air base during the Cold War.

For another decade and a half after the end of the Cold War, Rosie Roads had existed principally to oversee the bomb testing that had been ongoing on Vieques since the forties. And this was not your garden-variety ordnance. Some of those warheads contained depleted uranium, napalm, Agent Orange. They packed in the worst shit they could throw, over eighty bombs a day of it. There were still hundreds of unexploded bombs scattered around parts of the island, a twisted parody of an Easter egg hunt gone horribly wrong—contamination, the islanders claimed, that produced the unusually high cancer rates on Vieques.

Isla Nena, the Viequenses called their home. Little Sister Island.

And for more than six decades, the navy had used Little Sister Island as target practice.

Finn had nearly crashed a boat off Rosie Roads during a SEAL workup, just months before massive protests finally shut down US military operations there for good. When the US turned the site over to the island's residents, the Puerto Rican government announced an ambitious proposal to develop the area into a massive tourist center. A major boost for the economy.

Inertia and corruption scuttled the plan.

He stood for a while, gazing west, letting the information he'd collected on Pedro and Miranda's disappearance—or rather the lack of information—sift through his brain.

Contemplating the resources that sat just eight miles away, on the other side of the Sound.

The US military still had a reserve force of three or four hundred stationed over there. The Puerto Rico National Guard had a dive team and maritime engineers. There were cops and Coast Guard and border patrol personnel. It was a gold mine of potential rescue resources.

He should be able to pop over there right now, enlist a reserves crew, commandeer a search team. He was, after all, still a US Navy chief.

He was, after all, still a SEAL.

Except that the moment he showed his face they'd cuff him, fly him back to the States, and lock him up for the rest of his life.

Or maybe just shoot him on sight.

He turned and walked back the way he'd come.

4

The two Americans emerged from their tinted-glass taxicab and stood on the narrow bluestone sidewalk, blinking in the sunlight like lizards.

Actually blinking. ¡Dios!

Jesús chuckled quietly and fell into step forty feet behind them as the two turistas collected themselves and began bumbling up the street, gawking at everything. Fresh from the airport, he'd bet his ten best fake Rolexes on it. The 7 A.M. nonstop from Miami, Frontier or JetBlue. Dropped their bags at the hotel while the cab waited, then straight to Old San Juan so they could get started on a week of gawking.

He closed the gap to thirty feet.

The couple was poking along, starting and stopping, staring at buildings, looking in shop windows. Jesús caught snatches of their conversation as they clucked and cawed at each other. The woman, a tall Amazonian blonde, was called Emma; her husband, a big pudgy balding guy, was Charles.

Georgia, had to be; that fat, lazy accent. Jesús knew his American dialects.

Not hard to see which one wore the pants in that house. What was it about Americans that made the women so masculine and the men so effeminate?

Must be something they put in the water. Or in the hog feed.

Jesús wouldn't mind spending a few hours in a shuttered bedroom alone with Emma the Amazon. Show her what a real man was all about. Could be an experience to remember.

He chuckled again.

But that was pure fantasy. Making Emma squeal was not on the menu. What was on the menu right now was that overpriced handbag hanging from her shoulder like a ripe papaya.

He quickened his pace and began closing the distance.

They still hadn't noticed him. As he knew they wouldn't. Turistas gringos: so ripe for the plucking, it almost hurt to watch.

The pair leaned closer into a shop window, which Jesús took as his cue. Accelerating as smoothly as a heron taking wing, he breezed by the couple, deftly lifting the bag from her shoulder as he went.

This was why he was never caught in the act, he thought as he felt the strap settle into his palm. He had a knack for targeting not only the richest marks, but also the easiest. Americanos, so full of themselves, so confident, so clueless. What was the expression? Like taking candy from—

"Ow!"

His arm jerked, rotating and yanking back behind him as his feet left the ground and he felt his body swing around in a tight arc—and in the next moment he found himself slammed against the woman, her arm wrapped around him like an iron band, her breath hot in his ear.

"Do not fuck with us," she whispered in perfect

Spanish. "Go home, puta. Hang laundry. Do something useful."

Jesús heard someone behind him softly chuckling. The woman's husband, still peering in the same shop window, having a quiet laugh.

The next moment he felt himself abruptly released, the handbag no longer in his hand. Without looking around, he took off at a brisk walk, putting as much distance as possible between himself and the crazy bitch, and doing so as quickly as he could without drawing further attention to himself. As he fast-walked through Old San Juan, a single thought spun over and over in his head.

What the hell just happened?

It wasn't until he'd gotten a hundred yards or so away that he slipped his hand in his pocket and realized.

His wallet was missing.

5

Leaving the pathetic pickpocket behind, the couple continued up the street for a block, then took a left down a cobblestone side street.

"Under the radar?" the man said.

The woman shrugged. "Nobody noticed."

As they took a right at the next block the man added, "His wallet? Seriously?"

She handed the wallet to him as they walked. "You can give it to whatsisname. A party favor."

The man pocketed the wallet and shaded his eyes with one hand, squinting ahead, then gave a grunt of confirmation. "Speak of the devil."

He nodded toward a trim Puerto Rican gentleman, about fifteen feet ahead, carrying a bright green umbrella and a folded newspaper under his arm.

Lord, the woman thought. *An actual newspaper. Like we're in a Cold War spy movie.*

They fell into step with the guy, one on each side. The Puerto Rican startled slightly as they appeared on his flanks, but kept walking.

"You are enjoying our beautiful city?" he said, eyes forward.

"It's everything advertised and more," the man replied quietly, also looking straight ahead.

" 'Charles' and 'Emma,' I take it?" said the Puerto Rican, still looking straight ahead.

"Tha'd be us," drawled the man.

The woman said nothing.

They walked on, the narrow sidewalks forcing them to break in and out of single file.

"Dar Adamson," the bulky man said.

"Toño Rivera, SIB," replied the other man. "Special Investigations Bureau."

"Toño, you said?"

"Short for Antonio. My mother says they named me after Antonio Paoli, the King of Tenors—Puerto Rico's first world-famous musician. My father says they named me after Toño Bicicleta, Puerto Rico's most famous outlaw."

"How's your singing voice?"

"It's actually pretty good. That's how I conned my wife into saying yes." He grinned.

The bulky man smiled.

The woman just walked.

"So, big picture, what exactly does Special Investigations cover?" inquired the Americano.

"Organized crime, terrorist groups, white-collar crime. And, of course, fugitives."

"Ah," said Adamson. Now he understood why the bureau had selected this man to be their liaison.

The three walked on up the Old San Juan street in silence. After a minute Adamson handed over the purloined wallet. "For your friends in PRPD. Pickpocket, four blocks east of here, by the Plaza Colón."

They walked another block, then at a nod from Agent Rivera took a right that brought them up a side street and out onto another fired blue-brick avenue. A few doors in they took a table at a small sidewalk café.

"Sorry for the cloak and dagger," Adamson said as they sat. "It's necessary. Under the circumstances."

Rivera waved one hand in a vague gesture that said, No hay problema.

"Our guy is a master of surveillance and countersurveillance," Adamson continued. "If he knew we were here, he'd be in the wind before we got within a mile. So no APBs, no circulated photos, no alerts. Nothing. It makes our work harder. But, big picture, it's how we need to go."

The SIB agent nodded.

"And nobody else knows we're here? Other than my bureau contact?"

"Only God and the angels."

A server appeared, placed water glasses and menus, and disappeared.

"So, Special Agent Adamson," Rivera said quietly once they were alone again, "what can you tell me about this serial killer whom you and your partner have come to—"

"War criminal."

They were the first words the woman had spoken since they'd met.

Agent Rivera turned to her. He had to angle his head slightly upward to meet her gaze, forcing him to shield his eyes from the glare of the morning sun.

"¿Perdóname?"

"War criminal," she repeated. "Not just serial killer. The man slaughtered an entire village of farm families in Yemen, then murdered his lieutenant and three teammates to cover his tracks."

She tilted her head sideways, indicating Adamson. "And he's not my partner."

Rivera looked over at Adamson, who shrugged and said, "Colleagues."

Rivera turned back to the woman. "Of course. I'm sorry. And you are?"

"Halsey, Monica," she said. "US Navy JAG Corps. But think of me as the Royal Canadian Mounted Police."

Rivera frowned and cocked his head. ¿Perdóname?

"We always get our man."

6

Thwack! The kid gave the ball a solid hit, then pulled the bat back for the next pitch as his line drive hit the rusting cage with a clatter.

Finn stood at the edge of the field, watching the kid facing off with the pitching machine. According to him, Pedro and Miranda had been there the morning before for an hour, maybe two, playing a pickup game with their friends before it got too hot to play. He hadn't seen them since.

No, he wasn't sure which way they were headed when they left.

Pedro and Miranda were crazy in love with baseball, although Pedro frankly wasn't that good. Miranda was a star, way better than her big brother. Drove Pedro crazy.

Finn almost smiled, thinking about it.

Miranda reminded Finn of himself at that age: a windup toy that went at top speed and never ran down, with an endless appetite for all things physical. He knew this only distantly; his memories of himself as a child were like looking the wrong way through a telescope—with a few cracks in the lens. But he remembered being fearless, too, when he was eight years old.

Maybe that was it. Why he seemed to feel some kind of connection with them. Because they reminded him of himself and Ray at that same age. Miranda was a ball of energy, and Pedro knew things. That was him and Ray in a bullet casing.

The sky burst open and poured down rain in fat, hot gobbets.

The kid gathered up his bats and baseballs and took off, splashing through puddles that weren't there just moments before.

Finn left the field and walked toward the center of town.

He'd already combed the beaches and landmarks to the east. Caracas Beach, Blue Beach, Secret Beach, Hidden Beach, Silver Beach. Even checked the old abandoned lighthouse on the way back.

Nothing.

Now he walked the little grid of streets by the shore, stopping to talk with whatever locals he could find out and about, sitting on covered porches or huddled under awnings. Which, this being Esperanza, with a total population of fewer than six hundred, was not very many people.

Isabel Segunda, the town center up on the north coast of Vieques, was where the bulk of the island's resident population lived. Named for the nineteenth-century queen of Spain, Isabel was where you'd find the municipal buildings, the post office, the island's only ATM; where you'd catch the ferry to la isla grande. The place had the feel of a sleepy seaside Spanish village.

Here on the opposite coast, six miles to the south, Esperanza had a more honky-tonk vibe. Something like Key West—if you shrank Key West to a quarter of its size and average income level. You could make the little winding road that connected the two towns in twelve minutes, but the trappings of civilization still felt light-years away. In Esperanza there were no gas stations, no traffic lights. No bank. No post office. Chickens ran wild in the streets.

Expats and tourists tended to gravitate here, both for the exotic beaches and for the sense of total seclusion. A taste of the better life. A glimpse of salvation, maybe even paradise.

Esperanza.

Spanish for "hope."

The moment he stepped inside the door of the Paper Mill, the smell of fresh coffee hit his nostrils.

Finn had traveled the world, but he had never smelled anything like homegrown Puerto Rican coffee, and there were few smells he loved as much. Though he never drank a drop. Caffeine monkeyed with the calibration of his perceptions.

"Hola, Mimo." Hugo, the store's proprietor, sitting behind his tiny counter.

Finn nodded in reply.

The Paper Mill was where Finn bought his sketch pads and charcoal pencils. It sold postcards and suntan lotion to tourists, an eclectic assortment of essentials to residents. Out in back, behind all the racks of paper goods and insect repellent, bananas and mangoes, flip-flops and beach hats, was Esperanza's version of an internet café. The internet part came and went, but the coffee was perpetual.

In the back, Hugo also "sold" books (used) and comics (new and used) to the kids in town, although money rarely changed hands, and most of the reading happened on-site.

To Pedro and Miranda, the back of the Paper Mill

was a portal to other universes, where they would go to spend hours reading everything from the latest anime to threadbare volumes of nineteenth-century swashbucklers. Miranda's favorite were graphic novels. Pedro liked big adventures—Jules Verne, Alexandre Dumas, Tolkien.

Finn gave another nod, this one to the nameless old woman sitting in a motionless rocker in a corner behind Hugo. She glared back at him, one of her go-to responses. Finn knew her only as "Hugo's abuela"; Hugo himself called her either "anciana" (old woman) or "vieja" (again, old woman). It wasn't clear to Finn what her role in the store was. Her principal function seemed to be to provide running commentary on whatever caught her attention in the moment, always in muttered Spanish, very little of it connected to anything like reality, as far as Finn could tell.

Finn explained to Hugo that he was looking for Pedro and Miranda.

The man nodded. "They were here around lunchtime yesterday, stayed a few hours. That's all I know." Hugo avoided Finn's eyes. He seemed ashamed that he couldn't provide more useful information. "The lieutenant was in, earlier."

The island's de facto chief of police. Finn knew the lieutenant by sight—on Vieques, everyone knew everyone by sight—but that was the extent of it. He'd made an effort not to cross paths with police of any stripe. The less visible he stayed, the better.

Finn's impression of the man was that he was soft-spoken and thorough.

So the lieutenant had come down in person from Isabel to look for the missing children. Which meant that, sooner or later, he would be having a conversation with Finn.

Probably sooner.

"Your abuela," said Finn. "Could she have seen anything? From up top?"

Hugo and his grandmother lived up on the second floor over the store, and above that was a covered widow's walk where she liked to sit and grumble at the ocean. Her husband was not, in fact, a sailor lost at sea. Just a shopkeeper, lost to cancer, like so many island residents.

"Nah," said Hugo. "I don't let her up there anymore. Too dangerous." He leaned in and whispered, "She might forget where she is and walk off the edge."

"La Bestia," the old woman muttered. *The beast.*

Finn looked over in her direction. Was she referring to him? Or the lieutenant?

"La ramera cabalga sobre La Bestia," she spat. *The harlot rides the beast.*

"¡Cállate, anciana!" said Hugo amiably. *Shut up, old woman.*

"Ehhh," she growled back, with a dismissive wave of the hand.

Hugo shrugged at Finn. "Bible shit, you know? End times. El apocalipsis." He got up from his stool and took the old woman's hand. "C'mon, anciana. Let's get you a coffee."

"No me mandes," she grumbled as she took his hand and stood. *Don't patronize me.* As they strolled together to the back of the shop she turned back to glare at Finn again. "La Bestia," she muttered.

When Finn stepped outside the Paper Mill he found the rain had stopped, and the setting sun had cast the wet streets in a pale red glow.

El apocalipsis.

He headed for the old café on the outskirts of Hope.

7

As he approached the weathered little clap-board structure that housed Papi's Café, Finn could see lights on in the kitchen. Which meant there was someone in there with the old man, who normally cooked with the lights off when by himself.

He climbed the three little steps to the front porch and entered by the front door, its little bell giving up a mournful *ding*. The place was empty. It was after seven, normally the height of the dinner crush. Not today, though. Today, people were giving Zacharias some space. Word traveled fast on an island.

He heard the indistinct murmur of conversation out back.

Pushing through the swinging door that led to the kitchen, he found Zacharias conversing with the lieutenant as he stripped two small plantains out of their peels. Next to his prep station, a wide fry pan of achiote oil sat heating on the stove.

"Mimo," said the lieutenant with a nod.

Finn returned the nod and regarded the man sitting on the stool at the back of the tiny kitchen. Elongated oval face, dark eyes, and thin lips, framed in a black mustache and goatee weathered with gray.

"I was just telling Papi," the lieutenant said, "it is

a television cop-show myth that a person must be absent twenty-four hours before police will look into the matter. Particularly when children are involved. Technically speaking, a child is considered 'missing' the moment the primary caretaker does not know their whereabouts. You were right to call this morning, Papi." (This, to Zacharias.) "That gave us a jump on things. We've covered a lot of territory today. This is a good thing."

Finn said nothing. He knew how this kind of interview worked. He understood that "this is good" really meant "this is bad." They'd covered a lot of territory—and found nothing.

"Toss me a garlic?" said Zacharias.

Finn picked a firm bulb out of a little hanging basket, looked over at the old chef, and underhanded it in his direction.

Zacharias snatched it out of the air.

Finn almost smiled. Never got tired of watching the old man do that.

He had once asked his employer exactly how he was able to sense objects in his environment with such precision, even when they made no sound.

"You have to feel the space around things," was all the old man had said.

Zacharias crushed and peeled the garlic, then tested the hot oil by dropping in a single slice of plantain. It sizzled. He added the rest of the pieces he'd cut, moving them gently from time to time to ensure that they fried evenly.

"Los pollitos will be hungry when they come home," he commented.

Finn and the lieutenant looked at each other.

"As I was just explaining to Papi," said the lieutenant gently, "in a situation such as this, we typically consider five scenarios, in decreasing order of likelihood."

He held up an index finger—for Finn's benefit, no doubt, since the gesture would be lost on the blind chef. Or perhaps it was just the way the lieutenant's methodical brain worked.

"One. They got lost. This comes first, as it is the most common explanation."

He held up two fingers.

"Two. They've been injured."

He didn't add the words *or drowned,* but Finn knew he was thinking them, and he was sure the old chef knew it, too.

Zacharias bent down, opened a little under-the-counter refrigeration unit, pulled out a piece of red snapper, slapped it on his cutting board, and sliced it neatly into two pieces, then seasoned it with salt and crushed pepper, cumin, and oregano.

The lieutenant held up three fingers.

"Three. They've run away."

Another finger.

"Four. Parental abduction."

He made a fist and stuck out his thumb.

"And five . . ." Here he hesitated. "Non-parental abduction."

The old chef gave the fish a quick sear in a second, smaller fry pan, then slid it into the oven to finish. Turning back to his prep station, he placed a handful of the fried plantains in a large pilón, the traditional wooden Puerto Rican mortar and pestle, along with the garlic, some achiote oil, salt, and pepper, and began methodically mashing.

"Now, looking at each possibility," continued the lieutenant. "And forgive me, Papi, I know this is painful, but you know your grandchildren better than anyone else on the island, so your viewpoint here is essential. Taking each point in turn—"

"Lost?" said the old chef, as he continued his work. "On Vieques? Not possible. Injured? Possible, one or the other of them, but not both at the same time. And if one were too hurt to move, the other would come for help. So, no to your scenarios one and two."

"Yes," said the lieutenant. "Which brings us to number three."

Zacharias formed the mashed plantain mixture into two spheres, each roughly the size of a baseball, then placed each on its own plate.

The lieutenant's third scenario was "run away."

"I realize," the lieutenant continued, "that no parent, no grandparent, wants to think this could ever be the case with their own child. But is it possible they got a ride up to Isabel, took the ferry over to the big island? Even snuck onto the ferry without being seen?"

"Pedro and Miranda, running off? Without telling me?" The old man shook his head. "I know these things happen, Héctor. But, no. Not these two. Unthinkable."

As far as Finn knew, Zacharias was the only person on Vieques who dared call the island's chief of police by his first name.

"I understand," said the lieutenant. "Still, we have to think the unthinkable. That's what police do."

Zacharias picked out a fresh lime, placed it on the board, and sliced out two wedges.

"Point four is obviously off the table . . ." the lieutenant continued.

No need to elaborate there. Hard to have parental abduction when both parents were gone.

"Which leaves scenario number five."

"Non-parental abduction? On Vieques?" countered the old chef. "Who would do this? Where could they possibly go?"

"I understand," said the lieutenant softly. Meaning, Finn assumed, *I understand that you can't even look at that possibility right now.*

It occurred to Finn that there was a sixth possibility, every bit as likely as being abducted. But he said nothing.

"Don't worry yourself, Papi," added the lieutenant as he rose from his stool. "In most such cases, we find the children have simply wandered off. And in any event, we'll find them. It's good that you called us so early."

The old chef removed the fish from the oven, placed the two pieces carefully atop the two plantain balls, adding one of the lime wedges to each plate, then moved the two dishes to his sideboard and covered them to keep them warm.

Then turned to face the lieutenant.

"Pedro and Miranda wander off every day, Héctor. They also wander back."

"Yes," said the lieutenant, after an awkward silence. "Well." He hesitated, then added, "I'll leave you to it, then. Of course I'll let you know the moment I hear anything."

Finn walked the lieutenant back out through the swinging door and empty dining room, through the front door with its doleful little bell, then stopped outside on the front porch to talk for a moment.

"What are you thinking?" he said.

"I am thinking we have a job to do. There are two children missing."

Finn let the lieutenant's evasive words hang in the air for a moment before speaking again.

"Scenario three? Or five?"

The lieutenant sighed. "We have been looking since early this morning, nearly twelve hours now. Tomorrow we will look again—in Destino, Barriada Monte Santo, Santa María, everywhere on the north side, as well as down here. We are coordinating with Fish and Wildlife, and two federal marshals will fly in tomorrow to help explore the preserve. We don't know where they are, so we will look at every possibility. If they're here, we'll find them."

Not an answer to the question.

"Okay," said Finn. "But what do you think? What's your professional opinion?"

"Opinions are for politicians. Police do not have the luxury of opinions."

Finn looked at him. "Okay," he said again.

The lieutenant nodded a *buenas noches*, stepped off the little porch, and walked up the street toward wherever he'd parked his car.

Finn watched him go.

Police do not have the luxury of opinions.

Finn didn't buy it. The man was thinking something, and Finn couldn't read what it was.

Which bothered him.

8

The room measured seven by nine, a postage stamp. Wood plank flooring, bare. Mat with bedroll, backpack next to it; card table with a single wooden chair. Shiplap walls, white paint long worn through, currently papered with pinned-up nine-by-twelve artist's pad pages filled with lists of locations, addresses, personnel, phone numbers, URLs, dates, and other assorted data, all in neat hand lettering.

Plus three portraits, side by side, sketched in charcoal pencil.

On the little card table: small stack of sketch pads, cup holding a dozen charcoal pencils; Coleman lamp, unlit; small laptop, open and running. The laptop's screen was divided into four windows, three showing regular sequences of video feeds from dozens of locations, the fourth a real-time scroll of GPS coordinates, each line coded with a "K," a "D," or an "M."

K. D. M. His mantra.

A little over seven months earlier, one morning in an office somewhere in Tampa, an admin's computer screen had gone blank, then immediately refreshed itself, the contents of its display uninterrupted—except for the simple transposition of two lowercase letters. In the lengthy URL displayed in the browser's address bar, "service" had become "serivce." Otherwise, the two screens were identical.

The admin had just taken a sip of mocha latte, extra shot, and never even noticed.

And just like that, Finn was in: full admin access to an intranet that posted travel itineraries and meeting schedules for every officer in the US Navy. Nothing classified or especially weighty; no real content. Just who would be where, and when, and with whom.

Not much, but a place to start.

In the months since his little phishing operation penetrated SOCOM headquarters, Finn had built on that start by cobbling together a patchwork of video feeds that allowed him to monitor his subjects as they moved around, sometimes in the US, sometimes overseas. He'd even managed to worm his way into audio feeds in several spots. No secure or personal communications, nothing high-level or especially revealing; he was still on the outside looking in.

But looking in with a thousand eyes.

For the past eight months Finn had been on a long-distance stakeout, tracking three officers up his chain of command. He hadn't learned anything relevant. Not yet. But sooner or later one of the three would slip and reveal a minor detail.

That detail would be the loose thread Finn would catch on to and pull.

And when the whole sweater came unraveled, Finn would know which one of the three it was. He would know who was behind the slaughter in Mukalla that they were now pinning on him.

Lieutenant Kennedy had known. That's what got him killed.

Kennedy.

The concept of "friendship" had always been foreign to Finn. It wasn't a skill set he grasped. At least he'd never thought so. But events of the past year had forced him to reconsider that assumption. In Reykjavík, someone he barely knew had left him a note saying, *You are good friend.* And he'd known she meant it.

Finn had always seen Kennedy as the man he looked up to most, after Ray. It was only now that he was gone that Finn understood this inconceivable truth: They'd been *friends.*

Best friends.

And he owed it to his friend to find the man responsible for his death.

He'd already ID'ed their old teammate Paulie as the probable triggerman. Tracking down Paulie, alive or dead, was his second priority. But not his first. Because Paulie was only a puppet.

Priority 1 was the puppet master.

Identifying the man who'd pulled the strings was also a matter of survival—it was the only way to clear his own name and avoid life in a maximum-security cell the size of this tiny room. That, or death by lethal injection.

Or death by some other, more clandestine means.

The military wanted to arrest him and take him to trial. But there was another party with a different agenda. A party who didn't want Finn arrested. Who wanted Finn erased.

Finn fired up his Coleman, turned, and looked at the sketched portraits on the opposite wall.

Keyes, Dugan, Meyerhoff.

Three men, all in uniform. Each bearing the features of leaders, men who bore great responsibility with grit and discipline. Dedicated men. Respected men.

But was any of that true?

Had Finn drawn what was there, or what he'd been told was there?

In sniper school, a surveillance instructor had shown them two reproductions of famous paintings, a portrait by Vermeer and some cubist nightmare by Picasso.

"I know what you're thinking," he said. "The first one looks like a very pretty photograph. The second one looks like the guy holding the brush was having a psychotic break. But look closer.

"From a sniper's perspective, the Vermeer is useless. All soft focus and luminosity and projection. All subjectivity. Vermeer's showing you what he wants you to see. What he feels about the subject.

"The thing about Picasso, he didn't paint what you want to see, or what you think you see, or how you look at what you see, or even what the camera sees. His thing was to paint what's actually there."

Finn wasn't sure about the man's take on cubism. But he never forgot the lesson.

Don't draw what you think is there. Draw what's actually there.

He looked at the three men again.

Keyes. Dugan. Meyerhoff.

K. D. M.

Finn had done the math. There were only three officers in positions of authority relative to his platoon who could possibly have been the one calling the shots.

Three men. Two solid. One rotten.

Which one?

The pencil sketches danced in the kerosene lamp's soft glow.

Don't draw what you think is there. Draw what's actually there.

Tommy Keyes, the platoon's CO, directly above Kennedy. Task force commander on base in Yemen. Keyes was the very definition of a straight arrow. A guy with an Olympic-level pole up his ass. If Finn had to guess, he'd say Keyes didn't have the imagination to pull off something so devious and intricate as a massive cover-up.

No, not Keyes.

Commander Dugan, the O-5 above Keyes. Finn had known Dugan way back in the early days of SEAL selection, and later in Iraq. Finn didn't have a great deal of experience with the concept of "kindness," but he'd seen it in Dugan. The man was tough, but fair. To some of the guys in the course, Dugan was the father they'd never had.

Couldn't be Dugan.

Admiral Meyerhoff, then, the O-7 in charge of it all, stationed in Bahrain. Meyerhoff was a force of nature. A legend. If they took the entire US Navy, ships, planes, guns, and all, melted it down to a slurry, poured it into a man-shaped mold, and let it cool, it would be this guy. Finding out it was Meyerhoff who'd masterminded this whole thing would be like learning that water ran uphill, that gravity was an illusion. That the center of the sun was ice-cold. Not possible.

It couldn't be Meyerhoff.

It couldn't be any of them.

But it had to be one of them.

9

"You want to talk about it?"

"No."

They continued eating in silence.

They'd spent the better part of the day walking around Old San Juan as "Charles" and "Emma," getting the lay of the city while Toño Rivera, their SIB contact, marshaled the resources they'd requested. Now they were having a shared room-service supper in Monica's hotel room. Agent Rivera was personally setting up Dar's room, what they called Room B, as their satellite data ops center.

The food was fresh and fabulous. The conversation, mostly monosyllabic.

The two had agreed to kick off their investigation by splitting up and pursuing the paths they each knew best. For Dar, ever the analyst, that meant doing an exhaustive search of data. In this case, CCTV images from the entire island—traffic stops, ATMs, casinos, government buildings, retail stores, whatever Rivera could get him—from the past eight months. It was an incomprehensibly vast data set, one that would take a supercomputer capable of trillions of floating point operations per second.

Rivera said he could manage access to such a

computer through their mutual contact at the San Juan FBI office. The challenge was transporting the actual data. He would have to load the search results onto hard drives and physically cart them over to Dar's hotel room, where they were setting up a bank of laptops and color laser printers to work on the second-tier sort.

Given the scope of the operation it would take days, not hours.

And while they were doing all that, what would the lady from JAG require?

The lady from JAG. Adventures in Macholand.

Shit fire and hold the matches.

"I just need a helicopter," Monica had replied. "With a pilot who knows the island and can keep his mouth shut."

Since handling their requests had taken Agent Rivera the balance of the day to arrange, there was nothing much else the two could do until the following morning. It was driving her nuts. They had one week, and the first day already felt like a waste.

And she couldn't help resenting Adamson's civilian presence. She didn't like being babysat. Which she knew made no sense at all; strictly speaking this was his gig, not hers. She was the one they'd sent along to ride shotgun, because of her experience. Not as a pilot. Because she'd actually known the subject.

She shuddered.

"Wish I'd never laid eyes on him," she murmured.

Dar said nothing, just hoovered up another spoonful of asopao, Puerto Rico's national soup.

"When I told him what I'd worked out—"

"I thought you didn't want to talk about it."

"I don't."

Silence descended once more.

Broken once again by Monica.

"That day, on the ship," she said. "When I told him that someone had sabotaged that Knighthawk before he ever came on board? That I'd realized none of it could've been him? He looked *relieved.* Like he hadn't been sure himself whether he'd killed those people."

"But he didn't, right? It was the other guy. Stevens."

"Yeah. Evidently." She speared another bite of garlicky deep-fried plantain. "I didn't know about Mukalla at that point. Didn't know about it till three weeks ago."

"He saved your life, though, no?" he persisted. "With the captain, on the fantail?"

"Yeah. Probably."

"But you still want to bring him in."

She put down her fork and looked at him.

"Did you see the photos?"

That shut him up.

Yeah, he'd seen the photos.

This was, after all, his show.

It was Dar who'd figured it out.

DIA had picked up their quarry's trail on the East Coast, briefly, then again in Reykjavík, where they'd confronted him at the airport trying to escape the country.

And he'd slipped through their fingers like water.

No one could understand how it happened. They'd pored over every plane manifest for every flight that left Reykjavík that day, finally found him on a flight to JFK traveling under a fake name. The flight touched down in New York, then continued on to Miami and San Juan—but Finn wasn't on it.

He got off at JFK . . . and vanished.

For months, they'd examined CCTV footage from all over the airport, trying to pick up a lead. Nothing. And no explanation. Not even a hypothesis. No one had the faintest whisper of a clue as to how the man could just evaporate like that.

Until Dar came up with a theory: What if he didn't?

What if he stayed on the plane?

Impossible, they said. He would have showed up on the manifest, and every single passenger had checked out. No fakes. No way.

Yeah, but what if he did the impossible? He'd done it before.

So Dar went back and personally reinterviewed every member of the flight crew. This time one of them happened to ask if they'd talked with "that nice pilot."

Nice pilot?

You know, the one who deadheaded through on the jump seat.

The jump seat?

Turned out the elusive Chief Finn had lifted a flight bag with a pilot's uniform, hidden in a bathroom during the chaotic reboarding at JFK, put his own photo on his clip-on ID, and emerged as an off-duty pilot looking to deadhead to the Island of Enchantment for a day's well-earned R&R.

And they gave him the jump seat.

The freaking jump seat.

Just like goddamn Frank Abagnale.

Adamson had pulled footage from every CCTV in both Miami-Dade and Luis Muñoz Marín airports for the three hours surrounding the time that flight touched down that day. Found shots in San Juan of a pilot he was convinced was Finn, although, infuriatingly, the man's face never showed up on camera. Somehow he'd managed to keep his head lowered just enough for the bill on the captain's hat to hide his features every single time he was within image-capture range.

Dar's conviction that this was their guy was viewed at the bureau as sketchy at best. It took him six weeks to persuade them to let him fly down and take a look around. He'd finally worn them down through sheer persistence.

Adamson, as Monica was already learning, could be one infuriating son of a bitch.

"One week," they'd told him. "You've got one week to find your ghost." A week, period, and then their superiors would pull the plug and reel them both back home.

"So," said Dar, "combat helo pilot to JAG investigator. Hell of a left turn. What made you make the switch?"

She was grateful for the change in topic, though this one wasn't much easier for her to talk about.

Her brother Sloane thought she was flat-out crazy when she announced her intentions back in the fall. Her mother's only comment: "It won't bring your friends back, you know." Vanessa didn't use the word "impulsive" in that particular phone call, but that'd always been her stock assessment of her daughter's career choices.

Which Monica found infuriating. It wasn't impulsive. It was just that flying didn't make sense anymore, not after the events on that accursed deployment aboard the *Lincoln*. And somehow, JAG did.

"Your father was a lawyer, right?" Dar noted. "So I guess, justice runs in your family?"

The guy had done his homework on her. Before joining the navy, she'd followed her father's footsteps and gone into law school, done two years before bailing to go enlist and chase her wings.

"Something like that," she said.

Her father would've understood her abrupt career change.

Wish you were here, Dad. Maybe you could explain it to me.

"Well, whatever your reasons, it's a good thing for us you did." Dar pushed his chair away from the room-service cart and stood to leave. "Early start tomorrow."

At the door he stopped and turned.

"You know, Emma, to keep up appearances, I should really stay in here with you."

Monica blanched.

He grinned and chuckled. "Oh, c'mon, Lieutenant. Sense of humor."

She blushed, chiding herself for letting him get under her skin.

"Take a breath," said Dar. "Yes, our clock is ticking. But we're gonna find the SEAL. We're gonna find him, and we're gonna haul him back to the States to face a panel of his peers. All right?"

She flashed a thumbs-up and tried to look positive.

She didn't want the SEAL to face a panel of his peers.

She wanted to shoot him herself.

10

The streets of Esperanza were still warm, though the midnight breeze had cooled the air a bit. He took a few breaths and began walking. He couldn't have lain on that bedroll in that tiny room for another minute.

Finn had a long history of claustrophobia. That he'd made it through SEAL training and deployment without the condition's detection had to be some kind of miracle. For the past year the symptoms had ebbed. Not altogether disappeared, but slipped into the background. Most of the time, at least. When he worked on his surveillance project, they receded. When he closed the laptop and lay back on his bedroll, they came creeping back. Sometimes, like tonight, they drove him out onto the darkened streets.

On those walks, he mostly thought about the past. About what he remembered, and what he didn't.

Finn was a haunted man.

Over the past year a series of critical memories had come back to him, resolving questions that had hung over him for thirty years like a kettle of vultures. Yet the revelations hadn't made the torment magically disappear. There were layers to his haunting, sediments of suffering that had grown around him over the years like barnacles, and they clung with a fierce persistence.

Carol said it started in the hospital, when he was eight.

"Nobody came to rescue you. I think that's why you became a rescue swimmer. You do for other people what no one was there to do for you."

But of course, Carol hadn't known about what happened just before the hospital. What landed him there in the first place.

He hadn't remembered himself until a year ago.

He walked to the center of town and down to the Malecón, the tile-floored boardwalk that abutted the Caribbean shoreline, then down a set of tile steps and out onto Esperanza Beach. He took a right and headed west, toward Black Sand Beach.

The evidence—or lack of it—said they were dead. Yet he didn't think so.

Which surprised him.

Finn did not generally take an optimistic view of life. Although it would not be accurate to say he took a pessimistic view of life, either. He did his best not to take any view of life at all, but just see things as they were.

This was his sniper training. That was the point, after all, of sketching an area of operation. You went into a territory and sketched the AO to reveal what you were dealing with. Not what you hoped you were dealing with, or feared you were dealing with. Not the best-case or worst-case scenario.

No scenario at all.

Don't draw what you think is there. Draw what's actually there.

But right now he was making an exception to that

practice. Right now he was holding a picture of an optimistic outcome.

He didn't know why he was doing that.

He just had to.

Playa Grande . . . Playa Vaca . . . Playa Vieja . . .

As the sand gave way to rock, Finn began climbing again.

Got lost. Injured. Ran away. Parental abduction. Non-parental abduction.

And then there was that sixth possibility, the one the lieutenant hadn't mentioned. The one on which Finn was rapidly becoming an expert.

On the run. Hiding from a predator.

The clock was ticking, and each tick cut deeper into his chances of finding them alive. If they were still alive.

He had to believe they were still alive.

Tick, tick, tick.

He pulled his pocket flash to help him see over the treacherous terrain. One-thousand-lumen LED, solid steel body. Most reliable illumination he knew. Also one of the best pocket weapons. Blind your assailant, or whack him with the steel casing. Dual purpose.

Finn had bought it online on his laptop using a fake account, had it shipped to a post office box he kept in Isabel Segunda. Along with his new razor-sharp four-inch steel ring knife and a few other essentials, all of which he stored in his backpack.

The laptop itself he'd purchased on the computer at the Paper Mill, using a VPN, or "virtual private network," and a brilliant little piece of software called TOR, which stood for "The Onion Router," so named because it channeled the user's online activity through a sequence of layers like an onion.

Rendering the user, for all practical purposes, invisible and untraceable. Popularly called the "dark web." Regularly employed by desperate citizens in authoritarian territories. Also by drug dealers and purveyors of extreme porn.

Created by US Navy researchers.

Your tax dollars at work.

The Onion Router was Finn's exclusive connection to the outside world. He used it for everything he did online, keeping his footprint as close to zero as possible.

Although in truth, there was no such thing as zero footprint. Finn knew this. Especially when you went on the hunt. All surveillance entailed risk.

When you searched, you made yourself searchable.

He cleared the last of the large rock formations and reached semi-sandy beach on the island's west side, most of which was off limits to civilians. Back in the day, the navy's actual target sites—what they called the "live impact area," or LIA—had been located on the eastern tip of the island. But there was plenty of activity on the western side, too, including tons of storage and disposal. Some on land, some in the water. No one really had a full account.

He kept walking.

Halfway up the western shore, he stopped.

He clicked off his flash.

Stood still for a minute, waiting for his eyes to adjust. Then walked on in the darkness. Stretching out his senses.

You have to feel the space around things.

In the distance, Finn spotted a telltale scatter of white. A pod of dolphins, out hunting for an early breakfast.

The night sky was crystal-clear.

Finn felt something brush the outside of one foot. He froze.

Something pliable, like seaweed fronds. But not seaweed.

He clicked on his flash again, pointed it down at his feet, and saw, there in the pebbled sand, what the incoming tide had washed up.

A pink snorkel.

Tuesday

T minus 5

Early this morning, Invest 95L's winds began to organize, creating the well-defined center or "eye" that defines an atmospheric disturbance as a "tropical cyclone." The storm is now racing west at forward speeds of up to forty miles per hour, twice the speed of the average cyclone's forward motion.

It is not yet known whether Invest 95L will reach the Caribbean Basin or dissipate its energy over the Atlantic.

11

Finn awoke screaming.

Not out loud, of course. Silent screams that shivered through his body and finally shook him out of sleep. Now he lay silent, sweat-soaked in the still heat of the room, staring up into the darkness.

Trying to remember their faces.

One of the nurses had been kind enough to talk to him, to explain, in hushed tones, why it was they strapped him down and shot him full of sedatives when he awoke screaming for his parents.

"We do it to protect you," she'd said. "You're having night terrors."

Young Finn didn't understand. "Night terrors" about what? He didn't remember the dreams once he was awake. He didn't remember how he got to the hospital, or what happened before. He had a memory of his father telling Ray and him, "We should be back in a day, two at most." That had to be at least a few days ago. Right?

So where were they?

Why were these people keeping him a prisoner there? Why wouldn't they let his parents in to see him? He kept expecting them to walk through the door and lift him off that hospital bed, take him out of here, bring him home, and make everything back the way it was.

But they never came.

Why wouldn't his captors let them in to see him?

He found out, of course, eventually. His parents weren't being kept out. They just never came. He never saw them again.

And now, thirty years later, he couldn't remember their faces.

"The man with the million-dollar memory." A nickname they'd given him in sniper school. He could surveil a territory once and reproduce it in detailed sketches with startling accuracy.

And he couldn't remember his own parents' faces.

"It makes sense, though." This was Carol speaking, when he had confessed this to her years ago. "They abandoned you. Left you there, alone in that scary place. So you erased them. It hurt too much to remember."

But they hadn't abandoned him, Finn objected. Or at least, eight-year-old Finn didn't know that. All eight-year-old Finn knew at that point was what eight-year-old Finn had been told, which was basically nothing. "They can't come right now . . . Later, be patient . . . You just need to rest."

It wasn't till weeks had passed, still in the hospital, that he'd finally gotten an answer to his question. That he finally found out why they never came to see him.

It happened one night when they all thought he was asleep.

"Poor kid . . ."

Disembodied voices, floating somewhere above him. He kept his eyes shut. By this time he'd taught himself how to breathe in a slow, semi-fitful way that aped a drugged sleep. He'd learned how to fool them, how to make them think he was asleep when he wasn't, how to make them think he was panicked when he wasn't, and how to keep them from seeing he *was* panicked when he truly was.

"It was the only thing you could control." Carol again, and as usual, she was right. He was helpless in that hospital bed. Even when he sat up to eat, they hovered, watching him like prairie wolves, strapping him down and jabbing him with needles when he got too loud.

But they couldn't see inside his thoughts.

So he'd been lying there silent, secretly awake, when he heard the voices floating above him.

"Poor kid. You hear about his parents?" whispered one voice.

"I know," a second voice whispered. "Hit by a fuckin' *truck*!"

It had taken every ounce of eight-year-old willpower to keep still when he heard those terrible words.

Once he was sure they'd left the room, sure he was alone in his cold cell with no one around to hear, he let a few sobs escape, then reined himself in and lay silently weeping in the dark until he fell into an exhausted sleep.

Later, in his first foster home, he'd pieced together a picture of what happened.

They'd been on one of their road trips when they'd heard the news about the accident at home. Turned the car around and headed back. It was late at night. There was a thunderstorm, driving rain, visibility near zero. On a long curve in the road, an eighteen-wheeler slammed into them.

Those details came to him only in bits and pieces,

long after he'd finally left the hospital. All he knew in that moment, lying stone-still on his cold prison bed with the hushed floating voices, was those five words.

Hit by a fuckin' truck.

For the next five years he'd been tormented by a recurring dream: the car, threading its way along a highway through the Oregon woods in a blinding thunderstorm, going into that long curve—and the massive crash when the two vehicles collided head-on.

And Finn would wake up sweating, screaming in his head.

And now, the past few months here on Vieques, the dream had been coming again, and Finn didn't understand why.

Because it wasn't true.

None of it.

It was a fantasy, a fiction eight-year-old Finn had invented to preserve his sanity. It wasn't until Finn was in his teens that the reprobate who ran his third (and final) foster home told him what really happened.

"Yer ma and pa, they's fugitives, boy, wanted in three states. When you hit the loony bin, they just run off."

The moment the man said it, Finn knew it was true. The isolated cabin. The barrels of fertilizer in the shed. The closet full of guns. *Wanted in three states.* His parents hadn't been killed in a crash. When they heard there'd been an accident and the police were at their cabin, they'd just stepped on the gas and kept right on going.

And that whispered conversation had come back to him then—the true, unedited version.

"Poor kid. You hear about his parents?"

"I know. Fuckers. Would've been better for him if they'd been hit by a fuckin' truck."

Would've been better.

"They call it 'magical thinking,'" Carol told him. "Something you make yourself believe because you don't want to face what really happened."

She was right; he'd known it even then, at the age of eight. That was the reason his life came unmoored, why he'd drifted at sea ever since.

There was no thunderstorm. Just one long empty night, and a car's taillights disappearing off to points unknown.

While an eight-year-old boy lay screaming in a hospital bed.

Even after he learned the truth, he still thought of himself as an orphan. He still thought of them as dead. He'd even put down "orphan" on his enlistment papers, more out of habit than anything. As Carol said, he erased them. They abandoned him, so he abandoned them back.

And even now, try as he might, he still could not remember their faces.

12

Still dark out.

Finn set his backpack down on the little skiff's wooden floor, gave the fuel hose pump two squeezes to prime the line, and pulled the choke. One tug of the starter rope and the little engine awoke with a quiet purr. He rolled on the throttle, carefully so as not to wake the town residents, and eased out of the harbor, sifting and weighing the air, assessing conditions.

Winds out of the north at less than five knots. No swell activity.

A calm morning, just as the NOAA forecast had promised.

NOAA weather was good, but not as reliable as his own senses. And winds in the Sound could spring up without warning. Today, though, NOAA and the wind seemed to be in agreement.

The smell of old fish hung in the air. There were no sounds but the cries of terns and *slap!* of pelicans hitting the water, and underneath that the soft thrum of the surf, the ocean's heartbeat.

Normally, a scene like this would recalibrate all his internal gauges to perfect stasis. According to Carol, seawater ran in Finn's veins. He'd taken her on a canoe trip around Lummi Island one day. She'd watched him the whole time, her expression unreadable as a cat's. When they docked, she gave up the faintest hint of a smile. "If you spent too much time on land," she observed, "you'd drown in it." Right again. Being in or on the water was his reset button.

But not this morning. Right now, not even the perfection of a solo boat trip in the Caribbean predawn was sufficient to dispel his looming sense of disequilibrium.

Finn was reluctant to leave the island. With a single exception, it would be the only time he'd ventured off Vieques since he'd arrived.

Talking to the lieutenant at the café was one thing. The Vieques police didn't interact much with the big island. It was like a closed system. As long as he stayed put, cooked at Papi's, and kept his head down, he'd felt relatively safe, or at least concealed.

Once he hit the other side of the Sound, it would be a whole different scenario.

Wiping the saltwater sting from his eyes, he pointed his craft west and goosed the outboard up a notch for the sixty-minute run.

As he rounded the western tip of the island and arced north, he clocked a Coast Guard cutter trolling the waters off the western beaches. CUTTYHUNK, said the big letters on the transom.

Picking up the search where he'd left off.

After finding the snorkel the night before, he'd spent the next few hours there diving, looking for bodies. Didn't find any. Not that he'd expected to. Diving alone, in the dark, was no way to conduct a search. Besides, the currents there were unpredictable. They could just as easily have been carried out deep into the Sound.

But Finn didn't think so.

He thought they'd been taken.

He'd told the police about the snorkel, of course, and they'd immediately contacted the Coast Guard. The lieutenant might stick to his no-opinions position, but the Coast Guard clearly had an opinion. They believed the kids had drowned.

Hugo and the other townspeople Finn had spoken with believed they were still somewhere on the island, maybe lost in the preserve, maybe hurt (maybe dead, though nobody was voicing that latter thought out loud), and that sooner or later they'd be found.

Not Finn.

His instincts said they weren't anywhere on Vieques. They had left the island. And not of their own volition.

She would not have left that snorkel behind.

He slowed to no-wake speed as he approached the little harbor at Fajardo. He'd made good time. The place was just barely coming to life, as he'd expected.

He'd wanted to dock somewhere he'd face the least scrutiny possible, yet still keep his boat secure enough that it would be there when he got back. He'd picked the marina at Puerto Chico, a small facility to the north, over the larger and more well-trafficked harbors of Sunbay and Puerto Del Rey. The fewer people, the fewer questions, the better.

As he cut the engine and glided to the concrete dock, he heard the familiar *chree, chree, chree* of the coquí frogs. Little buggers were everywhere on the big island, silent during the day but dominating the sonic landscape at night.

"That's our national symbol. You knew that, right?"

Pedro's earnest soprano, clear as a glass bell in Finn's ear.

Eight weeks earlier, he'd taken the two niños—or *nenes,* as they said in Puerto Rico—across the Sound for that Fourth of July outing. Against his better judgment, but he'd wanted to do something special for them. He'd taken them for lunch at a seaside café in Palmas del Mar, farther down the coast. And bought them a Fourth of July present.

A pair of matching snorkels.

"You know how they got their name? The coquí?"

Pedro's solemn eyes always took on an electric excitement when he explained things.

Finn had just listened. No need to say, *No, how?* When Pedro was all primed and ready to spill, he didn't need any prompting.

"So, this goddess falls in love with this young guy named Coquí, the chief's son. She told him she would come for him that night, but before she got there someone else showed up—the evil Juracán, deity of chaos and disorder."

Finn had nodded. Chaos and disorder. He was familiar with the concept.

"The sky went black and the winds rose up hard. The goddess tried to protect the man she loved, but Juracán snatched him away—and they never saw each other again! And the goddess, I guess trying to cope with her loss, she created this little frog that would call out his name forever—*Co-KEE! Co-KEE!*"

Finn suppressed a smile. The boy did such an earnest frog imitation.

"Although, there's this other legend, too," Pedro

added. "That one says another evil god named Guahoyona abducted all the women from the island, leaving the men to take care of the children. But the men didn't do a very good job of it, and pretty soon the children were all hungry, and they started crying, 'Toa-Toa,' meaning 'Mother, Mother!' And since their fathers didn't know how to take care of them, the children all turned into frogs."

The boy's face fell as he went silent for a moment.

"That one doesn't really make sense, though. And Toa-Toa isn't even the right sound."

Finn tied the little fishing boat off to two big cleats, slung his pack over his shoulder, and stepped out onto the dock.

No, he thought, it didn't really make sense. But the boy had told the abduction story anyway, hadn't he.

The boy whose madre and abuela were both long gone, abducted by cancer, leaving the men to take care of them.

Finn turned back to the water and sniffed the air again. Sifting, weighing.

Five knots, no swell.

He left the boat behind and headed inland.

13

Just north of the marina stood a good-sized hill, heavily treed, no structures on it. Finn had located the spot online before setting out; it was the highest elevation in the immediate area. In the distance, he could just see the hazy outline of the El Yunque mountains.

From this vantage point, he now stood looking out at the landscape spread around him.

These smaller population centers weren't what people in the States would think of as "cities." More like sprawling villages that crept over the hillsides like vines, hamlets tucked into gullies and ravines and isolated spots where the jungle allowed little clusters of humanity to coexist with the island's native wilderness.

Directly below, half a klick to the south, two enormous smokestacks towered over the ruins of an abandoned sugar mill, surrounded by a maze of streets dotted with mostly abandoned houses.

The travel agents called Puerto Rico the "Island of Enchantment," because of its tropical beaches and breezes, its waterfalls and caves, its bioluminescent bays and breathtaking pageantry of exotic flora and fauna.

Seen from the inside, it was a different story.

"Remember the Boston Tea Party, the colonial Americans' big beef with Britain? 'No taxation without representation,' right? That right there? That's us . . ."

This was Tómas, one of the SEALs who'd been part of that boat exercise at Rosie Roads, the one where they'd all nearly drowned. Tómas was a Puerto Rico native; he'd shown Finn and a few other guys around the island, the best surfing spots in Rincón, the best nightlife in San Juan. Nobody knew how to party like puertorriqueños, he'd told them. "We invented the concept."

Later that night he'd shared some of the grittier realities of life on la isla grande.

"Puerto Rico is basically a post-colonial colony. Ruled by a president we can't vote for and a Congress where we have no vote. We pay our taxes and serve in the military, but we're not allowed to ship in our own food. San Juan is the oldest city on American soil, and five in ten Americans don't even realize we're part of America. We're like an adopted kid who got left in the parking lot in a hot car by parents who went shopping and forgot about us."

There was a reason for the "Rico" in "Puerto Rico," Tómas said. At one time, more than a century ago, the place was an agricultural Eden, the most productive island in the Caribbean, doing a thriving export business in coffee, sugar, tobacco, and more.

"Shit, man, back then we grew all our own food. Now we have to import everything. Our agriculture got stripped, our economy got choked and bled. We got three strata to this island's class system. The wealthy. The tourists. And everyone else."

That was 2003. Since then the government and

national utility had both gone bankrupt. One in every three residents now lived below the poverty line. And they still couldn't vote.

Island of Enchantment.

Island of Abandonment.

Finn turned to face north, toward the resorts, the golf course, the four- and five-star hotels, the tracts of pricey homes. The boating crowd kept their yachts there, in striking distance of the islands—Vieques, Culebra, and the Virgin Islands beyond. Up in that neighborhood, sightings of Hollywood celebrities were everyday events.

He turned back and looked south, toward the ancient town center and its outlying barrios, where the poorest residents lived.

Mapping out his strategy.

Assuming the kids were taken, the central strategic question became, Why? Answer that, and you'd find the who and the where.

So why were they taken?

It didn't seem like a planned event. No one would have had any way of knowing in advance that these two children would be out there in that specific location, at that specific time. Let alone any conceivable reason to set up a kidnapping, even if they did know.

Which meant it happened on the spur of the moment. Whoever took them hadn't expected them to be there. And their presence was not simply unexpected but unwanted.

Ergo: The kids were taken because they saw something they weren't supposed to see.

Such as what?

The obvious answer would be a drug-running operation in progress. The passages around Puerto Rico were notorious waterways for the drug trade. The big island served as the perfect gateway between Colombia and other South American countries to the lucrative US markets. Once you got your contraband into Puerto Rico's harbors or airports, you were already on US soil. You didn't need a passport to fly from San Juan to Miami. It was like flying from Atlanta to New York.

That was why they called Puerto Rico "America's third border."

Could it have been something else the two children witnessed, something other than drugs?

Sure it could. Finn could come up with half a dozen alternative scenarios. A murder. Politicians having an onboard orgy. An alien invasion. But none of those seemed likely.

When you hear hoofbeats, don't look for zebras. Something he'd heard Kennedy say more than once. Kennedy had been trained as a corpsman, and apparently it was a saying among medical people. Their version of Occam's razor. Given a range of possible solutions, go for the most obvious.

If these hoofbeats were horses—if it was drug runners he was dealing with—then his mission was simple: Find whoever was in charge of running drugs in the Sound.

Find him, or them, and he'd find Pedro and Miranda.

And take them back.

That was the strategy.

Now he just had to work out the tactics.

Exactly how should he locate and confront his drug-running capo?

Talking to the police was out. No passing out

photos of Pedro and Miranda or putting up posters saying, HAVE YOU SEEN THESE CHILDREN? No going to the media. He couldn't do any of that.

For one thing, it wouldn't do any good. Not if he was dealing with the kind of people he thought he was dealing with. The attempt would only increase his own odds of being scooped up by the multiple military intel forces already scouring the planet for him, which would take his odds of finding Pedro and Miranda down to a big fat zero.

No, no cops, no newspaper or television sleuths. No anyone.

He'd have to execute this stalk on his own.

Crime networks had their hubs in big cities. The top dogs of Puerto Rico's crime families all lived somewhere in high-rise beachfront condos in and around San Juan. Just an hour away by car. But San Juan was also where all the island's law enforcement, intel, and military communities were headquartered. About as far from "lying low" as you could get without putting up billboards saying HEY, IT'S ME, CHIEF FINN, HERE I AM!

Finn would not be going to San Juan.

Besides, a frontal assault would only get him shot, even if he knew which doors to knock on. Which he didn't.

All of which was why he was right now standing on a wooded hill overlooking Fajardo.

When it came to the drug trade, Fajardo was like a battery, its north pole the rich boating crowd, a prime market for cocaine, pills, and pot. Its south pole, the projects. Meth and crack. In between, the nodes of distribution. The dealers.

His tactical target.

That much he could see from a map.

Here was what Google Maps didn't show: A territory was a living, breathing fabric. A web. If a fly stumbled into it on the far edge, the spider instantly knew it. Events made ripples; nothing happened in a vacuum.

So how did you find the spider at the heart of a criminal network?

You didn't.

You let the spider find you.

A crisp trade wind blew cooling salt-clean air in from the ocean as the late-August sun burned away the sea mist blanketing the village below.

Finn set his backpack down, withdrew a few simple bits of tactical equipment, and began assembling them as he waited for the little town of Fajardo to wake up and start its day.

14

Pedro had been awake for an hour.

He'd been having a nightmare, bull sharks standing on their tails, dancing in a chorus line to reggae music, circling them. Louder and louder, closer and closer, dancing and singing and clicking their big teeth—

When he awoke he made no noise, the way he'd learned from Mimo.

At first he kept his eyes closed. He heard a TV going in the next room, or maybe it was a radio. The sound was too muffled to make out what the show was.

Then he heard a voice, also muffled. From the tone, it sounded like the man was complaining. After a minute, a second, quieter voice answered. He couldn't quite hear what either of them were saying.

Pedro's head ached. His mouth felt like it was stuffed with cotton. He smacked his lips a few times and rubbed his tongue around his mouth to get some saliva going. Yuck. There was a nasty taste on his tongue.

Pedro was pretty sure they'd been drugged.

He heard the sound of Miranda breathing and listened for a moment. She was still asleep, right next to him.

When he felt sure there was no one in the room watching them, he opened his eyes and looked around.

He was in a small room, lying on a folded worn cotton blanket. The wood floor was painted an ugly green. Miranda lay on another blanket, on her side, still asleep, her face sweaty, frowning. She was having bad dreams, too, though he couldn't tell if they were as nightmarish as his.

There was no closet in the room. No furniture. In the corner, a cardboard box with a few old toys. Picture books for toddlers. A magnetic alphabet board, half the letters missing.

There was a single dirty window on one wall, covered in bars that ran up and down on the outside. Opposite the window, a single door, from behind which came the sounds of the TV or radio—radio, he thought, definitely a radio—and the two men talking to each other.

He didn't bother going over to try the doorknob. He felt sure it would be locked.

There was a bottle of water next to his mat. Seeing it made him realize how thirsty he was. He opened the bottle and drank and drank, until the bottle was half empty. He put it down without a sound.

The voices continued. Mostly the louder one, now and then the quieter one answering. Once or twice Pedro caught a few words. The louder guy was complaining about his bowels and cursed a lot.

He had no idea what they looked like, but in his mind he saw them as orcs. Loud Orc and Quiet Orc.

He got on his hands and knees and crawled around Miranda, careful not to wake her, then to the window. He stood, feeling a little woozy, and peered out through the dirt and the bars.

There was a backyard of mostly broken-up asphalt and weeds. One car parked there. No other houses or buildings that he could see, just wild-looking grasslands and rolling hills, and beyond that, trees. Trees and trees and trees. Some regular. Some huge. Like the jungle around Pirate Mountain, only more so.

El Yunque. It had to be.

They were on the edge of El Yunque National Forest!

Pedro had never seen the rain forest before, not in real life, only in books and on websites. Even through this dirty window, it looked so much realer than he could've imagined. And so big! Like Fangorn Forest in *Lord of the Rings*! He couldn't stop staring at it. He almost said *Wow!* out loud, but then he remembered where he was, and he didn't say anything.

Silently, he got back down on all fours, crawled over to Miranda, and gently shook her awake.

Her eyes sprang open.

"¿Qué está—" she started to say—*What's going on?*—but he put a hand over her mouth and the index finger of his other hand to his lips. "Shhh."

Her eyes went wide. She looked around, taking in their surroundings, then nodded solemnly.

"Drink," he whispered. He handed her the half-full bottle. She polished it off.

"I think we've been kidnapped," he whispered.

She nodded, her eyes wider now. She sat up and looked at him. "For ransom?" she whispered. Then she grinned. "How is Papi going to pay, in fish heads?"

"Yeah, maybe," he murmured. Her joke was making him think. They were poor. Why would anyone kidnap them?

Why were they there?

And most important: What was going to happen next?

He crawled to the door and pressed his ear to it so he could hear the voices a little better. Loud Orc was wondering how long the two of them would have to wait.

Wait for what, Pedro didn't know.

He knocked hard on the door.

Someone turned the radio way down.

"We have to pee," he said, loudly.

"Fuck," he heard one voice mutter. Loud Orc, he was pretty sure. Even when he was quiet, he sounded loud.

Footsteps. A key slid into the door and unlocked it. Pedro hurriedly backed up a few steps. The knob turned and the door swung open.

A man stood there. Thin. Kind of short. Thoughtful eyes in a blank face. Even before he heard the man say a word, Pedro guessed this was Quiet Orc. "I'm taking you one at a time," the man said, then nodded at Pedro.

Pedro was vaguely offended that the man was taking him first, and not his sister; she was obviously a lot younger than him. But he didn't say anything. The truth was, he was eager to get out of the little bedroom and see whatever else he could of where they were.

He stepped forward. Quiet Orc gripped his shoulder with one hand and led him through a larger living room, out the front door, and around to the side of the house, where a little shack stood. Even from a few feet away, the smell told him it was a latrine. So, no bathroom in the house.

The man opened the outhouse door and pushed

Pedro in. "I'll be standing right here," he said, then closed the door.

It smelled terrible.

Pedro peed. He looked around for some way to wash his hands, but didn't see any sink or towels or anything. He pushed the door open again.

Without a word, the man led him back inside the house, back into his room, and took Miranda.

Pedro sat and waited, telling himself not to worry, so anxious he wanted to scream. After a few minutes, to his great relief, the door opened and Miranda came back in. Before Quiet Orc had a chance to close the bedroom door again, she turned to look at him and asked, "Why are you keeping us here?"

He looked down at her. "Don't worry," he said. "You just lie down and rest. You'll be going home to your mamá and papá soon enough."

The door closed and Pedro heard the key turn in the lock. As Miranda sat down next to him, he thought about what the man had said.

You'll be going home to your mamá and papá soon enough.

He knew the man was lying. They didn't have a mamá and a papá. These men didn't even know who they were.

For a minute, neither one said anything.

"He seemed nice," Miranda whispered.

Pedro didn't say anything back.

After another minute she whispered, "Mimo will find us."

It doesn't matter, he thought. *They've let us see their faces.*

Pedro Ortega was only eleven years old, but he knew what that meant.

15

An hour after the stranger from the marina as-cended the hill, a scruffy-looking individual walked back down. Dirty blond dreadlocks. Puffy cheeks. Hunched shoulders, slightly uneven gait. Cotton drawstring pants topped by a T-shirt sporting some obscure eighties rock band.

Tactical equipment.

Finn rarely used disguises. He didn't need to. If he walked through a room of twenty people and you asked all twenty for a description, some would say he had light brown hair, some would say blond; there would be at least one who insisted he was a redhead. He was short; no, medium height. Skinny, wiry, medium build, muscular. If you asked your twenty witnesses to close their eyes and try to get the picture in focus, you'd be wasting your time.

Because you can't remember something you never saw in the first place.

Finn had a face that looked odd if you focused on it—but you wouldn't. Your eyes would slide off the moment they made contact, like a surface too slippery for your hands to get a firm grip.

That ability to evade notice and slip into the spectrum of invisibility had, like his prodigious memory, made him something of a legend in sniper school. (The joke was, anyone could disappear in a crowd; Finn could disappear in a crowd of two.) Yet this was not something he learned in sniper school. He'd learned it as a boy, over the years he went from foster home to foster home in eastern Oregon. In those environments, invisibility was a survival skill.

This situation was different. Today he *wanted* to be noticed.

Not by the people who were looking for him. By certain people who didn't even know they were looking for him. At least, not yet.

The lift in the shoe, the cotton balls in the cheeks, the dreads, should keep him invisible to the former, and put a target on his back for the latter.

At least, that was the plan.

Walking through the outskirts of Fajardo was like visiting the set of a post-apocalyptic movie. Finn had read that the little city had a population of twenty thousand. He wondered where they all were.

The grassy plaza at town center was about two klicks away. Ringed by wood-and-iron benches, shaded by ancient ceiba trees with trunks like brontosaurus legs. A statue of some war hero mounted in the brick-paved center. Arrayed around the square were the Fajardo town hall, the legislature and other government buildings, and of course the Catholic church.

A handful of people populated the plaza this morning. Two women in scrubs, employees from the clinic across the street, taking a coffee break. A family of tourists. Two local men, just sitting, playing chess on a beat-up board. One wore nice tennis shoes and a discreet gold chain around his neck. Discreet but unambiguous.

Like hanging out a shingle.

Finn approached them and spoke to the man sporting the chain.

"Excuse me, sir," he said in bad Spanish, hobbled by Finn's best take on a Danish accent. Finn's Spanish was actually quite good, and in his eight months he'd gotten a good handle on the idiosyncrasies of the local dialect, with its truncations and Spanglish and slang. But bad Spanish better served a scruffy Dane expat with limited brain power. "If I wanted to buy some groceries, who would I talk to?"

The man gave Finn a bored glance, then looked back down at his game.

"Groceries," repeated Finn. "You know what I'm saying?"

The man gave an insouciant shrug, nodded his head to the west. "Así son en la tiendita." *Store's that way.*

"I'm looking for some, you know, special groceries. Probably won't find them in a tiendita."

The man moved a pawn, ignoring him.

By "groceries" he was really talking about cocaine, of course. Or at least that's what Finn assumed. Though the other man may have been thinking he meant heroin. Or meth. Or pills. It didn't really matter to Finn what the man thought he was talking about. As long as it was illegal.

Finn drew closer, breathing heavily, and dropped his voice a few decibels.

"Actually, I have a friend, from overseas, who wants to *bring in* some groceries. A *lot* of groceries. Specialty stuff. And he'd rather ship it here direct. If you know what I mean."

The other man knew what he meant, all right. Anyone in Puerto Rico would have known what he meant.

Under a century-old US law called the Jones Act, any goods imported into Puerto Rico had to be carried by US-owned and -crewed vessels—at significantly higher rates than foreign carriers. It was the central buckle in the island's crushing economic straitjacket.

In other words, Finn's clumsy inquiry was a straightforward one: *We wanna smuggle in some dope, you know a buyer?*

No answer.

"So, you know of anyone who could hook us up?"

The man's friend moved one of his pawns. The drug dealer studied the board for a full minute, then made his next move. Knight takes pawn.

Ignoring Finn completely.

Which was fine with Finn. He expected no different.

"Hey, okay," he said. "I'll swing back later."

He'd wriggled one strand of the web. Sooner or later the spider would come poking around, see what sort of fly was making all the noise.

Sooner or later.

Although he couldn't afford later. How to make sure it was sooner?

Wriggle more strands.

Leaving the plaza, he headed a few blocks south to a "check-cashing store"—in other words, a loan shark—just off the big highway. He'd found it online early that morning. "They result to illegal and abusive methods in order to get their moneys irregardless of how big or small is your debt," an irate customer had posted. "Employees are very rude as well. Stay away!"

Perfect.

He went inside, found the place empty of clients. Approached the man behind the counter and repeated the conversation: groceries, friend, specialty stuff. Ship direct. The man acted like Finn wasn't even there.

Finn promised a return visit.

As he left the loan-shark operation and headed up the street, Finn felt a hot prickling up the back of his neck. He recognized the feeling.

Finn knew when he was being watched.

Next, he visited a seedy-looking pawnshop five blocks to the north.

Then two bars that, incredibly enough, were already open this early. One featured posted hours of 3 A.M.–12 A.M. Pillar of the community.

Nobody gave him so much as the time of day.

He headed back toward the center of town, stopping in at a respectable boat repair shop. An establishment that would be a nexus point for the wealthier dope-seekers from the resorts and hotels. Here he got a marginally more polite silence.

The whole operation, start to finish, took no more than two hours. It was enough, he figured, to set the whole web humming.

He'd swing back that way in the evening, see if anything eight-legged was there to greet him.

Finn stopped in at a store in the Plaza del Mercado, purchased half a dozen prepaid Android knockoffs, and stashed five of them in his backpack. The sixth he used to set up an Uber account and order a car to take him sixteen miles south, past Ceiba and Rosie Roads, to Humacao.

He stood outside the store, thinking about his encounters so far.

Finn had spent his teen years on the docks. Most of his friends had either OD'ed, died a violent death on the streets, or ended up on the inside. Finn himself had escaped that fate by the fortunate fact of his aversion to drugs. But he knew that world. He knew how the process worked.

It was normal to be cautious. To not respond on the first pass. To take one's time, check out new faces carefully. Still, he sensed that what he was running into was more than the normal caution. There was something else lurking behind all that stony silence.

It began to rain, a furious, full-fisted rain that pummeled the pavement like artillery shells.

Finn stepped back into the store's doorway and waited for his Uber.

16

". . . It was Puerto Rico that lifted America up from its provincial status and onto the world stage. As spoils from winning the Spanish-American War in 1898—the same year, by the way, it annexed Hawaii—the United States took possession of Guam, the Philippines, and, you guessed it, Puerto Rico. Which put the US on the map and created what would become known as the American Empire. Throughout the twentieth century, Puerto Rico served as a key strategic naval—"

"Franco?" she said into the little boom mic on her aviation headset.

"¿Señora?"

"Stop."

The pilot glanced at her and hesitated. "¿Señora?"

"The tour-guide patter. Can it. Please just tell me what we're seeing."

"Sí, señora."

Monica had spent the night before poring over maps of the island, working out her route for the day. If you're going to look for a needle in a haystack, she figured, might as well start by taking a tour of the haystack.

At Dar's insistence, Agent Rivera had set her up with a little civilian R44, on loan from a private tour company, rather than run the risk of using a police helicopter. All the pilot had been told was that "Emma" was a logistics rep for an unnamed American pharmaceutical company that was quietly scouting out possible site locations.

She'd divided up the island into sectors, like a search grid. Something she'd done over a dozen times in search-and-rescue ops from the pilot's or copilot's seat of her Knighthawk. Only this was a search for someone who didn't want to be found.

Algebra, Mon. Quantify the knowns, then solve for X.

Monica had a gift for mathematics. She'd been through officer training, pilot training, and now legal training, all of them extensive—but she still approached every new situation as a math problem. Algebra. Find for X.

"You've got a remarkable mind, Em." That was her daddy, the most successful trial lawyer in Amarillo, on the eve of her first semester of law school. "But if you want to become a great trial lawyer, you can't rely on brain power. Rationality'll take you only so far. You've got to trust your gut."

But what if your gut is wrong? she'd thought.

That was the beauty of mathematics. It was never wrong. The key to finding the unknown was the knowns. Quantify the knowns, and you'll find your X.

Algebra.

All she had to do was look at the knowns of Chief Finn.

Which were what?

Navy SEAL, obviously, decorated. Rescue swimmer. Swam like he'd been born and bred in the water. Preternaturally adept at stalking. Awkward looking as hell, but moved like a mongoose when he had to. Didn't consume caffeine or alcohol, but not a religious thing, and not a health nut. Orphan. Quiet, rarely said much.

And he'd slaughtered an entire farm village, children and all.

". . . More than sixty percent of Puerto Rico is forested," the pilot's voice was saying in her ear, "its forested mountain ranges running pretty much clear across the length of the island . . ."

They were making a complete counterclockwise circuit of the island, mostly staying close to the coastline, but right now, as they swung back east on the southern side, he had pulled inland a little bit to get the mountains into view.

She let him drone on, watching the lush countryside slip by beneath them, looking for . . . for what?

For something to go *click*, she supposed.

". . . We're now passing along the southern edge of El Yunque National Forest. Twenty-eight thousand acres, the only tropical rain forest in the US national forest system. One of the richest, most biodiverse rain forests on the . . ."

After Chief Finn jumped ship a year earlier and vanished into the night, investigators from DIA had done a deep dive on his background. Or as deep as they could, anyway.

The man was a cipher, his past mostly a trail of question marks.

They'd tracked down the retired navy psychologist who'd been at Coronado when Finn went through BUD/S and talked to him. Didn't get much, but every scrap helped.

He'd cut his teeth on the California docks, done a stint working on a dive boat, none of which was as romantic as it sounded. Tough childhood. Most of the kids he hung out with ended up dead or in prison. Finn had survived by going into the service. The psychologist had no trouble remembering him.

"Something fractured about the guy," the man had said.

No shit, Sherlock.

". . . Every year a huge yellow dust plume drifts over the island, sand and soil, straight from the Sahara, blown clear across the Atlantic." This pilot didn't have an OFF switch. "When it passes over the mountain ranges, the cooler air precipitates out the minerals, and all those nutrients dump onto El Yunque. Incredible to contemplate, isn't it? To think that the African desert can have such a profound impact on this ecosystem thousands of miles away? . . ."

What else did she know about him?

He had claustrophobia.

Now, *that* was a pretty serious psychographical tidbit, one that by all rights should have kept him out of the SEAL teams, maybe out of the military altogether. Except that nobody knew it. Somehow, he'd successfully concealed that dirty little secret from every soul he encountered. Except one: Stevens, the ship psychologist on the *Lincoln*, had figured it out.

She'd overheard him say so.

And it made sense. No wonder the SEAL was always walking the decks like an insomniac, or sitting out on some gun mount looking out at the ocean. He had trouble with enclosed spaces.

She made a mental note to share this with Adamson. Was surprised she hadn't done so already. Not like her to let something that significant slip her mind.

Dar believed Finn would be right there in San Juan. "Pretty easy to get lost in a city of a quarter million people," he'd said. She couldn't argue with that. "And immediate proximity to the airport and major harbors would mean he'd have ready access to rapid exfil, if he ever needed it. Which we both know he almost certainly would." All good points.

But Monica didn't think so.

Big cities also meant more exposure. Proximity to the heart of intel and law enforcement. The FBI, SIB, state and municipal police, border protection, Coast Guard—they all had their headquarters in San Juan. She didn't think Finn would opt to hide out in San Juan or any of the other major cities of Puerto Rico, like Ponce or Mayagüez.

Not the claustrophobic Chief Finn.

No, he'd go for smaller cities and more open spaces.

". . . Now I'm taking us over the Greater Humacao area, very strong site location opportunities here, local airstrip . . ."

Which left her with what? Three million people scattered over five thousand square miles and seventy-eight municipalities. And they had a week to find him.

Correction: six days.

They crossed into the Humacao airspace at its northwest corner and headed toward the center of town.

17

As his Uber approached Humacao from the east, Finn observed a parade of big-box American franchises sail by: Sears, Walgreens, Walmart, Marshalls, Home Depot, Ralph's. On the outskirts of the city, a halo of manufacturing, tech, and pharmaceutical companies clustered around the local airport—Medtronic, Microsoft, Bristol Myers Squibb. The Humacao landfill. A Chili's.

Finn had the driver drop him off at the baseball field on the edge of town, so he could walk from there into the heart of the city.

His mission in Humacao was a little different.

Humacao was a hub, on multiple levels. Two major highways converged there, plowing right into the heart of the city. The regional FBI satellite office was located in Humacao; so was the regional Catholic diocese. The city featured its own coliseum, a university, and a gaggle of tourist attractions; the island's most chichi resort and a handful of its poorest barrios. And it opened onto the Sound—in fact, it sat due west from Vieques.

An act like kidnapping was like dropping a stone in a still pond. Finn was betting there were people somewhere in central Humacao who would've felt the ripples.

And not only criminals.

Rather than tweaking the drug-trafficking network, in Humacao he wanted to make contact with a different underground: the network of the dispossessed.

Those who lived on the fringes knew things mainstream people didn't. People tended to ignore them, treat them like they didn't exist. They became invisible.

Much like Finn himself.

And invisible people saw and heard things—often things no one was supposed to see or hear.

Like the crime web, the street web had its nodes. Not top dogs, exactly—not like the bosses, officers, or corporate executives of the visible world. People closer to the action, those who knew what was going on and made the whole thing run. Every human structure had them. In the drug world it was the dealers. In the army it was noncoms, in the navy, chiefs.

There were chiefs among the street people, too.

Finn just had to find one.

As he walked toward the plaza at the center of the city, Finn watched and listened. There was an electricity in the air, and not a friendly one. The jokes seemed muted, the smiles brittle.

The sound of Puerto Ricans in conversation had always fascinated Finn. To him it was like listening to a fast-moving mountain stream, swirling through eddies, spilling over rocks, hurtling through narrows and rivulets.

Today the stream was at a slow trickle.

He passed a shopkeeper. Put on a smile and nodded. The shopkeeper returned the nod. No smile.

Finn could sense a quiet anxiety in the air. It didn't feel like Puerto Rico. It felt like Prague in the fifties, Germany in the thirties, a people on edge, a place on the brink of war.

He'd felt the same thing in Fajardo.

He wasn't sure what to make of it.

Reaching the plaza, he took a seat on one of the cement benches catty-corner from the stunning white-and-tan New Gothic church, withdrew an artist's pad from his backpack, and began making a sketch of a pachydermal ceiba tree across the way.

In the distance, Finn became aware of a faint humming sound.

Growing louder.

18

"Wait. Could you repeat that?"

"¿Señora?"

Monica frowned. What had he said? "About Humacao."

"Ah. I was just saying, quite a few American companies have located here in this little city—Medtronic, Bristol Myers Squibb, and so on. You have a decent airport, excellent highway access, nearby ports—"

"Take us down."

"Sorry?"

Smaller cities. Especially those near ports and with local airport access.

"Right now. Please. Take us down. I want to see."

The pilot looked confused but began descending, dropping from a thousand to five hundred feet, bringing the buildings surrounding the city plaza into view.

"Lower."

"Um . . . they're not too crazy about people flying too low here, I mean right over the city . . ."

She wasn't listening.

She was looking down at a man with blond dreadlocks who was sitting in the plaza, sketching something.

19

Finn felt a hot prickling up the back of his neck.

Resisting the impulse to turn and look up behind him, he homed in on the sound of the nearing helicopter.

No reason to be concerned. He could tell by the distinctive *whirrrr* that it wasn't a police chopper. The PRPD used Bells. This was a Robinson R44: a tour helo. Which made sense. There were a handful of popular tourist attractions nearby. National parks. The nature reserve. The Pterocarpus Forest. Cayo Santiago, called Monkey Island for its hundreds of macaque monkeys.

The helo could be headed for any of those spots, or half a dozen others.

But why was it flying directly over the city center?

Acting on instinct, he scooped up his pad, slipped it in his pack, and stood, then strode across the corner. At the foot of the church he made an abrupt right turn, hoofed up the wide marble steps, pushed open the two great wooden doors, and ducked into the interior.

20

"¿Señora?"

Monica didn't hear the pilot. She was turning in her seat, following the disappearing figure of the Rasta sketch artist.

Hearing something in her brain go *click*.

"¿Señora?"

She was thinking about Finn, remembering him sitting out on the big gun mount attached to the side of the *Lincoln* like a steel barnacle, gazing out at the ocean—and sketching.

What's that, she'd said, *some kind of meditation?*

Thinking back over his file, over what the retired navy psychologist had told them.

Cut his teeth on the California docks. Stint working on a dive boat.

"¿Señora?" the pilot repeated again, a little louder this time.

Monica turned and looked at him.

"If I were going to work on a charter fishing boat, where would I go?"

"Um . . . Ponce, I guess, or Rincón. Or actually, Fajardo—we'll be flying over Fajardo in a few minutes."

Ponce. Rincón. Fajardo.

"Okay," she said. "Good. Please tell Mr. Rivera I'll need a car tomorrow. Just a car. No driver."

21

Finn stood inside the big church doors, waiting for his internal alarm bells to silence.

The place was all smooth white concrete, the lighting in its soaring interior supplied by the building's numerous windows and reflected by the blue-and-white polished-marble floor, bathing the entire space in a soft radiance.

Finn realized he had seen all this before, when Tómas took a few of them on a brief tour of his stomping grounds back in '03. "How come they always built these old cathedrals with all that freakin' wasted empty space up top?" one of the other guys had asked. "To leave room for God, moron," Tómas replied.

Looking up toward the altar, Finn realized there was a service in process.

On the left, up at the front, he spotted a woman, a redhead, dressed all in black and wearing a black veil, sitting straight as a kommandant. There were several people arrayed directly around and behind her, whom he assumed were friends and family of the widow, and perhaps half a dozen others scattered through the back rows who seemed to be there on their own. Locals, he guessed, paying their respects.

On the other side of the aisle, eight or ten uniformed men sat at attention, unmoving as statuary.

Police officers.

Finn felt a nearly overwhelming urge to slip right back out the door again. The last thing he wanted right now was for a squad of policemen to turn in their seats and look his way.

Yet there was something about the ceremony going on at the front of the space that compelled him to stay.

He walked silently up the center aisle, stopped a few pews in, and took a seat.

An enormous man in crisp police uniform, minus the hat, stood at the altar, silvery tears marking the lines of his broad, kindly face. Though he spoke softly, his deep voice carried clear back to where Finn sat.

"Like all of you"—he nodded in the direction of the other officers—"I am a family man. I look at you, I see my own sons, and I am proud. Proud of every one of you, the service you give, the sacrifices you make."

Nobody in the congregation moved, not a twitch. If Finn hadn't known this was happening right now, right in front of him, he could have sworn he was viewing a still photo.

"Today," the big man continued, "we have lost a good officer, and a good man. I could even say, a great man. And today, I have lost a son."

Perhaps this was a prearranged cue, because at that moment an organ joined the speaker as he slipped into song. Something about the wind at your back and the rain falling at your feet, and God holding you in the palm of his hand.

The man had an extraordinary voice, rich as raw honey and thick with emotion.

One or two of the seated officers joined in, but halfheartedly, barely mouthing the words. The rest just sat, lips pressed tight, almost as if in protest.

The widow herself sat like a stone. Which didn't surprise Finn, at first. He'd seen an awful lot of death, and he knew the wide range of responses it could evoke in those closest to the departed.

This was a new one on him, though.

As best as he could read from her posture, she was sitting rigid with fury.

When the song concluded, the big man left the altar and a priest took the helm, wading into a discourse on the sorrows of the world and joy at being released from its chains. Didn't sound too cheerful to Finn, but then there wasn't a soul in the place who seemed receptive to any cheering up at the moment.

The priest couldn't have been much over thirty, yet Finn was struck by how old he looked. Like a young tree that had already been battered by a legion of storms and expected to face more of the same. Finn's impression was of a man who carried the world's weight on his young shoulders. Or at least this part of the world.

The service didn't last long. As he sensed it nearing its conclusion, he slipped out of his pew and back to the rear of the chapel, near the big double doors, where he stood watching. Soon the last benediction was uttered and the congregants stirred and stood, murmuring among themselves. The police on the right side clustered in place. Waiting for the big man who'd spoken, Finn guessed.

Those seated toward the back were the first to

leave. As they walked out, they avoided looking at him. Or at one another. Or at anyone. Mostly they looked down.

Finn overheard one ancient parishioner's muttered prayer as she dipped her fingers in holy water while exiting the chapel.

"Por favor, Dios, no más gárgolas."

Please, God, no more gargoyles.

Her companion hurriedly shushed her. They both left the building with their heads down.

Gargoyles?

As far as Finn knew, there were no gargoyles anywhere on the island. This was Puerto Rico, not medieval Europe.

The young/old priest walked back to where Finn stood, leaned in, and spoke in a hush.

"Excuse me, señor, may I ask, how did you know the deceased?"

"I didn't."

The man looked at Finn as if trying to decide what to say. He straightened up, looked around behind him at the milling congregation, then back at Finn.

"You should go."

He looked frightened.

22

Caleb "Calypso" Cordova was having a bad day.

Problems at work. Problems at home.

Things had started off on the wrong foot. That morning, while he should have been getting out the door and off to the precinct, he'd had to step in and referee a knock-down drag-out fight between his wife and their oldest boy, Carlos. It took five minutes of listening to them both shouting for him to work out what it was all about.

Apparently Carmelina had found a box of condoms in the boy's nightstand. Which was a mighty dumb place to keep them, as far as Cal was concerned, but that was an observation he kept to himself.

Cal invariably played the role of peacemaker, both at work and at home. Though he was more successful at breaking up street fights and bar brawls than family battles, and it hadn't gone well. Carmelina was a good mother, and an intoxicatingly beautiful woman, but she could be a hard woman, too. Cal felt bad for the boy. He expected Carlos would grow up and choose someone exactly like her for his own wife. Wasn't that what kids did?

The day went downhill from there.

For the past twenty-four hours, he'd been monitoring the situation in the Sound and dealing with its implications. None of which were good. The Coast Guard was still out there, searching. Chances were good that as long as the two kids were still missing, they'd keep on looking. And Coast Guard presence in the Sound was a problem right now. Even if it lasted no more than another few days, the timing could not be worse. The Venezuelans were not happy.

The boss was not happy.

And losing the deputy director of the Ports Authority? A necessary thing, but inconvenient, to put it mildly. That was making operations at the docks a lot more complicated. With the Venezuelans skittish and personnel issues on the harbor side of things, they were being hit on both receiving and shipping ends at the same time.

And because Cal was director of HR—obviously not a real title, but wasn't that what it came down to?—it was all in his lap.

Problems at home. Problems at work.

What he wanted to do was drive straight from the memorial service in Humacao back to San Juan, sit down, and have a clarifying conversation with Carmelina. Then go find Carlos and have a different kind of talk, father to son.

But all that would have to wait.

He pulled off the dirt road, over the gravel drive, and around back onto the pitted blacktop behind the house. Got out, and walked around to the front entrance.

One crisis at a time.

"They panicked, I guess. No way anyone should have been out there, been out anywhere near there, and the fucking thing had to come up for air, you know? And before you know it, out of nowhere, here are these two kids. So they grab them, I don't know, I guess because they have the brains of a fucking—"

"Okay," said Cal, meaning nothing by the word beyond the desire for the other man to stop talking. He shot a black look at the radio that was still filling the room with its noise. Adriano, the one who hadn't yet said a word, noticed and hastily shut it off.

Cal knew these two. Had stood up at both their weddings. They'd both been decent officers, not outstanding but adequate, until their positions fell to the budget axe. Adriano was quiet and dependable. Steady. Cal was godfather to his three nenes. Paco was smart, in a mean, reptilian, rat-in-a-corner way, but he was also a motormouth and something of an ass, in Caleb's opinion.

But you worked with what you had.

"Okay," he repeated. "But why bring them here?"

"I told them it was a shit idea," said Paco. "Two local kids? Jesus, you guys, what the fuck were you—"

"In their situation, what else were they going to do?" This was Adriano. "Better than killing them outright." He looked back to Cal for agreement.

Cal gave his head a small tilt to the right, then to the left. *Maybe. Maybe not.* "Kids drown. It happens."

"That's what I said." Paco again. "You take 'em back out there at night, hold 'em under for a few minutes, then leave 'em out by, I dunno, Boca Quebrada or somewhere up there, and bing-boom!"

Bing-boom? Cal closed his eyes. Misericordia.

"So you're saying, they suddenly show up," he

said, "after being missing for nearly forty-eight hours, after the guardacostas have thoroughly scoured the entire area. This is, how did you call it, bing-boom?"

Paco was silent. Small mercies.

"We could take them back," offered Adriano, "drop them drugged in the middle of the reserve. They got lost, fell asleep. They wake up with some story about being in a house somewhere, but nobody believes them, and pretty soon they stop telling it. I mean, what did they really see?"

"Adi," said Cal gently; he understood. Adriano had kids about that same age. But still. "They saw what they saw."

"So we take 'em back, snuff 'em, *then* leave 'em in the reserve." Paco just would not shut up. "Sooner or later someone finds 'em. Kids got lost, died of exposure. Maybe insect bites, or, you know—"

"If someone did drown in the Sound," Adriano mused, ignoring Paco, "couldn't their bodies end up somewhere else? Yabucoa, Emajagua, somewhere on the coast down there? You know how the currents run."

"Yeah!—get a few uniforms down there at first light to 'discover' the bodies." Paco made air quotes with his fingers, to ensure that his meaning was clear.

Cal suppressed his irritation and considered the idea. It actually wasn't terrible. They'd have to ensure that the drugs had left their bloodstream, that there was no food in their stomachs or intestines. The timing might work.

He looked at his phone.

No signal.

"Where do I get reception?"

"Out front," said Paco.

He looked up at the two men. "Wait."

He walked outside and stood in front of the house while he composed a brief text.

> Suggest disposal tonight along southeastern coastline. Yabucoa, Emajagua, Lamboglia. Approve?

He hit SEND.

Nothing happened.

He sighed. Blasted infrastructure. Nothing in Puerto Rico was dependable anymore.

He went back inside.

"All right, I need to head back to town for a few hours. I'll be back. We'll take care of it tonight."

He opened the door, then turned back to the two men. "Don't feed them."

The door closed.

For a moment, the two men were silent. Then Adriano said, "This is fucked up."

23

At first, he'd thought they were saved.

When Pedro heard the car coming down their road he'd wanted to scream out, shout for help, bang on their dirty little window. He hadn't done any of those things.

For one thing, he doubted anyone in the car would hear him. And besides, he was terrified of what the men in the next room would do if they heard him. Which of course they would.

If he had magic powers, like the elves in *Lord of the Rings,* he would reach out with his mind and try to persuade the driver to stop, turn around, and go get the police.

He closed his eyes. *We're two kids, being held here, kidnapped!* he thought furiously, then immediately felt foolish. What was he, a child? He prayed Miranda wouldn't notice and ask him what he was doing.

And then, wonder of wonders, he heard the car slow down, then the crunch of gravel as it rolled over the driveway and came around back.

It was stopping!

His eyes snapped open. Was it possible they'd actually heard his thoughts? He hurried to the window, just in time to see the car come into view and stop. The engine cut out. The door opened. He heard a creak of springs as the driver hauled himself out, shut the door, then walked around the car and back around toward the front of the house.

As he passed out of view Pedro caught a glimpse.

The man was enormous. Navy-blue pants, black stripe running all the way down the side of the leg. Gun at his belt, covered by a leather strap. Broad, kindly face. And a patch on the arm of his shirt that read, PROTECCION. INTEGRIDAD.

"Police!" whispered Miranda, startling him. He'd thought she was asleep again, but she was standing just behind him. "We're saved!"

"Shh," he said. "Stay calm. Don't make a sound."

They moved back to the door and sat craning their ears, trying to hear the muffled sounds of conversation. Pedro caught only a word here and there, nothing that made any sense. But from the general tone of the conversation, it sounded like these men *knew* one another.

And then Pedro distinctly heard a few words that made his heart freeze in his chest.

"Kids drown. It happens."

That wasn't Loud Orc or Quiet Orc. It was a deep voice, like the horn on a big navy ship. El Gigante.

The big policeman was part of the whole thing!

Pedro could not wrap his young mind around this.

Part of it? Police were the good guys! Police *saved* people. Police were the people you could always trust. Everyone knew that!

He didn't know if Miranda had heard, too, but he didn't think so. He didn't dare look at her.

He pressed his ear harder to the door's worn wood surface.

"We get a few uniforms down there at first light to 'discover' the bodies."

Pedro felt a shiver run down his neck and all the way down his back.

For a moment he was sure he was going to throw up.

He heard the front door open. Then silence. After a minute he heard big footsteps come back in the living room.

Then a few words he couldn't hear.

Then a few he could.

"We'll take care of it tonight."

"Pedro?"

Miranda was watching his face.

He looked at her, then looked at the door. Then back at her.

"I'm thinking," he whispered.

24

Late afternoon. Things in Luis Muñoz Rivera Square were shutting down for the day. Almost time to go back north and check the traps.

Finn used the same burner phone to call another Uber. And waited, watching the woman in blue gather her bags, preparing to head off to wherever it was she went for the darker half of the day.

Wondering whether they would talk, and if so, how soon.

Tick, tick, tick.

After emerging from that peculiar memorial service, he had spent the next few hours sitting in the plaza, sketch pad on his knees, capturing various subjects' likenesses with his charcoal pencil, playing the role of transient sketch artist as he watched the comings and goings in the square.

He'd sketched three members of a family of tourists. Two hospital workers on a late lunch break. A young woman who appeared to be the girlfriend of the young man running the coffee stand on the plaza corner.

And her.

The homeless woman, dressed all in pale blue, surrounded by her cotton bags of possessions.

He'd noticed her immediately, sitting on a bench on the opposite side of the square. Feeding pigeons. Soaking in the sun. Every now and then someone would come up to her—another of Humacao's dispossessed, Finn guessed—and speak in low confidential tones. Then she would talk. The person would listen carefully. Nod. Receive a squeeze of her hand. And leave.

At one point two people came by together, their body language telegraphing mutual resentment. They both spoke, presenting their cases. She listened. It took more than twenty minutes. Finally she held up one finger and spoke for less than a minute. They both left, one looking darkly triumphant, the other defeated, but both seeming to accept whatever edict or decision she'd rendered without question or argument.

Like an audience with a judge. Or a priest.

She was the one he was looking for. Noncom of the homeless, chief petty officer of the marginalized. High priestess of the Invisibles.

He waited. Drew a few more sketches for passersby. In between these he stole glances at the woman in blue.

Her black hair, what he could see of it spilling out from beneath the pale blue head scarf, was liberally mixed with gray, yet her golden skin was as free of wrinkles as a lake's surface on a windless summer day. Fifties? Sixties? She appeared ageless.

As the afternoon drew to a close, Finn stood and walked across the plaza. Handed the woman in blue a piece of sketch paper, folded once. She took it without looking at him and unfolded it.

It was a portrait of her, sitting on her simple cement throne, with a small, neatly printed inscription at the top left that said, LA REINA DE LAS CALLES. The Queen of the Streets.

He had signed it, like all his other sketches that day, "Picasso."

She folded it again and tucked it into a bag by her feet. Not a word. Not a glance.

The artist sometimes known as Mimo and now Picasso traversed the square and retook his seat.

Finn had once lain still for eighteen hours, deep in enemy territory in southern Afghanistan, bolt-action Win Mag primed and cradled in his outstretched arms, watching a distant doorway, waiting to see who emerged. If it was Person A, he would watch for another hour, then slip slowly backward, fifty yards into deeper forest, and silently exfil. If it was Person B, he would take the shot.

No one came out.

He'd waited another four hours that day, for good measure. Later he learned that within an hour after Person A and Person B both entered the little house, everyone inside was dead. Poisoned by a third party. Finn never learned whether that "third party" was some rogue-state actor, a jealous local warlord, or a three-letter agency from his own government.

Some missions were like that. You go in, you wait, you leave.

It was already coming up on forty-eight hours since the children had gone missing. It had taken every fiber of self-control not to go up to her and just ask. Two little nenes. Taken Sunday, on the Sound. What have you heard?

But that wasn't how this worked. He knew that. A frontal attack would only be met with shuttered silence. You had to build trust. Let the other party make the approach. The SEALs had a saying: "Slow is smooth, smooth is fast." Sometimes the fastest path to your objective was to wait.

The coffee stand on the corner closed up shop, the young man and his girlfriend holding hands as they left.

A shift of workers departed the hospital across the street, replaced by new personnel.

A big clock somewhere nearby tolled five, echoed one by one by the shuttering of shops around the square.

The woman in blue gathered her bags and stood.

To come his way? Or leave the plaza?

Finn saw his Uber approach from a side street and pull up to the corner behind him. He stood and signaled to the driver, indicating he should wait a few minutes. Then turned back toward the empty bench where the Queen of the Streets had sat.

She was gone.

25

It had rained again by the time he reached Fajardo, a sly, sticky rain that did nothing to temper the cloying humidity.

Finn spent the next two hours retracing his steps from earlier in the day, looking for the people he'd encountered that morning.

The boat repair shop stayed open till eight, but the man he'd spoken with earlier wasn't there. Neither were the bartenders at the two bars he'd visited. Nor the proprietor of the pawnshop, which was locked up and dark, despite a sign on the door that proclaimed it was open from 9 A.M. to 9 P.M. Same with the check-cashing store.

The chess-playing man with the discreet gold chain had vanished.

No one who seemed remotely like a representative of any cartel or crime family, eight-legged or otherwise, approached him.

The spiderweb was silent.

Spatters of rain came and went as a wet, hot dusk fell over the little city. With the approaching nightfall it seemed that the temperature, rather than backing off, was only increasing.

Finn began walking northeast, back up toward the marina.

About five blocks into one of the little city's sketchier neighborhoods he heard the *click click click click* of heels. The glistening streets seemed to amplify the footfalls' echoes. He turned the next corner and froze.

There was an assault in progress.

Correction: Not quite in progress. But about to be.

A petite woman with long dark hair walked briskly up a side street, coming in his direction on the other side of the street. She was alone and clearly oblivious to the two men casing her.

Finn put the woman at about his age. Unadorned T-shirt and chinos, black choker, simple studs in her ears, the tiny gemstones throwing off faint sparks as she moved. Small handbag slung over her shoulder. Her outfit was plain but well put together. Like she had money but was going out of her way not to broadcast it.

The first guy was coming up from behind. The second approached from the opposite direction, on Finn's side of the street. As the rear flank guy neared, the other guy began crossing over to the woman's side. Triangulation. Rock and hard place.

Finn saw the moves unfolding like a chessboard.

For the past six months, Finn had been teaching Miranda martial arts. Pedro had been teaching Finn chess. And he had seen Pedro make this exact move, boxing in Finn's king with two pawns, using two seemingly insignificant pieces to end the game. Evidently it was as classic in chess as it was in combat and urban street crime.

The well-dressed woman was walking into a checkmate.

Not his problem.

And yet.

If he didn't act, this woman would be robbed, possibly hurt. Possibly raped. In the next thirty seconds. While he stood by and did nothing.

But if he did act, he put himself out in the open as someone with sufficient training and skill to put down two attackers at once. Not something people would fail to notice. Could lead to questions he would prefer didn't get asked.

A lose-lose proposition.

He couldn't allow the two to complete their move. But he couldn't fight them, either.

At least not in the way he would if he were being himself.

Stepping back out of sight around his corner, he pried up a piece of brick and slipped it into his backpack, then set out for the guy on his side of the street at a brisk clip, flipping open his burner phone with one hand and pulling out his steel-shanked thousand-lumen flash with the other, keeping his eyes on all four would-be muggers' hands.

He couldn't tell if they were armed, but had to assume so.

"O-yay!" he called out in bad Dane-inflected Spanish, holding his open phone out in front of him as he walked. "Excuse me! Excuse me! I think I'm lost!"

He saw the man look back his way and hesitate. It was all Finn needed.

He picked up his pace. "Hey, thanks! This Google Maps thing has its head totally up my ass . . ." He held out his phone for Mugger 1 to look at and raised his flash, snapping it on just as it pointed directly into the man's face.

The guy screamed "Fuck!" and jerked backward, flinging his hands up to his face.

Now Mugger 2 broke into a trot, crossing over toward them. As Finn had figured he would.

"Sorry! Sorry! Oh, Jesus, I'm sorry, man!" Finn cried, and as he lurched forward to help the blinded Mugger 1 he swung his backpack around just as Mugger 2 reached them.

He heard the soft *thud* as the padded brick made contact with the man's head. It dazed the guy and knocked him off balance.

"Ah shit!—*Jesus,* I'm sorry!" Finn cried, as he began to turn back to face Mugger 1, hands spread wide, his face a billboard of mortification.

And took a punch to the gut. The man had gotten his sight back.

Finn knew it was coming and tightened his abdominals, hardly felt it, but he let out a huge "Oof!" and fell backward, hitting the ground hard and clumsy.

The woman stood still on the far side of the street, rooted to the pavement, her face frozen in shock and dismay.

He felt the kick coming. Sensed it. Knew it was there before it landed. The countermove unfolded automatically in his mind—his open hands taking hold of the oncoming ankle, pulling the leg with him as he rolled away from his attacker, pure muscle memory, letting his body weight slam down on the helpless leg, snapping it in two like kindling—

The kick landed. Square in the small of the back.

And then another. And another. And another.

It took an act of will not to move, not to leap to his feet and immobilize these two, to let the screaming pain be what it was and mount no defense.

One last kick, and then he heard the first guy saying, "Enough, man!" followed by the scatter of retreating footsteps.

Silence.

Then the *click click click click* of approaching heels.

"¡Ay mi Madre!" the woman's voice said. A firm hand on his shoulder. "Can you move?"

Finn rolled over on his back and looked up.

Her hair was coal black and curly, framing handsome features around a sharp nose that gave a patrician cast to her face. Not precisely attractive, not in the classic sense, yet not remotely unattractive, either. There was something captivating about her face, something he couldn't quite identify.

"I'm fine," he said as she helped him up to a sitting position. "Geez Louise." The winces took no acting.

"Oh my God, oh my God," she murmured. "We have to get you to a hospital!"

Finn put up one hand. "No need. I'm good."

"Or at least a doctor! You should be looked at!"

"Really," he said. "I'm fine."

"You are very brave," she said as he got to his feet.

"More like very stupid. I had no idea what I was walking into. Who *were* those guys?"

She shuddered and looked back around her. "I don't know and don't think I want to know." She turned back to him. "I'm so sorry. This is all my fault, isn't it. I shouldn't have been out here walking alone like that." She put out her hand. "I am Graciela Dominguez."

The way she said it, he had the sense she expected him to recognize the name.

"Picasso," he replied, shaking her hand.

"Picasso," she echoed, a musical lilt to her voice as she said the name. She smiled. "A painter, then?"

"Amateur."

She smiled again, then frowned. "I feel terrible about this. Do you live nearby?"

"No, just visiting."

"Can I help you to your hotel? Or wherever you're staying?"

"I appreciate it. Really. But I'm fine."

"Ah," she said. "Well, then." She nodded uncertainly. "Buenas noches, I suppose. Thank you for your gallantry, Señor Picasso, intentional or not."

The woman gave him a full thousand-watt smile and an adiós nod, then turned and walked away.

26

Adriano was ready to scream.

They'd been at the so-called safe house now for two days straight. Cell signal came and went, and he'd been able to speak with Angelique only once, briefly, as she was picking up the kids from school. There was no TV here, no reading materials, nothing but the radio and endless inane conversation with Paco.

If you could call it a conversation. More of a monologue, really. About everything—the fucking governor, the fucking utilities, the fucking United States, the fucking PRPD, the fucking radio stations. His wife's cooking. His wife's looks. His wife's complaining. (Now, there was some rich irony, totally lost on Paco.) But mostly his own bowels.

It was driving Adriano crazy.

He wished the man would just go out to the crapper and not come back till he'd worked it all out. So to speak.

And then something happened that very nearly made Adriano believe God was actually listening. As if in answer to his silent prayer, the man stood up and announced, "I'm heading out to the shitter."

And out he went.

Silence, blessed silence. Adriano switched off the damn radio, just to give himself a little peace and quiet, if only until Paco came back. Which, if God really could hear his thoughts, would not be for at least ten minutes.

The peace lasted barely sixty seconds.

A sound. From outside? A wounded animal?

It took him a full five more seconds to realize it was the little girl in the next room. She was crying. He went to the door and listened. The boy was hushing her, but she wouldn't be consoled. Now she was getting hysterical.

Suddenly there was a loud *thump!* like something hitting the floor, and the boy cried out, "Miranda! *Miranda!*"

Oh, shit.

Adriano tore open the door and burst into the room just in time to see the girl collapsed on the floor, the boy standing frozen, horrified, helpless.

Shit, shit, shit!

He stepped over to her, knelt down, and bent over her prone figure—

Miranda kicked.

What the Quiet Orc saw was not a girl collapsed on the floor, but a spring coiling into itself. Like a snake preparing to spring. As the man bent over, shifting his weight awkwardly onto one bent knee, the snake uncoiled and struck.

She spun around and punched her leg straight upward, slamming her bare heel with every ounce of her eight-year-old fireball's strength into the underside of the man's jaw.

And Miranda packed a ferocious kick.

The force of the blow sent a shock wave from the tip of his chin to the back of his jawbone, pinching the nerve cluster under his ear, which in turn shot a series of neural impulses screaming along the vagus nerve to the brain stem, tricking his body into believing that his blood pressure had suddenly skyrocketed into the danger zone, triggering response signals that instantly caused his blood pressure to plummet, sucked blood from his brain, and plunged him into unconsciousness.

Quiet Orc went down without a murmur.

Miranda fell back on the floor, breathing heavily. She looked up at her brother, who had gone a little white around the gills.

Pedro silently nodded, willing the queasiness in his stomach to be still. Then bent down to help her up.

She stepped softly through the open door, then looked back at Pedro, who was rummaging around in the toy box. "What are you *doing*?" she whispered.

"Hang on," he murmured. He fished out one of the alphabet board letters and a paper clip, which he tucked into the waistband of his swim suit, then turned and stepped out the door with her into the little living room.

The radio was shut off. There was no one else there.

They burst out the front door, ran around the house to the far side, facing away from the outhouse, and stood for a moment, Miranda looking at Pedro, Pedro in an agony of indecision.

His every impulse told him to grab Miranda's hand and run out to the road as fast as they could, follow it to the nearest town, and get some help.

But he didn't dare.

He'd spent ten long minutes after the big policeman left in his car, thinking about this, reasoning it through. They knew that at least one policeman was working with whoever kidnapped them. Which meant they couldn't afford to trust *any* policemen. And they couldn't even risk any regular people recognizing them as the two missing children, either—because the first thing any well-meaning citizen would do would probably be to alert the police.

Kids drown. It happens.

We'll take care of it tonight.

They needed to hide somewhere, and fast. But there was nowhere to hide. Now that they were out front he saw a handful of other houses nearby, but they didn't dare take the time to find out which ones were occupied and which weren't, and besides, even if they found one that was empty, the huge policeman would search them all anyway. There was no shelter nearby where they could hope to be safe.

They wouldn't be safe till they got back to Papi's.

And there was only one way to get there.

"We can't use the road," he said.

Miranda accepted his verdict without comment, just a solemn nod.

They both turned and looked behind them.

At the massive trees beyond the wild grasses.

El Yunque National Forest.

"We can sneak through," he said. "We'll stay far from the trails."

She looked up at him.

"It's only a few miles," he added. "We'll be safe."

Miranda said nothing. They both knew that wasn't true. It was already getting dark. The rain forest was huge and unknown.

Still, whatever dangers might lurk there, they did not loom as large as the big policeman with the booming voice and kindly face who was coming any moment to kill them.

And then Pedro heard the sound he desperately did not want to hear. A distant hum, growing louder.

An approaching car.

"El Gigante," he whispered.

Miranda took his hand, and they ran together toward the jungle.

27

Caleb knew something was wrong long before he reached the house. He could feel it. By the time he pulled onto the gravel drive and screeched to a halt, the signs were confirmation of his worst expectations.

Silence. No radio. The front door slightly ajar.

In two strides he was inside the house.

The living room, empty.

Service weapon out, round in the chamber.

Made the bedroom in two strides—

Adriano, on the floor, out cold.

No Paco.

No nenes.

A voice behind him. "Oh, fuck."

He turned to glance at Paco, who had just rushed in, still buckling his pants, and now stood aghast, looking past Cal into the bedroom at the evidence of disaster.

"Correct," said Cal.

The plan had been approved. Drown the little ones and leave the bodies off the coast of Yabucoa, where their bodies would be found by morning. Fine plan.

But now they had no little ones to drown.

Paco looked up at Cal.

"Ohhhh, *fuck*."

Cal grabbed Paco by one ear and dragged him

outside and onto the front drive. They stood looking out at the road. Cal frowned.

Turned and looked back at the house.

Then out at the rain forest.

"There," he said, nodding into the distance. He looked down at Paco. "Go get them."

"Me?" the man said. "Fuck, man. What do I know about tracking in the forest?"

"Learn."

Cal gave the man a hard kick in the ass that sent him flying.

Paco grunted as he hit the ground. He picked himself up and stared at Cal, then back at the jungle, then at Cal again. "What. *Now?*"

Cal said nothing.

"But I don't—" Seeing the look on Cal's face, Paco stopped himself. "*Fuck.*"

He turned and took off at a measured trot toward the tree line.

Cal waited until he'd seen the man disappear into the thick darkness, then strode back into the house.

"Adi. Adi . . ."

In his dream, Adriano's papá was shouting with joy. They were at a ball game, at the big stadium in San Juan. He was twelve years old and their team was just about to win the game. It was one of the best days of his life.

"Wake up, Adi."

Cal, shaking him gently.

"C'mon. Wake up."

Adriano had taken his own boys to that same stadium just last year to hear Bad Bunny in concert. But wait. Then how could he and his papá be . . . ?

It took him another moment to emerge all the way out of that weird half-dream, half-waking state, where he wasn't sure if he was with his father, or he *was* the father, or somehow both at once. And why was Cal there? He smiled, or rather, he tried to smile, but it hurt too much. His jaw was throbbing.

And then it all came rushing back.

The two nenes.

The little nena.

Mierda.

"Where's Paco? I—" He struggled to get to a sitting position, but found he couldn't move. Something was constraining his wrists. "What happened?"

"They're gone, Adi."

All at once he realized why it was he couldn't move his arms. He was zip-tied, wrists and ankles.

Besides, there was no point trying to move.

He knew how this worked.

He sank back onto the floor. Felt a single tear leak out and dribble down his cheek.

Silently, he watched Cal reach into an inside jacket pocket, withdraw a small leather case, and zip it open.

Watched him remove five stainless-steel tools.

A scalpel.

Three sleek surgical chisels of varying thicknesses.

And a little steel mallet.

"I will look out for the boys, Adi. And I'll talk to Angelique."

Adriano's eyes darted around, hoping at least for some sign of anesthesia—a little bottle, a pill, a hypodermic.

There was nothing.

And then the pain began.

28

They had just stopped running and stood by a giant tabonuco tree, catching their breath, when they heard it. A harsh, chilling sound, like a hawk calling its mate, only long and wobbly and horrible.

Pedro had seen a gangster movie once that had a scene in a restaurant where someone shot someone else, and just before he did it there was this terrible screaming of subway brakes on the sound track.

This sound was like that.

It lasted for only a few seconds, and then suddenly stopped. For a moment, there was nothing but silence. And then the frogs picked up their chant again.

co-KEE! chreech-chreech-chreech co-KEE!

Miranda looked at Pedro.

"Macaque monkey," he said. "Or a screech owl. Ignore it. It's just a sound."

He knew the macaques mostly lived on an island off Humacao, miles away. And they didn't scream like that.

Neither did screech owls.

Without another word, they pressed farther into the thick cover of the trees, just far enough until it felt safe to stop and catch their breath again. Pedro knew it was dangerous to keep going after dark. There were deep clefts that even in daylight lay hidden under a camouflage of thick foliage. At night it would be impossible to see.

Plus, in the dark they could easily end up walking in circles. Which, in its own way, might be even more dangerous than the hazard of falling into a ravine.

Temperatures in the rain forest could drop into the sixties at night. Not that cold, but certainly cooler than anything they were used to. And both of them still in the bathing suits they'd been wearing since Sunday.

"We need to dig in," he whispered.

He started gathering giant ferns, spreading them out like blankets on the mossy forest floor. Foraged a handful of big elephant-ear teak leaves. "We can use these for blankets."

Miranda took the leaves.

They both lay down on their fern mats.

"We'll get through it tomorrow," Pedro said softly. "It's only a few miles."

He squeezed Miranda's hand.

As night fell, the forest lit up with a ghostly illumination cast by millions of click beetles and fireflies. Millions of moths and other insects filled the air. Bats and owls emerged from their slumber and fluttered through the trees, gobbling up their flying breakfasts. Tens of thousands of tiny coquís clambered up into tree branches to feed and sing.

Less than two minutes went by before he heard the soft rasp that told him his sister was asleep. Miranda could fall asleep at the snap of your fingers. They were both so exhausted, he should have dropped off as fast as she did. But he didn't.

He lay awake, eyes alert, listening to the hypnotic chorus of frogs.

chreech chreech chreech chreech chreech chreech

co-KEE! chreech-chreech-chreech co-KEE! chreech-chreech co-KEE!

He thought about how far they had to go, tried to sort and catalog everything he'd ever read about El Yunque. There were no wildcats or bears. Snakes, but not that many dangerous ones. Insects, some of them bad, some of them really bad. Lots of ways to get lost.

He thought about what he'd told Miranda, that it was only a few miles, that they would be safe. Part of him believed it.

He thought about the sound they'd heard, which he knew wasn't a macaque monkey or a screech owl.

Yes, he decided, they were definitely safer in the forest.

He stayed awake awhile longer.

Pedro was terrified of more than a few things, but he was not afraid of the dark. He had lain awake like this, many times, in their little bedroom at home, staring up into the night, wondering what it was like to be Papi and see nothing at all.

29

She lay there, wide awake, staring up into the semi-darkness of her hotel room.

She couldn't shake that photograph.

It haunted her when her head hit the pillow at night, wrenched her out of bed in the predawn darkness. It was the sightless eyes, staring up from that dirt floor into a future of nothing.

The photo was taken less than ten hours after it happened, according to the classified report they'd shown her. Some local cop who'd been called in when a supplier stumbled upon the scene. There were dozens of photos, in fact—bodies in the front courtyard, bodies lining the interior hallways—but the one image she couldn't shake was taken in a little inside room. Two kids, lying on their backs on the packed-earth floor, couldn't have been older than four or five. Sightless eyes, bloody slits where their ears had been.

What kind of monster would do that?

And what horrors had those eyes seen, in the moments before they dimmed forever?

She thought back over a comment Dar had made over dinner. "You're a hard case, Lieutenant." Was that true?

Maybe so, on the outside. But Dar didn't see the amount of concealer and Visine it took every morning to look like she hadn't sat up half the night weeping.

Monica had been through more grief than she could manage. A whole crew from her helo squadron. Her best friend, Kristine, murdered. And Scott, a man she'd cared about, or begun caring about. And before all that, just weeks before deploying on the *Lincoln,* the cancer had finally taken her father, the best man she ever knew.

She missed him so, missed him more than she thought a human being could bear.

She missed Kris.

Hell, she missed flying.

Had her grief hardened her? She thought that was probably true—but on the inside she felt like jelly half the time.

After things blew up on the *Lincoln* she was benched for a full ninety days. "Take the time off, Lieutenant. You earned it." Which she understood to mean, *You need it.*

They'd wanted her to get some counseling. She didn't want counseling. She wanted to forget about the USS *Abraham Lincoln* and every single thing that had happened there.

Like the fact that she'd been forced to kill a man. Not in the heat of combat, and not from up in the sky at the pilot's seat of a Knighthawk. No, she'd shot a man point-blank in the gut. With a speargun. And watched him die. An American. Yes, a murderer. But still. An experience like that didn't just go away.

As she was learning.

Needed or not, that furlough they'd forced on her

didn't go the full ninety days. After three weeks on land she walked into her air wing commander's office and announced that she'd enrolled in an accelerated course at William & Mary Law. Six months later she'd knocked out her 3L and passed the bar. By June 15 she was a fully frocked O-3 navy JAG lieutenant.

Five weeks later, two guys from DIA knocked on her door with a folder of photos, and it all came rushing back at her again.

"It's natural to want to punish someone, Lieutenant."

Her air wing commander, the day she informed him of her decision.

"I don't want to punish anyone, sir. I'm not lashing out at the world. I'm fine. I just . . ."

He'd waited.

"I just want to serve the best way I can, sir. And I think I can do more in a judicial court than in the cockpit of a Knighthawk. That's all."

She told him that she was going over to JAG because it satisfied her mathematical nature. Find for X. That was, after all, what justice was all about, wasn't it? Solve the puzzle. Fill in the blanks. Balance the scales. Create parity on both sides of the equation.

That's all.

And she'd almost believed it herself.

Until she saw the photograph.

The guys from DIA had shown her a few other photos, too. A SEAL lying prone on a snow-covered hotel rooftop in Iceland. Two more SEALs, jammed into a small closet like demented puzzle pieces, limbs askew, eyes staring.

They also had physical evidence that placed Chief

Finn at every one of these crimes, they said. That proved beyond any doubt that it was all his work.

She hadn't wanted to believe it.

But she had.

And having once seen the photos, she couldn't unsee them. The two SEALs in the closet. The SEAL lying in a pool of his own blood. The farmers' bodies in the courtyard and hallways.

But mostly it was those kids.

Their sightless faces.

Goddamn SEAL. She wished she'd never laid eyes on him.

30

Finn stepped into the old chef's little skiff and pushed off, then began rowing his way out before firing up the outboard.

A big face poked up out of the water and stared at him. He looked back. A manatee. They were all over the island, like roving underwater cows.

As the creature swam away a trail glowed behind it like strings of tiny mercury vapor lamps, sparkling for a few seconds before winking out into darkness.

"It's called bioluminescence, and it comes from plankton!"

Pedro again, in encyclopedia mode.

"They say it's caused by this light-emitting molecule called luciferin, you know, like Lucifer? It's kind of like a disguise. They say the plankton use it for camouflage, distraction, and misdirection."

Camouflage. Distraction. Misdirection.

He thought about his sketches of the three officers' faces on the wall of his cell-sized bedroom.

Keyes: All straight lines and right angles. Pole up his ass. Moral rectitude. Dugan: All chiseled planes and rounded corners. Tough but fair. Father figure. Meyerhoff: Eyebrows like hawks' nests, stone jaw. Epitome of military excellence. He'd served with all three, trusted them, followed them. Admired them, even.

And one was corrupt to the core.

He tried to identify the feeling.

Moral outrage . . . disillusionment . . . thirst for revenge . . .

Nothing quite clicked.

He focused on the most vivid details—the bodies in Mukalla, his last conversation with Kennedy, the images he'd seen of the memorial service—and ran the list again.

Moral outrage . . . disillusionment . . . thirst for revenge . . .

It was a process he'd learned from Carol. Go through a list of emotions until you reach one that clicks. Like twenty questions. He'd resisted, at first. It seemed childish, for a man who could surveil an insanely complex theater of operations and remember every detail days later.

But then, Finn had never been adept at tracking his own feelings.

"It's like asking a blind man to describe color," he'd told her.

"No," she'd replied. "It's like asking a man who's had his eyes shut for years to open them."

He couldn't argue. Carol knew him better than he knew himself.

They'd been together since they were teenagers, both refugees from the land of shattered childhoods. Yet when the other Team guys ragged on him for not hitting on other women and probed him to explain what the deal was with Carol, he never knew what to say.

What they had together, as Carol had explained it, was a kind of shared loneliness. Which was a concept Finn had never quite grasped. He didn't understand what it meant to be lonely, had never been able to isolate and identify the sense of it.

At least, not until these past few months on Vieques, spending time with Pedro and Miranda.

Because in those moments, that feeling vanished.

He turned his thoughts back to the events of the day, to everything he'd witnessed so far and what intelligence he might glean from it. He'd spent the day thrumming that web, feeling that hot prickling up the back of his neck that told him his wriggles were being watched—but gotten zero response from any spider. Two things were clear.

Everyone knew something.

And no one was saying anything.

He hadn't been able to put a name to that pervasive unease he'd sensed that morning in Fajardo, that afternoon in the streets of Humacao. At the memorial service, in the priest's face. In the strange hush over the neighborhood when he returned in the evening. Now he could.

Terror.

Whatever that spider looked like, it had people terrified into silence.

Finn put his face into the wind.

Five knots. No swell.

He gave the starter rope a tug and the little engine sprang to life.

Behind him, unseen as he motored out of the harbor and into the Sound, the water glowed a ghostly green in his wake, the bioluminescence whispering its luciferous messages.

Camouflage! Distraction! Misdirection!

Wednesday

T minus 4

Record-warm ocean temperatures have continued to pump energy into the Invest 95L system, causing accelerating winds and increased evaporation, releasing more heat and generating a cycle that feeds on itself.

By mid-morning Invest 95L was upgraded to "tropical storm" and given the name "Will."

The National Weather Service has issued a tropical storm watch for the Caribbean Basin.

31

. . . from the French "gargouille," meaning "throat" or "gullet," derived from the root word "gar," meaning "to swallow," said to represent the gurgling sound of water . . . In ancient and Medieval times, gargoyles served two purposes: practical, as water spouts to project rainwater away from buildings so as not to erode the walls' masonry; and symbolic, principally as terrifying beasts to scare away evil spirits. Sometimes called the Devil's Mask—

Finn became aware of a presence outside his door a few seconds before he heard the voice.

"Come eat."

The Devil's Mask.

He closed his laptop, pushed away from the little card table, and stretched in his chair, arms straight up, his back a sheet of pain from the beating he'd taken the night before.

He stood and followed the voice out into the tiny kitchen, where he took a stool and watched Zacharias at work. Steaming bowls of crema de arroz appeared, accompanied by small plates of cold smoked conch and sliced mango.

Finn ate, grateful for the nourishment. He hadn't had anything to eat since the lieutenant's visit two evenings earlier, hadn't even thought about it. He wondered where the two children were at that moment and what their condition was, when they had last eaten, if they were still—

That line of thinking isn't useful.

He buried the questions and ate, thinking about his objectives for the day.

Zacharias interrupted the silence.

"Why did you come home last night?"

Finn hadn't been expecting the question and paused to consider it.

The old chef replied for him. "You came back to check on me."

Not true, Finn silently countered. He'd come back to check on Keyes, Dugan, and Meyerhoff. To do the same thing he'd done every night for the past eight months: reach out through the vast faceless anonymity of the Onion Router universe and attempt to push his investigation a few inches further. To move one step closer to ID'ing the individual responsible for a farm settlement full of slaughtered families—for snuffing out the life of the best man Finn had ever known and burying Finn himself in a cloud of accusations and indictments out from which he didn't know if he'd ever be able to crawl.

Except that he hadn't.

It occurred to him only now that for these past hours, he'd done nothing but hunt for whatever scraps of information he could dig up that might help him find the two children.

He'd read pages and pages of background on the

major crime families of Puerto Rico, pored through histories of the island's drug trade. Read up on the Catholic Church in Humacao and its role in the community. Found the identity of the slain cop and looked up his widow in San Juan. Even did a search on "Graciela Dominguez Fajardo" and discovered that there was a good deal more to the woman in the plain T-shirt and chinos than met the eye.

He hadn't given the three naval officers a thought.

"You think," the old chef added, "that whoever took los pollitos may come after me, too."

Finn paused, fork midway from plate to mouth. Set the bite down, uneaten.

Whoever took los pollitos.

He hadn't told the old man anything of his thoughts about what happened out there on the Sound. Clearly, though, Zacharias had come to the same conclusion as Finn had himself.

Pedro and Miranda had been unwitting witnesses to something criminal, and the men involved had taken them.

And might come after Papi, too? He had no reason to think so. But once he made himself a target, didn't that automatically put anyone close to him at risk?

Wasn't that why he'd waited to get up onto that wooded hill before altering his appearance? Because he didn't want to run the risk of being spotted getting out of his boat or coming through the marina with his dreadlocks and limp? Didn't want "Picasso" to have any link back to Vieques?

He looked over at the old man, his straight-backed posture as he ate, the knots of ropy white scar tissue where his eyes had once been. The old chef who saw things more clearly than most sighted men.

"Protecting me is a distraction," Papi continued. "It's not like you to be distracted. I'll be fine. Or not. It doesn't matter."

Finn took another bite of the cold fish and said nothing.

"Don't come back tonight, Mimo. Stay over there. Do whatever you have to do."

Finn gave a quiet grunt that could have meant anything, or nothing at all.

Zacharias polished off his crema de arroz and set his empty bowl down on the counter, in the precise center of his empty plate.

"Héctor has been asking around Esperanza. Talking to everyone."

"As he should."

"He's been asking about you."

Finn made no reply.

Of course the lieutenant was asking about him. Finn could guess what the man was thinking, too. What were the odds of this newcomer, this mystery man, finding that snorkel out on the western tip of the island? In the middle of the night, in the dark? Out in an area where the lieutenant's own officers had already looked?

How exactly did that happen?

Finn had told him he'd just gone out there on a hunch. Went to walk the beach where he thought the kids might have gone, and there it was. Which, as far-fetched as it sounded, was the truth.

It was just that when it came to tracking, Finn's hunches were better than most people's.

"Hugo told me he came into the store and asked, how often did he see you and los pollitos together?"

So there it was.

"*Scenario three?*" he'd asked the lieutenant. "*Or*

five?" A case of runaways, or a "non-parental abduction"? The canny policeman had claimed he had no opinion. But he did.

Finn was not only on his radar. He was a suspect.

"You can check on me by phone," the old chef said, and he stood to take the empty dishes to the sink.

"I don't have a phone, Papi," Finn lied.

Papi gave a dismissive snort. "Vamos," he said.

Back in his bare room, Finn took down all his sketches, maps, and carefully hand-lettered lists from the wall, one by one. At his card table desk he pried open his laptop, removed the hard drive, and slipped it into his backpack.

He left the laptop, now an empty shell.

The smart move would be to pull out right now, hard exfil, take his precious hard drive and all his work with him. Spin the globe; be on a different continent before the next sunrise.

That would be the smart move.

He took the stack of papers out back and set them on fire, then walked around front to the empty street and down to the dock. Set his backpack down on the little skiff's floor, gave the starter rope a tug, and slipped away from the shore.

Closed his eyes and felt the wind on his face.

Five knots. No swell.

Halfway across the Sound, he dropped the hard drive over the side.

32

"We've spoken with everyone who worked the ferries over the past three days, both this side and over in Ceiba. So that avenue, at least, is closed."

Zacharias knew what the man was driving at, long before he came to the point. But he let him take his time and do it his way.

"The two marshals will resume this morning, and the Fish and Wildlife people. And our officers, of course."

But . . .

Zacharias heard the unspoken word as clearly as the bland, diplomatic ones Héctor was speaking aloud.

The lieutenant had stopped by to report on the search activities. Doing his job, keeping the family up to date. But that wasn't really why he came.

"You know, Papi, it has been over forty-eight hours now . . ."

And there it was. *Time to start facing facts. Prepare ourselves for the worst. Temper our hopes with the need to accept, to grieve, to move on.*

The lieutenant wasn't there to update him, he was there to *handle* him.

"Héctor," he interrupted. "This isn't necessary. I

appreciate your coming over, but you are wasting both our time. You have a job to do. So do I. Yours is to figure out why they haven't come home. Mine is to be here for them when they do."

And then, seeing or not, he stared the man down.

After a long pause—perhaps uncomfortable for the policeman but entirely at ease for the chef—the lieutenant murmured, "Of course, Papi." He stood and walked to the front door. Then turned back and said, "Is Mimo about?"

"Out on the water," said the old cook. "Another day, more fish to catch."

Héctor nodded. "Could you have him give me a ring later? When he's back?"

"Of course."

The lieutenant nodded once more, knowing there were still words unsaid, but they would have to wait for their time. He opened the door, its little bell ringing its melancholy goodbye, and disappeared.

Zacharias stood for a moment, listening to the silence in his café.

He couldn't go out and physically investigate, the way Mimo was doing. He couldn't travel, and he certainly couldn't go looking for clues. But over the decades since the accident, he'd gradually learned to ignore all those things he couldn't do and focus his attention on those he could.

He could listen. And while he couldn't use his eyes, he could see with his mind.

People said, "Seeing is believing."

In Zacharias's experience, it was exactly the other way around.

Which was why he had spent the minutes since Mimo's departure, at least until Héctor's arrival, sitting in intense concentration, picturing in his mind's eye his two grandchildren—faces he had never laid physical eyes on—in his kitchen, laughing, cooking, Miranda teasing solemn Pedro, making Zacharias smile when they thought he was out of earshot.

He could see it all as clearly as the sound of a silver spoon against the rim of a champagne glass.

Because believing was seeing.

And listening?

Well, he'd heard it said that blind people could hear like bats. Zacharias could hear better than that. He could hear what people said and, more important, what they didn't. What they were feeling but concealing, what they thought and also what they believed, sometimes without even being aware of it themselves.

Héctor was a cagey one, but it wasn't difficult to hear the direction the man's thoughts were traveling at the moment.

Returning to his favorite seat, a well-worn armchair in a back corner of the little dining area, he thought about his quiet employee.

The man was Serbian, someone said they'd heard back when he first showed up in town. Or maybe Albanian. Or Portuguese. There were conflicting stories, but no one really cared. At first they had called him El Extraño—the stranger—but that had lasted only a few days.

It was Miranda who coined the name "Mimo," because he spoke so little (she said) that he reminded her of a mime.

It wasn't till a few months later that a second meaning of the name emerged. One day Zacharias overheard his two grandchildren out behind the kitchen, convulsed in giggles. It took him a good minute to figure out what he was hearing: His hired help was doing impressions of several townspeople, so spot-on it was like hearing the playback of a recording. The most astonishing mimetismo he'd ever heard.

"Mimo," he'd murmured.

He understood that Mimo was an intensely private person. Aloof, even. He never asked the man anything about his past life, knowing it was a door he would rather keep closed. Which was no problem, as far as Zacharias was concerned. He could fish. He could cook. And the old man sensed he could trust him.

He'd hired him the same day he first showed up at the café.

Zacharias was a good judge of character. This had not always been the case. As a young man, he'd understood no one very well, least of all himself. But the years and circumstances had forced him to take a deeper look at things.

The old chef didn't know what Mimo was looking for on the laptop he kept in his room, but he knew how single-minded the man's focus was. He'd been on a mission these past eight months. A hunt for something that mattered to him more than anything else in the world.

And now that mission had been supplanted, it seemed to Zacharias, by a single-minded focus on finding los pollitos.

He hoped his young friend was not putting himself at too grave a risk in doing so, but he also knew that hope was not the force that ran the universe. The world was a dangerous place, at times terrifyingly so. The forces that allowed one to navigate the tempest and come through it intact, in Zacharias's weather-worn experience, boiled down to two:

Love.

And *believing.*

He quieted his mind and opened up a picture of Pedro and Miranda, wherever they were, waking up now, one day closer to being home again.

33

"I'm hungry."

Pedro hadn't realized she was awake. He'd been lying on his back, listening to the silent forest, gazing up at the dark green canopy soaring above their heads like a great cathedral ceiling, shutting out the sky. He knew it was morning but couldn't see in what direction the sun had risen.

Now he looked over at her. "Me too," he said, and as he said it his hunger came rushing at him like an enormous wave. How many days had they gone without eating? The day they were caught in the Sound was Sunday. The day they woke up in that little bedroom prison, was that Monday? Or did they spend all of Monday in a drugged sleep?

He quit trying to work it out and got to his feet, a little unsteady and ready to eat a tree.

The two gorged themselves on sour-sweet bananas, ripe mangoes, starchy breadfruit, and yagrumo fruit, those leathery fingers with their sweet syrupy jam inside. They ate so much Pedro thought he would be sick, but once they started walking, he didn't even feel full.

As they slipped through the shadowy forest Pedro thought of the Narnia books, and of being in a gigantic wardrobe, somewhere between reality and magic.

They passed what looked like a collection of broken umbrellas hanging from branches that rustled slightly in the breeze. Except there was no breeze. Pedro came closer for a better look. He could just make out what looked like a little gray fox's head tucked into each "umbrella." Bats. Just settling in to sleep as he and Miranda were starting their day.

As they kept walking the ground grew wet, mossy, and pebbly. "That means there's a river nearby," he said.

And sure enough, in less than fifty yards they heard the rush of water, and in another fifty yards they were staring at it.

Miranda looked at him. "Is it safe?"

Pedro nodded. "Río Mameyes," he said. "I'm pretty sure. Cleanest water in the forest." They both dropped to their knees and drank.

After they'd satisfied their thirst, Pedro began searching along the riverbank. "There!" he said after a few minutes, stopping at a spot where a stream branched off and formed a little pool to the side, no more than two feet wide and a foot deep.

"Help me dam it up," he said. "So it's completely still."

Miranda helped him gather up some small branches and large stones, leaves and moss, mashing everything in place until the pool was completely sealed off, its surface still as glass.

He reached inside the waistband of his bathing suit and fished out a little piece of colored plastic, long and thin.

The capital letter "I" he'd taken from the toy box in their bedroom prison.

Next he fished out the paper clip and took a minute to straighten it out.

He sat down on the forest floor, placed one end of the straightened paper clip on his knee, and held the other between his fingers. Holding the magnet "I" with his other hand, he brushed it sharply down the length of the paper clip, over and over, six or seven times, as if he were sharpening a kitchen knife.

After stuffing the magnet letter back into the waistband of his suit, he placed a small green leaf on the water's surface and carefully set the paper clip down on top of the leaf. And watched.

At first, it sat still on the water's surface, then slowly rotated a few degrees to the left, like a clock hand moving from noon back to ten o'clock.

Pedro looked up, frowning, following the direction the paper clip pointed, and his heart sank.

He'd had them way off course.

"That way," he pointed in the paper clip direction, "is north." Then turned and pointed in the opposite direction. "We want to go south."

Miranda had watched the whole thing with fascination. "Did Mimo show you that?"

He shrugged. "He does this sometimes, when he's out camping."

They set off, heading south, according to Pedro's paper clip compass, taking in all the sights of the rain forest as they walked.

There were orchids everywhere, some no bigger than his fingernail. A giant snail the size of his fist. Giant ferns. Huge tree trunks wound around with vines, and the canopy high above, draped with great masses of hanging moss and bromeliads.

They'd walked in silence for about twenty minutes when Miranda said, "I don't think he was camping."

"Who? You mean Mimo? Of course he was."

They walked on another little while before Miranda spoke up again.

"I think Mimo is a spy."

Pedro smiled at his sister's imagination. Mimo, international man of mystery!

Miranda suddenly stopped.

"What?"

She bent her head and put up one index finger to shush him, like she was listening for something. Then looked up at him.

"Are there any jaguars in El Yunque?"

Pedro shook his head.

"Wolves?"

"No, Mira. There are no wolves anywhere in Puerto Rico. No jaguars, no tigers, no jungle cats at all. None of those." He frowned. It wasn't like her to worry.

He glanced behind him. Covered in mosses, ferns, and bright-colored mushrooms, the scatter of fallen limbs made him think of a nest of giant tarantulas.

"C'mon," he said. "It's only a few miles."

"Okay," she said softly.

They kept walking.

And listening.

34

The wind, man, the wind has a mind of its own . . .

As Finn skirted the tip of Ceiba on his way north he caught a glimpse of the piers where the old Rosie Roads base used to be, and he thought again about that boat exercise all those years ago.

Before Finn became a SEAL, he'd been a rescue swimmer. According to Carol, that was still who he was. Maybe she was right.

If so, he was a failure.

He had saved a lot of lives over the years. As a SEAL, he had taken lives, too. He still remembered the faces of some he had killed, but none of those haunted his dreams. What tormented him were the lives he had tried to save. Tried and failed.

Like Tómas.

"The wind, man, the wind has a mind of its own."

It's as loud as a factory floor inside that fat four-prop C-130, but Finn is seated hip-to-hip with Tómas, and the dude has a voice that could penetrate steel.

"Especially in the Sound, man. You got the Atlantic to the north and Caribbean to the south, with

wind currents from all over the fucking planet, and it's all being jammed through this shallow little channel, like two big-ass brawlers walk into a dark alley, you know? You don't know what crazy shit's gonna go down in there. But the one thing you do know is it's not gonna follow your plan. I'm telling you, man. Freakin' mind of its own."

The "plan," in this case, is a long-range boat nav course.

Simple concept: Drop eight guys with two Zodiacs—inflatable rubber raft, the definitive Spec Ops sea craft—into the Caribbean just off St. Croix and then navigate the sixty-odd miles back to Rosie Roads. With a storm on its way.

Hooyah.

They push the two Zodiacs out the back of the plane and watch the chutes bloom like fireworks. Jump, pull their rip cords, and splash down as close to the boats as they can.

Except the wind has a mind of its own.

Just as they're lining up to jump, the wind decides to pick up, hard. They hit the water five miles farther south than planned. Which means that once they reach the boats, they now have an uphill drive into the swell.

And when the Zodiacs' chutes deployed, something punctured one of their gas tanks.

And by the time they've rationed the gas and refigured their course, the storm has accelerated to near gale force and veered in their direction.

And halfway to Rosie Roads, both boats are hit by a rogue wave and take on blue water—"blue water" being the nautical term for a catastrophically bad shit-ton of deep water filling your craft. Their nav charts are yanked out by the wave and washed away by the sea.

A few of the other guys start losing their shit. Tómas snaps them to attention.

"Everyone start bailing," he yells. "¡VAMOS!"

Once they've bailed enough to get back under way, they discover that both engines have completely flooded.

"Hey," says Tómas as Finn hands him the engine repair kit. "You know how to say 'hooyah' in Puerto Rican?" Finn waits for it. "¡Hooyah, cabrón!"

Tómas is the best outboard motor mechanic in the Teams, but still, pulling off a boat repair in these high seas is a nightmare. Fixing the engine would normally take fifteen minutes. In this storm-torn chop it takes an hour, Finn following his stream of instructions, dishing out spare parts like a scrub nurse. Screw driver. Carburetor. Hose clamps.

Tómas gets the first engine fired up. The second one's flatlined and not coming back. They rig a towline, then swap their one remaining functional gas tank from the dead boat to the lead, and set off again, soon rounding the corner of Vieques and into the Sound.

Where the wind has a mind of its own.

Fifteen-foot swells crash down on them as thirty-two-knot winds buffet from every direction. It's like being tossed in a food processor with a lunatic's finger on the PULSE *button. Visibility is down to yards, then feet.*

And somehow, they make it.

After tying off the lead Zodiac, Finn and Tómas haul the dead boat out onto the dock. Tómas turns to Finn and grins.

"Live to fight another day, bro."

—

Finn cut his motor and coasted into the dock at Puerto Chico, still adrift in the treacherous channels of his memory.

Tómas did live to fight another day. And another, and another. Until he didn't. A year later, on the streets of Fallujah, a squad from Finn's platoon got ambushed by a vehicular IED, blowing off one of Tómas's legs at the knee.

Their CO lay forty yards off, knocked unconscious from the blast. Bleeding from a bad head wound.

A band of insurgents was approaching full-tilt, shooting off their AKs.

Finn started toward his fallen teammate to haul him out, but Tómas waved him off.

"I'll hold them. Get the CO!"

Finn hesitated for a split second.

"¡VAMOS!" Tómas screamed.

Finn vamosed.

He sprinted the forty yards, got the CO in a fireman's carry, heard the *ssssnap!* and *crack!* of insurgents' bullets striking around him—and then the ear-shattering blast of two grenades going off in rapid succession.

Tómas, a grenade in each hand, had waited till their attackers got close enough and then taken them all out together.

Hooyah, cabrón.

"¡Hola!"

He had just tied off his skiff and slung his pack over his shoulder when he heard a voice from behind. He turned to see an old man stumping down the quay, straight for him.

He stepped out onto the dock to observe the man's approach.

Mid- to late sixties, was Finn's guess. Shock of white hair. Rolling gait of a man who'd spent the better part of his life on the water. Finn noticed a slight hitch in his step and reflexively wondered what put it there.

"Back again," the man growled as he drew close enough to not have to shout.

Finn nodded.

The marina's dockmaster. Finn hadn't seen him the day before. Probably holed up in his little guard shack up by the main gate when he saw Finn coast in. Up close he revised his estimate of the man's age upward by a decade.

"Saw you docking your yacht. Sniffing the air."

Finn waited. Was the man making a point?

"Yeah," the old man said. "I don't trust NOAA, either." He squinted out at the water, then back at Finn. "You back tonight?"

"Can't say just yet. Have you got a more long-term spot I could use?"

A little more out of the way, in other words.

The old dockmaster turned and nodded with his chin toward one of the farther docks. Finn saw the empty slip he was pointing out.

"Gracias," he said.

The man grunted something that sounded like "De nada." Finn had just turned back to his skiff when the dockmaster spoke up again. "Tropical storm watch coming."

"They call it?"

"Not yet. But they will." He turned and stumped back up to his office.

Finn got back in his boat, pushed off, and re-docked at the far slip. Then got out, walked up the dock, and headed inland, aware of the dockmaster's eyes on his back as he went.

He climbed his wooded hill, donned the dreadlocks and cotton balls but skipped the lift in one shoe. He wouldn't need to fake the limp today; he was still recovering from the previous night's tune-up at the hands (and feet) of Mugger 1 and Mugger 2.

After a twenty-minute wait he descended to the street again and began walking toward town.

Before he'd gotten two blocks, he heard a car screaming up the narrow street, heading straight for him.

35

It was a BMW. Metallic green, tinted windows, pimped-out wheels with spinner rims.

The car banked and braked into a sideways skid, coming to a halt six yards in front of him. The passenger's side front and rear doors both swung open and two men got out.

Pressed dark jeans, sharp T-shirts. Guy on the left wore expensive shoes, polished to a sheen. Guy on the right, shitkickers. This one also had a few gold teeth, a thick neck hung with four or five gold chains, and a Glock 41, a ridiculously large .45-caliber monster of a handgun, held a foot or so out from his side, presumably to give it maximum visibility.

Shiny Shoes and Gold Tooth. Front man and enforcer.

The driver stayed in the car. A bull in a seat harness. Probably carrying ten Glocks. Maybe a Howitzer.

Shiny Shoes—doubtless also packing, though less showy about it than Gold Tooth—spoke up.

"You going around town, talking about groceries an' shit like this." He spoke softly, for effect, was Finn's guess, like a movie bad guy, so bad he didn't need to raise his voice to terrify you. "Not a smart idea, bro."

Finn put out both palms. "Hey, I don't want any trouble, guys. It's just that I've got this friend, from overseas—"

"He *said* not a smart *idea,* bro." Gold Tooth, earning his pay. He grinned his sparkly grin and took a step closer.

"Situation here is complicated, amigo." Shiny Shoes again. "Messing with shit you don't understand."

"You feeling us, bro?" Gold Tooth took another threatening step.

Finn didn't even look in the enforcer's direction, just stood still and kept his eyes on Shiny Shoes.

Gold Tooth visibly bristled at the slight. Finn could practically feel the temperature on the guy's neck rising from where he stood. The man took a few more steps, halving the distance between them as he brought up his cannon and growled, "Need you to get *down* on the *ground,* bro."

When Gold Tooth got within three feet, Finn began looking alarmed. He put his arms up in that palms-out position again and took a step backward. "Hey, hey, back off, huh?" His voice rising to whine.

"I said DOWN on the GROUND!"

When you've got a cartel foot soldier shouting at you and pointing his big Glock in your face, you don't typically have a lot of options.

Finn stuck his hands up in the air, eyes gone wide as silver dollars. "Please, man . . ." His voice was shaking now. ". . . please don't point that in my direction."

Gold Tooth flashed a gleaming grin.

Took one more step.

Then slowly, deliberately, lifted his gun hand and

stuck the Glock directly in Finn's face. Close enough to touch.

So Finn touched it.

In a single burst of motion, he grabbed the man's gun hand in a two-fisted grip while simultaneously pivoting himself to the left and out of the line of fire—

—then twisted gun and gun hand back toward the other guy's forearm—

—drove the barrel to the outside with his right hand while pulling the guy forward with his left—

—and used the man's momentum to spin him 180 degrees, throwing his left arm around the guy and clamping him to his chest as he stuck the gun up under Gold Tooth's chin and spoke a single word:

"Don't."

The other men froze.

The whole thing had happened so fast, none of them had the chance to react until Gold Tooth's Glock was already in Finn's hand. The driver stood half out his car door, Shiny Shoes halfway into pulling his own weapon.

"Don't," Finn repeated.

For a few seconds the only sounds were the rising breeze in the trees and the distant shouts of two unseen boaters calling to each other out on the water as they worked their rigging.

Finn broke the silence.

"You," he said, nodding at Shiny Shoes. "Please toss that over here."

The man hoisted his gun over to the ground at Finn's feet, looking at him curiously.

Finn nodded at the driver. "All the way out. Leave the door open. And toss your weapons over. All of them."

The driver stepped out, stood, and tossed over two handguns. No Howitzer.

Finn felt in Gold Tooth's pockets, removed his phone. Looked over at Shiny Shoes.

"Tell your capo I'd like to meet with him. No weapons. Just the two of us. I'll be brief. No one will be harmed. I have some questions."

He held up Gold Tooth's cellphone.

"He can reach me at this number."

He looked over at the driver. "You. Call me."

The driver looked at Shiny Shoes, then at Finn. "You mean, like, now?"

"Yes. Like now. Carefully."

Looking uncertain, the man carefully pulled out his phone, keyed in a number, and pressed SEND.

The phone in Finn's hand buzzed.

He thumbed the TALK button to establish the connection, then clicked off.

"Good. What's your name?"

The driver looked even more confused. "Garcia."

"All right, Garcia. Now I have your number. When I finish with the car I'll send you a text, let you know where you can pick it up. I'll take good care of it."

Now he released Gold Tooth with a shove, pushing him toward Shiny Shoes. He pointed at himself as he looked at both of them.

"Picasso," he said. "Not 'bro.' Not 'amigo.' Picasso. Good?"

He got no response. Hadn't expected one.

He motioned the driver to join the other two on the far side of the road, then picked up all the guns, one by one, tossing each into the car, and got in behind the wheel. Emptied each gun in turn, letting the ammunition fall onto the car floor. Then dropped the empty weapons out the car window, so that the three could have them back—albeit empty—after he left.

This wasn't what he wanted to do. His every impulse was to have them take him directly to their capo right then and there. Pedro and Miranda had been missing now for over forty-eight hours. There wasn't a minute to waste, let alone hours.

Tick, tick, tick.

But three on one in an enclosed vehicle was a fool's scenario. If he brought all three along, they'd find a way to jump him. And if he took just the driver, leaving the other two behind, they'd get a warning back to their home turf within minutes.

Besides, even if he did make it to San Juan, the capo would be too well protected there.

Either way, Finn would be dead within the hour.

So he'd have to settle for waiting to be contacted. Or ambushed. Either one was fine with him, as long as it moved the pieces on the board forward.

Slow is smooth, smooth is fast.

"Hey, Picasso," Shiny Shoes called out. "You for real, man?"

Finn backed into a turn and braked, then looked over at the man. "What do you think?"

He put the car in drive.

"Hey," Shiny Shoes said again. He narrowed his eyes. "You with El Rucco?"

Finn didn't answer. Instead, he held up Gold Tooth's phone and said, "Tell your capo."

He took off, less than 100 percent happy about how that had played out.

The man who'd asked the question wasn't stupid.

You with El Rucco?

Finn hadn't had a clue what he was talking about. And Shiny Shoes knew it.

36

It surprised Pedro how quiet the place was. Aside from an occasional chirp or two, the noisy coquís were mostly silent now. There was sporadic birdsong, but it was hushed, almost as if the birds themselves didn't want to disturb the magic. Butterflies darted in and out among the patchy beams of sunlight.

As they picked their way through the foliage, Pedro thought he could hear the scuffle of small animals slithering away from them under the quilt of dead leaves and fallen plants that blanketed the forest floor. The ground underfoot was muddy, and they both slipped and fell a few times before getting their forest legs.

Every few meters they had to halt their progress to clamber over fallen tree trunks.

As they went deeper into the forest, the vegetation changed. The banana, bamboo, and yagrumo grew scarce, giving way to tall tabonuco trees covered in thick, woody vines, their canopies soaring thirty meters overhead. The forest floor grew gnarled and knotted in vines and cool underfoot, the matting of leaves slippery, giving off a smell like something fermenting.

After what Pedro guessed was a little more than an hour, Miranda stopped suddenly.

"What?" said Pedro.

"Shhh."

He listened. Heard nothing.

They resumed their hike.

Twenty feet on she stopped once more. Then looked up at Pedro.

He'd heard it now, too, a distant thrashing. Moving closer.

"I think it's tracking us," whispered Miranda.

Pedro felt a bubble of panic rising in his belly.

There were no bears in El Yunque. No jaguars. No wolves. The thing tracking them went on two legs, not four.

Could it be a forest ranger, maybe? A lost tourist? Sure it could. But it wasn't. Somehow, Pedro knew it in his gut.

Should they run? Try to hide? If they ran, would whoever was tracking them hear them and start running, too?

Miranda tugged at his arm and pointed. Off to their left, a great fallen tree trunk lay amid a dense thicket of ferns. She looked up at him, questioning. *You think?*

He took a deep breath, then put up a finger. *Wait.*

He set off at a clumsy run to the right, through the ferns about thirty feet, disturbing as much foliage as possible, even bending down to break small branches and fronds as he went, then stopped and retraced his steps, running swiftly and carefully, doing his best to place his feet in the same tracks he'd just made.

Next, he set off straight ahead in the direction they'd been walking before, and fast-walked another forty feet, this time making an effort to leave a visible but less blatantly obvious trace, and carefully doubled back again.

He grabbed Miranda's hand and together they slipped over to the fallen tree, stepping as cautiously as possible, trying not to leave any tracks at all.

They clambered over the trunk and crouched down behind it.

And waited.

Pedro heard something slither through the ferns behind him. A moment later he felt a cool, undulating weight slide across his foot. He clenched his teeth, fighting the urge to look down. Whatever kind of snake it was, he'd rather not know.

They heard the thrashing approach, getting louder and louder and now accompanied by a quiet muttering, until it stopped, right at the spot where they'd been standing just moments earlier, no more than twenty-five feet away.

Pedro could hear heavy breathing. Then:

"Fuck!"

Quiet or not, Pedro recognized the voice.

He held his breath.

It seemed like minutes ticked by, though Pedro knew it was probably no more than eight or ten seconds. Finally they heard the man mutter, "Fucking cucarachas," and start moving again. It sounded like he went off in the same direction they'd been walking.

Pedro waited an eternity. Could he dare hope his idea had worked? Finally he poked his eyes above the line of the fallen tree trunk.

The man was gone.

It *had* worked. He saw Pedro's clumsy rightward fork and figured it was an attempt to fool him, that they'd really continued south. He'd fallen for it and gone south after them.

Pedro let out his breath.

They had tricked Loud Orc!

They heard the thrashing diminish until it had passed out of hearing.

They waited a full five minutes before stepping out from behind the fallen tree. Then took off, forging a new westward path.

37

Ten minutes south of his encounter with the cartel foot soldiers, Finn pulled off at an abandoned convenience store and drove around back. He parked the car and popped the hood.

Going around front, he disconnected the car's battery. While waiting a few minutes for the airbag system's reserve electrical charge to dissipate, he collected a few tools from the rear trunk, then returned to the driver's seat. Using a flat-head screwdriver, he popped the retaining springs on the steering wheel airbag, cautiously jimmied the airbag itself free from the steering wheel, then turned it over and disconnected its wires.

The process felt much like disabling a roadside bomb. Which was what it was, essentially. One wrong move and that thing could kill you.

He placed the disabled airbag module in the trunk.

For the driver's side door, he first removed the handful of bolts that held the side panel cover, then the cover itself. The side airbag was held in place by three hex bolts. He carefully removed the bolts, then disconnected the wires and stashed this module, too, in the trunk.

Finn was a fan of seatbelts. Airbags, not so much. Yes, they could save your life. But in combat circumstances they could also restrict your movements when you most needed them unrestricted.

And you never knew when combat circumstances would present themselves.

He reconnected the car battery, got back in the driver's seat, and withdrew the burner phone he'd used for Uber the day before.

And looked at it.

He stepped out of the car again, extracted the phone's SIM card and crushed it with his heel, then pitched the empty phone far off the road into a weed-filled empty lot. Then got back in the car.

Finn hadn't owned or used a phone the entire time he'd been living on Vieques, and he was reluctant to start now, even with burner phones he could trash the moment he used them. Phones were like spotlights. The last time he'd relied on one, the DIA had homed in on his location within minutes.

But he had no choice. At least he could get rid of the phone after he finished with it. And it was a relief not to have to use the ride-share service again. Drivers had memories. He didn't need the exposure.

Not that driving a stolen cartel blingmobile was exactly discreet.

He pulled out a fresh burner phone. Looked up the number for the mayor of Ceiba, keyed it in, and pressed SEND.

"¡Buenos días, oficina del alcalde!" said a cheerful voice. *Good morning, mayor's office!*

"Is the mayor in today?"

"I'm sorry, not until a little later this morning. Did you want to make an appointment?"

He declined and thanked the nameless voice, disconnected the call and pocketed the phone, then gunned the BMW back onto the road and headed south toward Ceiba. Just above the first exit for Rosie Roads, he pulled off the highway onto a side road, wound west for a few minutes, and turned off at an upscale gated community whose address he had pulled the night before.

He stopped at the security gate and identified himself as a friend of the mayor's.

"I'm sorry, sir," the rent-a-cop said. "The mayor isn't taking visitors this morning. Perhaps you can make an appointment at the mayoral office downtown?"

"Of course," said Finn. He backed out, turned, and parked a few hundred feet down the road around a curve.

The "security fence" wasn't very secure. He hopped the thing and ran, silent and low to the ground, around the inside of the perimeter until he came to the mayor's little villa tucked away at the very back of the property.

The place was built on the low end of luxurious: on grand enough a scale that constituents would be suitably impressed, yet not so opulent as to suggest graft or corruption.

Classy, but not over the top.

He tracked around to the front of the house, where he was not that surprised to find the front door unlocked. The place was outfitted with a mid-level security system, but it wasn't activated at the moment. The mayor evidently felt no need to lock the door or arm the system while at home, in the morning, inside a gated compound.

Finn quietly entered and walked straight back to the kitchen, where a woman stood on the far side of a butcher-block island, her back to Finn, looking out through sliding glass doors at a small enclosed courtyard, sipping a cup of coffee.

"Señora Dominguez," he said.

She turned around and her face lit up with that thousand-watt smile. "Picasso!"

It was the woman from the night before.

38

"Please call me Graciela," she said. "How are you feeling this morning?" She set her coffee down and rushed to pull out a tall counter stool for him. "Please, sit." She didn't seem startled to see an intruder suddenly appear in her kitchen. Or maybe she just hid it well. "Would you like some coffee?"

Finn stepped into the kitchen and took a seat on the stool. "Water's fine."

She came around the island to the refrigerator and poured him a glass of ice water as she talked.

"I mean it—how *are* you feeling? That was horrible, what those men did to you."

"A little sore, but I'll live. Gracias," he added as she set his water down on the butcher-block surface. "You didn't tell me who you were."

She settled onto her own stool and picked up her coffee mug again, cradling it in both hands. "To tell the truth, I was a little embarrassed. I knew it wasn't the safest neighborhood to be out walking alone. I'm sorry my carelessness got you in trouble."

"Who were those two? Why did they target you?"

"Delincuentes. Just out making trouble. I don't think they even knew who I was."

"They didn't recognize the mayor?"

"I try to keep a low profile. It makes it easier to spend time out where the people are, without any fuss or bother. Clearly, though, last night was a bad idea. And again, I'm so sorry." She took a sip of her coffee, looking at him as she did so, a smile dancing at the corners of her lips.

"So, are you here in your official capacity as an artist, Señor Picasso?" she said. "Come to paint my portrait?"

"As a journalist, actually," he said. "Freelance. I'm researching a piece on crime in Puerto Rico since María. For a Dutch magazine. Though I'm actually hoping to sell it to *Rolling Stone*."

Dreadlocked Dutch journalist, itinerant street artist, drug broker . . . sooner or later his conflicting cover stories would start crashing into one another. Finn didn't care. He'd worry about cleaning up his footprints later.

"Ah," she said. "Crime in Puerto Rico. A sad story, I'm afraid." She took a sip of coffee and paused, as if gathering her thoughts. "There are two essential, underlying causes of crime. Do you know what they are?"

"Tell me."

"First is the fallen nature of humanity, which goes back to Genesis. There is little we can do about that. But there is also a second cause, and that is money—or rather, the lack of it. The great American philosopher Mark Twain had it right when he said, 'The lack of money is the root of all evil.' And there is a great deal we can do about that. Tell me, in your research, have you read about our P3 initiatives?"

Finn nodded. "A little."

The mayor, he'd read in his online hunt the night before, was on a mission to transform Ceiba through a series of public works—expansions to the local airport, turning it into a full-service international hub; reliable high-speed internet throughout the region; support for local farmers growing indigenous crops through sustainable agriculture; renewable energy projects, especially solar and wind ("It's insane not to do this, with all our abundant sunshine and wind!" she'd been quoted in one article), and meanwhile burying all their power lines ("And it's insane that we haven't *already* done this—every time a storm blows through our lines go down again!").

These projects she aimed to accomplish through systemic collaboration with big corporations and generous billionaires—public-private partnerships, dubbed "P3."

"Half the Puerto Ricans you talk to claim they want independence," she was saying. "The other half clamor for statehood. I just want them to have electricity and decent jobs. But our economy has been systematically destroyed over decades. Textiles came and went. Manufacturing came and went. Pharmaceuticals and high tech are already halfway out the door. There are only two industries that have come and stayed: drugs and tourism.

"The first is killing us. The second will save us."

It had the universal cadence of the political pitch, the kind of rhythmic oversimplification that rallied masses of hearts and votes. A chicken in every pot. Together, a new beginning. Yes we can. Make America great again.

Though he had to admit, coming from her, it had a clear ring of sincerity.

"Am I hearing a policy platform?"

"You are, and I make no secret about it. The drug trade is a horribly destructive force. Our people cannot thrive by exporting drugs. We can only thrive by exporting beauty and joy. In a word: tourism.

"Tourism is the future of Puerto Rico. The north's endless appetite for the exotic south—one of the earth's great inexhaustible resources." She smiled. "And to rebuild a robust tourism, you have to get crime under control. Which is why you found me out walking around a dubious barrio in a neighboring city.

"As mayor of one little town, frankly, there's a limit to how much I can do. But if we can make a difference here, perhaps that small difference can make a big difference."

Finn was no political savant, but it was impossible not to hear the woman's ambitions bleeding through her rhetoric.

"Puerto Rico is a small island," he said. "It's only an hour's drive from here to the governor's mansion."

She smiled, shooing away the thought with a wave of her hand. "Let's not get ahead of ourselves." She set her coffee down and stood.

"And with that," she said, "I really must go. If you have more questions, or need to clear any quotes or fact-check particulars, you can make an appointment with my office." As she spoke she began to shepherd him toward a side door.

"One last question?" said Finn.

She gave a little laugh. "A true journalist, I see. Okay. One."

"Who, or what," said Finn, "is El Rucco?"

Her smile dimmed. She sagged back against the butcher-block island and shook her head.

"¡Ay! ¡El Rucco!" She gave a heavy sigh. "Ay . . ."

she repeated. She picked up his water glass and ferried it to the sink.

"El Rucco is a phantom. An urban legend. Parents tell their children stories of the bogeyman to frighten them and keep them in line, yes? Our culture has its own versions of these myths. The one you mention is the latest incarnation, only it's one told by adults, to adults. Who should know better.

"We have enough problems with the criminals we have, Señor Picasso. We don't need to invent those we don't."

She glanced at her slim wristwatch.

"I'm so sorry, mi amigo, but I'm already running late." She plucked out her cellphone as she opened the door and ushered him out. "Can I call you a car?"

Finn stepped outside. "That's okay," he said. "I have one."

39

Heat hung over the city like a steam press, the famous Caribbean breezes smothered and stilled for the moment. The super-saturated air seemed to amplify the ambient sounds. Or in this case, to highlight the lack of ambient sounds. There were people on the streets, here and there, but on the whole the place felt deserted.

On the road to Humacao, Finn had considered his two encounters with Graciela. He found himself strangely drawn to her, though he did not understand why. It wasn't sexual, and "attraction" wouldn't be the right word. But there was something almost electric about her face, something magnetic that drew him, yet at the same time repelled him. He couldn't put his finger on it.

She'd exhibited the same sort of evasiveness he'd seen in all his encounters the day before. Not exactly terror, in her case, but some undercurrent he couldn't quite identify. As if she had more to say, but something had prevented her from saying it.

Gold Tooth's phone had not buzzed.

No word from the gangbangers' capo.

Not so far, anyway.

The car's radio, which Finn had on low, caught his attention.

"... National Weather Service has issued a tropical storm watch for the Caribbean Basin ..."

The dockmaster was right.

Finn parked his purloined BMW in a day lot, paid with cash, and walked to the church at the plaza. The big front door was open, the place once again aglow in that soft morning radiance. Nave and sanctuary were both empty. Finn walked all the way back through the altar and through a small arched door on the left that opened onto a small chamber.

The room was carved in the same luminous white concrete and blue-and-white polished-marble floor tiles as in the sanctuary, the walls lined with furnishings, mostly cabinets of various sizes, made of mahogany or cocobolo or some other tropical hardwood. A small prayer bench, currently unoccupied, sat in the very center of the room. A hardwood desk was built into the wall opposite the door, covered in a scattered mess of papers and matched with a stark straight-backed wooden chair, upon which sat the young/old priest, bent over his work. Maybe writing a sermon. Or balancing the parish budget.

Finn scuffed a foot to make himself audible, and the priest turned around in his chair with a start. His face lit up with a smile.

"¡Buenos días! How may I help you?"

In the next instant his expression darkened as he recognized Finn from the day before, and he stood, stiffly.

"Sorry to bother you." Finn spoke in what he'd come to think of as his journalist voice: casual, breezy, yet rapid and purposeful. "I'm a journalist, actually, researching an article on crime in Puerto

Rico since María. If you're not too busy? I just need a few minutes."

"I don't think I'm really—"

"It's just a few questions. And then I'll leave you alone."

The priest hesitated. "Very well," he said, his discomfort palpable. "What would you like to know? I'm certainly no expert on crime."

As he spoke, the priest slowly sat again, though Finn noted that he wasn't offering a seat to his visitor.

His third standing interview of the day. If you counted Shiny Shoes and Gold Tooth as an "interview."

"The memorial yesterday. It was for a police officer?"

"Yes."

"Local?"

"No, San Juan. He grew up here. In Humacao, that is."

Giving the briefest answers possible.

"Why the hostility?"

"Excuse me?"

"Yesterday, I mean. The feeling I got from the congregation was not what you'd call comradely. Which surprised me. Those were fellow officers, right?"

"I—I don't see how this helps your—"

"Just background, human interest, that sort of thing." Finn had no idea what "human interest" meant, but it seemed like something a journalist would say.

The priest hesitated again, then spoke carefully, as if feeling for the combination of a safe that might explode if he got it wrong. "According to what I've been told, the deceased was an officer who had fallen in with some unsavory characters. I should really—"

"And how did he die?"

"Done in by those same unsavory characters, I would imagine. Was there anything else—"

"Did this have anything to do with someone called El Rucco?"

The priest's transformation was more dramatic than Graciela's. He abruptly shot to his feet again and put up both hands, as if to stop an oncoming truck. "I have no idea who that is. I'm so sorry, I wish I could be more helpful . . ." He began walking Finn toward the door.

At the door to the sanctuary Finn turned and said, "Father, can I ask you something else, completely unrelated?"

The priest hesitated. This made hesitation number three, by Finn's count.

"I heard someone in town refer to 'La Bestia,'" he said. "Like it was something ominous. New Testament, yes?"

The priest ushered him out of the vestry and began walking him toward the front of the sanctuary as he talked.

"Well, yes, it certainly could be. The Revelation to John, the final book of The Book, which talks about the Beast in the end times. But there's also a local legend about a sea monster, sometimes described as a giant squid, sometimes as half dragon, half octopus, the accounts vary. Supposedly, La Bestia lives deep in the Muertos Trough and trolls the Caribbean looking for victims."

Now that Finn had him talking about mythology instead of crime, he seemed to have relaxed into it.

"Muertos Trough?" prompted Finn.

"Yes—you've heard of the Puerto Rico Trench, just north of the island? Over five miles deep, the deepest spot on the Atlantic floor. The Muertos Trough is a similar trench, running east to west just below the island, not as deep but still more than three miles down. Some call it 'Devil's Ditch.'

"There's another version of the legend that talks about a man-eating whale—some say sent by the devil, others call it the Devil's Ride—accompanied by an entourage of sharks, or perhaps demons with pitchforks."

"The Devil's Ride," said Finn. "Wow."

" 'Where La Bestia goes, the waters boil.' So they say."

"That is seriously fascinating. Hey, can I ask one more question? What do you know about gargoyles in Puerto Rico?"

The priest jerked like he'd been stung.

"I'm sorry," he said, dropping all pretext of politeness and pushing Finn brusquely toward the outer door. "You have to go."

40

When Finn emerged from the church, he saw the woman in blue watching him from the opposite end of the plaza. Taking that as a tacit invitation, he crossed the tile square to where she sat and hunkered down facing her.

Without looking at him she began speaking, as if they'd known each other forever and were just picking up a conversation where they'd last left off.

"A great number of people have left Puerto Rico."

Her voice was soft and light, yet it somehow seemed to carry great weight.

"When I say 'a great number,' I'm speaking of several hundred thousand, this in a population of scarcely three million. Since María, they say, one in every six Puerto Ricans has moved away. There are a lot of empty houses on this island."

That there were. In his brief tour so far, Finn could attest to that. A ton of vacant storefronts, vacant homes, even entire vacant blocks.

"About thirty miles east by southeast of San Juan, on the outskirts of the town of Río Grande, near the entrance to El Yunque, there is a stretch of land that is home to dozens of abandoned houses. Some have been vacated as part of that general exodus. Some are tied up in an eternity of probate." She briefly glanced his way. "Puerto Rico's rat's nest of estate laws comprise a maze so byzantine it would have stymied Theseus."

She paused. It felt as if Finn ought to nod, so he did. Theseus. Labyrinth. Got it.

"There is a cluster of such buildings," she continued, "around the end of Route 731. Most of one-story cement construction, but there is one wood-frame farmhouse, surrounded by a stand of yagrumo. Built in a fit of nostalgia by some wealthy dreamer transplanted from the States, vacant for years now."

And she stopped talking.

Finn waited a full minute for her to continue. When she did not, he understood that this was her entire message to him.

"And I should go there," he said.

She reached into a bag and scattered a handful of whatever was in there on the ground. Several pigeons strutted over and pecked at it.

"And if I do?" he prompted.

"You may find what you're looking for."

"And how do you know what I'm looking for?"

She finally looked up at him.

"You are Mimo," she said. "From Isla Nena. You're here for los nenes."

Finn took a slow, deep breath. Then got up and took a seat on the bench next to the woman in blue.

He'd tapped into the network of the dispossessed, all right. And it was even more informed than he'd expected.

"They're not in that house," she said. "But somewhere close by. This is my understanding."

Finn nodded. So the wood-frame house was his

landmark. If she was to be believed, and he saw no reason to doubt her.

"I have no information on who has them," she added, "or why."

He nodded again. "May I ask you something?" he said. "You don't have to answer."

She tilted her face in his direction.

"Who, or what, is El Rucco?"

A shadow fell across her otherwise serene visage. "El Rucco." She gave an infinitesimal sigh. "El Rucco is a scourge upon our people. A plague. Do you know the meaning of the word?"

"I don't." He had never heard the term before today. It wasn't any Spanish word he knew.

"'Rucco' is Spanglish. Puerto Rican slang. It means 'rook,' a con man or swindler—or castle, as in a game of chess. Puerto Ricans take their castles seriously. Calling himself 'El Rucco,' he has cloaked himself in an image of impregnable power, which he wields to inflict unspeakable pain and suffering."

She paused.

"It would be best if you had as little to do with El Rucco as possible."

Finn sensed that she knew a good deal more than she was saying, but had already taken a significant risk in saying as much as she had. Or perhaps she believed saying more would put *him* at risk.

Still, she'd already said a mouthful.

The priest had been too terrified to talk about it at all. The mayor, who didn't seem to fear anything or anyone, was either in denial or simply didn't want to admit to the man's existence in front of a journalist because it was bad PR.

But the woman in blue had spoken freely.

"Why aren't you afraid to talk to me?"

A faint smile lit her face briefly, like the moon showing through a scud of clouds.

"In the States, you cross the line when you kill a cop. In Puerto Rico, you cross the line when you hurt a nun."

Finn raised his eyebrows in question. *You're a nun?*

"A fallen nun. I had an affair with a married man. Now"—she gestured with one hand, taking in the tiled plaza with its pigeons and cypress trees—"my church is here."

They sat silent together for a moment. Then she reached out and took one of Finn's hands in hers. The skin of her palms felt soft yet strong, like worn denim.

She gave his hand a squeeze.

Finn felt a jolt of something like a static charge shoot up his arm. His lungs inhaled sharply, and his brain seemed to light up for a moment.

"Go find them," she said.

41

Pedro was going insane with anxiety.

They'd been hiking for hours, changing their path forward, zigzagging every few minutes, doing everything they could think of to make sure they'd lost their pursuer.

His plan had been simple. Head west for a while, long enough to make sure they'd gotten well away from their pursuer, *then* cut south and keep going until they were out of the forest. And then? Well, he would worry about that when they came to it.

But it hadn't been nearly as simple as he'd thought.

For one thing, the terrain didn't cooperate. He could draw nice straight lines and clear compass directions in his head as much as he liked, but the forest was full of slopes and slants, sharp cliffs and treacherous ravines, and the farther they went, the less sure he was of their direction. He worried that they might be going in circles, even heading straight back toward the man they were trying to escape.

What was worse, it had started to rain, and it rained and it rained and it rained, which made the ground muddier and more slippery, and also drowned out any other sounds they might have heard, which made it impossible for him to know for sure whether they were alone.

Finally the rain stopped and fingers of sunlight poked through the canopy. They stopped to rest for a moment by a stream and drink some more of that wonderful mountain water.

And then, just as they were starting to feel safe, they heard it again.

The distant thrashing, far behind them. Coming their way.

Miranda leapt to her feet and turned to head south, downslope—but Pedro stopped her with a harsh whisper.

"*Wait!*"

She froze and stared at him.

He was looking at the stream, studying it intently.

The water had turned brown, silty, cluttered with fresh leaves flowing down from upstream.

He looked over in the direction of their pursuer, then off to his right, to the north. Then back at the stream.

The water level was visibly rising, its faint gurgle turning to an excited babble.

He jumped to his feet and grabbed Miranda's hand.

"Run!"

He pulled her off their path and to the northwest, up a steep slope to their right, as they heard the stream rise from a babble to a loud chatter.

"Flash flood!" he shouted.

Pedro knew about flash floods. They weren't just strong, they were like freight trains made of water. A flash flood could tear up trees by their roots, push boulders, carve new riverbeds, trigger deadly mud-slides.

And the very worst thing you could do was also the thing that your instincts told you to do: try to escape by running downhill. Because that would always be the same way the water was going—and the water would always, always outrun you.

"We have to get up higher!"

They ran up a slope that almost immediately dead-ended in a series of rock cliffs, impossible to scale.

Pedro turned and stared at the oncoming churn. In just minutes the stream had swelled to triple its size, sweeping tree branches and debris in its onrush. The hours of accumulated rain had unleashed a watery monster.

They were trapped.

"Here!" shouted Miranda. Pedro glanced back and saw her shimmy up a tree trunk that reached up to the cliff overhead. He followed. They scrambled over and around the rocks, climbing higher and higher, until the ground leveled off into a steep but walkable incline.

And kept going.

As they climbed, the forest changed. The substrate thinned to nothing but sparse grasses, rocks, and hard soil. The trees grew shorter and shorter. The tabonuco and other more familiar trees had long since disappeared, replaced by soaring Sierra palm, like the masts of great schooners, and then those faded, too, gradually giving way to strange, stunted creatures, their trunks and limbs twisted by the constant wind, more like spiky shrubs than trees.

"Némoca . . . Guayabota . . . Camasey . . . Limoncillo . . ." As they walked Pedro whispered their names, like a roll call of gods on a mythic mountain.

The air grew clammy, cold, and thick with mist.

Miranda shivered.

"Cloud forest, they call this," said Pedro, his voice hushed as one would speak in church. "We must be eight hundred, nine hundred meters up. Maybe more. Maybe close to the summit."

They were both still barefoot, still in the swimsuits they'd put on three days earlier. Pedro was all scratched up from pushing through dense thickets as they'd run from their pursuer.

They were both exhausted.

It was growing dark.

"We have to stay up here tonight."

He looked at Miranda, who frowned.

"He has to stop at night, too," he added.

She looked at him closely. "You're sure?"

"Yeah," he said, though what he thought was, *No, I'm not sure at all.* He knew he would be sleeping very lightly that night. If at all.

42

It was already going dark but still hot as a steam bath when Monica pulled into the marina at Puerto Chico. Monica was no stranger to hot climates; she still remembered the summer when she was twelve and the mercury on their ranch hit 114 degrees. But even in the worst heat, Muleshoe, Texas, was dry as the outside of a cactus.

The heat in this place made her feel like a chuck steak in a pressure cooker.

She'd spent the better part of the morning debating her next move. Her role in this investigation was designed to be a limited one: review the collected footage and stills, identify the target, assist in the arrest. But so far that footage was still being collected. There was nothing to identify and no arrest to assist. She had, in other words, no official use.

Being useless was not in Monica's playbook.

The day before, she'd flown the length and breadth of the island, familiarizing herself with the lay of the land, using mathematical logic to sniff out what to her seemed the most likely areas where Chief Finn might go to ground.

Now she wanted to do something about it.

She parked, found the door to the little office of the dockmaster, and knocked.

After a moment the door swung open. The man who faced her looked like the title character from *The Rime of the Ancient Mariner.* White hair like a shock of sea spray, deeply weathered dark brown skin. Face like a topographic map of the Atlantic floor.

"Help you?"

He invited her inside his sparse office, offered her a seat in his rolling desk chair. He sat on the edge of a metal desk that looked like it was about to be overtaken by corrosion from the salt air. Behind him, a window opened onto a view of the harbor.

She introduced herself as Emma Halsey, said she was looking for her brother Marlin (the alias Finn had used in Iceland), who was in trouble with the American authorities, and needed to find him before the law did.

"Although, knowing Marlin, chances are good he's going under a different name, I have no idea what."

She'd put some thought into her story, and the phrasing was intentionally vague. Puerto Ricans' loyalties to "the American authorities," she guessed, might be decidedly mixed, and she hoped to find sympathies tilted in the lost brother's favor.

If anyone asked what kind of trouble, or specifically which authorities, she had an elaborate backstory concocted, but she hoped not to have to deploy any of it. The more detail she gave, the more easily the fabric would come unraveled upon closer inspection.

Then she handed him a photo of Chief Finn.

It wasn't a very good shot, a blow-up from an old

BUD/S class photo taken some two decades earlier. But it was all she'd been able to sneak from their set.

If Dar knew what she was doing, he'd pop a vein.

He was still insisting on keeping their mission 100 percent under wraps, and would have shit ten kinds of bricks if he'd known she was actually showing the man's photograph. But they had just days left to find their subject before they got called back to DC. If they were going to accomplish their mission, it was time to put on their big-boy and big-girl panties and get it done.

And she didn't especially love Dar's assumption of authority here. Yes, it was technically his operation, and again, she was supposed to be playing a supporting role. But they answered to two entirely separate chains of command.

And yes, he was fairly senior, as FBI special agents went. Monica herself had been official JAG for less than three months, and normally a freshly minted JAG would start out at the bottom of the pecking order, which in this case meant being assigned to tasks barely above the level of paralegal.

But Monica's situation wasn't normal. Her existing service record meant she automatically commanded far more respect than any normal line officer. She felt she'd earned the right to make some decisions here.

So she told her story—and handed over Finn's photo.

It wasn't an ideal shot for ID purposes, the enlargement of his face making it even grainier than it was to start out with. And it was twenty years out of date. It would have to do.

The dockmaster took it from her and gave it a long, careful perusal. Then looked back at her.

"Navy?"

"Sorry?"

"You got the feel of an officer about you. Navy?"

"No, I'm—actually, I'm just a lawyer." (God, she was such a terrible liar.) "But I grew up around boats. My brother and I."

"Naval Station Great Lakes," he said, setting the photo down on the surface of his desk. "Pass-in-review March of '69. Served in 'Nam, if you can believe that. Took a hunk of shrapnel when an outpost shelled my PBR in June '71. Purple Heart."

"Well. Thank you for your service."

"You know who fired the first shot in World War One? On the American side?"

"I'm sorry, I don't."

"A Puerto Rican lieutenant. Officer of the day at El Morro Castle in Old San Juan. Led to the capture of a German supply boat."

"I did not know that."

The helo pilot had given her a geography lesson. Now she was getting a history lesson.

So this was how investigations went.

Slowly.

"Sixty-five thousand puertorriqueños served in World War Second, sixty thousand more in Korea, and another forty-eight thousand in Vietnam. It was Puerto Ricans trained the Tuskegee Airmen. You've heard of them."

"Of course. That's—well, that's all amazing."

"There's some in the States don't even realize this island is part of their country. You gotta wonder about the state of education these days."

At that, he fell silent. Monica didn't see what she could possibly say in response to all that, so she waited a few moments, then said, "So . . . the photo. Have you seen him?"

He picked up the photo again and scrutinized it once more. Looked up at her again. Shook his head.

"Sorry. Afraid I haven't seen him, young lady. But I will definitely keep an eye out."

He held the photo out to her.

"That's for you," she said. "My phone number's on the back. In case you hear or see something. Call me anytime, day or night, at that number."

After she thanked him and left, he studied the picture of the young man again for a moment. Then tucked it into a drawer in his salt-rusted desk.

43

It was already coming on dusk, but the brutal heat of the day had hardly diminished.

On his way the sky had opened up and poured out an ocean of hot rain, great drops smacking the highway's asphalt like a battalion of nail guns. On and on it went, battering cars and trees and roadside rooftops until it stopped as abruptly as it had begun, leaving the air as hot and heavy as before.

As Finn drove into the countryside in his borrowed BMW, the highways quickly gave way to pitted streets, barely patched together with asphalt, blocks of homes overgrown with weeds, wild dogs roaming the front yards, some inhabited and quite a few not, judging by appearance.

He turned onto Route 731, which wound through the wild territory like a blacksnake in tall grass, and took it right to the end, where it abutted the border of El Yunque.

He had no problem finding the old wood-frame farmhouse, exactly as the woman in blue described. What she hadn't described was its condition. "Surrounded by yagrumo" was one way of putting it. To Finn it looked more like it was being slowly absorbed by the plants. The path leading to the front porch was barely discernible through the tangle of weeds. The porch itself looked like it was about to detach and float away. The entire house sagged to one side. If it had ever been painted, the long years of tropical weather had pretty much erased the effort.

The place looked as if it had been transplanted here from a gothic horror tale set somewhere in the Jurassic era.

He drove through the tangles of trees and giant ferns around to the back and parked his car in a spot where it wouldn't be visible from the road. After confirming that the house was empty, he climbed up onto the dusty second floor—more attic than finished space, but with good window views—to survey the territory and map out his route through the more than two dozen squat cement and stucco buildings in the immediate area that all sat staring back at him with vacant eyes.

He crept back downstairs and cautiously moved out, then spent the next two hours searching, building-to-building, never sure they were truly vacant until he'd taken the time to clear each one. It was a simple but time-consuming operation.

He'd cleared all but three or four when he came to the one he was looking for.

He knew it by the smell.

Finn was well acquainted with the smell of death. When you got a full-on hit, it didn't leave your nostrils for hours; even if you showered until the hot water went cold, the stink still wouldn't completely wash off. If you met up with enough of it over time, it got to the point where it never left you.

It was, in Finn's experience, the most terrible smell there was.

Hurricane shutters and bars, like all the others.

Not to keep out crime. To keep out flying debris in a hurricane. The cement construction that had become almost universal in Puerto Rico was a mixed blessing: Cement houses were better able to withstand hurricanes, but they also trapped heat, especially when they were shut up tight. As this one was.

He didn't want to enter the building.

The door was unlocked. Small living room, sparsely furnished. Kitchen, no bigger than a closet. No bathroom.

One bedroom.

Which was where the smell was coming from.

Finn had found dozens of dead bodies over the course of his career. Hundreds. But there were two he didn't think he could bear to find.

He didn't want to go into that room.

He stepped up to the door and pulled it open. And sank to his knees, head down.

It was a man, lying dead on his back.

Not los pollitos.

Someone else.

He took a few long breaths despite the stench, which was ten times worse in there than it had been in the living room, then got back to his feet and went in to inspect the corpse.

The sight was worse than the smell.

The man lay stretched out, his upper body propped up partway against the far wall. There was a puncture wound in the front of his neck, dead center, just below the Adam's apple. His eyes stared out with an agony Finn could only guess at. But what was most striking was what he found between the puncture wound and the eyes.

Or rather, what he didn't find.

The lower half of the mouth was completely missing. So was the jaw. The tongue spilled out obscenely, like the raw stamen of a blossoming flower in hell, the severed muscles and gaping maw where the chin and mandible ought to be causing it to lurch outward.

The overall effect was horrifying. Terrifying. Something that would frighten away evil spirits.

Like a gargoyle.

There was dried blood pooled around the man. A lot of dried blood, enough to indicate definitively that the man had bled out. Death by exsanguination.

Which meant he had been alive when this was done.

Hence the staring eyes.

Finn searched the room, what there was to search. Cardboard box of old toys. Two worn cotton blankets, folded to make two flimsy mats on the wooden floor. A few empty water bottles. And one very dead man.

He withdrew a third burner phone, cut a notch in its side so he could distinguish it from the one he'd used to call the mayor's office, and took a series of photos with it. Moving carefully around the body. Touching nothing.

Then went back outside.

Had Pedro and Miranda been held there? Good chance; the two blankets suggested so. Had they been killed there, too? He saw nothing to support that conjecture.

Assuming the kids had been there, where were they now?

Finn saw three possibilities.

The people holding them could have moved them to some other location. Which would put Finn back at square one.

Except that it seemed likely to Finn that this guy had been guarding them. And had been murdered. Why? Because someone else came in, killed him, and took the kids. Which would mean there were now two different parties after them, and this second party had stolen them away and taken them to some other location.

Which would also put him back at square one.

Or, the third possibility, the guard had been punished by the people holding them in the first place. Because he'd fucked up.

Because they'd escaped.

And gone where?

If they hit the road on their own, walking the miles on Route 731, they would have easily been caught by whoever came back looking for them. Which would put Finn back at square one.

Unless they'd hitched a ride.

Square one again.

And if they escaped but didn't hit the road? Could they have . . . ?

He turned and looked out at El Yunque National Forest, just visible under a waning moon. Twenty-eight thousand acres. Of an entirely unknown environment.

With a tropical storm coming.

It was difficult to say with certainty, given the extreme temperatures in that buttoned-up concrete bunker of a house, but his best guess was that the body had been lying there for at least twenty-four hours. Which meant that wherever they had in fact taken off to—or been taken to—they would already be a full day into their journey.

A full day or more.

Fighting off the sense of defeat, he limped back to the wood-frame ghost house, went inside, and set up a spot by his second-story lookout window where he could sit and think about what to do next.

44

"People die here," said Miranda.

Building mats to sleep on in the cloud forest wasn't as easy as it had been down at the forest's edge, but they'd managed to scrounge enough loose foliage to get themselves bedded down, tucked into the crook of a fallen tree. Now they lay on their makeshift beds under the faint light of a waning moon, Pedro on his back, Miranda squished up against him for warmth.

A faint wind moaned in the shrunken trees.

Pedro shook his head. "C'mon, Mira . . ."

"They do!" she insisted. "Hugo said so! At least a few tourists in El Yunque die every year because they go off the paths."

"I know, but that's only because they don't understand where they are."

She frowned, but didn't press the point.

"You know where the name 'El Yunque' comes from?" said Pedro.

"No, Profesor."

"It's a Taíno word. Yúcahu."

"*Yúcahu,*" she repeated softly, like an incantation.

"According to the Taíno, a spirit called Yúcahu

lives up here on his mountaintop throne, watching over Borinquén, protecting its people."

The Taíno were their ancestors, as Papi had told them both a hundred times, maybe a thousand times. "Borinquén" was the Taíno word for what the Spanish called "Puerto Rico."

"Yúcahu was responsible for everything good. He kept the peace. Kept the farms fertile and productive. And that's why Boricua are a happy people, even now. Because we can still feel the presence of Yúcahu there, watching over us."

"Okay."

They fell silent. Listening to the alien wind, Pedro could guess what she was thinking. *If everything is so happy, why are we running from some cursing man? Why is there a bad policeman who wants to kill us?*

Why did Mamá die?

"But it took work," he added. "Yúcahu had to do battle with another spirit, the god of chaos and"—he couldn't quite find the word he was reaching for—"of everything going wrong and falling apart. His name, the bad god, was 'Juracán.' "

"Juracán," she murmured.

He turned his head to look at her.

"Do you remember María?" he said softly. "The storm, I mean?"

"Of course," said Miranda. Her voice no more than a whisper.

Pedro looked back up at the sky. He didn't think she did.

Miranda was not yet three years old when the big storm blew through, leveling the island's infrastructure, killing more than three thousand people, and knocking out everyone's power for months on end.

There were people who depended on that power, people in hospitals and places like that.

People like their mamá.

"Well," said Pedro, "Juracán is where the word 'hurricane' comes from. That's the god of chaos."

They lay silent for a while.

Mayhem, he thought. That was the word he'd been looking for. *The god of chaos and mayhem.*

He listened for the telltale rasp that would tell him his sister was asleep, but it didn't come. He could tell, from the silence next to him, that she was going to speak up again.

In another few minutes, she did.

"Pedro?"

"What?"

"What if Yúcahu is only pretending to be good, and is really even worse than Juracán?"

45

Sitting up on his makeshift bedroll at his lookout spot by the window of the abandoned farmhouse, Finn pulled a fourth fresh burner phone from his backpack and placed a call to Zacharias.

"I'm glad you called," the voice said. No greeting, no identifying himself or asking who was calling. As if he could tell who it was from the ring alone.

"Anything new?" said Finn.

"I tried a new recipe today, with the snook you brought me. Skin off, a little sazon rub, grilled with butter. I toasted you."

Finn said nothing.

"Héctor stopped by this morning, after you left. And again at suppertime, but I had nothing to offer him."

Finn heard the old man moving around.

"Where are you right now?"

Finn heard a quiet huff. The old man having a laugh.

"Where I always am. In the dark. The question is, where are you?"

"I think I'm getting closer to finding them, Papi."

That was a lie. Why did he say that? Because he couldn't bear to tell Papi the truth.

"I am sure you are," said the voice. "I've not doubted it for a moment."

Finn didn't know why he'd called. Perhaps to reassure the old man. Offer him a measure of hope. As if Papi were the one who needed it.

"Is it lonely?" he asked. "Being blind?"

Zacharias was silent for a moment. Finn heard a slight sigh and recognized it as the sound Zacharias made when he settled himself back into his favorite armchair.

"When I was a boy," the old man said, "I used to lie in bed at night, staring up into the dark, listening to the bombs fall."

Finn knew some of the old cook's history from Hugo and a few other islanders, but he'd never heard him speak of it till now.

"Sometimes, when the scream of the jets overhead woke me, flying so low, so fast, I would be confused, think at first that I was hearing screeches from the witch that inhabited my nightmares, coming to steal me away. And then the bombs would hit. The shock waves from the blasts shook our house as the explosions lit up the night sky. I remember the terror of it, lying in the dark, never knowing when another apocalypse would fall. I grew up terrified of the dark. To me, the night always meant more bombs might come.

"And, of course, some years later, one of those bombs finally found me."

Movement outside caught Finn's eye. A police car, then another. They rolled up outside the little cement death house and stopped. The driver of the first police car got out and came around to open the passenger's door. A woman stepped out. He led her inside the house.

"In my twenties," Zacharias was saying, "I

worked for the navy on an ordnance crew. I don't know if you knew that, Mimo. We were supposed to locate and mark, then move on, leaving it for the EOD techs to contain and remove. It was coming on dusk, and they were pushing us to make one last round. Nobody would go. But I was young and arrogant and macho. So of course, I went. An undetonated piece of ordnance blew, and when it exploded into the sky it took my sight with it.

"From that time on, I have been surrounded by night."

Finn heard a distant, unearthly scream, the cry of an animal being mortally wounded. He instantly pressed the MUTE button on his phone so Papi wouldn't hear. The scream broke into a wail, so desolate it could have melted the bars from their cement casings, and then collapsed into sobs.

Zacharias, unaware of this aria of fresh grief, continued recounting the tragedies of the distant past.

"Those first few years after the accident, I was very angry. I couldn't work, and I felt a great shame about that. I drank. I argued politics with anyone drunk enough to listen. I spent so much time feeling sorry for myself that I had more or less abandoned my young wife.

"And then she died. Cancer, they said, caused by the contamination left by those same bombs that had so terrified me as a child."

The policeman escorted the woman, bent and broken, out of the house and back into the car. Two more officers emerged from the other vehicle and entered the house. A moment later they came out bearing a body bag, which they loaded into their trunk. The little convoy backed out, turned, and drove off the way they'd come.

Why had they waited twenty-four hours to retrieve the body?

Maybe they'd left it in place as a means of intimidating the widow, in case her silence needed a little persuading.

"Now I had a wife to mourn and a daughter to raise," the old man continued. "I learned to cook. I learned to be a papá. And then, after years, she died, too—but not before giving birth to two little pollitos."

Finn heard him take a sip of something. His traditional nightcap of pitorro and Angostura, no doubt. Puerto Rico's own moonshine.

"I lost my sight long before they were born, Mimo, so I have never seen their faces with my eyes. But I learned them through my fingertips. If you put one of your pencils in my hand, I could draw them. They are imprinted in my bones.

"So I ask you, how could I be lonely?"

Finn thought about the woman being driven away in the police car, about whether she had any little pollitos of her own, and whether she would ever be able to forget what she'd just seen.

He thought about his old friend, learning the contours of his grandchildren's faces through the touch of his fingertips.

If you put one of your pencils in my hand, I could draw them.

Finn had no doubt that he could.

And Finn, who had eyes to see with, couldn't remember his own parents' faces.

What did that say about him?

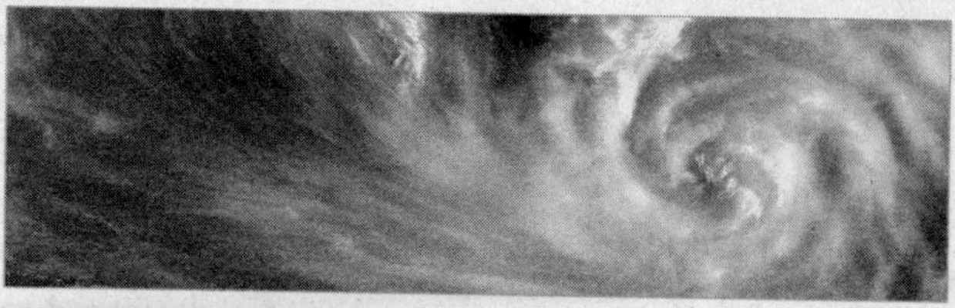

Thursday

T minus 3

Thursday morning Tropical Storm Will's wind speed exceeded seventy-four miles per hour, triggering the designation "hurricane." The Weather Service has upgraded its tropical storm alert from "watch" to "warning." There are divergent views on where Hurricane Will will make landfall:

The Global Forecast System (the "American model") projects it will skim along the bottom of the Caribbean and barrel directly over the so-called ABC Islands—Aruba, Bonaire, and Curaçao.

The European model has it veering northwest, hitting Jamaica and the Caymans before moving out into the Gulf of Mexico.

The National Hurricane Center splits the difference, putting landfall somewhere between Belize and Cancún.

All three will prove wrong.

46

Pedro awoke with a soft gasp.

The cloud forest.

He took a few long, slow breaths, the way Mimo taught him, feeling his heartbeat slow back to normal.

He'd been having a nightmare. El Gigante, the big policeman, had turned into a giant snake and come into the forest looking for them.

He's not here, he told himself. *It was just a dream. You're in the cloud forest, you and Mira. You're safe.*

The dawning sun felt cold and distant in the mist. He glanced at Miranda, stretched out on the ground next to him, still asleep.

Her hand twitched.

He blinked and stared. No, it was still.

He saw it again.

A little twitch.

And then it appeared.

Not her hand twitching at all, but something else, something poking up just above the horizon of her thumb. A thin, waving little stick, then another. Then a pair of mandibles. And now the face behind it.

An insectile face, huge, flanked by wicked, curving poison fangs.

I'm still dreaming, he thought.

The thing kept coming, crawling up and over Miranda's hand, now wiggling its way up her arm, inch by inch, more of it revealing itself as it pulled itself up and onto the full length of her arm. Another pair of legs. Then another. And another.

Not a dream.

He was awake, and he knew what he was seeing—an Amazonian centipede. *Scolopendra gigantea.* Native to El Yunque. Largest centipede in the world.

The beast was still coming, growing longer and longer, more legs and still more legs, climbing his sister's arm.

All twelve terrible inches of it.

Kill it! Stop it!

He couldn't move. He lay frozen, staring at the beast.

He'd read about this thing of nightmares—*The giant centipede has been known to kill and eat tarantulas, frogs, mice, small birds, even bats; at least one fatality has been reported, a four-year-old child*—but he'd never seen one in the . . . would you even say "in the flesh"? In the scales. A dragon. A monster.

You have to do something, NOW!

He took a shaky breath, steeling himself to move.

The monster stopped.

And then it lifted its front few inches off the surface of Miranda's arm, detaching and swiveling its upper body around so that its head now faced Pedro.

Looking at him.

Don't you dare.

It swiveled slowly back, planted all its horrible feet again, and resumed its climb, up, up, toward Miranda's neck and face.

Pedro lay paralyzed with horror.

Miranda started with a jerk.

The thing bit down, hard.

"Ouch!"

Her eyes flew open and fastened on the creature with its mandibles sunk into her upper arm.

She screamed.

The sound jolted Pedro into motion.

He leapt to his feet and swatted at the thing with his hand, knocking it to the ground, then stamped on it as it wriggled away. He could hear its exoskeletal body crunch under his bare foot, and once, just once, the thing jerked like a whip, trying to catch Pedro's foot in its jaws but failing as Pedro stomped and stomped, killing it with his bare heel.

He turned, pale and shaking, to look at his sister, who had gone silent after that one piercing scream.

"Thank you," she whispered.

47

The heat wave continued, with temperatures expected to climb into the high nineties toward the coast. There were three armed robberies last night in San Juan. A stabbing attack in the Bayamón projects, two arrests made, victim in critical condition.

And that was it.

No murder. No grotesque mutilation or ritual disfigurement. No gárgola.

Finn folded the newspaper and placed it back on the passenger's seat.

There'd been no connectivity when he awoke early that morning in the empty house, so he'd driven in to the nearest one-stoplight town to pick up an actual newspaper.

Which had reported exactly nothing.

He wondered if this one would get a memorial service, with a song about God holding you in the palm of his hand.

Once he was in range, before buying the paper, he'd used Gold Tooth's phone to scour the internet and found no mention of any grisly death in an abandoned house near the entrance to El Yunque.

It was as if the whole thing had never happened.

The news also informed him that the National

Weather Service had now upgraded the storm watch to a storm warning, meaning it had gone from a possibility to a certainty. Projections put Hurricane Will passing harmlessly through the Caribbean and making landfall somewhere far to the south and west of Puerto Rico.

Finn didn't trust the projections.

He got out of the car and did a series of stretches. He'd pretty much worked out the stiffness from the attack two nights earlier, but his body still felt old and tired.

He sat against the hood of the BMW and pulled out burner phone #2, the one he'd used to call the mayor's office the day before.

He couldn't wait forever for the capo whose car he'd stolen to make contact. He badly needed to make some progress here. Contrary to his nature though it was, he was going to have to trust someone.

He pressed REDIAL.

"¡Buenos días, oficina del alcalde!" It was the same cheerful staffer he'd gotten twenty-four hours earlier.

"Hi, me again. Is the mayor in this morning?"

"Actually, she is, lucky you! Who should I say is calling?"

"Picasso. We've met before. Several times, actually."

"Lucky you!" the cheery voice said again. "Isn't she amazing?"

Before he could reply Finn was put on hold. Less than thirty seconds later the familiar musical voice came on the line. "Picasso! Where are you?"

"I need your help."

"Anything," she said. "What can I do?"

"It's about the two missing children from Vieques."

There was a pause, and when she spoke again her voice was a good deal more muted.

"¡Ay, Dios!" she murmured. "Those poor little nenes. I've been following the Coast Guard's search-and-rescue effort. Officially, they are still considered 'missing,' but most people here fear they have drowned in the Sound and may never be found. Is this somehow connected with your article?"

"I can't reveal my sources, but I have reason to believe they may be somewhere here, on the big island."

"*Here?* How? Why?"

"They may have been witness to a drug-smuggling operation."

He figured she could fill in the rest.

"And you think . . ." Her voice trailed off as she saw the whole scenario. "I see. Have you talked to the police?"

"About that. May I speak frankly?"

"Please."

"I have reason to believe there may be some members of the San Juan police force involved on some level."

"Jesús," she murmured. To Finn she sounded stricken, yet not entirely shocked.

"You're not surprised?"

He heard her let out a sigh, followed by a brief silence. Then:

"You know about PROMESA?"

"La junta," said Finn.

That was what the locals called it. A classic government acronym: the Puerto Rico Oversight, Management, and Economic Stability Act, cleverly packaged to sound like a "promise." In fact, it was a federally run oversight board that allowed Puerto Rico to declare bankruptcy and then became its de facto economic dictator. Hence, "la junta."

"Unfortunately," said Graciela, "the 'promise' has proven to be mostly brutal austerity measures and cutbacks. Police budgets have been slashed, their ranks reduced by pay cuts and 'accelerated retirements,' and suddenly we have far fewer officers making next to nothing while they see the criminals they're charged with containing make ten, twenty times the money. The temptation to cross the line, I'm afraid, has grown great."

She was silent again. Finn could feel the weight of her thoughts.

She sighed again, then said, "You said you needed my help. What do you want me to do?"

"Is there someone in DEA, or in your own border patrol in Ceiba, who might have any insights on who might be behind this? And who would keep your confidence about it?"

"Yes, of course," she said, distractedly. "Jesús."

"There is also a possibility that they escaped and are hiding somewhere in El Yunque."

"Oh, my." A pause while she digested that. "So, park rangers, then. Okay. I can do that, too. Though in terms of keeping that channel confidential, I need to think about how best to manage that."

"Understood. And one more thing."

"The true journalist," she said, and he heard a bit of a smile come back in her voice.

"Graciela. Who is El Rucco?"

There was another silence.

"Not now," she said, her voice now barely above a whisper. "Call me later, on my cell. We'll talk then." She gave him the number. "And, Picasso—I will do what I can."

Finn used his fifth burner phone to place one more call, which took no more than two minutes to complete. He then destroyed that phone's SIM card and pitched the empty phone, climbed back in the BMW, pulled out onto the highway, and continued west.

He needed to know more about the police's role in all this. Which meant it was time to do that thing he had promised himself he would not do.

Go into San Juan.

The capital city. Ten percent of Puerto Rico's population jammed into a landmass the size of Madison, Wisconsin. The island's financial and industrial center, heart of the law enforcement and intelligence communities, Coast Guard, FBI, Homeland. Rumored NSA and CIA presence. Thousands of CCTV cameras.

Last place he wanted to go.

But he didn't have a choice.

He didn't know if the woman he'd seen the night before—the one he'd heard pierce the night with wails of grief and horror, the one who'd been escorted in and out again by a convoy of police—would ever say a word to anyone about what happened or who was behind it. He doubted it.

But the widow he saw at the church in Humacao would.

He knew this, because he'd just called her on burner #5 and asked.

And she said yes. “Only be careful when you come,” she’d added. “They’re watching.”

Finn glanced in the rearview. A charcoal-gray Lexus had pulled onto the highway shortly after he did. Now keeping a careful distance. Going his exact speed.

He was being followed.

48

It didn't surprise him. These guys were pissed off that he'd taken their car. Their pride was wounded. Maybe they'd been tracking Gold Tooth's phone. Maybe the car itself had a tracking device on it. Whatever. Of course they would've been looking for him.

Which normally wouldn't be a problem. But he didn't have time for this. They obviously didn't have their capo with them—if they did, they wouldn't be skulking back there, trying not to be noticed. And Finn had somewhere he needed to be.

If this were the movies, he would suddenly swerve off the highway and a high-speed chase would ensue, ending only when the other car plunged off an embankment in a fiery explosion while Finn sped safely away.

Most of the time reality was more complicated than the movies. In this case, it was a little simpler. And a whole lot less noisy.

First he had to confirm that the gray Lexus was in fact following him. Two box turns would do it.

He pulled off the highway at the next exit, at a modest speed but without signaling. Staying in the right-hand lane, he took a left at the first intersection, drove a short block, then paused briefly, as if changing his mind, and took a second left, again without first moving into the left-turn lane, and headed back toward the main road.

The Lexus followed from a discreet distance.

Surveillance confirmed.

He turned right and went down a narrow dirt road, then turned onto a secondary highway heading south, keeping things relaxed so as not to spook his prey.

He sped up on the roadway's single southbound lane, moved out and passed the car in front of him, an aging Honda, then gently applied the brake pedal, creating a slight, gradual decrease in speed and forcing the Honda to slow down with him.

Two cars back now, the Lexus had no choice but to pass them both, or it would've become too obvious.

A mile later the Honda turned off, leaving just the two of them on the road, Finn behind and the Lex "tailing" from in front. A minute later Finn saw a crumbling cement package store up ahead on the right with a set of abandoned filling pumps out in front.

Perfect.

He accelerated and swung up from behind.

The key to a successfully executed PIT maneuver—precision immobilization technique—was to maintain speed at a maximum of thirty-five miles an hour. Anything greater would be liable to send the other car into a roll, with resulting injuries and possible fatalities. Finn didn't want to kill these guys. He was already wanted for the murder of quite a few people he hadn't actually killed. If possible, he'd prefer not to complicate things further.

He just wanted them out of the way while he went about his next order of business.

He brought his right front wheel even with the other car's left rear wheel and gave the steering wheel a quick yank, knocking the front of his BMW hard into the other car's rear wheel well. As the Lexus lost traction and started into an uncontrolled 360, Finn backed off for the count of three, then made a sharp right and rammed into the other car's center frame, at the point between the rear and front doors where there was adequate reinforcement, so that he would have maximum force on the car but minimum risk of injury to its occupants.

Then hit the accelerator, pinning the car against one of the old pumps.

The Lexus's airbags all detonated at once.

Finn's did not.

His airbags were sitting in his trunk, disarmed and dormant.

The other driver looked dazed. The front- and backseat passengers struggled to exit the vehicle, but between Finn's BMW on one side, the defunct gas pumps on the other, and the inflated airbags filling the interior, they were all completely blocked in.

Finn shifted into reverse and shot backward for three car lengths, keeping the speedometer under thirty to maintain control, then rapidly shifted into neutral and yanked the wheel all the way to the left, holding it there without braking until the BMW had completed a 180-degree turn, then shifted back into drive.

Time to *vamos*!

Or so he thought.

As he hit the gas to exit the scene and get back on the highway, a blacked-out Toyota Land Cruiser pulled out from behind the package store and rolled in front of him, blocking his passage.

Finn braked to a halt. Impressed.

The gangbangers tailing him had been smarter than he'd given them credit for. He hadn't lured them in here after all.

They had lured him.

That was some damn good chess.

49

The Land Cruiser's driver killed the engine. A lone passenger stepped out and walked toward him. Pressed slacks, French cuffs. Light silk jacket, tailored.

The driver stayed put.

Finn put his BMW in park and stepped out, too. Best guess: He was about to have his meeting with the cartel gang's capo, second only in stature and authority to the top dog in whichever crime food chain this was.

The man stopped six feet from Finn and opened his jacket, showing he was unarmed.

"You wanted to talk. Talk." He spoke in a smoothly accented Spanish, a voice that could have charmed the ladies even as it froze the trees and caused birds to fall dead from their branches. No doubt the effect Shiny Shoes had been going for, only this was the real deal.

Finn stood motionless by his car's front fender. Standing farther back, with ready access to the driver's door, would have signaled cowardice; any farther forward, disrespect or aggression.

"I understand you have something of mine," he

said evenly. "Acquired in error, I'm sure. No offense taken."

The capo's gaze sharpened, a faint frown touching his eyebrows. "Something of yours," he repeated. After a beat, when Finn made no reply, he added, "Such as?"

"Dos pollitos. Pecking outside the border of their yard. Purely unintentionally."

A silence.

"Dos pollitos," the other man repeated.

Again Finn said nothing.

After a long pause the capo said, "Why are you here, really?"

Finn spread his hands. *I've already said.*

The man scanned the scene to his left with mock caution, then to his right, then back at Finn.

"Look around you."

Finn didn't move. Didn't look. Figured it was rhetorical.

"You will see," the cartel boss continued, "there are no police here. No TV cameras, no media, no helpful civilians going about their business. No bystanders. You are in my world. When I put out my hand, like this—" He held one fist out in front of him, his thumb jutting out on the horizontal. "— and go like this—" He dipped the thumb down and back, just a teasing degree or two. "—a high-speed, steel-jacketed round strikes your temple with a thousand foot-pounds of force. Hollow-point. The skull explodes like a ripe melon."

He raised the fist to just above eye level, holding the thumb steady, as if it held the pin to a grenade hung around Finn's neck.

Which, in a sense, it did.

Finn didn't have to look around to know. There

would be one sniper perched on the low roof of the crumbling cement package store, well concealed. And at least one other gunman, stationed somewhere else at similarly close range. Probably more than one.

So much for "no weapons."

"But you won't," said Finn.

The man's stare bored into him.

Finn looked back, his eyes flat as the sky.

"No?" The capo raised his fist a few inches higher. "And why is that?"

Finn waited five seconds.

Ten.

Then cocked his head, just a teasing degree or two.

"Because you don't yet know who I am."

The man's face darkened.

"Señor Picasso, I will suggest you return to whatever whore's den you crawled out of and don't let your face appear within a hundred miles of this place again. And tell your 'friend' his business is not welcome here."

Finn held the man's eyes. "The 'specialty groceries' business, my overseas 'friend,' this was all horseshit. I assumed you knew that."

The man's face colored slightly, his black eyes sparking fury, but he said nothing.

Finn continued. "I have no business with you. I have no business on your island. I'm here for one reason only. Which I've already stated. Though I will add this: If you have any knowledge about these two nenes, their whereabouts, or who holds them, El Rucco would be . . . grateful."

It was a calculated risk. Finn had been caught off guard when Shiny Shoes had asked if he was with El

Rucco. Which of course this man would know, and therefore be likely to take this last veiled threat as a bluff. But on the other hand, he might reason, if this Picasso really *were* in El Rucco's employ, would he have so readily tipped his hand to a mere messenger?

Finn kept his eyes locked on the other man's—but his attention was fully focused on any movement in that thumb.

The cartel boss took a slow breath, the fire in his eyes cooling to a glow of calculation.

And slowly lowered his fist.

"I have, quite frankly, no idea what you are talking about. But if your business is, as you say, with that gentleman, then I say, Vaya con Dios." He took a step back, made a half turn, then turned back to Finn.

"Keep the car. Consider it our gift."

He turned, walked back to the Land Cruiser, and got in.

The car backed into a K-turn and drove off.

As Finn watched them shrink and disappear he thought about the calculation in the man's eyes.

I have, quite frankly, no idea what you are talking about.

Could be pure posturing. But Finn didn't think so. And now he knew two things about the man.

He didn't have Pedro and Miranda.

And he was as terrified of El Rucco as everyone else.

50

As a rule, Cal avoided lying to the boss. Doing so could be hazardous to one's health. There were dozens of people who could attest to that. If they still had jaws to talk with.

Plus, he believed in telling the truth. Cal still went to confession every week, and he had never once had to squeal on himself for telling a falsehood. A record that to Cal was a source of some personal and professional pride. When he said something, he meant it. His word, as the saying went, was his bond.

Lies by omission, on the other hand, he considered a gray area.

Such as not mentioning to his wife their son's plan to move out of the house this weekend and in with his girlfriend.

Or the conversation he'd just had with his boss.

Apparently Venezuela was nearby but holding off "until tomorrow." Which meant they were holding off, period, until they judged conditions safe for them to move.

This was a problem. The Venezuelans' merchandise made up a critical percentage of the total shipment. The rest of the cargo, collected from a handful of other sources, was already assembled at the dock, ready to load and go. But they couldn't move without Venezuela. And Venezuela wouldn't budge. They would keep sitting down there to the west, off the southern coast of the Dominican Republic, pretending to drop fishing nets and circling back to check on them, until they were certain the coast was clear. That, in this case, not being a figure of speech.

Cal had to get the Coast Guard to stand down. The only way to do that was to resolve the issue with the two children.

And Paco wasn't responding to his texts.

That was his lie of omission. No need to let the boss know his man hadn't reported in for a full thirty-six hours.

El Rucco was viewed by all as a force of nature, remote and terrible, a force that could reach out and touch anyone, anywhere, anytime. A god, basically.

By everyone but Cal.

Cal was the only person on earth who knew El Rucco's true identity. Or at least, since Sunday night, the only person with that knowledge still breathing oxygen. To Cal, El Rucco was very much a human being, and one, like Carmelina, to whom he saw no reason to give unpleasant news when it wasn't absolutely necessary.

Even gods could get in pissy moods.

Still, he couldn't just sit around waiting on Paco. Which was why he was now in his car, driving down into the heart of the rain forest, a pair of binoculars sitting on the passenger's seat next to him.

He took PR 191 about a third of the way into the heart of the forest, stopping when he reached Yokahú Tower.

The Yokahú observation tower rose seventy feet from the ground, to an elevation of nearly sixteen hundred feet above sea level. Still less than half the height of Pico El Yunque, but tall enough to command a serious view. On a clear day you could see all the way out to the Virgin Islands from up here on the tower's crenellated roofline.

Today was not exactly clear, not in El Yunque; it had rained on and off for the better part of the last two days. But he could still see for at least a mile around. Better than slogging through miles of ferns and mud, as Paco was doing.

Putting the binoculars to his eyes, he began scanning in a slow 360-degree arc. He scrutinized the smooth Palo Colorado forest to the south and soaring canopies of tabonuco to the east. The solid green tracts of Sierra palm on the steeper slopes. Finally, up on the highest elevations, the crowning patches of cloud forest.

After ten minutes, he lowered the binoculars.

This was futile. "Like looking for a unicorn in a forest of pricks," as his great-grandfather would say when they were out on the plantation, his great-grandmother not around to box their ears. He'd probably repeated the phrase once or twice himself for his own sons' great amusement.

The thought of his sons made him smile.

The thought of the two pint-sized fugitives made the smile disappear.

These were smart little mocosos. Paco and Adriano were competent guards, and yet the children had found a way past them. Paco had been on their trail now for thirty-six hours—and so far, evidently, they had eluded him.

Which frankly surprised him. Paco was a nasty piece of work, and persistent as a cockroach. And smart or not, the two nenes were, after all, only children.

He climbed back down the one hundred steps of Yokahú's spiral staircase and approached the park ranger sitting in his Jeep at the foot of the tower with the windows down, talking on his radio.

He waited for the man to finish his conversation, then asked, "How's it looking out there?"

"Not great. Had some bad flash floods yesterday, worst of the season. Washed out a few roads and trails. Had to rescue a family of tourists over at La Mina Falls." He nodded to the south. "Still looking for a young couple reported missing out toward El Toro, strayed off the trails, apparently. Honeymooners," he added, shaking his head. "With a hurricane out there."

"That's supposed to go well south of us, though, no?" said Cal.

"Supposed to," the ranger agreed. "Like tourists are supposed to stay on the trails."

Yeah, thought Cal. Like Paco and Adriano were supposed to sit on the two nenes. Hopefully Paco was on them at this very moment. But there was nothing he could do at that moment but go back to San Juan and wait.

Cal had no problem doing that. He was a patient man.

51

The way down was harder.

As they descended the trees grew taller and denser, their canopies thickening overhead. The air grew hot and sticky, the exposed soil slippery underfoot again. Everything felt wilder, as if the rain and flooding from the day before had washed them back into some prehistoric era.

Pedro half expected dinosaurs to emerge from the thickets of giant ferns. He started to smile at that idea, until the thought of dinosaurs brought back an image of the giant centipede biting down on Miranda's arm.

They'd been on the hike for at least two hours, maybe three. Maybe four.

It was hard to keep track of time.

Twice, they'd had to cross over hiking trails, and once over one of the few roads that ran through El Yunque. The section of road where they crossed had been freshly washed out, probably by yesterday's flash flood, Pedro guessed.

Soon after crossing the road they came to a little river that Pedro was pretty sure was the Icacos, which he knew flowed south, unlike the Mameyes and Río de la Mina, which both flowed north. They stuck close to the river, figuring that it would lead them down and out of the forest somewhere in the middle of Naguabo, the next district over from Ceiba.

As they went, he tried to think about what they should do when they reached Naguabo. If they reached Naguabo. But he had trouble focusing his thoughts on any kind of practical strategy.

All he could think was, *We'll still be so far from home.*

Suddenly Miranda froze in place and grabbed his hand, hard.

He glanced at her and followed her gaze.

His heart stopped.

Twelve meters downriver from them a man lay asleep on his side, his feet toward them, his face obscured from this angle.

Miranda looked at him, her eyes wide. *What do we do?*

Pedro struggled not to panic, furiously trying to think.

The river ran on their right, a gently sloping incline to their left that ended in a small rock cliff about fifteen meters in. He thought about quietly fording the river, putting it between themselves and the man, then slipping away on the other side. But the river's current was still pretty strong, and he didn't trust it. Besides, what if they couldn't help splashing as they crossed, and the sound woke him up?

He put one finger to his lips, then nodded forward and to their left.

They would have to sneak around him.

Miranda made a circle with her forefinger and thumb—*okie dokie!*—and grinned, and before Pedro could make a move she started up the incline, quiet as a shadow.

Pedro followed, his heart in his throat.

Keeping as wide a berth as possible, they crept

forward till they had come nearly level with the man's head—

And Pedro slipped.

The wet leafy floor gave way underfoot and he slid several feet downslope before coming to a halt on his hands and knees.

For a moment, the world stopped.

Pedro's heart hammered in his chest as he steeled himself for a sprint. Then he forced himself to dart a quick glance toward the river.

The man hadn't moved.

"Pedro!" Miranda whispered sharply.

He put his finger to his lips again, then slowly began edging down the incline toward the man, barely breathing, staying alert to the slightest movement. It wasn't until he got to within four or five meters that he could see him clearly in the dappled light.

The man was surrounded by a wash of scattered tree limbs and broken twigs and pebbles, a few small branches lying across his legs—a tide of debris washed up by the flood as it roared through, carrying him with it.

His head had come to rest against a large rock. His eyes stood wide open, staring at nothing.

Flies buzzed and flew and crawled.

A convoy of beetles trundled across his lips, in and out of his mouth, into his nose.

The world started going dark around the edges of Pedro's vision. He thought he was going to faint.

Instead, he threw up, violently, twice, three times.

As he sat up, breathing heavily, he became aware of Miranda, who had come down the hill to stand at his side. They looked together at the man's face.

The cursing guard. Loud Orc.

"I'm not sorry," Miranda whispered.

52

Old San Juan was a quilt of contradictions, seventeen sloping blocks of cobblestone antiquity and bright pastel gentrification, surrounded by thick walls and massive stone forts to keep out centuries of foreign aggression, and shot through with the unapologetic fever of commercialism.

This was the city that captured her heart, then broke it, the city where she found her life calling and her true love—a love that had now been ripped away forever.

Lucy Santiago stepped out of her apartment and picked her way down the blue-brick streets, past funky storefronts selling hand-rolled cigars cozied up next to high-end brand-name jewelry stores, little cafés run by tenth-generation baristas and sparkling new Starbucks outlets, ethnic marisquerías and chi-chi cocktail lounges.

She walked past the ancient St. Francis of Assisi Parish and a Mr. Weenie Waffles, then turned downhill and across the marble tiles of Plaza Colón, where the imposing Santiago Gate once stood, granting or barring entrance to the walled city. Today it was the spot where tourists congregated and walking tours began and ended.

She found a bench on the south side of the plaza and chose a seat next to a bald, blind man who sat taking in the sun.

After a few minutes of silence, the old man said softly, in English, "I saw you at the service in Humacao."

"Really," she said. "I didn't see you."

They both looked straight ahead, showing no sign that they were conversing.

"That was Tuesday," Lucy continued. "Less than forty-eight hours after he died. He has brothers, you know, in New York and Miami. They'd've been here, too, if they'd held the service even a few days later. Bastards did it on purpose, of course. Sooner he was in the ground, the better."

She was silent for a moment, then added, "Motherfuckers."

The blind man retrieved a small loaf of bread from a paper bag, tore off some crumbs, and tossed them on the ground. Eager pigeons waddled in and snatched at them.

"Tell me," he said.

"What did you hear?" she said bitterly. "That Nico was part of it? Nico was not part of it."

The old man said nothing, just fed the pigeons and listened.

"They're saying Nico was working for El Rucco, and at the same time in bed with the cartel. That he was trying to play both sides against the other and make a fast buck selling each the other one's secrets. And when a government official found out what he was doing, he shot the man. All of which is complete bullshit. I say that not because he's my husband. I say it because of who Nico is."

A few years before they met, Nico had a big sister

who disappeared while working as a singer on a Caribbean cruise ship. Whether she fell overboard, or was raped and then drowned at sea, or kidnapped and trafficked—a not uncommon occurrence in those parts—nobody knew. She was never found.

"It killed his parents," she said. "To find out your child has drowned or been killed in an accident, that's a horrible thing. Even to learn she was murdered. You never get over that—but it has a conclusion. It's finite. But for your child to simply disappear? To never know what happened? To know she could be out there right now, alive, suffering every day at the hands of some monster? It was too much to bear. They never recovered."

In fact, that was how she first got to know Nico and his family. Lucy was a pediatric surgeon from LA who'd come to San Juan post-María to do her residency. She'd also begun doing volunteer work for a local nonprofit, helping families deal with the emotional and financial impact of violent crime.

"But I couldn't help them. Their way of dealing with it was to withdraw from life altogether. Nico's was to become a cop. He couldn't bring his sister back, but he could help purge the kind of corruption and cruelty that took her. Nail those who prey on the innocent, bring them to justice."

"Get the motherfuckers," murmured the blind man.

"You got that right. And he was *good* at it. Made arrest after arrest, most of which led to convictions—"

She abruptly fell silent as two patrolmen rolled by on bicycles.

They stopped in the shade about ten paces away and stood there, straddling their bikes, while one finished eating a Popsicle, then tossed the stick in a trash receptacle.

They rode on.

"And then?" the blind man prompted.

"And then, El Rucco." She sighed and looked down at her hands, as if trying to organize her thoughts.

"About three years ago, things started getting uglier. You have to understand, crime is a part of ordinary life here. Just like any big city. People hate it, but they've learned to live with it. Not anymore. Because El Rucco, whoever he is, doesn't play by the rules."

Historically, she explained, crime families in Puerto Rico directed their violence toward rival gangs and organizations, and mostly left ordinary citizens alone. A kind of self-sustaining ecology of violence, power, and relative safety.

El Rucco flipped that tradition on its head. Ignoring rival gangs and crime families, he turned his acts of terror on citizens and his own people. Anyone who failed him, who gave even a hint of betraying him, anyone who got too close to his business, anyone he perceived as a threat, he had murdered, using his signature method of retribution and mass intimidation.

"The face is slit open horizontally, from the corners of the mouth out to the neck on either side." She spoke in a monotone, as if reading from an autopsy report. "The ligaments of the temporomandibular joint are severed and the mandible, or lower jaw, chiseled out and removed so that . . ." She stumbled for a second, then continued, ". . . so that the tongue protrudes.

"A local blogger was the first to report on it. He

was the one who coined the term 'las gárgolas.' He also referred to El Rucco as 'El Sico,' the Spanish for 'psychopath.'

"Sometimes they perform this obscenity postmortem, after shooting their victim." She paused, then added, "Like Nico." She looked down at her hands again. It took a few moments to compose herself. "So there's something to be grateful for. Sometimes they do it while the person is still alive. Those poor souls either suffer a heart attack from the ungodly pain, or simply bleed out."

The bald man tossed out a few crumbs, then leaned forward and spoke as if addressing the pigeons.

"How is no one talking about this? I saw a victim myself, last night, out by El Yunque. PRPD was there. This morning, it's as if nothing happened."

"PRPD," she said, her voice dripping with venom. "Those officers you saw at the memorial service? Every one of them is on this man's payroll.

"El Rucco runs his organization on fear, discipline, and secrecy. Nobody knows who's in and who isn't, so no one trusts anyone. Divide and control. And that secrecy goes right to the top. He's obsessive about his own anonymity. No one has ever seen the man's face. He runs his organization by text, never in person, not even on voice calls. Except for maybe one or two trusted lieutenants, nobody knows his real name."

She took a deep breath, closed her eyes, and rubbed her temples. Then straightened again.

"Among that first wave of gárgolas were two reporters who were digging a little too close, and that blogger I mentioned. You see?"

He saw.

Her voice dropped to barely a whisper, yet every syllable crackled.

"I hope you find the motherfucker. I hope you end him. That's all. Just end him."

The blind man scattered the last of his crumbs, sat back, and let the sun beat down on his face.

"Tell me what Nico was working on," he murmured.

53

Monica was going stir-crazy.

Agent Rivera's supercomputer had finished crunching through its first mountain of data, which meant that Monica had spent the last two hours in Dar's war room setup, staring at a few thousand still images of men from all over Puerto Rico at all times of day and night who all shared one singular trait: None of them were Chief Finn. An officer in the United States Navy, Monica was no stranger to burrowing through reams of onscreen data, but still. She'd been staring at this parade of futility for two hours now, Dar thoughtfully resupplying her with enough Puerto Rican coffee to fuel a Cessna.

She was starting to feel like a puma in a cage.

"You lost a few friends in that whole cockup on the *Lincoln,* right?" he'd commented that morning at breakfast. "And your dad, just before the deployment?"

Monica answered with only a nod, furious at herself that she had to fight back tears at the memories.

Dar handled it sensitively, pretending not to notice. He handled everything sensitively. So much so that it was making her cabin fever worse.

Monica understood machines, from ancient tractor engines to $5 billion helicopters. It was what she loved most about flying. She missed being around them. She didn't care if it was a socket wrench in her hand or a trig calculation in a crosswind correction, she missed the logic of them, the consistent reliability. The tangible *there*ness. And she was brilliant at it.

What she was not so brilliant at was human beings. "You're a freakin' genius at everything mechanical, Buffy," as her brother Sloane had told her at least four dozen times, "but you're shit at people."

Like Dar, for instance. Who was making her both more comfortable and more uncomfortable with each passing day. The man was considerate to the point of solicitousness. He certainly knew how to be an empathetic listener.

She didn't want empathy. She just wanted competence.

She wondered if he "had intentions," as her daddy used to put it when she was fifteen and the high school boys were hitting their hormonal prime.

She hoped not. He was not her type. Not that she could have said with mathematical precision exactly what *was* her type. But Special Agent Adamson definitely wasn't it. He reminded her more of a big teddy bear than anything conspicuously manly.

And anyway, the idea of getting closer to Dar—of getting closer to anyone—freaked her out enough to put the kibosh on any amorous possibilities. It didn't take a doctorate in psychology to understand why. The last time she started having feelings for another officer, he ended up with a charcoal pencil jammed through the eye socket to the brain.

Which, by the way, she still wasn't 100 percent sure was not also the SEAL's doing.

She went over it all again in her mind, for the hundredth time.

A year ago, an act of sabotage killed four in her crew, including one of her cabinmates. But that was weeks before Chief Finn even came aboard. Obviously, he had to be innocent of that crime. So she'd leapt to the conclusion that he was innocent of all the crimes that followed.

But those photos had made her reassess everything that happened to her on the *Lincoln.*

Her best friend had been murdered, and the man who killed her had paid for it with his life, shot by a speargun from her own hand.

Or so they said. But could she really be sure he'd been guilty of that crime? The man had never confessed; there hadn't been time. She'd shot him before he could say a thing.

Who had told her the man was guilty? The goddamn SEAL had. Who gave her the weapon that killed him? The goddamn SEAL did. Who was there with her when he died? The goddamn SEAL was.

Algebra, Mon. Knowns, and unknowns.

No, he couldn't have sabotaged the helo. Fact. But what about the other murders? Kristine? Schofield? Scott? Those poor E-2s running the incinerator? The SEAL had known things about those murders nobody else knew. Found evidence nobody else found. And it *had* all started just days after he came on board.

What if he was the guilty one all along?

"I gotta get out of here." She abruptly pushed back her chair. "I'm gonna get some air."

Dar hopped to his feet.

"I'll go with you."

54

Finn shuffled down Calle de la Fortaleza in his bald wig and cataract-filled contacts, away from Plaza Colón and toward the docks where his BMW was garaged, thinking about what Lucy had told him.

"*No one has ever seen the man's face,*" she'd said. Finn wondered if that was somehow related to El Rucco's choice of ritual murder. If maybe he had a thing about faces, perhaps because his own face had been disfigured at some point.

Though he felt a little out of his depth playing armchair psychologist. Hard enough understanding his own motivations, let alone unraveling those of some unidentified sociopath.

Finn had frankly not the first clue to the mystery man's identity.

But he did have an idea how to gain access to him.

According to Lucy, Nico had gone undercover, created a relationship with some high-up port official who was corrupt as a game of three-card monte and played some significant role in the El Rucco operation. La Empresa, they called it. The Enterprise.

Through this contact—the same guy Nico had

supposedly shot to death—he'd learned that El Rucco was amassing a huge cargo to ship out of pier 9 any day now, bound for Miami for distribution throughout Florida, Texas, New York, and who knew where else. It was the biggest single operation they had mounted to date. They called it simply "el cargamento." The cargo.

"Drugs?" he'd said, to which Lucy had shrugged and replied, "What else?"

Nico couldn't get warrants to search any of the hundreds of shipping containers sitting at the docks, but he had managed to have drug-sniffing dogs brought in to do a tour of piers 8, 9, and 10, without his contact knowing he had anything to do with it. They found nothing. But he was still convinced their big shipment was being assembled somewhere right there.

That was all Lucy knew. Except that Nico had been acting completely on his own.

Really? That had surprised Finn. Hell of a personal and professional risk, mounting an op like that as a sole operation, without any support. Insane, really. Almost like something a SEAL would do.

The department had vetoed the whole idea, saying it was too dangerous. His partner practically begged him to let the thing drop.

His partner?

"You would have seen him at the service," she'd said. "Big guy, delivering the eulogy."

Finn remembered. The huge man with the deep voice and tears streaming down his kindly face.

Don't draw what you think is there. Draw what's actually there.

And then, as Finn took a left onto a little side street two blocks southwest of the plaza, he suddenly found himself staring at the face of a tall blond American woman.

It took every ounce, every atomic particle of training not to turn and run, to keep the shock from registering on his face. Because he knew her.

What was worse, she knew him.

55

Dar and Monica stopped briefly to admire the Iglesia Santa Ana, one of the oldest churches in America, then took a left at a little side street named Calle de San Justo. As they neared the end of the block, they passed a blind man coming the other way.

They took a right on Calle de Fortaleza and went eight paces farther when Monica stopped dead in her tracks.

Dar took another step or two, then stopped and looked back at her. "What."

"You see that blind guy?"

"The one we just passed?" He looked back, squinting into the stream of turistas. Dar had been sweating profusely from the moment they stepped out of the hotel, and he seemed to be losing a grip on his normally bottomless well of annoying patience. "Yeah. Don't see him now. What," he repeated.

"We saw him before. Somewhere."

Dar frowned. "Don't think so."

They went another few paces—and she froze. "*Shit!*"

She ran back to the corner and stared back down San Justo.

That face.

She knew that face.

"Mother*fucker,*" she said. "He's here."

"Who's—wait. *What!*" he said as it dawned on him what she was saying. "Are you *serious?*"

They ran back down the little side street, dodging through the slipstream of tourists and barking apologies. They burst into a few clothing stores along that side of the street, coming up empty-handed each time.

"We need to split up!" Dar shouted as they reached the end of that block.

"Aye aye," she replied reflexively. She shot an index finger up that street—*You try that way*—then turned and headed the opposite direction to clear the contiguous block.

They met up back on the corner of San Justo and Calle de la Fortaleza, both of them swiveling back and forth, looking in every direction.

"Shit!" said Monica. "He'll be miles away by now. *SHIT!*"

56

In fact, he was twelve feet away.

Twelve feet up, to be exact. Lying on the floor of a Juliet balcony outside the little condo on the corner, directly above where they were standing.

The moment he'd seen her face, Finn's years of training had kicked in. Keeping his face forward and stride unbroken, he walked on past for eight or ten feet, then ducked to the other side of the street and melted into the scenery.

His every instinct was to book out of there completely, put as much distance between himself and the blond woman as possible. Yet it was the capacity to resist his instincts, completely and instantaneously, that had saved his life more times than any other single skill.

It was a trait Finn had been developing since the age of eight.

And he needed to get confirmation of that brief glimpse.

He ducked behind a trash bin, yanked off his shirt and bald cap, swapped them for the blond dreads and the eighties-band tee, and popped out his contacts, stashing it all in his backpack, all while watching the two of them on the far side of the street down the block, popping in and out of retail storefronts.

He saw them split up at the end of the block, hoofed back up to the Fortaleza intersection, hopped onto the hood of a parked minivan, and took a leap that put his hands on the balcony's lower rail. And pulled himself up from there.

Then lay down and waited.

Sure enough, a minute later they met back up, breathless from dashing around their respective blocks, right at the same intersection. Right under his balcony, in fact.

Close enough to hear their hushed conversation.

He knew the voice. It was the helo pilot from the *Lincoln*, all right.

"West Texas," he'd called her.

He didn't know who the man was.

That would have to change.

As West Texas fumed and the man kept looking around, he reconsidered the situation.

Her being here could be a coincidence. But why would the navy station an active-duty helo pilot in San Juan? Right at that moment he couldn't come up with a single viable reason.

Other than because she could identify Finn.

The guy she was with was clearly military, or something close to it.

The smart move would be to abort. Not just get out of San Juan, get out of the Caribbean. If they knew he was here, they'd find him. By the time they ran his trail to the ground in Vieques, he'd do well to be in Kazakhstan, or Karachi. Or Columbus, Ohio.

But he couldn't. Not with Pedro and Miranda still unaccounted for.

He watched the two give up the hunt and head west, down Fortaleza.

A minute later, he hopped down from the balcony and followed them.

57

"I screwed it up."

"You did not screw up anything."

"We shouldn't have been out there walking around, out in the open."

"Oh, c'mon, Lieutenant. This is pointless."

"I should've . . ."

Rather than fumble for an intelligent conclusion to that sentence, Monica took another slug of her drink.

The moment they'd gotten back to their hotel, Monica had headed straight for the bar in the lounge, thumped down on a stool, and ordered a Cuba Libre, adding, "Don Q, Añejo."

Dar had hesitated, then held up two fingers, more in solidarity, she suspected, than enthusiasm. So far he hadn't touched his. He seemed to be having trouble recovering from the heat of the streets, the meat-locker-level AC in the bar notwithstanding.

"Don't get offended," he said, "but are you even sure it was him? A hundred percent?"

"Yes, I'm sure!" She glared at him. Then closed her eyes and sighed. "Shit. No, not a hundred percent."

She had, after all, spent the morning staring at roughly a billion images, hunting for Finn's visage lurking in every one of them. Had her trigger-happy brain sparked a false positive once they got out on the street?

No, goddammit—it was him, she was dead sure.

Almost.

Shit.

She took another slug. "Call it ninety-nine and forty-four one-hundredths," she growled. "Like Ivory soap."

Dar signaled the young woman tending bar. She came over and he quietly ordered a bowl of salted peanuts.

"Listen," he said. "Say it *was* him. Did *he* know you recognized him?"

"Huh." She thought about that. "Hard to say. I didn't even know it at first, not for a good eight or ten seconds."

Dar nodded thoughtfully as he munched on a handful of nuts. "Okay," he said. "So basically, you've gotten us confirmation that he's here. Which is half the battle. So, nothing changes. We push on. Somewhere in those millions of stills we're gonna find something that tells us exactly where this guy hangs his hat."

Monica gave a grudging nod, caught the bartender's eye and held up her glass.

They sat in silence for a moment.

"He really got to you," Dar observed quietly. "Didn't he."

She waited until the barkeep brought her a refill. She sipped at it, then set it down and took a long breath.

"I trusted him."

Dar popped a few more peanuts, munched, and listened.

"I mean, I hated him. But . . ." She paused. But what? "I thought he was a good person."

She sipped at her fresh drink, then set it down.

"I should have trusted my gut."

Dar nudged the bowl of nuts an inch closer. "Maybe that was the problem. Maybe you did."

She shot him a dark look. "Yeah. I guess." She looked at her glass and decided she might as well go ahead and say it. "I spoke with a few dockmasters yesterday, when I was touring the island."

Dar's face went still.

"In Ponce, Rincón, Fajardo. A few other spots. I told them I was looking for my missing brother." She paused, then said, "I showed a photo."

"Christ." He put his drink down with a thud and inhaled through his nostrils, his lips pressed to a slit. "I thought we were clear, *Emma.* I mean, holy *crap.* One hundred percent confidentiality, we said. Toño Rivera, period, we said. No one else. Nothing."

She ate a peanut. "Yeah," she said. *Though now I wonder if showing a picture will do any good.*

"F/X," she murmured.

"Say what?"

"That's what the psychologist called him. 'Hello, F/X,' he said. Special effects."

"Huh," said Dar. "Like disguises, for example."

"Like disguises."

They both sat quietly for a moment.

"He had a brother," she said.

"Really. I did not know that."

"Nope. Neither does anyone else."

"It's not in his file."

"Nope."

"And you know this, how?"

"He told me. Ray. Former SEAL, 'moved on to bigger and better things.' "

"You're kidding."

"So he said. Here's the part he didn't tell me. One fine day when they were still both kids, the future Chief Finn picked up a handgun and put a bullet in his brother's head."

Dar stared at her. "You effin' kidding me?"

She took another slug of drink number two. "Killed him just as dead as those three SEALs. Dead as those kids in Mukalla."

He went on staring at her for a moment. Then let out a breath and faced forward, elbows on the bar. "Whoa. That's *definitely* not in his file." He looked at her again. "And you know *that* how?"

"The psychologist again. Confronted him about it, that day on the *Lincoln*. I overheard."

"And the good doctor never thought to mention this to anyone else?"

"Didn't have the opportunity. Two minutes later I shot him with a speargun."

For a moment he was silent. Then said, "Yeah. Heard about that."

"So this is what you guys in the States call lunch?"

They both looked around as Agent Rivera took the seat next to Dar and hoisted a slim attaché up onto the bar. "Next batch, kids." He signaled the bartender. "Coke." He patted the attaché, then set it down on the floor, under the bar. "And you should have the last batch tomorrow morning."

He looked from Dar to Monica and back to Dar. "Everything all right here?"

Dar looked at Monica.

"Stellar," she said. She pushed back her barstool and stood. "Let's go stare at some screens."

58

Finn was not a highly skilled lip-reader. Still, over the past two decades he had spent a lot of hours staring at a lot of people's faces through a spotting scope. When the decision whether to squeeze the trigger and end someone's life depended on what those lips in that tiny circle were saying, you developed a fairly intimate relationship with fricatives and sibilants and the vowel sounds that connected them.

Even without a spotting scope, he caught a few critical words and phrases.

UNKNOWN GUY: You've gotten us confirmation that he's here. Which is half the battle. So, nothing changes. We push on . . .

WEST TEXAS: Killed him just as dead as those three SEALs. Dead as those kids in Mukalla . . .

Just a few snippets—but it was enough to establish beyond any doubt her reason for being here.

He'd saved her life, that day on the *Lincoln*. And she'd saved his. But that was all water under the aircraft carrier. She knew about the three SEALs in Iceland. She knew about Mukalla.

She'd been told what she'd been told, and she believed what she believed.

He still didn't know why they would send a helo

pilot to help track down and arrest a fugitive. Made no sense. But it didn't matter. There was something he knew about West Texas: She didn't stop until she got what she was after.

And right now, what she was after was him.

His concealment wouldn't hold much longer. If he could see their faces in the mirror behind the bar, they could see his, too. Yes, his dreads and dark glasses would deflect their notice at first glance; their brains' selective attention was tuned right now to notice "bald and blind" in the environment, not "Rasta white guy." But he was standing on mighty thin ice.

He raised the notched burner phone he'd used to photograph the body, pretending to hold a conversation on it, and clicked a few photos of the two at the bar. That was all he needed.

He was about to slip away when another man joined them.

Finn risked one last shot, then slipped the phone in a pocket and disappeared.

Out on the streets, the early-afternoon sun shone hard on the swarms of sweltering, sunblock-lathered tourists streaming along the sidewalks like ants at a picnic. Something about the light felt profoundly false. Like a smile that hid dark intentions.

Finn walked up the west side of Old San Juan toward the old cemetery and entered La Perla at its western tip.

What had Nico Santiago been doing there in the middle of the night? Meeting that corrupt port official, the one greasing the wheels for the big operation at pier 9? Or stalking him?

He walked east along the rocky Atlantic coast.

Halfway up the cement boardwalk he stopped. Closed his eyes. Imagining the hot dark of night.

Pounding surf, sprinting footsteps, ragged breath . . .

He opened his eyes and began walking again.

A minute later he reached the neighborhood's eastern terminus at the foot of the towering San Cristóbal castle.

He took a hard right, heading back into the tangle of shacks, then stopped at the mouth of another narrow alleyway, a fold in the urban fabric where the sun's insistent rays failed to penetrate. Closed his eyes again.

No fleeing footsteps, no scrambling over cobblestones . . . only a dog barking and the distant curses of locals rousted from a hungover sleep . . .

The fine hairs on his arms stood at attention.

This was the spot where Nico died. Right here.

Finn didn't know how he knew it, but he trusted the knowledge.

He reversed course and wound his way back out of the maze. Thinking about what Lucy told him.

His partner practically begged him to let it drop.

Kindly face, streaming tears.

Exiting La Perla, he walked south, skirting the western edge of the Plaza Colón. Walked through a full recon of the neighborhood.

Zone 1 police precinct, Nico's precinct, sat three hundred yards south of the Castillo San Cristóbal. Three blocks to the west of the police station he found the coffee shop where, according to Lucy, Nico and his partner would meet for coffee every morning before going in to the precinct.

Both were a stone's throw from pier 9.

59

He stopped in at an electronics shop and paid in cash for a high-megapixel digital camera, something with significantly denser resolution than his cheap smartphones.

Standing at the counter, he took one of the store's business cards, turned it over, and on the back of the card wrote out a brief message in block letters.

He picked up a few fried bacalao, salted plantains, and two bottles of water. Ate the bacalao and stashed the plantains for later. He hadn't eaten since breakfast the day before, and this might be his last chance for a while.

He walked a few blocks to the Plaza de Armas. Sandwiched in between city hall and the State Department building, this was not a location he'd anticipated visiting voluntarily.

The plaza was ringed by four statues representing the four seasons. Working his way around to the *Winter* statue of an old man huddled in a cloak, he took out the notched burner, the one he had designated as his photo-taking phone. So far he had trashed the Uber phone (#1), the Zacharias phone (#4), and the Lucy phone (#5) the moment he'd finished using them. He was going through phones almost as fast as identities.

He propped the business card up at the base of the statue, off to the side like a random piece of litter, then stepped back just far enough so that when he framed a photo that captured the entire statue, the handwritten text was just visible at the edge of the shot.

Clicked a few snapshots. Selected the best one, zoomed in to make sure the message was legible at maximum zoom.

Satisfied with his work, he walked a few blocks to a little cybercafé, tearing up the card as he went and dropping the pieces into several trash bins along the way.

At the café he ordered one of their bottled waters and drank it while waiting for the computer farthest toward the back wall to become free. It didn't take long.

He sat down at the computer, opened up the browser, and navigated to The Onion Router. From there he downloaded an "amnesiac" operating system so that his work would be forensically untraceable. Probably overkill; he didn't expect anyone to trace his message to this shop, let alone perform a forensic analysis on the machine. But when it came to communicating with Stan L., there was no such thing as too careful.

There were two people in the world he trusted. Carol was one.

The other was Stan L.

Not his real name, of course. Stan was a huge Spider-Man fan and practically worshipped the late, great Stan Lee. More of a Peter Parker type himself, but in terms of what he could do in the world of electrons, ones and zeros, he was as close to a superhero as anyone Finn had ever met.

Finn had contacted Stan L. soon after landing in Vieques in January. Stan had let him know that he'd been promoted in the blue-ribbon defense intel firm where he worked, which meant he now had more access than ever. That was the good news. The bad news: He was also significantly more visible. Which meant running back-channel intel for Finn was going to be even harder than it had been before. And riskier. Both for Finn and for Stan L.

They both knew the DIA—Defense Intelligence Agency—had a major bug up their ass for Finn, especially since he'd embarrassed them by slipping out of their noose in Iceland. He had no doubt that they would be throwing the weight of the entire US military intelligence community at their manhunt.

Apparently, though, they hadn't yet connected the faint dots between Finn and Stan.

The two had never served in the same platoon, not even in the same SEAL team. They'd crossed paths in a brief training evolution. But they'd clicked, and stayed in touch ever since. Which neither the DIA nor anyone else seemed to have figured out. Stan didn't think they ever would.

Finn knew there was no such thing as "never." So he had vowed not to play the Stan L. card unless it was critical.

This was critical.

Their past methods of covert messaging wouldn't be sufficient, not this time. Hence the business with the camera.

He opened a fresh message in the amnesiac browser, addressed it to stanl3099@gmail.com.

No subject line.

There was no text, just five photos, which he first sent to his online self from the notched burner phone and then attached to the message. One shot of the bartender, with West Texas and her two male companions visible in the mirror behind her. Three more of the bartender herself, at various positions along the bar, including one close-up on her face.

And the shot from the plaza.

The statue would place him in San Juan, which was risky but necessary in order for Stan to understand the context of Finn's questions.

The choice of *Winter,* rather than any of the other three seasons, could mean any number of things. It was the only one of the four figures with a full beard. It was the only one fully clothed. Winter was the season diametrically opposite from August, which was when the shot was taken. An analyst could spend days trying to crack that particular code.

Of course, it meant absolutely nothing.

Aside from giving his general location, the photo itself was all about the message on the business card:

> "El Rucco," major local ski lift operator.
>
> Ebert fan. Shy.
>
> Et al.

Stan L. would understand.

"Ski lift operator" = drug dealer (cocaine being "snow").

The legendary film critic Roger Ebert was probably the best-known person to undergo a mandibulectomy (medically managed)—thus, "Ebert fan" to describe the man's signature executions.

"Shy" meaning no one seemed to know who this character was.

The bartender, like the *Winter* statue, was a decoy, the extra shots of her designed to make it look like she was the object of scrutiny in all four interior shots. Stan would understand that it was the three in the mirror Finn was interested in.

Hence the "Et al."

He spent the next few hours researching the cargo piers that lined the Port of San Juan, running along the southern end of Old San Juan abutting San Juan Bay. General layout, storage capacity, security, possible surveillance posts, everything he could find online that might be useful.

Then deleted every trace of his work, deleted that batch of photos from the phone, closed out the computer, and left the cybercafé.

He began walking a circuit of the old city, winding his way through the interior streets, staying alert for any police presence. He needed the anonymity of the outdoors for an important phone call.

He was past due his check-in with Graciela.

60

She answered on the first ring and got right down to it.

"Have you learned anything new about los nenes?"

"Nothing," he said. "You?"

She gave a small sigh. "I've spoken with a close contact at DEA, as well as someone I know at Homeland, and with the regional head of our own border patrol. All in strictest confidence—and these are people I know and trust. We've put together an unofficial task force, just the four of us, each working with our own resources and pooling what we know. But no, I've got nothing to report so far. We're looking. I'm afraid that's all I can promise."

"And El Yunque?"

"This is a little trickier. But yes, I've made progress there, too."

The resources of three powerful agencies, and possibly a fourth. It was more than Finn could have hoped for. Some sense told him it wouldn't be enough.

"Talk to me about El Rucco."

"I—I'm sorry I was evasive about that before. You have to promise me, none of this can go into your article."

"Understood."

"This . . ." She sighed. "This *sociopath* has his reasons for keeping his existence unknown to the outside world. And I'm afraid to say, we all collude with that silence, for our own reasons. If his crimes, his reign of terror, were widely known . . ."

"The resulting PR disaster would scuttle all your public works efforts."

She sighed again. "Sí. Something like that."

"So talk to me. What do you know?"

She paused again, as if deciding exactly where to start.

"Tell me," she said, "do you know what commodity it was that first drew the Europeans to Puerto Rico, more than five hundred years ago?"

"Sugar?" guessed Finn. "Coffee? Tobacco?"

"Gold," she said. "It was rumors of gold that triggered the collapse of the island people's autonomy and ushered in half a millennium of foreign subjugation. In 1503, fifteen years after Columbus himself set foot here and gave Borinquén a Spanish name, one of his lieutenants heard about rich deposits of gold running under the feet of the 'ignorant natives.'"

As Finn walked, a thick bank of clouds blew in, blotting out the darkening dusk. Lights winked on everywhere—storefronts, apartments, streetlights—until the city was a sparkling disco ball of nightlife.

Graciela's voice in his ear continued narrating their history of enchantment and abandonment.

"You know how it goes, with Europeans and gold. They went crazy. Within five years they had mined over a million ounces. Lust for gold soon overflowed into lust for tobacco, cocoa, coffee, and sugar, and the massive income flow they produced.

The local population was turned into a slave labor force.

"When that lieutenant arrived here with pick and shovel, the native Taíno population numbered about thirty thousand. Within a single generation they were nearly gone, wiped out by concentration-camp living conditions and European diseases.

"Still, a remnant survived. Even today, five hundred years later, six out of every ten Puerto Ricans have the genetic markers of Taíno blood. Some take that more seriously than others."

"Like El Rucco?"

"El Rucco, whoever he really is, takes it seriously to the point of fanaticism," she said. "El Rucco sees himself as the anti-Columbus. The Spanish turned us into plantation slaves. The Americans trashed the plantations and turned us into urban slaves. To El Rucco, the Puerto Rico of today is an abused child addicted to the affections of its abuser. A Stockholm syndrome survivor. El Rucco is a liberator. His mission, in his twisted mind, is to rescue Puerto Rico from its abuser and come into its own again."

"By selling drugs?"

"It's not about drugs. It's not even about money. In his mind, it's about liberation. El Rucco sees himself as a kind of Robin Hood. Taking the money of the rich northern nations to benefit the people of Puerto Rico. He has claimed that none of his enterprises harm Puerto Ricans. He imports his merchandise from other places—Colombia, Bolivia, Brazil, Venezuela, the DR—and sells to rich Americans, Europeans, and Asians."

"And you don't know who he actually is? Or where?"

"I know this: Whoever he is, he has a grandiose

view of his own stature. People think he must be some big, strong man. Like a castle. I don't think so. I think he is a man who stays hidden in the dark and lets others do his dirty work. A coward."

There was no mistaking the venom in her voice. She might be an unwilling participant in his code of silence, but her hatred for the man was palpable.

"Do you know what he does?" she said. "To the people he wants to punish?"

"I do." He'd seen it with his own eyes.

"If your nenes are still alive and El Rucco has them, we have to find them as soon as possible! The idea that such barbarity could be inflicted upon innocent children is . . ." Her voice cracked. "This would be more than I could bear. I can't . . ."

After a moment, Finn said, "All right. Thank you."

"Where are you now?" she said. "What are you going to do?"

"What investigative journalists do. Investigate."

At a nearby hardware store, he bought a hundred-pack of heavy-duty cable ties, a can of light brown spray paint, a set of wire cutters, and a small pair of binoculars. He would've preferred a spotting scope but was not in a position to be choosy.

He then walked to the coffee shop where Nico and his partner met every morning and thoroughly cased the place, noting the number and position of all the tables, in relation both to one another and to the front entrance, location of restrooms, and range of interior view from the front window.

Then he left for the docks.

It was going to be a long night.

61

Cal nodded. "That's him."

He and the park ranger from earlier that day stood in the darkening forest, looking down at the body stretched out by the streambed, the top of its head crushed in by the rock against which it had so lethally come to rest.

Another widow to comfort, a few more children to look out for. *Take care of the widows and orphans in their misfortune,* as Santiago—Saint James—wrote in his epistle.

"Have any other bodies been found?"

"No, not so far, and believe me, we've done a good amount of looking."

"Well, that's a relief." *Shit.* The kids were alive, he felt it in his gut.

Of course, they could be dead somewhere else in the forest, fallen into one of its many hidden crevices and ravines, say, or bitten by a snake.

But Cal didn't think they were dead.

He thought about their situation as he and the ranger walked back to the other man's Jeep to ride back to the Yokahú Tower, where Cal's own vehicle was parked.

If he were a scared little boy, out in the wilds with

his little sister, desperately trying to get back home to Vieques, what would he do? He would stay off the trails, head due south, and hope to find a ride once he emerged into the open.

A ride to where?

To Ceiba, where I would sneak us onto the ferry back home.

Their only choice, really.

The southeastern border of El Yunque was a lot of open territory to cover. Impossible to stake out the entire thing. But if the two little cucarachas did get out, they would have to make their way to a major road, and there weren't that many to choose from.

Seven officers should cover it.

As he climbed back in his police car, Cal began mapping out all the viable exit points in his mind. He headed back to San Juan to start making his calls.

Once they crept out of their hiding places, even cucarachas could be killed.

62

"I'm hot."

Miranda pushed off the cover of giant leaves and turned on her back, then flopped to her side.

Pedro waited to the count of ten, then quietly slid the leaves back up to cover her. She was already asleep again, a fitful, fidgety sleep.

They'd finally made it out to the forest's edge, but it had taken hours, and once they breached the perimeter he realized they had to stop for the night, so he took them back in a few hundred yards for cover, then went about foraging for their makeshift bedding while she sat watching him, her eyes dull.

Hardly a word had passed between them since finding their former guard dead by the river. Pedro had never seen a dead body before, and he was sure Miranda hadn't, either. Despite her fierce denial ("*I'm not sorry*"), he could tell she was shook up.

And now she was getting sick.

He lay on his back, desperately trying to remember everything he'd ever read about Amazonian centipede bites. He knew they were toxic, dangerously so. But what were the symptoms? How quickly did they come on? What was the prescribed treatment, and how long could you wait to apply it before things got really bad?

He wished they were back home with Papi right now.

He wished that terrifying thing had never crawled up onto Miranda's arm.

He wished, more than anything, that he could have a chance to do that part over again. This time, he wouldn't freeze up. This time, he wouldn't hesitate. The second that ugly thing appeared he would leap to his feet and slap it away. He would take *action,* that's what he would do!

But you don't get another chance.

And now she was sick.

Pedro fought back the tears. If he started to cry now, he was afraid he would never stop.

"Pedro?"

He looked at her in alarm. "What? You okay?"

"I'm sorry."

"*You're* sorry? For what, Mira?"

"I never should have swum out there to see that whale. When you said we should go home, I should have listened."

"No no," he said. "You didn't . . ." He felt his voice starting to crack, and stopped talking.

You didn't do anything wrong. It was me. I should have done a better job watching out for you.

A few minutes later she murmured, "Pedro? Tell me about Mamá. I forget."

Pedro started quietly talking to her about their mamá, about how she smelled like mangoes and woodsmoke and cinnamon, how she used to sing to them and tell them stories of mischief and enchantment.

He looked over at Miranda. She had sunk back into her troubled sleep.

What if Yúcahu is only pretending to be good?

"Please let her be okay," he whispered. "Please don't let her die."

He tried to take comfort in the words.

But to whom was he praying?

63

There was a bank of public restrooms set back from the water on pier 8, the adjacent dock. He scrambled up onto the roof, shook off his backpack and set it down, then lay prone, rested his binos on the pack, and started looking.

His first question was, Why pier 9?

According to Lucy, Nico had mentioned that dock specifically, but if he'd known the reasoning behind it, he hadn't shared it.

There were nearly eleven miles of dock spread around the shoreline of San Juan Bay. If it were Finn setting up a clandestine drop zone for illegal cargo, he would choose some spot deep in the sprawling stretch of docks along the southern edge of the bay, where there was space for thousands of shipping containers. Looking for a smuggling operation there would be like hunting for a grain of sugar on a beach of white sand.

Piers 8, 9, and 10, clustered together up at the top of the bay, were tiny in comparison. Worse yet, they were far more visible, only a stone's throw from piers 3 and 4, where the big cruise ships dumped their daily catch of tourists. This seemed to Finn the least likely choice for a drug lord's smuggling op.

So why?

After sixty seconds of surveillance, he had his answer.

Control.

El Rucco was powerful, but not omnipotent. The crooked port official who'd been murdered on Sunday had no doubt opened a chink in the port's security armor, but Finn suspected that it would've had to be limited in scope.

And it would be far easier to control a piece of real estate as small as pier 9.

The Port of San Juan was watched by a system of more than 150 closed-circuit cameras, but that system was spread out over nearly eleven miles. Finn noted the location of each camera on pier 9. There were a total of five. There'd be a central office somewhere with an overpaid security guard munching on Burger King and fries, tasked with watching the monitors for all 150.

Finn was willing to bet that he was paid a little something extra (or perhaps not so little) to ignore the video feeds from pier 9.

There were also two guards on premises, manning a tiny security booth and climbing into a Kia hatchback with AUTORIDAD DE LOS PUERTOS painted on both sides to make one full circuit of all three docks every half hour.

Finn didn't think El Rucco could control eleven miles of security guards. But two guys, covering a few thousand square yards?

No hay problema.

A little more than a football field away on pier 9, rows of shipping containers, shaped like train boxcars and serving much the same function, were lined up in a central dockyard surrounded by old barbed wire. Dozens of them, more than that. Finn stopped counting at 175. Only a fraction of the thousand-plus lined up two miles away along the south side of the bay. But still enough to hide a few aces in the deck.

If they were going to make a move, it would be at night. He felt fairly certain about that. Had it already happened? His instincts told him no, not yet. There was still too much tension crackling in the air.

Was it about to happen tonight?

Time would tell.

Finn lay on the rooftop, watching, aware of the passage of time but attaching no meaning to it.

When people heard the word "sniper," the first association they made was "expert shot." True enough, but that wasn't the principal skill set. What snipers excelled at was hypervigilant waiting. Cops famously hated stakeouts, not because the long hours were boring but because they were exhausting. Keeping your attention fixed on doors that don't open and cars that don't move for hours on end is grueling.

It was a sniper's superpower.

Finn watched, and waited.

Ate some of the plantains, finished off one of the water bottles.

A scud of clouds concealed the moon, then drifted past.

An hour went by. Then another.

He became aware of a distant figure in the dark. A man had slipped up on top of a parked trailer truck in the parking lot between piers 9 and 10. He was surveilling the dock, much as Finn himself was doing.

He couldn't quite see the man's face from this angle.

He descended from his rooftop perch and began moving silently through the shadows, avoiding moonlit open spaces, until he reached the top of pier 9, where he crouched in the lee of a dormant crane. It was slow going. He calculated that he was already at the edge of the other man's field of vision and would have to move with extreme care.

But this was what Finn did. There was no one on earth better at it.

He set up surveillance in his new location and watched.

Soon a glint of headlights from an eastbound truck on the road by the dock spotlit the man's face for an instant, and Finn recognized him.

The SIB man at the bar with West Texas and her partner.

Based on his position and behavior, Finn figured he was doing one of two things. Either he was watching to try to catch El Rucco's people in the act, just as Finn was.

Or he was part of it all, another corrupt cop, standing watch to ensure that their illegal operation went off without a hitch.

Who exactly was this man, and what was his game?

They both sat still, the one watching the dock, Finn watching the one watching the dock.

At about three in the morning, the man moved. Slipped down from his post and left the area, traveling on foot.

Finn followed.

Trailed him to the police precinct building. The same as Nico's and his partner's.

He watched the man enter. Two minutes later a light went on. After half an hour he still had not emerged. The light stayed on.

Dedicated public servant, burning the midnight oil?

Or embedded double agent, rotten as landfill?

Finn returned to the docks, took up station again.

The two security guys made their pointless little circuit every thirty minutes.

Nothing happened.

•

As he watched, he thought back over what little he'd gleaned from surveilling West Texas and her partner in the hotel bar. He'd caught a few other salient bits, too.

I spoke with a few dockmasters yesterday . . . Ponce, Rincón, Fajardo . . . I showed a photo . . .

So his dockmaster at Puerto Chico knew they were looking for him.

And then there was this one:

. . . picked up a handgun and put a bullet in his brother's head . . .

How could she possibly know about that?

She must have heard Stevens, the psychologist, talking to him when he was down in the flare magazine, being drowned and psychologically tortured. How Stevens himself knew about Ray, Finn had no idea. Probably never would.

Until that day on the *Lincoln*, Finn himself hadn't known.

In the aftermath of those endless twenty-four hours alone in the blood-spattered gun closet with his big brother's corpse, young Finn had shut up the memory of what happened as tight as one of those shipping containers. Lying imprisoned in his hospital bed, he'd had no idea what had happened to Ray, other than a few vague murmurs he overheard about his having "lost his family."

Lost them? he remembered thinking. *What, like a misplaced sock?*

All he knew was that there'd been some kind of "accident" at home that landed him in the hospital, and that he and Ray were separated.

So what happened to Ray?

At first, he figured they must have split them up and sent Ray to a different foster home. Then over the years, the boy assembled a "memory" of his big brother going off to join the navy, becoming a SEAL, and from there into military intelligence. High-level stuff, saving-the-world stuff. It was why Finn himself had joined the SEALs. So he'd told himself.

More magical thinking.

Deep down, a part of him always knew that none of this was true, but he never understood what had really happened to Ray—not until that day a year ago now, down in the lower decks of the *Lincoln,* when the memory burst open again, flooding his grown-up self with the poisons of thirty-year-old truths.

Ray had died, shot by Finn himself with one of their dad's handguns.

It was just a stupid accident. Which took away his brother and parents, his whole family, forever and ever.

Just a stupid accident.

But the fact remained.

If he hadn't shot Ray, maybe his parents wouldn't have driven off and left him there alone.

A whisper swept over the bay. The wind was shifting.

Finn closed his eyes and sniffed the air. Listened to the bay lapping up against the docks. The water was restless.

The storm was coming their way.

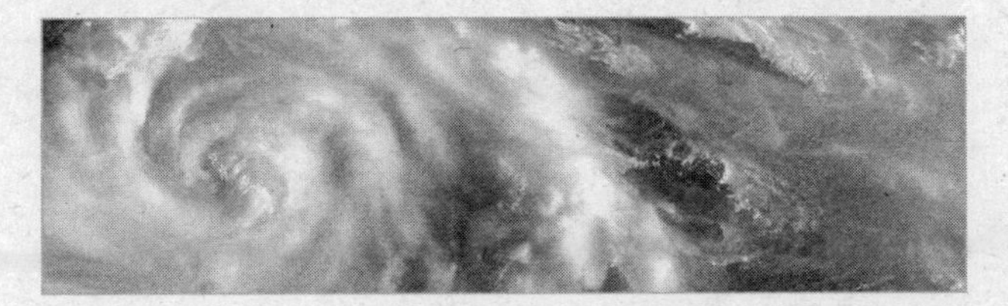

Friday A.M.

T minus 1

After crossing over Barbados early this morning, Hurricane Will halted in its tracks, gathering force as it sat stationary in a spot over the southern Caribbean, a hundred miles west of St. Vincent. By noon it had crossed the threshold into a Category 2 event, with winds of ninety-six miles per hour and above.

Its behavior has baffled meteorologists.

Populations throughout the Caribbean Basin are growing increasingly alarmed.

64

Cal carried his mug and pot of coffee to the empty table in the corner. The table that was always unoccupied and waiting for him at this time of morning, where Nico used to join him for a cup before the day got roaring. He took a seat and poured the rich hot brew into the mug they kept for him behind the counter. The big blue letters on the cup read:

El Mejor

PAPÁ

Del Mundo

The best DAD in the world.

He sipped and waited for the call.

The tourists all asked for their coffee "con leche," believing that to be the most authentic. If they'd put in extra time studying their travel websites, they might even ask for "oscuro" (a hint of milk) or "término medio" (equal parts milk and coffee), or even "café bibí," baby-bottle milk, milk with just a hint of coffee.

Coffee, with just a hint of smug superiority.

The turistas saw it through turista eyes, as something cute and endearing, a little tear-off strip of "the local culture" they could sample.

To Cal, the coffee of Borinquén was not cute. It was a battle scar, a link to generations of sweat and hard labor, of jíbaros working the sugarcane and coffee plantations, starting the day with strong coffee to sustain them through the unforgiving hours of labor ahead.

Cal drank it like his great-great-grandfather, a giant like Cal, who worked the soil and built a family: a big, full-bodied mug of black, with a single respectful spoon of sugar. Not enough to make it sweet; just enough to remind you of the pain and sacrifice of the sugar plantations.

The phone buzzed.

Cal picked up and put the phone to his ear. He said nothing, just listened. After a moment, he said, "Good," and ended the call. He let out a small sigh of relief.

Finally, some good news.

He thumbed in a number and placed a call of his own. Held the phone to his ear once more. When the call connected he said, "They're leaving." Then listened, stony-faced. "You're sure?" he said. Listened. "Very well," he said, and he ended the call.

He set his phone down on the table, peered out the front window of the coffee shop, took a sip of his cooling coffee. And softly cursed.

No one had ever seen El Rucco's face. That was the legend, and it was almost true. Cal was the only person on earth who knew El Rucco's identity. Or at any rate, the only person alive. There had been several others. Every one of them had at some point miscalculated. Grown overconfident.

Cal never miscalculated.

Never let himself become overconfident.

His unique knowledge notwithstanding, he communicated with the boss exclusively via text, just like everyone else in the organization. He could count the number of times they had met face-to-face on the fingers of one hand.

Actually, on the thumb of one hand.

He opened his phone again, then tapped on a different number to send a new text message.

Good news. Just spoke with our man in the Coast Guard. They're calling off the search. The Sound is clear.

Good.

However, Venezuela is still balking. They want to wait a few more days. Until the storm in the Caribbean has passed.

Unacceptable.

. . .

Cal waited to see what the alternative plan would be. He didn't have to wait more than a few seconds.

If we can't resolve within 24 hrs I will go down and offload the cargo myself.

¿Los nenes?

No longer a factor. When you find them, just take care of it.

Cal switched off his phone and slipped it back into an inside jacket pocket. Finished the dregs of his black coffee, then set the mug down empty and got to his feet.

This was all going to work out.

The shipment was almost ready to go, finally. The boss would handle Venezuela, one way or the other, and the thing would be gone and out of his hands within another twenty-four hours. The children would be found, today, and Cal would, as the boss had put it, take care of it.

This weekend his son would move in with his girlfriend, Carmelina would realize she had lost this particular battle, and the house would grow quiet and peaceful once more.

Even the weather had taken a turn for the better. The vicious heat wave had finally relented, letting the cooling ocean breezes back into the city.

Cal didn't think he had anything to worry about concerning the hurricane to the south.

As he stepped out the door he bumped into a blind man making his way in. "¡Perdón!" he said, as the man mumbled "Gracias" and steadied himself on Cal's arm. Cal held the door for him, then stepped out onto the sidewalk, looked up at the blue sky and took a deep breath.

Gracias a Dios, it was all going to work out.

It was a short three blocks to the precinct. Half a block from his destination he reached into an inside pocket for his phone to check for further messages.

It was gone.

65

Finn knew he had only a few minutes. Five at most. Probably less. He slipped into the tiny restroom and locked the door. A blind man staring at a smartphone screen would be mighty conspicuous.

He touched the screen and it came to life, showing a little padlock icon and below that the words ENTER PASSCODE, then the usual array of digits:

1 2 3
4 5 6
7 8 9
0

He'd set himself up outside the coffee shop for a bit of street-corner begging, keeping his contact-covered eyes glued on the figure of Cal at his table inside, watching for the moment the man would pick up his phone and enter a passcode. And sure enough, the moment had come—except that at the last minute a passing server had obscured his view, just as the detective's index finger keyed in the code's final digit.

Finn had three numbers.

But not the fourth.

He entered the first three digits and stared at the phone's little screen.

0 9 2 —

Oh-nine-two what?

He scanned back over what he'd learned about Nico's partner the day before at the cybercafé.

Caleb Cordova. Born March 15, 1978. Detective first class, PRPD. Twenty-one years on the force. Cal was named for his great-great-grandfather, whose birthname was Caobanex (pronounced *Cow-ba-nesh*), later Anglicized to Caleb. Family worked on sugar plantations just north of Ponce for generations. Grandfather served in World War II and Korea; father took a manufacturing job in the sixties and moved the family to San Juan. A classic Puerto Rico story.

Which left Finn where?

Three tries before the phone locked him out.

He thought back to the memorial service on Tuesday, when he first saw the big policeman.

Like all of you, I am a family man . . .

True, apparently. Five sons, ranging from five to seventeen, all with names that started with the letter "C." Finn had seen the pictures at commendation ceremonies: Cal in uniform, five handsome beaming boys, trophy wife. Carmelina Cordova, née Díaz, born September 28, 1983.

September 28.

Oh-nine-two-eight.

It seemed sentimental, for a killer. But then, brutal executioners came in all sizes and stripes. Finn had known sociopaths who would kill for their pet fish.

He keyed in a fourth digit:

0 9 2 8

The numbers shook twice, as if to say, *Uh-uh*.

The padlock remained locked.

Two tries left.

Five children. The three middle boys had birthdays in April, February, and June. Cal's youngest, Celestino, was born on September 24, 2018. And his oldest, Carlos, in 2006.

On September 20.

Finn felt like the guy on the TV show with wire cutters and a loud timer ticking down, going *The green wire or the yellow wire?*

Two sons. Two tries left.

If Cordova was using his family's names for codes, the chances were good he'd been using the same one for years. Try the oldest boy first.

He keyed in Carlos's birthday:

0 9 2 0

The phone shook.

The padlock stayed locked.

One more September son.

One try left.

Had to be it.

He tapped in the numbers . . .

0 9 2 —

And paused, his finger over the 4.

Family man. Who Finn suspected had either personally murdered the fellow cop he was eulogizing or ordered it done. His own partner. And carved him up like a Halloween pumpkin.

And today, I have lost a son . . .

Bullshit.

Finn's finger still poised over the 4.

Two minutes had gone by.

Think.

66

Cal stood rooted in place as pedestrians streamed around him, Moses parting the Red Sea. Eyes closed, trying to bring up footage of the last few minutes.

Where could he have left it? Could he possibly have dropped it?

He was furious with himself. Barely twenty minutes ago he'd been sitting on his rear end boasting about how he never miscalculated, how he was never overconfident.

Pride.

What was he always telling his sons? The worst sin is pride, because pride leads to carelessness.

He could not afford to be careless.

He began retracing his steps, block by block, eyes vacuuming up each meter of pavement as he walked.

Two blocks in he suddenly stopped again, struck by a terrible thought.

The blind man. Could he have . . . ?

The thought was so horrifying his breath caught in his throat.

He picked up his pace.

67

Finn's mind raced.

Cordova was a cop, a senior detective. But also, if Finn's instincts were correct, a top lieutenant for a drug kingpin and indiscriminate slaughterer of innocents.

What kind of mindset could keep that stark a contradiction going, year after year? Finn knew only one force that could drive behavior like that for decades on end.

Blind devotion to a cause.

What was Cordova's allegiance? To Puerto Rico, his homeland? Not to the government officials who signed his paychecks. Serial murder in the service of a drug lord was not exactly model police conduct. There had to be some kind of deep fanaticism in there.

Back to his bio.

Grandfather served the US government in two wars. Father left his roots to pursue Puerto Rico's version of the American dream, which soon became just another Puerto Rican nightmare. On the surface, Cal now served his government. Law and order. But whose laws, and which order?

Named for his great-great-grandfather. Caobanex, a Taíno name.

He remembered a comment from Graciela.

"Half the Puerto Ricans you talk to claim they want independence. The other half clamor for statehood."

Which Finn knew was not the whole story. In fact, a majority of Puerto Ricans shrugged and voted for a third option—leaving things the way they were.

Not Detective Cordova.

Cal's allegiance, if he had one, would be that of the aggrieved underdog, the outlaw, the revolutionary. He would view the US as a colonial invader. Ditto the Spanish Empire. His allegiance would be to his own bloodline, the original inhabitants of this fertile land, its soil plundered and soul enslaved for centuries.

I am a family man . . .

Which left Finn where?

Three minutes.

He popped out his contacts, swapped his bald cap for the blond dreads, and changed his shirt, and as he did he thought again of Pedro, the day Finn had quietly motored them across the Sound to the big island for their Fourth of July outing.

"Actually, some Puerto Ricans don't celebrate July Fourth."

The kid was so damn smart.

"They think American independence has nothing to do with us. Or like it's an insult. People who are into statehood celebrate July Fourth. People who support the status quo celebrate July 25, which is the day the Commonwealth was founded in 1952."

What about the independentistas? Finn had asked.

"Oh, they have a date, too. September 23, 1868.

That was the day of El Grito de Lares, the first major revolt against Spanish rule."

Finn stared at the phone's screen.

0 9 2 —

Where was Cal's allegiance? To his youngest son? Or to the revolution?

A four? Or a three?

Green wire or yellow wire?

Finn cracked open the restroom door, took a quick look out, making sure first that no one was standing around expecting a bald blind man to emerge, then stepped out—and caught a glimpse of Cal through the front window, striding back toward the front entrance.

One try left.

No more time.

Finn input the fourth digit—

0 9 2 3

The phone opened.

68

In the space of a single second, Finn scanned the most recent text thread and shut off the phone as he—

crossed over to within five feet of the table in back, the one where he'd seen the big cop sitting on a recon run half an hour earlier—

underhanded the phone onto the chair that still sat empty with its back to the wall as he—

pivoted and straightened up just in time to see the front door pushing open—

and saw Caleb Cordova, all six foot five inches of him, striding toward him. Nothing kindly about that face, not just then. It was the face of a killer, etched in shades of frantic fury.

Looking right past Finn, toward the table in back.

And the moment his eyes fastened on the phone, sitting idle on his chair, the executioner's face relaxed into an expression of relief, and he transformed once again into the fatherly senior officer of the law.

Finn ambled toward him and the front door beyond, his eyes resting on nothing at all.

The two passed each other, the big man in a beeline for the chair, the dreadlocked street artist cat-footing for the exit.

Reaching the table, Cal picked up his phone and frowned. He turned and looked around the interior of the coffee shop, but saw nothing and no one that seemed anything but normal.

69

Finn sat on the same bench in Plaza Colón where he'd sat the day before with Lucy Santiago, now in his blond dreads and eighties-band T-shirt, thinking about how to word the text message he was about to send.

He closed his eyes and felt the atmosphere.

The air was heavy. It smelled of pigeons and fish and car exhaust and coffee, the smells of a normal summer day in urban Puerto Rico—but there was atmospheric unrest behind it. A trace scent of ozone.

In his hands he held the notched phone, the one with the photos of the dead man. So far he'd not used it to communicate with anyone.

Opening his eyes, he gazed up at the massive stones of Castillo San Cristóbal, just visible through the trees that ringed the plaza. Nico Santiago's de facto tombstone.

He entered El Rucco's text number, then typed the words:

> I know all about La Empresa. El cargamento at pier 9. The Venezuela problem.

And pressed SEND.

He glanced at the paling sky. The vivid azure of an hour ago was fading to a washed-out powder blue.

The phone vibrated.

> Who is this?

Finn selected one of the photos of the defaced dead man and tapped on it to insert it into the text thread.

Pressed SEND.

There was another pause, this one a little longer. Then the previous message repeated.

> Who is this?

Finn replied:

> Call me
>
> . . .

He let the message hang there, so that wherever he was at this moment, El Rucco would have to sit there staring at the dot-dot-dot on his screen. So that he would have to wait.

Just to underline who was in control here.

After a full ten-count, he continued:

> Call me Picasso. I work for a three-letter agency, which one doesn't matter. I have deep contacts within DEA, FBI, and elements of the Puerto Rican intelligence and law enforcement community. They know you

exist, but not who you are. They suspect Cordova, but have no proof. They have an inkling of the scope of the thing. But they don't know what I know. Yet.

. . .

Another five-second pause, like a tug on a leash. Then:

By tonight, they will.

There followed the longest pause so far. No dot-dot-dot, just an empty screen awaiting reply. Finn had the man thinking. Good.

Then a single word.

Unless?

Finn took a breath and thought it through one more time before replying.

The thread on Cordova's phone had made it clear that El Rucco's people hadn't found Pedro and Miranda yet. Finn had to make sure that when they did, they would be under strict orders to keep them alive.

At the same time, once he revealed his own agenda, he would lose a critical advantage.

Telling Graciela that he was looking for the children was one thing. Telling the sociopath who was hunting for them, most likely so he could kill them, was something else altogether.

Right now he had the man off balance. To him, Finn was a complete unknown. An X factor. El Rucco didn't know who he was, where he came from, or how he had come into possession of his private phone number. He had no idea how much Finn did or didn't know about him and his operation. Most important, he didn't know what it was Finn wanted.

Know what someone wants and you can control them.

Once he walked through this door, there was no going back.

He typed five words and pressed SEND.

You have something of mine.

Do I?

Dos nenes.

Another long pause.

What do two little mosquitoes have to do with you?

That's my business. Return them, or I'll take down your business.

Where and when?

Rosie Roads. Visitors center behind the ferry building. Deliver them by ten o'clock tonight. When I have them, I forget you exist. Otherwise, I talk to my contacts and they shut your operation down.

How do I know you'll keep your word?

I have no reason not to. Your operation, your cargo, is not my concern. I have other interests. I'd prefer to stay under the radar. I'd prefer not to talk to my contacts, not disturb the water. But if you force my hand, I won't hesitate.

Another long pause. Then:

Duly noted. Adiós, Picasso.

And that was the end of it.

Finn took a deep, slow breath.

He was under no illusion that El Rucco would acquiesce to his demands, that patronizing "*duly noted*" notwithstanding. But it was possible that he might believe Finn hoped so. Perhaps he would send a contingent to Rosie Roads well ahead of the ten o'clock hour to ambush Finn, just in case he actually showed up there.

In any case, Finn sensed he was worried enough about what this "Picasso" did or didn't know, who he might or might not share that knowledge with, that he would take immediate action.

Finn didn't have the resources to find the children himself. Graciela might, but he couldn't count on it. Either way, El Rucco would be further along in the hunt than either of them, and Finn had just given him a nudge and a timeline.

And, hopefully, sufficient incentive to hold off murdering them—at least not for another twelve hours.

70

Cal was in the middle of delivering his morning roll call and briefing to the troops when his phone buzzed. *The* phone.

No more than half a dozen people knew of this private line, and every one of them knew never to call during his 9 A.M. briefing. He put up one finger to pause the troops and slid the phone out to take a quick look.

When he saw who it was, he turned the briefing over to a sergeant and exited the briefing room into a small hallway where he could be alone for a moment. He slid the phone out again and read the text.

> There's a man, calling himself Picasso. I've been hearing about him the last few days. The information I have is that he's been posing as a Danish journalist, or a street artist, and making noises about representing a foreign supplier.

Cal had heard about this man, too, from his own people in Humacao and Fajardo. It hadn't seemed significant. Why did something so trivial warrant breaking into his morning roll call? He texted a brief reply.

Go on.

I just had a disturbing text exchange with this man. He now says he is with a "three-letter agency," knows everything about our operation. I need to know if this is true or if he is bluffing. And he's asking for the two mosquitoes. What is his connection to them? I'm sending you a photo, taken Tuesday at one of our storefronts in Fajardo. Somehow, this man got my number. Which means there is a leak. Find the leak and plug it.

. . .

Cal waited for the thread to finish.

And we need those two mosquitoes—today. Alive.

Cal clicked open the image the boss had just sent over.

And his blood went cold.

The image showed a man entering a check-cashing store near the highway in central Fajardo. The man was medium height, wearing a T-shirt with some obscure eighties band. Blond dreadlocks.

He recognized the man.

He'd passed him barely half an hour earlier in the coffee shop, when he went back to get his phone. He was just leaving as Cal entered. He remembered having the fleeting thought that the man looked familiar. And now he remembered why.

He'd seen that same man at the back of the church, at the memorial service.

There is a leak.

That face. Put a bald wig and white contacts on it, and it would be . . .

The blind man he bumped into.

When his phone went missing.

His phone.

He was the leak.

71

Cal rushed into the briefing room where his sergeant was just starting to wrap up for the morning and abruptly retook the podium.

"Update, people. New development. We've got a killer on the loose right here in our neighborhood. Nationality unknown, possibly American, possibly Danish. A top lieutenant for El Rucco. People, this is the man who killed Nico Santiago. This guy killed my partner."

A murmur went around the room.

"If you see this man, call me immediately. He is believed to be armed and is extremely dangerous. I repeat, extremely dangerous. Do not approach him. Do not attempt to take him into custody. Call me. And if the immediate environment permits, take him down. Shoot to kill."

This was a grave command. Unheard of. Shoot to kill, in the middle of a busy city?

But Cal was taking no chances. He needed to make sure the man was not captured alive. The last thing he needed was for anyone to actually talk to him. He could not afford the slightest chance that the boss would learn where that leak had come from.

If he'd gotten El Rucco's number from Cal's

phone, that must mean he'd seen at least a portion of their text thread. How much had he read? How much had he learned? He couldn't have had the thing in his possession for more than a minute or two. But that minute or two could pry open a crack that would destroy him.

He had to find this man before El Rucco did.

Find him, and silence him.

He sent the snapshot on his phone to the precinct's private bulletin board, then looked up at his team.

"I've just uploaded his photo to the intranet. But be wary—he may have changed his appearance. That's it. Roll out."

Two-thirds of the officers nodded grimly. The other third watched Cal's face carefully for any signs as to what was really going on. He caught the eye of one and gave a tiny nod. They all understood. The part about the man working for El Rucco and being the one who shot Nico was, of course, bullshit, baby food for the other officers.

The part that wasn't bullshit was the "shoot to kill" part.

Cal left the briefing room and walked outside and down an alleyway that ran along the side of the building. The cubicle that passed for his office was nowhere near confidential enough for the next conversation he needed to have.

He couldn't quite get that single thought to stop echoing in his brain.

He was the leak.

The boss could not know this. It was bad enough that Cal himself knew it.

His shame burned deep.

Deep in the alley, he placed a call to his top contact at the cartel. When the other man picked up, he didn't identify himself. It wasn't necessary. When Cal was calling, it was never necessary.

"The man you know as Picasso."

"Yes," said the voice on the other end.

"We've come into some information. He is not who he says he is. The man is an American agent, here undercover."

"An agent for . . . ?"

"DEA. From what we understand, the target is you."

There was a brief pause. "He had given us to understand that he was with you."

"He has quite a collection of cover stories," said Cal. "The man is a chameleon. We have no interest in him. Think of this as a public service announcement. El Rucco wants you to know, he has no issue with your taking care of him."

"Received," said the voice on the other end. "Gracias, Detective." The line went dead.

"De nada, cabrón," Cal said as he pocketed his phone and headed back inside.

72

Once he felt sure his audience with the unseen El Rucco had come to an end, Finn pocketed that phone, saving it for further communications with the drug kingpin, then used his mayor phone, the one without the notch, to place a call to Graciela's cellphone.

"Graciela Dominguez," she said.

"Are you somewhere you can talk?"

"Hang on." He heard her put the phone down. *Click click click click*. It sounded like she was shutting the door to her office. "Things are hectic here, coordinating efforts for the hurricane—"

"I just talked to El Rucco."

He heard a sharp intake of breath.

"'Talked' is a little misleading," he added. "We exchanged text messages."

"Jesús," she said under her breath. "How do you know it was him?"

"It was him."

"Jesús," she said again. "How on earth did you find him?"

"I made an appointment to meet with him in person. Tonight, at ten o'clock. Outside the Medio Mundo visitors center at Rosie Roads."

"Dios mío. You waste no time, señor."

"He may or may not appear. If he does, he'll be expecting me. But he won't be expecting anyone else. As far as he knows I'm operating completely on my own."

"*All right, I'll be right there—*" This last bit sounded muffled, like her hand was over the mouthpiece. "Sorry, I have to go into a meeting in a moment. What can I do to help?"

"If he shows, he may or may not have the two children with him. My guess is not, and he'll be there solely with the intention of killing me. But I can't be positive."

"Jesús."

"I know we're under a hurricane warning. I know the timing could not be worse. But can you arrange to put a few people there on the perimeter?"

"*One moment—*" Another muffled aside. "Ten o'clock. Ay-ay-ay." He could practically hear her brain racing, trying to work out what resources she could marshal to put an undercover team in place—without the police knowing about it. "Okay. I'll get it done. But you, be careful. Listen to me, Picasso. This man has eyes and ears everywhere. You're not safe. No one is safe."

And with that, she disconnected.

Finn sat looking at the enormous statue of Cristóbal Colón—Christopher Columbus—that loomed over the plaza. The man who had arrived five centuries earlier, given the island a new name, and, wittingly or not, wiped out nearly the entire native population within a single generation.

Island of Enchantment. Island of Abandonment.

He noticed a pair of police officers step into the plaza at the northwest corner, and just seconds later, another from the east. Their eyes searching.

His instincts told him they were searching for him.

73

Dar had had only a handful of images to work with, none of them ideal. Grainy old photos from boot camp, that BUD/S class photo, a group shot from his first platoon. A few more recent shots obtained from the airport police at Reykjavík, both low-res video captures. And those CCTV shots from the San Juan airport, back in January, which were next to useless.

Starting with these, he'd had an FBI sketch artist work up a composite of Finn, current age, in a plain shirt. Your basic mugshot.

For the past three days, the agency's supercomputer had been churning through millions of possible sightings from all over the island, using the custom AI filters Dar had developed himself to winnow these down to the thousands of stills deemed worthy of review by an actual human being. Which was the main reason—probably the sole reason—Dar's superiors had consented to having Monica accompany him: She was the best candidate to be that human being.

After three days of data-crunching, the project had yielded a bumper crop of some seventy-two hundred possible hits, in three big batches. Monica had already been through five thousand of them. This morning she was poring through the final twenty-two hundred.

They'd started early. It took a few hours, but Monica had tossed out all but three dozen images, which Dar had printed out in high res on one of the laser printers Agent Rivera had brought in. She now went through these, one by one, giving each as much scrutiny as its level of resolution allowed.

She stopped at photo #27.

An interior shot, three figures, caught at an angle halfway between profile and back view. Probably from a cam mounted over the storefront's front door, so no clear view of facial features.

"This one," she said. "Do we know where it was taken?"

Of course they did. Dar had date, time, and location stamp information on every single one. He just had to wade through his hastily constructed indexing system to find it on a separate laptop.

"This one was . . . hang on a sec."

While he drilled into his index, Monica stared at the shot, half squinting to give the grainy image a sense of more depth and realism.

The figure in the center was a man, slender, with knobby joints. Hard to tell, with the lack of clear landmarks to provide any true sense of scale, but he seemed about medium height. Medium-length hair of medium color. Medium everything.

He was standing at a counter, holding out something that looked like a few slips of paper. Cash, perhaps. Like he was paying for something.

The two figures standing on either side were shorter. Youngsters. A boy and a girl.

"This one was from a seaside shop," Dar was

saying, "in Palmas del Mar, on the coast of Humacao . . ."

Palmas del Mar. Coastal resort in Humacao, upscale. *He'd cut his teeth on the California docks, done a stint working on a dive boat.*

"This one was taken on—"

"It's him."

Dar looked at her. "Are you sure?"

She looked at him. "It's the SEAL, Dar. It's him."

She peered at the printout, trying to see what it was the man was buying.

"This was July Fourth," said Dar. "Just eight weeks ago."

It looked like a pair of snorkels.

"Can we find out who the two kids are?"

Dar shook his head. "Don't know. My guess is that'd be pretty much a shot in the dark. All we can do is ask. Maybe Rivera can put some people on it, see if the store has any kind of sales receipts or other identifying documentation. Or if any other cameras from that day and location have better images of the two of them. But I wouldn't put any money on it."

He put a call in to Rivera, who was working out of a temporary office in the police precinct building on the other side of Old San Juan, just half a dozen blocks away. Dar explained what they were after.

"Give me twenty minutes," he said.

They waited.

It was a little awkward, sitting there with nothing to do but wait. Dar appeared to be in no mood for chitchat. In fact, now that they weren't actively engaged in the process of reviewing images—now that they weren't actively engaged in anything at all—it became painfully obvious that Dar was in some kind of funk.

Monica suspected he was still irritated over her admission from the day before, that she'd broken his protocol and shown Finn's picture to a few people.

Honestly, she was just as glad. She preferred this I'm-pissed-off-at-you Dar to the more patronizing I-might-be-flirting-with-you Dar. The Dar whose strongest curse word seemed to be "crap." That other Dar had really been getting on her nerves.

Less than fifteen minutes later Agent Rivera knocked on their door, walked into the room, and went straight to the computer that still displayed the image in question on its screen, then at the printout.

And gave a chuckle. "No, I'm not gonna put my people on this."

Monica felt deflated.

"I don't have to," he continued. "I can tell you exactly who they are."

"You *can*?" exclaimed Dar.

"Pedro and Miranda Ortega. They live with their grandfather on Vieques."

Dar and Monica looked at each other. How the hell did he know that?

"We need to get over there immediately," said Dar, "and talk with the grandfather . . ."

Rivera nodded.

". . . and those two kids."

Rivera pursed his lips.

"*That* . . . will be difficult. They've been missing since Sunday."

74

Finn slipped off the dreads before the police officers' scanning eyes reached him, stashed them into his backpack, and slipped on a pair of flat-lens glasses with thin wire rims. It wasn't much, but it was the best he could do. He joined a walking tour as it passed his bench and moved with the group out of the plaza, southwest on Fortaleza.

The sky was starting to cloud up with the telltale mackerel pattern of cirrocumulus.

Whatever he'd just set in motion, it would have less than twenty-four hours to play out.

A block later he separated from the group and doubled back a few blocks to risk a return visit to the cybercafé.

Hopefully there would be a reply from Stan L.

Same table, same computer.

Opened up The Onion Router.

Downloaded the amnesiac browser.

Went to the Gmail account he'd set up the day before.

There was now one new message. But it wasn't from Stan. It was from squidink28@gmail.com.

Carol's communications were always brief, usually no more than a single line. This one was classic Carol: two words. Yet the message itself surprised him.

Come home.

Had she ever used the word "home" to describe the place they sometimes shared, on those rare occasions he was able to stop and take a breath?

Not that he could remember.

To Finn, "home" was something he remembered dimly from childhood. Before the hospital. Home was a distant cabin in the Oregon woods. He hadn't experienced anything since to which he could affix the "home" label. And Carol's place up in Lummi Island? He didn't know what to call that.

He looked at the screen again.

Come home.

He hit REPLY and typed out the four letters S-O-O-N, then hesitated.

"Soon," meaning what? In a week or two? A month? Another year?

He deleted the word. Thought about typing *Can't yet.* But that was self-evident. Carol would know that. If he didn't, it meant he couldn't.

The lack of reply would be his reply.

He deleted her message—and as the mailbox refreshed, he saw that a brand-new email had just arrived.

It was, of course, from Stan L.:

Getting hot in here. Someone open a window.

That was it.

Which seemed a little odd to Finn. Stan was using

the same method he'd used just eight months earlier, in Iceland, which Finn had thought too risky to repeat.

He went to a Gmail account the two of them shared. The only time either one used it was to leave unsent drafts for the other, which were always deleted immediately upon reading. That way the email itself was never actually sent, so it was impossible to intercept—unless one had access to that account and its Drafts folder.

He opened the draft.

And was stunned at what he saw.

No code. No complicated spy-novel cryptograms. No enigmatic one-liners.

It was an actual letter, in plain English.

He'd never seen anything like it from Stan before.

Dear JJ,

Burn after reading. Burn it all. You are too hot. Fissionable materials hot. For that matter, so am I. May or may not be staying here at this cushy post. Too early to know. But I won't wait long.

To your questions.

The lady in the photo, currently traveling as "Emma," is one Lieutenant Monica Halsey, a helo pilot for the good ol' US Navy. But you already knew that. Here's what you maybe don't know: that's *former* pilot. Now she's a commissioned officer and attorney in good standing for the navy Judge Advocate General's Corps.

"Charles," the Teddy Ruxpin guy she's with, is Darwin Adamson of the Federal Bureau of Investigation. No clue how, but when DIA hit a dead end, it seems Special Agent Plush Toy ended up with your case.

The third wheel is Antonio Rivera. Works for the Special Investigations Bureau, aka Negociado de Investigaciones Especiales. These guys focus on organized crime, white-collar crime, terrorism, and, no offense, fugitives.

Current cellphones for all three attached.

Now, your ski lift operator.

Military intel here is dimly aware of the guy and his piquant way of saying goodbye. But as far as a real-world name, whereabouts, or any other useful information on this one, nothing but dead ends. Sorry, JJ. This one's on you.

One more thing. Your Fibber McGee used to work for ONI, did a stint at Kennedy Irregular. This was eight, ten years back, but do these guys ever really retire?

Hey: Do we?

That's a wrap here. Watch your six.

Nothing lasts forever.

Spidey

75

Nothing lasts forever.

It was a common SEAL saying, usually invoked in the context of excruciating discomfort, like the endless freezing nights of BUD/S or privations of the battlefield. The capacity to ignore temporary pain for the ultimate gain of a strategic win.

That wasn't Stan L.'s meaning here.

His opener was a clue. "Dear JJ." An inside joke, a dig at Finn: John Jonah Jameson, aka JJ, was Peter Parker's boss at the *Daily Bugle,* and also a longtime thorn in Spider-Man's side.

But it was also, in Stanspeak, a way of saying, "This is a Dear John letter."

Burn after reading. Burn it all.

Finn deleted the draft, then deleted the Gmail account altogether. And spent the next thirty minutes tracking through a handful of electronic pathways, revisiting every one of the dozens of mailboxes and secret message boards and other drop sites he and Stan had set up over the years, vaporizing them all, one by one. Erasing not their communication history—they had already been erasing that all along the way—but their means of communication itself.

It was the last time he'd hear from Stan.

Ever.

And it occurred to him only now, as he watched the man vanish from his life, what it was they'd had. A friendship. Stan wasn't just someone he trusted.

He was a friend.

And now he was gone.

Nothing lasts forever.

The trail of destruction complete, he sat back and focused on everything Stan had said. There was a lot to unpack there.

The guy with West Texas was a federal cop.

Fibber McGee and Molly.

And West Texas herself was now with JAG Corps. He'd wondered why the navy would send a helo pilot to track him. This explained it: They didn't. They sent a JAG officer, teamed up with the FBI guy because she could both identify him *and* arrest him under the aegis of a military court.

And then crucify him, based on the bits and pieces he gleaned at the bar and the look on her face as she said them.

But the bombshell of Stan's letter was the phrase "a stint at Kennedy Irregular." "ONI" was the "Office of Naval Intelligence." Among their various branches, ONI's Kennedy Center for Irregular Warfare was the one intimately involved with the comings and goings of Naval Special Warfare. SEALs.

Darwin Adamson was not the harmless teddy bear his appearance suggested.

And before disappearing from Finn's life forever, Stan L. had left one last crumb of critical intel. There was an attachment to his Dear JJ letter. Finn had pulled it out before burning down the house.

He clicked on the attachment.

It was a single image, a screenshot of a text thread

addressed to Special Agent Adamson. Sent, from what Finn could see, on a TOR-based message system on a secret site, exclusive to ONI. Stan had hacked it.

Even someone as preternaturally skilled as Stan wouldn't be able to do so from the outside without detection. He would have had only seconds on the account before the system recognized there was an intruder and locked him out.

Just time to take a screenshot.

Had the ONI system been able to track Stan down and identify him? Had Stan just committed career suicide, possibly made himself criminally vulnerable?

Finn would never know. He hoped not.

The shot included the most recent message and a fragment of the one immediately preceding it.

The message itself was just thirteen words, from someone identified only as "Papa Bear."

Papa Bear?

Didn't seem like the sort of call sign the FBI would use. It sounded more like some off-the-books military intel figure who had an inflated sense of his own autonomy. And who'd read too many spy novels.

So Special Agent Adamson was taking orders from two different bosses, with two very different agendas. One at 935 Pennsylvania Avenue. And one somewhere up the chain of command at Naval Special Warfare.

Responding to the previous message, evidently Adamson's latest report on his progress in Puerto Rico, Papa Bear had written:

> When you acquire the target, take it. And make it a clean sweep.

When you acquire the target, take it.

That wasn't from Adamson's Pennsylvania Avenue boss. Those instructions came from that other party. The one that wanted Finn dead.

"The target," of course, was Finn himself. And every sniper, every warrior, every hunter knew what "take it" meant.

And make it a clean sweep.

In other words, when you kill Finn, leave no witnesses.

Kill West Texas, too.

Friday P.M.

At 2:06 P.M. today, Hurricane Will abruptly arced northwest like a guided missile, hurtling directly toward the southeastern corner of Puerto Rico.

The governor's office advised coastal residents to evacuate, then within hours reversed its position and issued an island-wide "shelter in place" order, which people largely ignored.

Panic has set in. An exodus has jammed the airports. Thousands are running for cover.

76

After more than sixty hours in the wilderness, Pedro and Miranda finally emerged onto a little road somewhere in Naguabo. Their odyssey in the wilds was over; they were back in civilization, or at least its outskirts.

Pedro couldn't put it off any longer. He had to face the fact that he had no idea what to do next.

In the middle of the night, he'd lain awake, listening to her groan and murmur in her sleep, afraid she was so sick she wouldn't be able to walk. At some point, though, she must have fallen into a less troubled sleep, because she had grown quieter. Or maybe Pedro had just fallen asleep himself.

When he woke up she'd seemed a little better, better enough to walk, anyhow, if not at her usual teasing full-throttle pace. He didn't know if the fever had broken, but if it was still there, it seemed like it had to be milder than it was during the night.

That meant she was getting better, right?

Pedro desperately wanted to get them to the ferry in Ceiba. The ferry would take them across the Sound to Isabel, and he knew he could get them home from there. But he didn't really know where they were, and wherever it was, Ceiba had to be miles from there.

The wind was picking up, and the sky had gone gray.

Could they walk the whole way?

That's what he was fretting about when he heard the sound of an engine in the distance. He stopped and turned.

A gigantic Coca-Cola truck was coming their way.

The two turned and stood stock-still as the thing approached. What were they going to do, outrun a truck?

With an enormous wheeze of brakes, the truck slowly rolled to a stop.

The window by the empty passenger's seat rolled down. "You kids know there's a hurricane coming?" the driver called out.

Pedro had no idea what to say. No strategy, no plan. He was too exhausted to think.

The man leaned over in the cab and opened the door for them. "Why don't you hop on up, I'll get you where you're going."

Pedro's instincts screamed, *No! You can't trust anyone! Tell him thanks, but you live just down the road from here!*

The problem was, he knew they'd never make it to Ceiba on foot. Sooner or later, he was going to have to get them a ride.

"Gracias," he mumbled.

Miranda clambered up into the seat. Pedro followed and pulled the big door shut, trying not to imagine that it sounded like the door of a jail cell closing.

The driver took his foot off the brake and the truck started to roll. Barely a minute later they came to the main highway.

There were two police cars there, stopping traffic.

77

The driver slowed to a halt. When he glanced at his young passengers, he was startled to see the boy had turned white and scrunched down in his seat.

"Son? You okay?"

"Please . . ."

The kid looked positively terrified. Of what? The police?

"Please—please don't tell them."

The driver glanced ahead. One of the officers had stepped out of his car and was walking toward the truck.

The driver frowned. Before he could give himself time to reconsider his actions, he slid open the internal door to the cargo bay, looked at the boy, and gave a sharp nod toward the back. "Lie down. Take your sister."

The boy half led, half dragged his sister back through the open door.

The driver slid the door closed, thinking, *What in the name of God am I doing?*

The cop tapped on his window. He rolled it down. "Buenos días, Officer."

"Buenos días."

"Everything all right out there?"

"Everything's fine. We just have a couple of lost kids we're trying to find before the storm hits. You happen to see anyone on the road? A boy, about ten or eleven, little sister with him?"

A police roadblock? For two lost kids?

The driver made a decision.

"Damn, that's a shame. Sorry I can't help. Nobody out that way"—he nodded back over his shoulder to indicate the way he'd just come—"but a stray dog or two."

The officer nodded, handed the driver a card, and took a step back. "Well, you keep an eye out. If you see anything, give us a ring on that number."

They rode on in silence for another five minutes, Pedro and Miranda both lying still against the corrugated-metal floor of the truck, until the door suddenly slid open again, letting in a shaft of gray light.

Pedro and Miranda climbed back up into the passenger's seat.

The driver took one look at Miranda, pulled a thin jacket out from the overhead bin behind him, and draped it over her shoulders.

After another minute or two, he said, "Okay, boy. What happened?"

Pedro wanted to come up with a clever story, something that would fool the driver, but his brain wouldn't cooperate. All he could do was tell the truth.

Or at least, a little bit of the truth.

"We got lost and had to spend the night in the forest. She got bit by a giant centipede. We just need to get home."

"Where is home?" he said gently.

"Vieques." Pedro was silent for a moment. "Are you going to Ceiba? We need to catch the ferry in Ceiba."

The driver shifted through a few gears as he seemed to think that over.

"The ferry," the driver said.

"Yes, señor."

He glanced over at Pedro. "You know your sister needs to see a doctor, right away. Don't you, son?"

Pedro nodded miserably. Of course she did.

Miranda wasn't getting better. She was getting worse.

"Listen. I've got a cousin in Ceiba who's a doctor. Let's get you there. We can talk about the ferry after we see what she says. Okay?"

Pedro nodded again, automatically, and said, "Gracias, señor," but they were empty words.

They had made it through the forest without getting caught, and he knew he should feel good about that. But Miranda was sick, really sick. And they were still so far from home.

78

"Thank you for agreeing to speak with us."

Dar and Monica sat around a wobbly four-top with the old proprietor of the café and the local police lieutenant who had driven them there from the little airport on the north side. They had identified themselves using their real identities (no Charles and Emma this time), a concession Monica could see Dar was distinctly unhappy with, but they really had no choice.

Dar was directing the interview.

"We're so sorry to hear about your grandchildren."

"Thank you. But they are strong. We'll get them back."

Dar glanced at the lieutenant with a raised eyebrow. They'd already been informed that the Coast Guard had abandoned the search after four full days. Didn't the old man know this? The lieutenant shrugged, as if to say, *I've tried to tell him.*

"We're not here about them, however," Dar continued. "We're here in connection with a colleague of ours. Here in Puerto Rico for the past eight months or so, working on an intelligence matter. I'm afraid we can't say more than that. We lost contact with him four days ago, and it's essential that we find him. We believe you may have met him at some point. Medium height, light brown hair, may be going by the name 'Marlin Pike'—"

The old man huffed a laugh.

Dar and Monica looked at each other, then back at him. "¿Señor?" said Dar.

"Two fish," the old man said. "Perfect."

"You know him, then."

"He arrived, as you say, about eight months ago, shortly after New Year's. He was looking for work and a place to stay. He could cook; he could fish. I hired him. We call him Mimo."

"Do you know, or have any idea at all, where Mimo might be right now?"

"I'm sorry," the old man replied. "I haven't seen him since early Wednesday morning."

Monica noted that the lieutenant was studying the old man closely, as if weighing each word for its veracity. She decided right then and there that the lieutenant was a more savvy investigator than Dar.

"Do you know where he's been staying?"

"Right here."

"Here in Esperanza?"

"Here in this building. I rented him the room behind the kitchen. In exchange for his help in the café."

The two Americans glanced at each other again.

Monica spoke up. "Can you show us?"

The old man led them through the place and out back. Monica was impressed at how his step never faltered, how his hand never missed a light switch or doorknob by even a fraction of an inch. It was like he had sonar.

As they passed through the tiny kitchen, Monica

noticed two empty plates set out on the counter, and next to them what looked like the makings of mofongo: two small plantains, achiote oil in a fry pan, an old pilón. She couldn't help thinking the old chef had put them out in anticipation of the two children's arrival. What had he said? *They are strong. We'll get them back.*

Her heart ached for him.

If Chief Finn had done anything to those two, she'd strangle him with her own hands, SEAL training or no SEAL training.

The little bedroom behind the kitchen wouldn't comfortably hold all four of them, so the chef hovered in the doorway while the lieutenant remained behind in the tiny kitchen.

The walls were faded white shiplap, undecorated. Faint rectangular outlines on two of the four walls showed that they had been covered with what had probably been tacked-up photos and/or printouts. There was nothing there now but tiny tack holes.

Furnishings included a bedroll, neatly made, an old card table, and a single chair. Nothing else. On the card table there sat the empty husk of a laptop. The hard drive had been removed.

The place would have been bleak when it was inhabited. Now it looked like an Airbnb on the surface of the moon.

"The last time you saw him was when, again?" Dar said without turning.

"Wednesday morning. Early."

The man had already told them this. Monica figured Dar was repeating questions to see if his story held up. In her opinion, he needn't have bothered. This old man wasn't going to miss a step.

Now Dar turned. "Did he say anything at all

about where he was going? Who he might be going to see?"

The old man held out both hands, palms up. "I wish I could help. He did say something about going over to the big island. I assume to talk to people on the other side of the Sound, see if anyone there had heard anything about my grandchildren."

As they exited the room Monica gave Dar a look. This was getting nowhere.

Dar turned to the police lieutenant. "We need a moment."

"Of course," the man said softly.

Dar and Monica headed out through the dining room and out the front door to huddle on the front porch.

"I don't get this," Dar grumbled once the door was shut. "The man's grandchildren are missing, for God's sake. You'd think he'd be falling over himself to help us find him."

"They don't trust us," said Monica quietly.

"That's insane. Why wouldn't they?"

"Puerto Ricans tend not to trust Americanos. And on Vieques they're not huge fans of the US Navy, either. That's two strikes against us."

They were silent for a moment.

"I swear to God," Monica murmured, "if he's done anything to those two kids, I'll shoot him."

"They *like* him," said Dar.

"What are you talking about?"

"He got the people here to like him. Trust him. Like he's one of them now—"

"That's ridiculous."

"No, it's one of his specialties. HUMINT. Human intelligence. Network of local assets. According to his file, the guy has an uncanny knack for gaining people's confidence." He seemed about to say more, but stopped himself.

Like he did with me, thought Monica. *That's what you were going to add, right?*

" 'Mimo,' " Dar grunted. "Cheese and crappers."

Ding. The door opened a crack and the lieutenant poked his head out. "Pardon the interruption. May we have a few words?"

He stepped out onto the porch, closed the door, and spoke quietly.

"We just got word. Hurricane Will has turned in our direction. The governor just issued an evacuation order for coastal areas."

Shit! thought Monica. *Just what we need.*

"Crap," said Dar.

"Also," continued the policeman, "you should know, our office has put out an APB on your colleague. This will cover Vieques, Culebra, and of course the big island itself."

"No," said Dar immediately. "We can't allow this. This is a classified matter—"

"I'm very sorry," said the lieutenant. "But it's done."

Dar stared at the lieutenant with a blank face, but Monica could see there was a hell of a lot more going on in there than the word "crap" could possibly convey. He was barely containing his fury.

"It was sent out over an hour ago," the lieutenant added, "before your arrival. Papi doesn't know this. I would have mentioned it to the two of you myself on the ride over, but I didn't know your business." *Because you didn't see fit to share it with me,* he didn't add.

"This is . . . no. You have to rescind it. We have to keep this contained. You don't understand—"

"We have two missing children, Special Agent. We have a responsibility. In truth, I do not have high expectations for the results, not in the face of an impending storm of these proportions. In any case, I will keep you duly informed."

He gave a little bow and silently withdrew back inside the café.

Monica looked out at the ocean. A line of ice-crystal-white cirrus clouds rimmed the horizon, marching their way forward. The storm's vanguard.

"An effing APB," muttered Dar.

"Dar, he didn't have a choice. And besides, don't you think it's about time—"

"We've been through this, Lieutenant. We need to keep this thing *contained.*"

"Oh, for Chrissakes—we've got nothing to contain! The man is *gone,* Dar, and I guarantee you he has those two kids. We've got forty-eight hours left on our clock, there's a hurricane coming, and so far we've got *fuck-all.*"

Her phone buzzed. They glared at each other as she picked up.

"Señora Emma?" A voice she dimly recognized.

"This is she."

"It's the dockmaster at Puerto Chico. We spoke on Wednesday. I may have something for you."

79

Monica nearly dropped her phone. "Yes?" she said, while she urgently signaled Dar to be quiet. It was hard to hear the man.

"I shared your information with a few people I know around the island," said the old dockmaster. "Got messages here from two of them I wanted to pass on. One at the boat club in Arecibo, Paolo, and a friend works at the marina in Salinas, Miguel."

"Yes? What? Go ahead!"

"Both report they saw someone fits your brother's general description, asking about docking his boat and finding a place to stay for a few days to weather the storm."

"That's fantastic! Thank you so much." She covered the mouthpiece and whispered to Dar "A lead—*two*." Then, into the phone, "Do you know exactly when this occurred?"

"Hard to say. Just came in the last few minutes. Both sounded like they'd called me right away, soon as they saw him."

"Did your friends say if he was alone? Or if he had any—if there was anyone with him?"

She heard a regretful cluck of the tongue. "No ma'am, wish I knew, but that was all I got from the messages. I can try calling back, but don't know that I'll reach them. Got their hands full with the storm coming."

She thanked him once more and urged him not to hesitate to call again with any updates. Then clicked off and stared at the phone for a second.

"Wow," she said. She relayed the news to Dar.

"Well, aren't I the asshole," he said stiffly. "Looks like your insubordination may have paid off. I owe you an apology, Lieutenant."

Ignoring that entire line of BS—it wasn't insubordination (since he wasn't her superior officer) and he didn't seem remotely sincere about apologizing for anything—she mapped out in her head the locations the dockmaster had given her, working out distances and travel times. "Arecibo to Salinas, that's a two-hour drive. And they're on opposite sides of the island."

"Obviously they can't both be him."

"Or if they are, at least one of the sources must have his timeline off by at least a few hours. Shit!"

They couldn't afford to dismiss either lead, or even to pursue one first while delaying follow-up on the other. If they hoped for even the slightest chance of picking up the SEAL's trail in either location before the impending hurricane made it impossible, they needed to jump on both of them at once.

They would have to split up.

80

"Pedro, this is Dr. Sara. She'll take care of your sister. Sara, this is my new friend Pedro."

Pedro solemnly shook the woman's hand. "Gracias, Doctor. My grandfather can pay you, once we get home."

The woman exchanged a look with the truck driver. "Let's not worry about that right now, Pedro. Why don't we take a look at your sister."

The three stood jammed together in the tiny space that served as the doctor's treatment room. Miranda sat back in a chair, her eyes dull, almost as if she were unaware of the others or of where she was.

The doctor murmured words to Miranda that Pedro couldn't hear as she slipped a thermometer in her mouth and wrapped a blood pressure cuff around her upper arm.

The driver took Pedro aside, out into the equally tiny waiting room in this tiny house on the outskirts of Ceiba.

"Sara is my cousin," he repeated. "You'll be safe with her."

Pedro nodded, knowing he had to trust her. He had no other choice.

"I'll come back for you. But listen, you know

there's a storm on its way, right? A big one. If we can't get you on the ferry and back to Vieques right away, you can stay here with Sara until the storm passes. All right?"

Pedro nodded again.

"All right," the man said. "Don't worry, Pedro. Okay?" And he went back out to his truck.

Pedro reentered the treatment room and found the doctor studying Miranda's infected arm. It looked awful.

"Are you hungry?"

"No, señora."

She took out a hypodermic, prepared Miranda's arm—her other arm—and pushed the needle in. Pedro had to look away. When he looked back again, the doctor had Miranda lying down and covered up on the little table. She turned to Pedro.

"When did you last eat?"

Pedro shrugged. "This morning."

"This morning," she repeated. "In the forest."

He didn't know what to say, so he said nothing.

"Wait right here," she said. As if there were anything else he could do.

He sat in a chair and watched Miranda's sleeping face.

A few minutes later the door whispered open again and the doctor came back in, holding a steaming bowl of something that smelled incredible.

"Sopa de pollo Boricua," she announced. Classic Puerto Rican chicken soup.

He wolfed down five or six big spoonfuls, then stopped himself and put the bowl down, still mostly full. "Is there more? I mean, for her?"

"She'll eat later. Once she starts feeling a little better."

Pedro got up his courage and said, "She's not going to . . . ?" He bit back a sob. "Is she . . . ?"

"No, Pedro. She's going to be fine."

Pedro burst into tears.

The doctor opened her arms and folded him into a hug while he sobbed and sobbed.

81

"Goddammit to hell," Dar muttered as the fucking traffic lurched to a halt again. The island was under an evacuation order for coastal and low-lying regions, and every goddamn motorist was acting like they'd never seen a hurricane before. Or maybe they'd seen too goddamn many of them.

He was still barely a quarter of the way from the Ceiba airport to Salinas when his phone buzzed. He glanced down. A Puerto Rico number he didn't recognize. Rivera? Couldn't think of anyone else it could be. He tapped the TALK button.

"Adamson."

"Dar!"

It was Halsey. She couldn't possibly be at Arecibo yet—they'd just parted at the airport half an hour earlier, each in their own rental—so he didn't see what she could possibly have to report.

"What—"

"I've got him in my sights! And I mean that almost literally." She sounded breathless, whether with physical exertion or pure excitement, he couldn't tell. "Rivera called, long story—our leads are *both* cold, or maybe they were false leads in the first place, who knows, who cares. He's holed up *right now* in an abandoned farmhouse near the north entrance to El Yunque."

"Wait—Rivera?" Dar's antennae went up. "How does he—"

"They sweated some low-level cartel soldier. Turns out a guy matching Chief Finn's description to a freakin' T stole one of their cars, a pimped-out BMW, and it was just spotted out here, going south on 731. License plate confirmed. I need backup. And Dar—*stay off your phone.* Borrow one if you can, otherwise just go dark. I don't know how, but he's tracking our *phones.* I'm shutting down now and going in from behind on foot. I'll wait for you. Turn on your phone just for a minute when you get here and I'll ping you, so you know I saw you. Get here as soon as you can!"

She gave him an address. A run-down wood-frame farmhouse set in a stand of yagrumo, a few hundred yards in from the end of 731.

And clicked off.

Dar spun the wheel of his rented Volvo and screeched off Highway 53, yanked the car through a rapid K-turn, and pulled back onto the road heading in the direction he'd just come from.

Luck, he'd always heard, was the junction of opportunity meeting solid preparation. Well, he was as prepared as a human being got. He had worked his butt off to get this far. He'd known that if he could just get to Puerto Rico with a few resources behind him, all he'd need would be a sliver of opportunity.

This was it.

"Son of a *bitch*!" he said aloud, and he pounded the steering wheel. "Fuck, yeah!"

The fucked-up traffic was getting worse, but it no longer bothered him.

Dar was on the hunt.

An abandoned farmhouse near the forest—he couldn't've asked for a more secluded location. Finn, Halsey, and himself. Period, full stop, end of fucking sentence.

When you acquire the target, take it. And make it a clean sweep.

As he drove he played out the scenario in his mind. Halsey coming in from the rear. Dar's job being to rush the front, make a little noise. No problem there. This was exactly why he'd brought along a flash-bang. So he rushes the front, creates the distraction. Halsey comes in from behind, gun in a two-handed draw, yelling "Freeze, asshole!" or whatever dramatic bullshit she has in mind.

Or maybe she just shoots the guy. He wouldn't be surprised. She really had a hair across her ass about him.

Either way, didn't matter to Dar. "Chief Finn, I'm placing you under arrest—" and he puts them both down.

Pop, pop.

And the two kids, if they were there, too?

He wouldn't dream of shooting them. God, no. That story would never play. A child abductor wouldn't have shot the kids he'd abducted. Made no sense.

Strangling, though. That would work.

Kind of sucked. He didn't feel great about that. Choking two little kids to death was not exactly what you'd call "in his wheelhouse." But there was a bigger picture here to keep in mind.

Dar had always been a big-picture thinker.

82

Dar slowed the rented Volvo as he approached the end of Route 731.

There was the farmhouse Halsey'd described. Thing looked ridiculous, totally out of place among all these little cement bunker-style homes. Jesus Fucking H. Who was the architect on this disaster, Stephen King?

He pulled off to the side of the road a hundred yards before the house, doused the Volvo, and turned his phone back on, making sure the ringer was off. Exited silently and proceeded along the side of the road, plenty of tall grasses and jungle-edge foliage to cover. Fifty yards from the house he cut across a patch of wildly overgrown shit that had probably been cut back to nothing when they built that heap, but had long since gone feral.

The house was fronted by a wall with three sets of windows. The curtains inside were half drawn, but Dar detected movement behind the window right by the front door. Almost too good to be true: He now knew not only that the fucking SEAL was there, but which fucking room he was in.

He came even with the house's front corner, then slowly began his approach.

His phone buzzed once. He stopped and looked.

It was a text message, from the same number Halsey had called from before.

A single emoticon: thumb and forefinger curled into an "A-OK."

He sent back a thumbs-up, then switched off his phone. Wherever her own rental was, she'd hidden it well.

All in position.

The SEAL might be on the lookout, but Dar was no stranger to the surprise takedown. He knew how to move without being detected. And the wind was already creating a backdrop of constant motion in the jungle that might've once been called a front yard here.

He resumed his approach.

He hoped the door would be unlocked, though it didn't matter that much either way. He didn't have a breaching charge, but that was not a problem. This place was practically falling down. Dar's own bulk would be plenty enough to breach a door like that.

He drew even with the door. Stretched out his hand and—carefully, carefully—tried the knob.

It turned.

He pulled a set of ear protectors from a vest pocket, jammed them in his ears.

Readied the flash-bang in one hand.

Turned the doorknob all the way with the other.

He kicked open the door, pulled the pin on the grenade and hurled it inside, then flattened against the outside wall to avoid the worst of the impact and possible bits of shrapnel.

BLAM!

In that small front room the thing went off like a stick of dynamite. A single flash-bang emits a burst of light equivalent to seven million candles and a roar the decibel level of a rocket ship blastoff. An instant after impact, Dar whipped around the doorframe and charged into the room, both hands on his drawn Glock, eyes searching the dimly lit space through the swirl of residual smoke.

For an instant, he stood still, scanning the room.

Then felt the metallic chill of a knife blade pressed against his neck.

He froze.

"Hello, Darwin," he heard Halsey say in his ear.

He turned his head, cautiously, just enough to see behind him.

It was Halsey's voice.

But it wasn't Halsey.

F/X. That's what the psychologist called him.

Halsey's voice on his phone.

He could cook; he could fish. We call him Mimo.

The dockmaster's voice on Halsey's phone.

"Fuck me," he said. "Buenos fucking días, Mimo."

83

"Place the Glock on the floor, to your left," said Finn. Adamson was right-handed. Finn had noted this at the bar and seen it confirmed in the way he handled the flash-bang. "Then lie down, face-first."

Adamson slowly, carefully, got down into a crouch and stretched way off to the left with his left hand, placing the gun on the floor. He put his left hand down, palm to floor, to steady himself. Then slowly, carefully, righted himself.

And launched.

Ducking down and to the side to move his neck away from Finn's knife, he simultaneously lashed out backward with a razor-sharp blade of his own, pulled from a sheath strapped to his leg and now aimed at Finn's right thigh in a lethal strike to the femoral artery.

The man was fast as a snake and astonishingly agile.

Finn was faster.

As Adamson slashed backward Finn pivoted with a long step to his left, pulled his right arm back across his chest, and reversed the direction of his pivot, striking the other man on the left temple with his right elbow.

The elbow is the hardest and sharpest point on the human body. The impact, amplified by the momentum of Finn's sudden rotation, traumatized Adamson's brain sufficiently to put him out cold.

When he came to, Special Agent Adamson's hands were zip-tied behind him, his legs zip-tied together, and his entire body bound to a chair with long strips of cloth hacked from one of the front curtains. Another strip served as a gag.

Finn sat on the floor facing him, the special agent's wallet, phone, car keys, and blade sitting on the floor next to him.

The Glock was in Finn's hand, pointed at Adamson's balls.

"Hukh-HUU," Adamson said through the gag.

Fuck YOU.

"Let's talk this through, Baby Bear. Is it all right if I call you Baby Bear?"

Adamson said nothing. Even without the gag, there really wasn't much he could say anyway.

"I'm curious," Finn continued. "How did this land on your desk in the first place? I mean, DIA, yes. NCIS, fine. But exactly how does a rogue Navy SEAL become a case for the FBI?"

Adamson glowered.

"My guess is it landed on your desk because someone put it there. Someone who's gone to a shit-ton lot of trouble to put a target on my back and make sure it sticks. Maybe an old acquaintance of yours."

Finn knew he had only one shot at this.

He couldn't intimidate this guy. The Teddy Ruxpin looks were deceptive; the man was ONI, and while he might daytime as an analyst, he'd moonlit plenty as an operator. "Papa Bear" hadn't put him on Finn's trail just to crunch data. Darwin Adamson had been sent here to stalk him and kill him. Which Papa Bear had to have known was a tall assignment.

The last one who'd tried had ended up at the bottom of a lake outside Reykjavík.

So Adamson was a good deal tougher than he looked. Which meant Finn couldn't beat it out of him or bribe it out of him. Couldn't even torture it out of him. Could he bluff it out of him? Maybe.

But he'd have to get it right the first time.

So. Doorway number one, two, or three?

Keyes, the straight arrow, the officer with the perennial pole up his ass? Or Dugan, tough but fair, to some the father they never had? Or Meyerhoff, the incarnation of military culture, built of bolts, bullets, and bombs?

He'd have to take a running leap and hope his guess landed on the mark. If he missed, he'd lose the element of surprise and the bluff would go foul. He wouldn't get a second chance. One out of three. Thirty-three percent odds.

Which one was Papa Bear?

The riddle he'd been asking himself for eight months.

And then it clicked.

He'd just answered his own question.

Papa Bear.

The father they never had.

He looked at Adamson and said, "When you get to Leavenworth—or hell, whichever comes first—give my regards to Frank."

He saw it—just a flicker, like a nanosecond's strobe from an atomic clock, but it was enough. The man had tried to hide it, tried to will his nerves to stay still as stone, but it wasn't humanly possible.

Shock, fury, fear—all twined together into one micro-expression that said: *How the fuck did you know?*

Finn leaned in close, almost nose-to-nose.

"I didn't. But I do now."

And just like that, his search was over.

Everything he'd done, everything he'd been through since jumping ship ten miles off the coast of San Diego a year earlier—nearly killed and almost arrested in Iceland, more than a thousand hours bent over his laptop in that tiny room behind Papi's kitchen—and he'd finally learned the secret he'd been chasing.

When he wasn't even looking for it.

The irony almost made him laugh.

Now he knew.

The man responsible for the poisonous cloud that murdered those families in Mukalla, that killed his best friend Kennedy, that turned Finn from a war hero into a wanted man, finally had a face and a name.

Frank Dugan.

"When they held Lieutenant Kennedy's memorial," he said to the bound and gagged special agent, "the line stretched out of the church and clear around the block, and another three blocks beyond. Six hundred eighty-seven people turned out. They had to move it out of the church and onto the Commons to accommodate the crowd. I'll bet you didn't know that.

"I'm sure some of those six hundred eighty-seven people cheat on their taxes. I'll bet a bunch of them cheat on their spouses. Some are kind to strangers.

Some are assholes. I'm sure it was quite a cross section of humanity. But every single one of those people shared two things in common with the other six hundred eighty-six.

"Every one of them was there to honor a good man.

"And every one of them was told a lie."

Adamson glared at him.

"Oh ukh uh-huh."

Go fuck yourself.

"Oh, he did die a hero, but not the way that crowd was told. Not the story they fed to his teammates, to his own parents. He didn't die in some 'classified mission' in some 'unnamed location.' He died right there in Bahrain. Silenced while trying to expose the corruption in his own chain of command. He died trying to tell the truth.

"He was murdered."

"Ih-huh aw hoo, hukh-ih HOO-ih!"

If you're gonna shoot, fucking DO it!

Finn raised the Glock to eye level, aimed so that Special Agent Adamson could see deep into the big empty tunnel staring at him.

Held it there for ten full seconds.

Trying to identify the feeling.

Moral outrage . . . disillusionment . . . thirst for revenge . . ..

Nothing clicked.

He wished it made sense to pull the trigger. It would be so much simpler if vengeance were the point.

He lowered the gun and stood. Collected Adamson's car keys and other paraphernalia, and headed out the door.

Baby Bear could sit there and ride out the storm.

Right now, he would just get in the way. Finn would come back later, if possible, and collect him. He could prove useful, if Finn was ever going to build any kind of case against Dugan.

Kennedy's death had been hijacked by a lie. Like Nico Santiago's. It was too late to rescue Kennedy. But it wasn't too late to rescue his memory.

If he ever got off this island.

84

Cal was so frustrated he could spit.

His officers in San Juan had turned up nothing. And now some pendejo in Vieques, one of his own people, had taken it upon himself to put out an APB on the man, so now the entire police force—not just his own police, but *all* the police—were looking for him.

Plus the two Americanos.

Santa Madre.

The traffic on the road to Humacao had gotten so crazy in reaction to the coming hurricane it was tempting to switch on his gumball and siren—but on this particular mission, he didn't want to draw attention to himself.

According to his people, the man had talked with two individuals he knew in Humacao, one on Tuesday and both on Wednesday. How much had they told him? What had he told them? Cal needed to know—and he needed to know before anyone else did.

The prospect of this Picasso being apprehended by anyone but himself terrified him. Cal might be El Rucco's top lieutenant, but that wouldn't protect him, not if it was ever discovered that he'd been so careless. The boss held strands of power that reached everywhere. No one was safe. Not even Cal.

His phone buzzed. *The* phone.

He glanced at the screen and saw who was calling.

An actual *voice* call. That only happened when the boss was worried, which Cal had witnessed only twice before. That blogger. And then with Nico and Alejandro.

He pressed the button and tapped on the SPEAKER icon so he could talk while he drove.

"Progress?" said the voice on the other end.

"I've talked with my man in Vieques. The children's abuelo has an employee, going by 'Mimo,' who disappeared a few days ago. Evidently the man has been there for the past eight months. No trace of him prior to his arrival in January. We're still working on that. The police there seem to think the children are with him, that perhaps he took them."

He didn't mention the APB.

"Two Americanos showed up there looking for him. One from FBI, one from JAG. They claim he is a colleague, 'working on an intelligence matter,' but it seems more likely they are trying to track him down because he has deserted, or run afoul of the law in some way."

There was a silence.

"He doesn't know who you are," added Cal. "He's bluffing. Just a man on the run, playing every angle he can think of. Otherwise he would have moved on you already."

"He got this phone number." The voice spoke the words without inflection, yet the flat tone induced a sense of terror. Cal could feel his balls shrivel. "Where are we on the leak?"

"On it," replied Cal.

"He has to have made contact with one of our people. Santiago? Alejandro?"

Alejandro was the Ports Authority deputy director who'd gotten careless.

No, thought Cal. *Nico Santiago didn't have that information. And Alejandro didn't just know your number, he knew who you are.*

"I understand he spoke to a few people in Humacao," he said. "I'm on my way there now."

The call went dead.

He silently cursed the traffic. The governor, that first-class idiot, had now reversed his evacuation order and instead issued a "shelter in place" order. Which was basically like throwing the car into reverse while driving at highway speed.

The result, of course, was chaos.

Long columns of cars streamed north and west to San Juan, and an equal number filled the opposing lanes in the opposite direction. Everyone seemed hell-bent on getting somewhere else. He'd taken the fastest route, south to Caguas to 30 East, which would normally take just under an hour, far less at cop speed—but he'd already been on the road for nearly two hours and was barely two-thirds of the way there.

Cal cursed himself out loud.

He should have driven out there earlier. Days earlier. He should have known the man was trouble when he saw him lurking at the back of the accursed chapel on Tuesday.

And why did he want to get hold of those two children? To clear himself, because the Vieques police thought he took them? Possible. Or did he want to find out for himself what they'd seen, on Sunday?

Just how much *did* he know about El Rucco's operation?

What was his game in all this?

It really didn't matter.

The point was, Cal needed to find the man Picasso before anyone else did, and prevent him from saying anything to anyone, ever again.

85

"Goddammit! Goddammit goddammit *goddam-*mit."

She laid on the horn, knowing it would do no good, since the car in front of her was just as irritated at the car in front of them, who was just as irritated at the car in front of *them,* and so on for as far out on Highway 2 as she could see.

When she'd finally arrived in Arecibo, no one there had any idea what she was talking about. "Paolo," the man whose name the Fajardo dockmaster had given her? Didn't exist.

She whacked the rental's steering wheel in frustration.

It was him. Had to be.

The SEAL.

The goddamn SEAL.

The traffic lurched forward and she punched the gas, then hit the brakes after twenty feet as it all ground to a halt again.

She should have known. She shouldn't have been so gullible. Somehow he'd fed them what had to be bogus leads—either got the dockmaster to go along with him through his HUMINT juju, or faked the man's voice himself, which she had no doubt Mister

F/X could do. He'd split them up. Divide and conquer.

And now she couldn't reach Dar.

Arecibo was at least an hour from San Juan—when the traffic wasn't losing its shit in the face of yet another oncoming weather disaster.

She tried Dar's number once more. No answer.

The traffic started moving.

Driving one-handed, she keyed in another number on her phone and pressed CALL, then hit SPEAKER.

"Toño Rivera," the speaker said in the phone speaker's tinny little voice.

"Toño, it's Monica." The situation's urgency seemed to call for first names.

She quickly filled him in: the two leads, she and Dar splitting up, how she suspected the SEAL had somehow sent them both on a wild goose chase, and now her inability to reach Dar. "I know this sounds crazy," she said, "but I have a sinking feeling he may have been suckered into some kind of trap."

"You think so? It could just be his reception. Cellphone service on the island, I'm afraid, is susceptible to blackouts."

She ignored the polite skepticism.

"Can you put out an APB on his car? Pretty sure it was a Volvo, but I have no idea of the plate number."

"Sure. No problem. I'll call the rental place and get that information. Then put it out on the network—but I have to warn you, with the storm coming, our people will have their hands full."

"I understand. Please try."

She clicked off as traffic ground once more to a complete halt.

Dar Adamson was a royal pain in the rear, but he

was also the guy who'd located Finn when no one else could. And a comment he'd made the day before was still lodged in her thoughts like a stone in a riding boot.

When she was on the *Lincoln,* she'd said, she should have trusted her gut. To which he replied, "Maybe that was the problem. Maybe you did."

Had she?

Of course she had. She'd believed that Chief Finn was, for all his strangeness, a trustworthy person.

"You can't trust the evidence, Em." Another heart-to-heart with her daddy during her early law school days. "You sure can't trust the witnesses. You can't even trust the law." *You have to trust your client,* was what she'd expected him to say.

But he didn't.

Instead, he'd surprised her by saying, "And your client? You trust them least of all. You *believe in* your client. Of course. But trust? No, there's only one person you need to trust, and that's yourself. Consult the evidence. Consult the law. Consult your client. Then trust your gut."

She'd never known her father to give her bad advice, but the unspoken reply still nagged at her:

What if your gut is wrong?

Dar was right. On the *Lincoln,* she'd trusted her gut about the goddamn SEAL.

And look how that turned out.

"Gut be damned," she said aloud.

Trust the math. *Find for X.*

If only she knew how to do that right now.

86

The highway was a nightmare. Finn didn't care. He had to get to Humacao. There were at least three people who knew more about El Rucco than they were saying. He had to talk to them.

Especially Graciela. She had given him a detailed map of the man's mind and motivations. Finn sensed there was some kind of connection between the two of them, maybe points in their histories where their paths had crossed.

As he weaved and dodged, he tried calling her cellphone. It went right to voicemail. He called her office in Ceiba and got reception there, was told the mayor was tied up in teleconferences with some of the other mayors, police chiefs, and the Coast Guard, coordinating storm response. Couldn't come to the phone.

He had no phone number for the priest, didn't think he'd reach him by phone even if he did.

The woman in blue obviously had no phone.

The sky had turned a bilious gray-green.

He drove on.

And thought about Commander Frank Dugan.

Finn still could not remember his own parents' faces, but he had no trouble remembering Commander Dugan. Though he was still Lieutenant Dugan when Finn first met him during SEAL selection. They crossed paths again in Fallujah, when Finn served for a short time in a platoon there, the same platoon he served in with Tómas.

He thought again about the day Tómas's leg was blown off by that IED.

Finn shouldn't have done what he did. He should have simply returned fire. Everything in their training said so. "Stay in the fight until the threat is down—if you stop to patch up your buddy's injury, you're putting both of you at risk."

It was a snap judgment. There were just too many of them for one man to repel with return fire. He could save one of his teammates—maybe—but not both.

He'd chosen their CO.

In retrospect, he knew he'd made the right choice. And so had Tómas, when he set off those two grenades. The leg wound was too grievous. He would have bled out before Finn could've gotten him to medevac. Probably.

The CO was in grave condition, but he recovered.

Which was what Finn was thinking about right now.

If Finn had acted differently, that CO would be dead. Probably all three of them would.

But Kennedy would still be alive.

Because the CO of that particular platoon was Frank Dugan.

Finn heard the blatt of a horn just as someone slid in from the shoulder to get ahead of him. He stamped on the gas and yanked the Volvo's wheel hard to the right, bumping up against the guy's fender and shoving him out of the way.

And kept going.

87

"Fiat voluntas tua, sicut in caelo et in terra . . ."

The young priest knelt at the altar, his voice so soft it barely raised an echo in the hushed space. The troubled skies outside cast the altar in a strange, gloomy light.

". . . Panem nostrum quotidianum da nobis hodie, et dimitte nobis debita nostra sicut et nos dimittimus debitoribus nostris—"

He stopped, sensing a presence behind him. Turned and looked.

No one there.

He turned back and resumed his vigil. The Latin words gave him comfort. They had been mostly taken out of service and shelved decades earlier, long before he was born, but he knew them all by heart.

". . . Et ne nos inducas in tentationem, sed libera nos a malo—"

He looked behind him again, and this time he thought he saw movement at a back corner of the chapel. He stood.

"Hello?"

He had walked halfway down the center aisle when the figure rose to its full height and he saw who it was.

"I've come for confession," said the big man.

The priest stopped, looking at the man across the dim space between them. "Very well." He headed toward the confession booth at the rear corner of the chapel, but the big man stopped him with a raised hand.

"Not mine," the man said. He stretched out his hand with a gesture toward the altar. "Come, Padre. Let us talk in the vestry."

They walked together up the aisle in silence.

"There is a hurricane coming, Padre," the big man said as they entered the priest's private chamber. "Why aren't there people sheltering here?"

"They're all in their homes. They're afraid."

"Afraid? Of what? The church?"

Teasing him.

The priest said nothing, afraid to lie, afraid to tell the truth.

Of you.

The big man picked up the straight-backed chair by the desk and turned it around to face the center of the room. "Sit."

The priest sat.

The big man pulled up the prayer bench, turned it backward, and sat on it, pulled up so close that the young man's knees touched his shins.

"Good. Now. There was a man at the service on Tuesday."

"A man?"

Cal sighed. He was a patient man, but Santa Madre, this part always annoyed him. So childish. Cal had been a detective for more years than his eldest boy had been drawing breath, had questioned thousands of witnesses, suspects, and "persons of interest," as his profession called them. And still it was beyond him, this evasive impulse. As if the truth could somehow be avoided, sidestepped, tricked into not mattering.

He didn't understand it, but accepted it nevertheless. Part of the job.

"A man," he repeated. "He came to see you the following day. Calling himself Picasso. Hair . . ." Cal fluttered his fingers on both sides of his head, pantomiming dreadlocks.

"I said nothing."

"Well, let's take a look at that nothing. Walk me through it. What did he ask?"

"He said he was a journalist, writing an article on crime in Puerto Rico." The words came out in a flood. Cal did not interrupt. "He asked about Officer Santiago, if he was local. How he died. If it—" He stopped.

Cal nodded once. *Go on.*

"If his death had anything to do with someone called . . . someone called . . ."

"El Rucco," Cal supplied.

"Yes," the priest said. He appeared grateful for the assistance.

"And what else?" said Cal gently.

"He asked about a sea monster legend, I have no idea why."

"A legend," prompted Cal.

"La Bestia, they call it. The Devil's Ride. It's just a local superstition. Like the Loch Ness monster. And that was all."

"La Bestia," Cal repeated.

The priest nodded and gave a faint smile. He seemed relieved. As if perhaps the worst was over.

That futile avoidance of the truth.

Cal's face remained neutral.

"It would have been better if you hadn't talked to him at all."

"I . . ." The priest's smile vanished. "I didn't . . ."

Didn't what, Padre? Didn't say anything that could get you in trouble? Didn't mean to do it?

Like a child.

"You know, Padre, we have our own sacrament. A sacrament of silence."

He leaned forward as he spoke, his eyes on the priest's, until they were nearly touching. Then in one quick motion he reared his head back and snapped it forward, bashing his forehead into the young man's with a sharp *crack*.

The priest slumped back, dazed.

Cal caught him so he wouldn't slip out of the chair. Holding the man in place with one hand, he reached into a deep inside pocket and withdrew a pair of rubber tarp bands, which he wrapped around the priest's arms and torso, strapping him tightly to the chair.

The priest began moaning softly.

"Shhhh," said Cal, as he reached into a smaller inside jacket pocket and withdrew his little leather tool kit. He unzipped the kit and placed it on his lap, then removed the scalpel. "This won't hurt, Padre."

Seeing the blade, the young man's eyes went wide, and he immediately launched into rapid speech, so soft it was barely audible. "Ave-María-gratia-plena-Dominus-tecum-benedicta-tu-in-mulieribus-et-benedictus-fructus . . ."

Cal donned a pair of nitrile gloves, then placed the tip of the scalpel against the priest's neck, just below the Adam's apple—

"ventris-tui-Jesus-Sancta-María-mater-Dei—"

and pushed.

It was like pressing the MUTE button on his television at home.

The prayer instantly went silent.

A tiny bit of blood spurted out, followed by air.

In his early efforts, he'd tried severing the vocal cords, but that had proven time consuming and messy—they were too well protected behind the larynx. Self-taught through the University of YouTube, he'd learned instead to insert a scalpel or knife just below the thyroid cartilage, the so-called Adam's apple, and puncture the cricothyroid membrane.

Similar to a tracheotomy, only quicker and easier.

Result: air pouring out the front of the neck rather than passing over the vocal cords. The priest could say all the prayers he wanted, shout till he was blue in the face, and he would produce nothing more than a slight hiss.

"This next part, I'm sorry to say, will hurt a great deal."

The process was simple in concept, but took some care in the execution. Avoiding getting blood all over himself was part of the skill.

Mainly, though, it was the part with the chisels. That had taken practice.

As Cal worked the priest's feet drummed frantically against the tile floor, the cords on his neck tensing to their maximum, his screams chuffing soundlessly through the hole in his neck. He writhed and thrashed against the cords for a full minute, which was an exceptional length of time, in Cal's experience. He was young and strong, and the extremity of pain and terror sent a flood of adrenaline surging through his blood and tissues, prolonging his struggle.

After that, he was still.

Cal withdrew from the same deep pocket a packet of Sani-Wipes, cleaned the blood from his tools, then zipped the case closed and slipped it back into its pocket.

He removed the tarp cords, wiped them clean of blood, wound them into a small coil, and placed them in a plastic bag, which he slid into a deep interior pocket.

The jawbone he placed into another, larger plastic bag, which he would store in the trunk of his car for disposal later. He had an associate who ran a crematorium in Guaynabo.

His phone buzzed.

He removed the bloodstained gloves, turning them inside out as he did, and popped them into the plastic bag back with the jawbone, then took out the phone and pressed TALK.

He listened.

Said, "Put her through."

Then he said, "Detective Cordova."

And listened.

"No, you did the right thing. I'll be there as soon as I'm able. Say, ninety minutes. All right?"

Listened.

"Good."

He disconnected the call, then exited the vestry through a side door and went out to search the streets of Humacao.

He didn't think it would take long.

88

He was right.

He found her in less than ten minutes. It wasn't hard. He'd had a good idea where to look.

"Buenas noches, Sofía."

"Buenas noches, Cal," said the woman in blue.

"Long time," he said. "You're looking well."

"Go to hell, Cal."

He sat down next to her.

"Sofía," he said. "We need to talk."

89

He'd been there, strapped to the fucking chair, for over an hour when he heard the first car.

Thank fucking Christ.

He'd managed to stump the chair a few feet across the floor and near the front window, where fucking Chief Finn had torn down curtains for materials to bind and gag him. But he hadn't been able to work himself free from the fucking zip-ties and binding.

And he had to admit, he'd been getting a little worried.

He figured someone would eventually find him and help get him the fuck out of there. But however long that might take out here in El Buttfucko, or whatever this hill town was called, he wasn't sure if he could afford to wait that long. He could hear the roar of the wind outside, gusts of wind and rain spattering the walls with increasing urgency. He knew how hurricanes sounded when they were building.

And this was Puerto Fucking Rico.

Fucking hurricane fucking central.

The house he was in didn't exactly look like the third little piggy's house of bricks. If that thing out there started huffing and puffing like it sounded it was planning on doing, Dar didn't have a whole lot of faith that the place was going to stay standing around him.

Unless he could get out of here in the next few hours, he just might be screwed.

Which was when he heard a car pulling up outside.

Then a second. And a third.

Car doors slamming.

Men shouting to one another in fucking Spanish, talking so fast he couldn't understand a word of it.

But at least it was people. And not just people. They sounded like they knew what they were doing, and were in a fuck of a hurry doing it.

Which sounded a hell of a lot like police to him.

The cavalry.

Thank God and Sonny Jesus.

He couldn't reach his badge to show it, but they would doubtless frisk him and find it themselves. That was just about the only thing the fucking SEAL hadn't taken. And anyway, if they would just come in and take this motherfucking gag out of his mouth, he could talk his way out of anything.

He furiously jerked against his restraints, hiking the chair half inch by half inch closer to where the SEAL had torn down the curtains. They couldn't fail to see movement at the window.

"Ah ih HIH!" he shouted. *I'm in HERE!*

He couldn't tell whether his voice would carry through the moaning of the wind.

Someone outside was shouting, too. He could just make out the words.

"¡Di tus oraciones, Picasso!" *We're talking to you, Picasso!*

Picasso?

"¡Vamos a recuperar el auto, hijo de puta del

DEA!" *We're taking back the car, DEA motherfucker!*

What the fuck were they yelling about?

"¡Te vas a morir, Picasso!" *You're going to die, Picasso!*

Picasso? Who the fuck was Picasso?

"Ah HAH hi-HA-ho!" he shouted. *I'm NOT Picasso!* "Ah ih uh EH EE AHH!" *I'm with the FBI!*

There was a brief lull in the wind, and in that short space he heard a sound that made his blood run cold.

The sound of guns being racked.

A lot of guns.

That sound, and the certainty of what it meant, was so terrifying it triggered his autonomic nervous system. Everywhere throughout his body neurochemical electricity raced, impulses slammed into reverse and screamed countermanding orders, contracting smooth muscles and loosening sphincters. He smelled the sharp, acrid smell of urine and felt the warmth spread in his crotch.

"EHH!" he screamed. *WAIT!* "Uh EH EE AHH—"

The guns roared.

90

Pedro was beyond exhausted, but as much as he wanted to, he couldn't sleep. He had to stay awake. He had to watch over Miranda.

The last time he saw his mamá, she was reclining on a cot in a tiny room in what they said was a clinic, but as far as Pedro could see was just someone's crappy little casita. It was just a few weeks after Hurricane María, and the hospital was still closed. This little house was supposed to be a place where sick people could get better, but he knew she wasn't getting better.

What he remembered most about that day was being afraid. Her skin was like paper, dry and thin, not like her real skin at all. It terrified him, and he couldn't bring himself to touch it. Her real skin smelled like mangoes and woodsmoke and cinnamon; now she smelled like medicine.

He was afraid of her voice. It was dry and thin, too, like her skin, not the voice he knew, the one that sounded like music even when she wasn't singing and always made him feel like nothing could hurt him, ever. This wasn't that voice. This voice was low and raspy.

Most of all he was afraid he would never see his real mamá again.

"You have to be brave, tesoro," she said. "Be brave for your little sister. Watch out for her. And take care of your heart, too. It's okay to cry. It's okay to be sad—but don't let it break your heart. You're strong, my little man."

But he wasn't.

He wasn't strong, and he wasn't brave.

They should have been on the ferry home by now, they should *be* home by now. But Pedro hadn't acted in the moment when his sister needed him most. He hadn't watched out for her.

And now, instead of being home and safe with Papi, they were sitting in another crappy little doctor's office in another crappy little casita.

He could hear the wind outside, moaning and yowling. The ferry was already shut down for the storm, he was sure of it. They were too late.

This doctor, the truck driver's cousin, said Miranda was going to be fine, that she would be all better soon. But Pedro didn't trust doctors.

And he was tired. So tired.

The doctor had put another little cot in the room for him, but he'd stayed in the chair in the corner, which was uncomfortable, but at least it would keep him awake.

He leaned his head back against the wall and closed his eyes.

At home, there was a tree outside their bedroom that brushed against the window when the wind came up. During María it slammed the house hard, over and over, until Pedro thought it was going to break through the wall, but the little house held.

He was in his bedroom now, with María outside

again, whipping their little house. Hitting the wall now. And again. And again, louder, and louder.

Bam. Bam. Bam.

It's Juracán, he thought. *Juracán coming to knock our house down—*

His eyes snapped open.

Tap-tap. Tap-tap.

There was a soft knocking on the door.

He had no idea how long he'd slept.

"Pedro?" It was the doctor, whispering at the door. "Are you awake?"

He got up from his chair, crossed the little room, and opened the door.

The doctor wasn't alone.

"Pedro, cariño, the police are here. They say they can take you and your sister to your grandfather now."

The big man by her side smiled.

A big, kindly smile.

91

The church was empty. Which didn't surprise him. It was a big, strong, cement building, and normally a certain segment of the population would take refuge in community buildings such as this when the elements threatened. But these weren't normal times. Finn had seen the looks on people's faces. The fear in their eyes. Holy though it might be, this house was no longer a place of refuge for the meek and downtrodden.

The light inside the chapel was brooding and sullen, reduced by the bleak dusklight outside to sickly shades of gray. None of the interior lighting had been switched on.

The entrance to the vestry was open.

Finn found the priest's body slumped in his chair, in the same condition as the man he had found in the abandoned house on Wednesday. Punctured throat. Staring eyes. Jawless, with tongue grotesquely protruding.

The weight of the world's sins had finally caved in on the young padre, and his heart had given way.

Finn left by the side door.

—

There was no one in the plaza. No tourists, no baristas. No pigeons.

No woman in blue.

Of course not. Not with a hurricane coming.

It took more than an hour of searching door-to-door, through empty porticoes and abandoned buildings, before he found her, a few blocks away in a deserted clinic waiting room where she'd been seeking shelter from the storm. Lying on her side on a small love seat, in a pool of blood, wrists zip-tied together, her eyes closed.

He was surprised to see that her jaw was still intact. Her tongue, however, had been cut out, which Finn knew only because it had been placed on the pillow beside her head. For what reason the killer had not executed his usual grotesque disfigurement, he didn't know. Perhaps there was, as she said, a line you crossed when you hurt a nun.

And this was supposed to be, what, a kinder, gentler torture?

How long had she been here like this? By what margin had he missed being here for her when the big policeman with the kindly face had appeared to deliver his death sentence?

He knelt down next to her and gently cut the zip-ties with his ring knife.

As horribly as she must have suffered, somehow there was a look of peace on her face that gave it a quiet beauty. Finn couldn't have explained it if he tried.

He felt her hand. Still warm.

He put two fingers of his other hand to her throat, dreading the stillness he would find.

A *pulse*?

Given the amount of blood loss, it didn't seem possible.

She was *alive*?

And then he felt her hand close over his, giving it a squeeze. A faint spark shot up his arm, and the pulse stilled.

Go find them.

92

He walked back to the Volvo and climbed in as the wind whistled and keened through the empty streets around him.

What now?

Time was running out. He still had no idea who El Rucco was, let alone where. And so far, his efforts seemed only to have gotten some good people killed.

The priest. The lady in blue. One terrified, one fearless, yet in the end it didn't matter. They'd both died, and for the same reason: because they talked to him.

With Lucy, he had taken elaborate precautions. He felt certain that no one was aware that the two of them had spoken. But he had taken no such meticulous care in speaking with the priest, nor with the lady in blue.

Nor with Graciela, for that matter.

Graciela.

Oh, no. Not Graciela, too.

He had met with her twice, once in the streets of Fajardo and once at her home. Had they been observed, either time? He didn't think so, but . . .

The man has eyes and ears everywhere. No one is safe.

He yanked out his Graciela phone, the one without the notch, and called her cell.

It went right to her voicemail.

He tried her office again. Reached a different staff person this time, who told him the mayor had left the office over an hour ago.

"Has she called in since then?" he asked.

"Oh, yes," said the aide. "A number of times. Just a few minutes ago, in fact. It's a little crazy here, with the hurricane coming."

Finn asked the aide to convey a message that Picasso had called and it was urgent, then thanked her and clicked off.

He keyed in the digits for her cellphone number again, hoping her line would have freed up in the last minute or two.

He couldn't leave her unprotected. He'd failed the priest and the woman in blue—he couldn't fail yet one more innocent victim. El Rucco's executioner was well ahead of him, and if he was systematically interrogating and silencing everyone Finn had spoken with, then Graciela had to be next on his list. She was incredibly lucky that he hadn't killed her yet.

He paused, his finger over the CALL button.

Hadn't killed her yet.

He sat back in his car seat, finger still poised.

Why not?

El Rucco is a liberator, she'd said. *He sees himself as a kind of Robin Hood.*

He's obsessive about his own anonymity.

And all at once, Finn understood.

He pressed SEND.

—

She picked up on the first ring. "Picasso!" she said. "I'm so glad you called! I've got things all set up at the visitors center, just waiting for him to show. Where are you now?"

Where are you now?

It occurred to Finn that this was, by his count, the third time she'd asked him that question.

She seemed anxious to know the answer.

"I'm in Rincón," he said. "No, Ponce." He paused. "No, Bayamón."

Silence.

"I could be anywhere," he added. "And you, Graciela Dominguez. You could be anyone."

People believe he must be some big, strong man. Like a castle. I don't think so.

No, not big like a castle.

And not a man.

That first encounter Tuesday night, when he chanced by to rescue her from those two muggers in Fajardo, that wasn't chance at all. And they weren't muggers.

They were employees.

The fly had gotten the spider's attention right on the first day, after all.

The voice on the other end of the phone finally spoke up again.

"Buenas noches, Mimo."

"Buenas noches, El Rucco," he replied.

93

She'd told him. She'd flat-out *told* him. He just hadn't seen it.

I try to keep a low profile.

Hiding in plain sight.

"You know," he said, "you're doing the exact same thing to your people as the Spanish and the Americans did. Subjugate and abandon."

"Hold that thought. I have a friend who wants to say hello."

Finn heard scrabbling in the background, then loud breathing, like someone holding their mouth too close to the phone.

"¡Mimo!—"

And then she was gone again.

Miranda!

It sucked the air right out of him.

Finn had known guys in SEAL training who couldn't handle jumping from a plane at twenty thousand feet, or the intense roller-coaster stresses of rapid maneuvers in a jet aircraft, or who got sick and puked halfway through exercises in a zero-g simulator. None of it had bothered Finn.

But right now he felt like he was going to throw up.

Up till this moment he'd had no solid evidence

that Miranda and Pedro were still alive. But no solid evidence they weren't, either. The one thing he'd known was that El Rucco's people hadn't found them yet. It was only now, hearing her voice, that he realized how hopeful that had made him.

And felt that hope buoyed and crushed in the same breath.

They were alive.

And in the clutches of the spider.

He struggled to get his thoughts under control.

"I wasn't bluffing, you know," he said. "About those deep contacts at DEA, FBI, and all the rest. They're ready to drop the hammer. They don't know about pier nine. I do. They're just waiting for my word. Turn the children over to me and that word never comes. I disappear. I don't care about your business. Rosie Roads, visitors center, parking lot. Within one hour. Or your shit hits the fan."

"Really? I don't think so. I don't think you have the luxury of time. I think you need to disappear before the police pick you up for kidnapping. Or if not the police, your American friends. The two from JAG and FBI."

She knew about West Texas and Adamson. Of course she did.

The man has eyes and ears everywhere.

"You know what they told the police about you, in Vieques? That you were their colleague. That you've been here working on some secret assignment."

She laughed, a sound devoid of mirth.

The way a spider would laugh.

"The police may buy that story, but I don't. I think you are some kind of rogue actor who has run afoul of his own people. A fly in their ointment. CIA, military intel, Special Operations, whatever.

"I'll make this simple for you, little fly. Turn yourself in to me, and I'll get you safely off the island, far away, and return the children to their abuelito, once my shipment is gone. Or, don't. And then people you care about start dying, one every hour. The old man first. Then the boy. Then the girl. And then you, when I find you.

"And I *will* find you.

"Rosie Roads, little fly, one hour."

The call disconnected.

94

Finn hit the ignition and the Volvo roared onto the streets leading out of Humacao and onto the highway heading north.

The impossible traffic had started thinning to a more manageable mess, as people either got to wherever they were trying to flee or decided to hunker down where they were.

Public-private partnerships, he thought as he shot around the cars, looking for holes in the crush, slaloming through the diminishing chaos. *Couldn't state it more clearly than that.*

Graciela was the public, El Rucco the private. A partnership with herself.

It wasn't big corporations and generous billionaires financing Graciela's public works—it was her own criminal enterprise. The merchandise that "never harms Puerto Ricans." Sourcing from other countries and selling to greedy northerners. Robbing from the poor and giving to the rich. Her twisted version of Robin Hood.

She had been ten steps ahead of him the whole time.

The "attempted mugging" Tuesday night was a classic honeypot deflection. She'd been aware of him that first day, and staged the street assault to draw him into her orbit, where she could keep an eye on him.

Do you live nearby? Can I help you to your hotel? Or wherever you're staying?

Damsel in distress: the oldest trick in the book.

And the moment she knew he was looking for the two children, she gave him her cellphone—not so he could reach her, but so she could keep tabs on him.

Have you learned anything new about los nenes?

No. You?

She wasn't helping him find the kids, it was the other way around. She was using him to help find them herself.

Why had he trusted her?

She hadn't talked to anyone in the DEA or border patrol about the kids. There was no confidential task force. It was all horseshit. She had manipulated him.

She was a far better chess player than he.

He'd seen it all too late, far too late.

He was coming up on a series of Ceiba exits.

Rosie Roads. One hour.

He shot past the exit for Rosie Roads and took the next exit, heading west.

The one time he'd been at the villa, he'd seen no one but the mayor herself, and there'd been no evidence of any other presence. But if she were running her entire operation from there, she would almost certainly have a significant security staff on premises. Especially now, if she were holding two prisoners there. Even two small ones.

Finn reached the turnoff for the property, made the turn, and accelerated.

Four seconds later he rammed through the front gate.

In movies a maneuver like that would send pieces of the shattered gate flying and leave the car basically unscathed. This wasn't a movie. The gate gave way but each half stayed semi-intact, gouging great chunks out of the Volvo on both sides as he scraped it through, leaving the car pretty much a mess.

But still drivable.

Finn powered around the edge of the property's maze of streets and seconds later pulled in at the villa's driveway. Grabbed Dar's Glock and ran around to the side entrance that opened onto the kitchen, the same door the two of them had used to exit a few days earlier.

No time for finesse.

He fired a single shot into the lock assembly and kicked in the door.

No one in the kitchen.

Holding the Glock out in front of him, he swept from room to room through the place until he had cleared the entire villa.

It was empty. No security forces. No prisoners. No one.

What now?

Rosie Roads. One hour.

If he took off now he could just make it.

He drove back down to the development's entrance, which was unmanned in the face of the impending hurricane. Parked, got out, hauled one half of the gate all the way open. Got back in the car.

And sat.

The old man first.

Why?

Why not the kids?

Perhaps because, with all her intel resources and razor-sharp predator's instincts, she was not as sure of her position as she pretended. She had to be wondering how he'd gotten access to her number in the first place. How he knew about el cargamento, Venezuela, and pier 9.

She couldn't quite afford to call his bluff, at least not totally.

She wouldn't kill the children, not as long as Picasso was still in the wind.

And Zacharias?

Despite her threat, he didn't think the old man's fate rested on whether or not Finn showed up at Rosie Roads within an hour. He didn't think she expected him to show up at all. She'd put Zacharias at the front of her execution roster for a reason. Everything she did was strategic.

She would have sent someone to Vieques to kill Zacharias and ambush Finn when he showed up. Which she had no way of being sure he would. But it was her best play.

It was an obvious trap.

But what else could he do?

He pulled the last burner phone from his backpack, punched in the old man's number, waited for it to go through. No answer.

Tried again.

Nothing.

He opened an online app that showed current outages across all seventy-eight counties, blue for 100 percent power, dark red for 0 percent.

All of Vieques was blue.

Why wasn't he answering?

He shut off the phone and hit the accelerator again.

The storm was coming on fast, the winds picking up speed and force. In another hour, maybe sooner, flight to Vieques would be impossible. But the big cop already had a solid lead. There was an airport right there in Humacao, five minutes from where he'd murdered the priest and the woman in blue. Gaining access to a small plane on a moment's notice would have been no problem.

The executioner could be touching down at Isabel Segunda at that very moment.

No choice.

Finn got back on the highway and sped north.

95

Zacharias busied himself in the kitchen, cleaning up from the two uneaten dinner servings he'd set out hours earlier. He had done this every day since they disappeared, and he would continue doing it until they returned. Or until he died. Whichever came first.

As he moved, he held murmured conversations with Santo Thomas, patron saint of children; San Judas, patron saint of the lost and desperate; San Matías, patron saint of drunkards; and Santa Ana, patron saint of grandparents. Zacharias was not a particularly religious man, but he was not too proud to seek intercession on his grandchildren's behalf.

And besides, conversations with the unseen were normal for him.

He set out the makings of the next morning's breakfast—the coarse-ground rice, the vanilla, the cinnamon, the salt, the little pot, the two bowls. If tomorrow was the day the world returned them to him, there would be hot breakfast waiting for them.

The wind outside groaned.

As he worked, he thought back to the day he nearly killed his best friend Jose in a bar fight over nothing but foolish politics. They'd both been drinking for hours; then suddenly Zacharias was smashing a bottle over Jose's head, landing Jose in the ER on the big island and himself in the Isabel jail for the night. The next morning he learned that his wife was back in the hospital. Three weeks later, she was gone.

In the distance, through the shrill cries and low moans of the wind, he heard the faint sounds of a car pulling in.

Zacharias moved silently out to the dining room, sat in his big chair, switched off the phone in his pocket, and waited.

The old man had no regrets, not about any of it. He'd long ago learned that regret was just another form of self-indulgence. It was simply a matter of living with a day-to-day acceptance of what was true.

He hadn't been there for his wife when she needed him most, and he hadn't been there for his young daughter, at least not until the day he awoke in that jail cell. But he would always be there for Pedro and Miranda, whose faces he had never seen yet knew better than he knew his own.

All that was true, and it was enough.

The distant car door shut softly, as if trying not to make a sound.

Footsteps.

He sat in the dark, seeing his grandchildren's faces. Holding a space for them in his mind. But accepting whatever happened, without regret. Whatever would come, would come.

He was already at peace with it.

He heard the little bell on his front door make the

bare beginning of its usual announcement—the *di-* of its mournful little *ding!*—but then go silent.

As if someone had muted it by wrapping something around it to dampen the sound, like a towel.

Or a large hand.

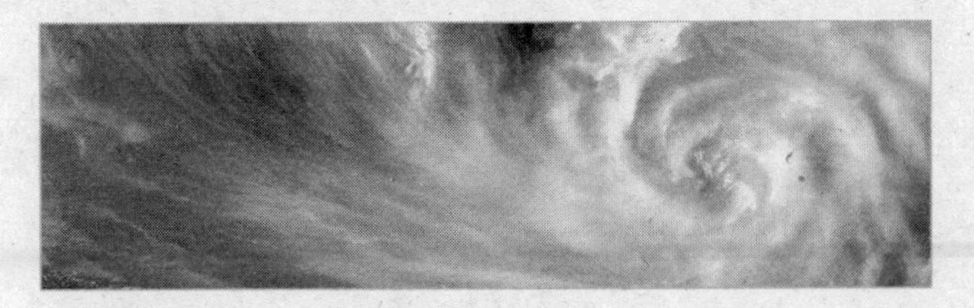

Saturday

Landfall

Hurricane Will's winds accelerated throughout the night, bringing bands of intense precipitation to coastal areas. By early morning the rainfall was horizontal in some locations, hitting in squalls like volleys of automatic gunfire. Standing upright was nearly impossible.

As it continues to drive toward the coast of Puerto Rico, Hurricane Will has been upgraded to a Category 3 event.

96

Here is the first warning sign that you shouldn't leave a harbor: if there are whitecaps showing up inside the harbor itself. Every sailor knows this. They learn it on Day One of Nautical Do's and Don'ts 101.

There were whitecaps inside the marina at Puerto Chico.

Finn stepped into the little skiff and secured the bowline to the rear seat, giving him an extra handhold. He expected he'd be needing it.

Hooyah, cabrón.

Dozens of boats sat snug in the harbor, the wind howling as it whistled through the dormant rigging. Among the yachts and daysailers and smaller service vessels he spotted a Coast Guard patrol boat, moored in tight and poised to launch its rescue efforts in the aftermath of the storm. Under the glare of the harbor lights, he could make out the name emblazoned along the rear transom.

The CUTTYHUNK.

Same cutter he'd seen out on the Sound, days earlier, searching for Pedro and Miranda.

He'd had teammates who would take that as a bad omen. Others who'd see it as a good one.

As far as Finn was concerned, the jury was still out.

He pulled on the engine's starter cord and it sparked to life, inaudible against the howl of the wind. He slammed on the throttle and the skiff took off, shooting out of the cove like a Tomahawk missile.

Within moments of rounding the outer jetty, he had to force himself to back off on the throttle to just over half speed. It was an agonizing choice, but he couldn't risk having the little boat plow into the surf nose-first and tumble end-over-end.

The reduced speed would add another sixty minutes to his ride. Minutes he couldn't afford to lose.

But he wouldn't do the old man much good if he dumped the boat halfway across.

The day he and Tómas nearly drowned, the sea state was bad. This was worse. If the hurricane did make landfall there, it wouldn't be for another eight hours or so. But the Sound was already at gale conditions, forty-mile-an-hour winds, waves climbing to twenty feet and more, generating millions of pounds of forward momentum.

"*Waves are created by the transfer of energy from wind to water.*" That was the first captain he'd worked for as a teenager, who'd taught him 90 percent of what he knew about boats. "*The wind is the general, the waves its battalions of infantry, its companies of cannons. You try to fight the waves, Bucko, and you're fucking with the wind.*"

And in the Sound, the wind had a mind of its own.

It was past midnight. What ambient light there was from the stars and waning crescent moon had been shut out by the soot-gray clouds and fitful blasts of rainfall. Using a light would just make things worse, like turning on a car's high beams in fog.

The ship's handheld GPS hung around his neck, a sailor's amulet against the chaos of the sea. The thing's LED display gave off a soft glow that extended no more than a few inches into the murk. Other than that, there was nothing but darkness.

He was flying blind.

There were the big sets, the twenty-footers plowing into him every eight to ten seconds in groups of four, five, or six, leading edges of the hundred-meter-long swells barreling in from the Caribbean. But there were also smaller sets from local swells, hammering at him at faster intervals from every direction.

Even at his reduced speed, punching through the swells felt like taking a half-track over speed bumps at sixty miles an hour. Water doesn't compress. Each new impact was equivalent to running full-force into a brick wall. His head throbbed with each smack of the bow as the skiff went airborne and then fell back to slam the water again. Finn did his best to anticipate the waves.

It took every calorie of neural energy he had to stay focused on keeping the little craft afloat and stable.

Yet he couldn't stop thoughts of Pedro, Miranda, and Zacharias from tugging at his attention.

And Graciela.

He should have worked this all out sooner. She'd showed up his very first day in Fajardo. He shouldn't have been so completely taken in. He should have seen it.

Then the people you care about start dying . . .

And she was right. He cared about the old man.

How exactly did that happen? He shouldn't have let himself get so close to these people—to this innocent, generous little family. But he did. And because of it, now the old man would probably die.

The wind increased. Spasms of hot rain battered him. The waves kept coming.

An hour ticked by.

Then another.

Coming up on the end of the second hour, he approached the western tip of Vieques.

And then something strange happened.

Just as he thought he'd spotted a few lights from somewhere on the island, Finn caught sight of something low and dark closing in from directly ahead. Some kind of shapeless mass or small cloud.

Coming in fast.

He squinted into the darkness.

Smack!

Something slimy hit him in the face—and from the smell he knew instantly what it was. A school of flying fish, freaked out by the storm, skipping out of the water and running scared.

Whack!

Another flying fish struck his chest. And another, and another, then three at once, nearly knocking him over.

Good omen? Bad omen?

Only the wind knew.

A few seconds later he was through the surreal gauntlet and could again make out the distant lights bobbing on the horizon, as he made his way east along the southern shore toward Esperanza.

Tick, tick, tick.

Now that he was in the lee of the island, the sea state began to back down—not much, but enough to make a difference. He rolled the throttle to three-quarter speed, the maximum he thought the little boat could handle in this chop.

He spotted a stretch of sand he hoped was close to town, tilted the engine release handle, and gunned it full throttle. Seconds later the skiff shot up onto the beach.

As he killed the engine and lifted it out of the water it gave up a loud cough. Not good. Not good at all.

No time to worry about that now.

Finn leapt over the side, staked the small skiff down hard, and ran.

97

He came in through the back entrance, tucked in between the big cooler and dry-goods pantry. The kitchen felt empty, but since it was pitch-black in there it was impossible to tell for sure. He strained to pick up any telltale sounds. The wheeze and groans of the wind outside made a mockery of his efforts.

Couldn't hear.

Couldn't see.

You have to feel the space around things.

He reached out his senses and began to move. Step. Step. Sink. Prep space. Step. Fryer. Griddle. Step. Straining to hear. Straining to see.

Nothing.

The kitchen was empty.

His outstretched hands met up with a smooth vertical surface. The swinging door out to the dining area. He pushed it open a crack.

And was flooded by the smell of blood and death.

He let go of the door and sank to one knee, his head in his hands.

Too late.

He took a slow breath in. And out. In. And out.

The killer would still be here, waiting for him.

Dar's Glock was back in the Volvo at Puerto

Chico, along with his backpack. He hadn't wanted to risk losing them to the gale on the way over. Figured he would rely on his four-inch ring knife, which he'd strapped to his thigh, to keep him alive. Wouldn't be the first time.

He steadied himself and tensed into a crouch.

Gripped the knife in his right hand, blade forward for thrusting, and placed his left on the door.

Another room he didn't want to enter, not because he feared death but because he feared the death that was already there.

He pushed open the door and slipped out into the dining area, close to the ground.

Straining to hear, straining to see.

The wheezes and groans of the wind.

The darkness.

The smell of death.

He felt his way along the wall to his right, approaching the corner where Zacharias kept his favorite armchair.

In the glimmer of illumination provided by a single distant shore light on the Malecón, the shape of the chair slowly materialized. As he drew closer, it resolved into two shapes. The chair itself. And the old man, whose body was still seated there.

He had been sitting up, waiting for his grandchildren. As he no doubt had been doing every night that week.

The shape of the old man was as still as the chair upon which it sat.

Steady.

Finn took a slow breath in. And out.

The giant was still here, somewhere, making no sound, or at least no sound Finn could detect.

Where was he?

As his eyes began adapting to the ghostly light cast by the far-off shore lamp, he began to make out the shapes of tables. Several overturned chairs.

And something else.

A long shape, on the floor.

Ready to spring.

He slowed his breath to near stillness.

Held the ring knife ready.

"Ah," said a voice at his ear. "It's you."

Finn whirled about.

The shape in the chair moved, and a light blinked on.

"I was expecting Héctor," said the old man.

Finn turned back and looked again at the long shape on the floor.

Drenched in the melted-butter glow of the old man's battery-powered camp light, the big cop lay stretched out on his back. A polished wooden haft protruded from his throat, both hands clasped around it, as if still in the process of attempting to pull it out. His face frozen in a stare of disbelief.

Finn looked back at his employer.

The man was breathtaking with a French knife.

Now he understood why the old man hadn't been answering his phone when he'd tried to call him. He'd had it shut off. He'd been sitting in his chair, quietly waiting.

Some sixth sense had told him he needed to stay silent.

"There is blood on those hands," said Zacharias, nodding in the direction of the corpse.

Yes there is, thought Finn. *A great deal of it.*

"But not pollitos blood," the old man added. "They are alive still. Aren't they."

Finn slowly nodded. "Actually, they are."

Zacharias nodded again toward the body on the floor. "I knew who it was before he opened the door. Not as quiet as he thought."

Finn looked at the giant's body.

A Taíno, felled by a Taíno.

"I called Héctor," Zacharias continued. "When you came in the back, I thought you might be he. But his noise is rowdier than yours."

Rowdier.

Underneath all that wind, he heard me coming, thought Finn. *And here I thought I was being silent.* Eight months of practice, plus an entire career as an elite scout/sniper before that, and when it came to silence and stalking, he was still nowhere near in the old man's league.

"Do you know where they are?" said Zacharias.

"Not yet. But I know who has them."

"Vamos, then. Before Héctor arrives."

Finn stepped over the dead giant and had gotten halfway to the front when another voice spoke up from the direction of the swinging door.

"Señor Finn."

The lieutenant with the oval face and gray goatee stepped out of the doorway and into the light, holding a service revolver pointed at Finn.

98

"Señor Finn," he'd said.

The man called him "Finn."

He hadn't heard that name spoken for the past eight months.

For a moment nobody moved.

The lieutenant looked over at Zacharias. Then at Caleb Cordova's outstretched body, where his gaze lingered. He let out a sigh. Took two more steps into the room, righted one of the overturned chairs, and sat down, the Smith & Wesson still pointed in Finn's direction.

"You are the SEAL who jumped ship off the coast of San Diego, one year ago."

The room was dead silent.

"The *Abraham Lincoln,* yes?" he continued. "The same ship where Lieutenant Halsey was stationed. Where, from what I understand, the two of you first became acquainted. And some unfortunate events transpired."

Finn said nothing.

Héctor shrugged. "I have friends in the navy, Chief Finn. I ask questions. Sailors talk."

"Fin," mused Zacharias quietly, and he huffed a laugh. "Like a shark."

The police lieutenant looked at Finn. Studying him.

Finn tightened his grip on the steel ring knife's handle.

"The Americanos tell me you are a wanted man," the lieutenant continued evenly. "For what, I do not know. Nor care, if I may be frank. You know me. I have no opinion."

He gazed evenly at Finn for another long beat, then nodded at the prone figure of the dead man. "I know about this one. There have been rumors. I am sorry to say, even one of my own men was with El Rucco and their 'Empresa.' I learned of this only yesterday, after your friends were here. I apprehended him in the process of making a clandestine report." He nodded toward the body on the floor. "To this one, I suspect. That officer is now in custody."

They both looked at the inert form of Senior Detective Cordova.

"Papi tells me he trusts you. I don't. If you were on the loose, I would be compelled to go looking for you and bring you in."

Finn eyed him carefully.

If you were on the loose?

"Of course, it could take me a day or two to organize the effort. Being distracted, as we all are, by the storm."

He holstered his weapon and crossed his legs.

"Papi tells me he believes you will find his grandchildren. That you are as stubborn as he is. I say he is a crazy old man. But I don't see any point in arguing."

Finn looked at Zacharias, then back at Héctor.

"I should add," the policeman said, "before I introduced him to the interior of a jail cell, my traitorous officer took it upon himself to send out an all-points bulletin on you. This was not by my order or design, but once done it's not practical to undo."

"Understood," said Finn. He gave a single nod and strode to the front door, which opened with its joyless *ding*. As he took a step out into the storm Zacharias called to him. "Mimo."

Finn turned back.

"Bring them home."

Finn took one last look at the giant's body with the old chef's French knife jutting out of his neck. Then looked at Héctor again.

"Nico Santiago tried to stop all this, and his partner killed him. Santiago was a hero. Make sure everyone knows."

99

Finn stood on the shore and felt the wind.

The horizon looked like Judgment Day. Less than six hours until landfall, and already the cyclone's spiral outer bands were sweeping overhead, bringing a sampling of the storm's full fury.

The day he and Tómas braved the Sound in their Zodiac, the wind had been at thirty knots, the waves pitching as high as sixteen, seventeen, eighteen feet. Now Finn pegged those numbers at double.

He pulled the skiff down the sand to the ocean's edge and into the water until he was up to his thighs, then climbed in over the rail.

GPS snug around his neck.

Bowline tied around his waist.

He clipped the ignition kill switch onto the throttle and slid its little red bungee bracelet over his wrist.

Pulled the choke to prime the motor, then lowered it into the water and pulled the starter.

The engine came to life with a cough, worse than before. He ran the checklist, purely by reflex—water in the fuel tank, air in the line, timing knocked off kilter by the beating the boat took on the way over—but it was pointless.

Too late to worry now.

He rolled on the throttle and crawled into the semi-darkness. Within seconds he had left behind the faint illumination provided by the shore lights of Esperanza, the town of Hope, and plunged again into the pitch.

By the time he was fifty feet from shore he had to slow down once more to half throttle. Then quarter throttle. The constant salt spray forced him to squint to keep his eyes from watering up. Not that it mattered much. All visual information had been erased, the faint glow of the GPS a pinprick of light in a sea of pure black.

He sat in the darkness, stretching out his senses, feeling the waves with his body the way a blind man uses a cane to negotiate the hazards of the city.

The big sets were now thirty- and forty-footers, hitting every ten to fifteen seconds in their deadly clusters, the smaller sets of ten- and twelve-footers crashing over him from all sides every two to three seconds.

Pitching and rolling on the surface of insanity.

Minutes ticked by.

Surfing down the front face of one monster wave, Finn slipped the engine into neutral, then reverse, where he idled for a moment, slowing the boat just enough to prevent the nose from catching and plunging into the ink.

Then back at quarter-throttle forward.

And was hoisted up twenty, thirty, forty feet—

And plunged down the face of the next to repeat the cycle.

The seconds felt like days.

His lips were cracked and bleeding from the salt

water. Both his eyes had swollen almost completely shut.

Every few minutes, he used the fingers of one hand to pry open an eye so he could check the GPS to make sure he was still on course.

Soon he was checking every ten seconds.

Feeling the waves, lunging with his body weight to compensate when he could, nudging the throttle back and forth—neutral, give her gas, back off—his tiny skiff no more substantial than a skateboard as he slid down the backside of another thirty-five-foot monster, choking on the saltwater spray, struggling to catch a clear breath, prying open one eye to check the GPS again, now coughing worse than the boat's engine—

WOOOSH

Finn surfed down the face of yet another big roller, his timing off by just a second or maybe two—

The bow dug in—

Inertia pitched him out of the boat and into the Sound.

The engine died instantly as the little bungee cord yanked at the kill switch.

Bobbing viciously in the welter of crosscurrents, he felt for the bowline at his waist and followed it blind, feeling his way back to the edge of the boat (*Theseus in the labyrinth*, he thought), then grabbed the rail and pulled with all his waning strength to haul his drenched body up and over the rail—

And found himself in six inches of water.

Alarm bells went off in his head.

(Blue water!)

The boat had taken on too much, way too much. It was going to founder.

VAMOS! screamed the ghost of Tómas.

He splashed and stumbled his way to the back of the boat, where his fingers found what they were looking for—an old white Clorox bottle cut in half and tied into the transom of the skiff.

The old man's bail scoop.

Counting the seconds between swells, Finn began bailing.

As he threw handfuls of water back out of the boat, the crash of the waves dumped more spray back in again, mocking his efforts.

Ten endless minutes later he'd bailed out about half the remaining seawater.

Not enough.

The boat was still dangerously overweight and destabilized.

He bailed for a few more minutes, then decided it was time. He jammed the Clorox half bottle back into its notch, then grabbed the engine start cord and gave it a hard pull.

Nothing.

Pulled again.

Nothing.

And again, *hard.*

Nothing.

He stopped, panting, his eyes glued shut.

If he couldn't get Papi's little fishing boat started, the hurricane would come and dash it to splinters.

One more time.

Blind and numb, he pulled.

The little outboard caught and sputtered to life—now coughing every other cycle. Finn knew that sound, the final gasps of an engine headed for the rebuild rack. The little skiff's death rattle.

"Hold on," he croaked. Speaking to the boat, to

himself, hell, to the wind . . . *Hold on. Just a little longer.*

He gripped onto the rails, letting go between each set to bail, grabbing hold again every time he skidded down the face of another monster wave.

He could have been bailing for hours.

Weeks.

The clock in his head had lost all track of time.

Finally he pried open one eye long enough to make out a harbor light, dead ahead.

Light at the end of the tunnel.

He increased his speed, blindly aiming toward the big white lights of Puerto Chico harbor. Straining through squinted eyes to locate the cement pier jutting out from the shore.

He couldn't see a thing.

C-R-A-A-A-C-K!

The instant he felt it, he realized his mistake.

Not the light at the end of the tunnel.

That wasn't the harbor lights he'd seen—it was a light marking the shallow coral reef at the harbor's northwest edge.

The lights warning mariners to stay away.

As the boat slammed into the reef, Finn was flung forward, out of the craft and into the crashing surf.

He surfaced and whipped around on instinct, just in time to see the skiff's hull hurtling toward him, lifted off the lip of the reef and then driven forward by another massive wave. He lurched to the side as the wave's fist slammed the boat back down onto the reef and smashed it into driftwood.

100

He lay on his back, unable to move. The rain lashed at his face as the surf boomed up around him.

Five minutes went by.

Ten.

Hooyah, cabrón.

Finn rolled over and got up as far as his hands and knees. Looked around, searching for lights. There. He had washed up about a hundred yards north of the marina, an undeveloped stretch of coastline bordering a forested area at the foot of his lookout hill.

He crawled half a dozen yards inland, just enough to reach cover, then collapsed on his side and rested as he tried to think through his situation.

West Texas had shown his picture to the dockmaster here. The man had talked with him face-to-face. He couldn't have failed to recognize him from the photo.

Plus, there was an island-wide APB out on him.

He had to get to the Volvo without anyone seeing him.

On his way out, he'd parked as far from the wharf as possible, up on a side street, and slipped down to the docks without being seen.

He had to get out the same way.

He took a series of long, slow breaths, then got back up on all fours, and from there up into a crouch.

Every time he moved, his body felt like a sack filled with broken glass.

Hugging the tree line, he began to walk. It was nearly a thousand yards to the car, over half a mile. The thinking part of his brain kept telling him he wasn't going to make it, not even halfway, not even a quarter of the way. But he knew how to switch that voice off.

Instead, he listened to his training.

His training told him, There is no thousand yards.

There is just this step.

And this one.

And this.

He didn't know how long it took, but it felt longer than the five and a half days of Hell Week. His mind stopped trying to keep track of time and sequence, and downshifted into a random series of freeze-frames.

He began to walk—

He was walking—

And then he was there.

He found the key where he'd stashed it, jammed in behind the license plate.

Once in the driver's seat he allowed himself one full minute of rest.

Where could she be holding them?

Pier 9, along with her shipment of merchandise?

It was the only target he could come up with.

He turned the key, put the car in gear, and drove.

101

Monica sat in her hotel room, oblivious to the outer bands of the hurricane raging outside her window, aware only of the equally ferocious maelstrom raging in her brain.

She was way past being worried and had crossed over into frantic.

For hours now she had alternated between being convinced Dar had somehow been set up by Finn, probably ambushed, possibly killed, and falling back on the simpler explanation, which was that he'd gotten stuck somewhere in the worsening storm—stuck, literally, in one of this place's abundant mudslides or on some washed-out road. Or gotten lost, his cellphone battery run down and nowhere to charge it.

Either way, she had no idea what to do about it.

She'd searched on foot—pointlessly, she was sure—and scoured half of Old San Juan. Called the car rental place three times. Checked in with the front desk at least half a dozen times. Called or tried to call everyone she had visited on her Wednesday tour by car around the island. And come up empty.

She reached over to the hotel phone to check in with the front desk again. Just as she laid her hand on the thing it rang, making her jump.

She snatched up the handset.

"Yes?"

"Lieutenant?" said the voice.

It was Rivera—no.

Wait.

Careful.

That definitely *sounded* like Agent Rivera's elegantly clipped Puerto Rican accent. But the dockmaster's voice on her phone the day before had fooled her, too.

"What did I tell you," she said, "the first time we met?"

There was a brief silence. Then: "Sorry?"

"What did I tell you, the first time we met?" she repeated. Then added, "Humor me."

After another pause the voice said, "That I should think of you as the Royal Mounted Police. Because you always get your man. And that you and the big guy weren't partners."

She took a breath and relaxed.

"Sorry. And thanks. Just wanted to make sure it was really you."

"Oh, it's really me," said Rivera. "And we just got a fix on Not-Your-Partner's car. A twenty-minute walk from where you are right now. If you don't mind a little weather."

102

His plan had been to shimmy up each pole and spray every one of the five security cameras with the brown spray paint. On the monitors, it would just look like they'd all gotten dirtied up and wouldn't draw much attention.

But that tactic was dubious in the driving rain.

And he didn't have time.

The hell with it.

After cutting his way through the barbed-wire perimeter with the wire cutters, he found the camera system's main feed and clipped it. The guy in the monitor station would notice, sooner or later, but Finn figured that with the full force of the hurricane just hours way, response time might be compromised.

Thursday night there had been close to two hundred containers there. Some had since shipped out, but there were still over a hundred.

He crouched down around the corner of the first container and waited.

A strange light seeped into the sky as dawn broke, argon purple.

The wind threw rivers of rain in all directions.

After a few minutes, he spotted the Kia hatchback

coming around. As it passed in front of the container he stepped out, aimed two-handed, and shot out both left tires.

The Kia skewed left and screeched to a halt, tilted halfway over on its left side.

He yanked open the passenger's side front door and stuck the Glock in the first guard's face.

"¡Sal! ¡Sal!" *Get out!*

The two struggled their way out of the vehicle. Finn got them down on the asphalt, zip-tied their hands behind them, took their keys and sidearms, then got them back into the vehicle, bound and gagged, stuffed on their sides on the front and backseats. Not too comfy. But they would survive.

He began walking through the aisles, not knowing what he was looking for but trusting that he'd recognize it when he saw it.

About halfway through the first row, he noticed that three containers were air-conditioning units marked SENSITIVE MATERIALS. Unlike the double heavy-duty cargo doors on the other containers, these were sealed with single steel "man doors," outfitted with standard lever locks.

Holding his flash in his teeth, Finn pulled the key ring he'd taken from one of the guards, sorted through them, and found one that fitted the door. The door opened outward—

And he was hit by a stench he hadn't expected.

Not death.

Not blood.

Shit.

Urine.

Fear.

In a crouch, he stepped cautiously over the sill and into the dark space.

Took the flash from his teeth and shone it directly in front of him.

At first, he didn't understand what he was seeing. Lumps, irregular shapes. Dozens of them.

Then, movement.

A face upturned.

It was a child.

Not Pedro. Not Miranda.

A little girl he'd never seen before.

And someone next to her, another little girl. And next to her, a boy. And another.

He swept the flash around the space.

Dozens of them.

More than a hundred.

El cargamento.

Not drugs.

El Rucco's business, her "merchandise," was *children.*

Finn felt a surge of emotion explode through him, a feeling foreign to him yet so vivid that it took no time at all to identify.

White-hot fury.

These kids had been stolen from their homes, from their parents, locked up inside this hell-hole for days, for who knew how long, surrounded by nothing but their worst nightmares about what might happen to them next. He couldn't begin to imagine the terror they'd felt, sitting there swallowed up in the pitch-black darkness.

The blind fear.

Crime, he could understand. Murder, even. But trafficking *children*?

It was beyond his comprehension.

The north's endless appetite for the exotic south . . .

He took a long, slow breath, and forced himself to focus.

Bring them home.

Shining his flash on child after child, murmuring assurances in Spanish words he didn't know if they understood and didn't know if he believed himself, he searched the entire container.

The two faces he was looking for were not among them.

If they'd been here at all, they weren't here now.

"¡Espera aquí!" he said. *Wait here!*

He stepped back out into the rain and ran to the second container. Tried the same key, and it worked—all three must have been keyed together.

The second container was empty.

He tried the third, and again found himself staring into a sea of terrified young faces.

Again, none were Pedro or Miranda.

El Rucco had taken them somewhere else.

Where?

And what could he do to take care of these two-hundred-plus that were here right now?

As he stepped out of the third container he heard a voice call out his name for the second time that day:

"FREEZE, CHIEF FINN!"

103

Before even hanging up the hotel phone she was out the door.

Dawn was just breaking when she pulled out onto the street—but it was like no dawn she'd ever seen before. An intense purple stain filled the sky. Along the far southeast horizon, which would normally be brightening from the rising sun, there stretched a ribbon of deep reddish black, the color of old blood.

It was a ten-minute drive. The streets were empty. Monica made it in three.

She skidded into the parking lot at pier 10 and pulled to a stop at Dar's Volvo.

Which was empty.

The rain was strong but intermittent, the wind coming in gusts that made it difficult to stand upright. She clambered up onto the Volvo's hood, standing low and bent-kneed to withstand the force of the growing storm, and scanned her perimeter. Nothing. No one.

A blast of wind nearly blew her off the car.

Wait.

She saw some sort of movement, out toward the end of the pier next door. Caught a brief glimpse of someone moving out from behind one huge shipping container and disappearing behind another.

Not Dar. Not big and bulky enough.

It looked an awful lot like the figure in the CCTV still.

The one buying the two snorkels.

"Oh, hell yeah," she said.

She jumped down and took off at a measured run, careful not to slip on the slick asphalt surface.

It was about a football field and a half from the top of the pier to the end, where the rows of containers were arrayed. She ran three-quarters of the way to where she'd seen movement, then slowed, moving cautiously, service weapon drawn.

And caught up to the figure just as he emerged from the third of three containers with air-conditioning units.

She stepped out, weapon out in front in the classic two-handed stance, and yelled, "FREEZE, CHIEF FINN!"

He stopped and looked up at her. She got a good look at his face—and in that purple rash of dawn she saw a flash of something she almost couldn't describe, an expression of horror mingled with unspeakable grief.

She trained her weapon on him. "Don't move!"

He didn't.

"Down on the ground," she said.

He made no move to comply.

"Take care of them," he said. "I have to go."

"Don't move, goddammit!"

He was studying her, as if weighing what she would do next.

"I will shoot you!"

He took a step to the side, away from the container, then another.

She fired off a single warning shot to show she meant it. It went wide by a good two feet. Zinged and ricocheted.

And in the next instant she heard an eerie sound arise from within the container, like a slow, high-pitched siren. Multiple sirens; an entire chorus of them. It took her a moment to understand what she was hearing. It was wailing voices. Dozens of them.

The voices of children.

"Jesus," she said, her voice a hoarse whisper that the moaning wind seemed to mock.

Jeee-sussss-jeee-sussss-jeee-sussss . . .

"What did you do?" she shouted at him. *"What did you do?"*

He didn't move. Made no reply.

Her weapon trained on him, she stepped over to the container door and looked inside.

Darkness.

She switched her weapon to one hand, still trained on him, flicked on her flashlight with the other, and peered inside.

And saw.

Her stomach convulsed—

And she realized her mistake.

She knew how lightning-fast Finn was. She'd seen him move before, seen him strike like a diamondback. That morning on the *Lincoln,* the morning he saved her life, he'd moved so fast it had seemed like a magic trick. In poking her head inside that container she'd let her guard down, given him a window, only split seconds, but time enough to close the distance and overpower her—

She whirled around and whipped her weapon

out in front of her, two-handed, finger squeezing, squeezing—

He hadn't moved.

He just stood there, looking at the open door, that map of grief and horror still on his face.

She motioned him farther away from the container with the barrel of her gun. "You're under arrest, Chief. Down on the ground."

He didn't move. Instead, he called out a phone number, then repeated it. "Name's Lucy Santiago. Call her. She's a pediatric surgeon, works with families of crime victims. She'll know what to do. If you can't get through, go find her. She lives three blocks away."

"Down on the ground, Chief!"

"Your boyfriend is in a house at the end of Route 731. Old wood-frame farmhouse. Careful, when you retrieve him. He's under orders to kill you, after he kills me."

A thousand questions screamed through Monica's mind and she struggled to sort them out. Dar? Under orders to kill *her*?

What in God's name was he talking about?

"I have to go," he said, and he took a step back.

"I will shoot you!" she shouted. "I am not fucking around!"

He turned to run.

She shot him.

104

Special Investigations Agent Toño Rivera sat on the edge of his crappy little particleboard desk, staring out the window at the vivid purple sky and watching the rain batter the building like random broadsides fired off by a squadron of psychopaths.

This wasn't, strictly speaking, *his* office. His actual office in the big Department of Public Safety building downtown was a primo piece of government real estate, a place that felt like one the job deserved. That desk, he'd picked out himself. Hardwood and leather. A desk that meant business.

But it wasn't close enough to the current action.

He'd gotten the Zone 1 precinct to give him this little cubby on loan, so he could stay right on top of things at the docks. After Sunday and the thing with Santiago and the deputy director, which was a disaster to the cause.

"No," he repeated wearily into the phone. "We don't 'wait out the storm.' The business we're in doesn't take coffee breaks."

He listened to his associate, who didn't seem capable of grasping that he was here to see this thing through, circumstances be damned.

"Listen, you can tell them I said—"

A sound at his back stopped him mid-sentence.

Chuck-chuck.

The unmistakable mating call of the Glock 17, chambering a round.

"I'll call you back," he said. He disconnected the call and slowly put the phone down on the desk behind him, then stood and turned.

A man stood in his doorway.

Toño immediately noticed three things.

One, this was the same man in the grainy photos, the war criminal the Americanos were looking for. *Alleged,* he reminded himself.

Two, the barrel of the Glock the man held pointed at his chest was trembling. Which didn't exactly bathe him in a warm glow of reassurance.

And three, the man himself didn't look so good.

"You don't look so good," he said.

"You know who I am?"

In fact, he looked like he was in pretty terrible shape. "Yes, Marlin, I know who you are. More or less."

More less than more, actually. "Marlin Pike," the Feeb had called him, noting it was just an alias. For whatever his reasons, the Feeb hadn't deigned to tell him the guy's actual name.

"I'll make you a deal," said the man.

"A deal? Oh, boy. Can't wait."

"I'll give up the gun. Let you hand me over to the Americanos."

"If?"

"I need you to help me do something first."

He looked like he was on the verge of passing out. Wait—had he been . . . *shot*?

"You all right, Marlin? You really look like you need to sit down."

"I'll live," the man replied.

"Well that's a relief."

The gun trembled. The wind howled. A wall of rain crashed against the window.

Marlin Pike said nothing.

Toño sighed. "Okay, I'll bite. Help you do what."

"What do you know about El Rucco?"

Toño stiffened. Now, *that* was unexpected. Never mind all the other questions—like, how did this guy find him? How did he even know who he was? What did he want with Toño, some kind of desperate hostage plan? If he had been shot, how bad was the wound, and who shot him?—no, more important than all of those was this one: What the living fuck did the Americanos' fugitive and alleged war criminal have to do with El Rucco?

"What makes you think I know anything at all?" he said.

"You're SIB. Organized crime. Terrorism. And I saw you, the other night, at pier nine."

"Ah. Of course."

A gust of wind screamed. He felt the window behind him shudder.

Buy time.

"Why don't you tell me what it is you want?"

In reply, Marlin Pike just waggled the gun barrel. *Start talking.*

It felt like a test, only Toño didn't know which answers would earn him a pass. Though he had a pretty good idea what would happen to him if he got it wrong.

"Let's do this. I'll tell you what I *don't* know. I know the crime families leave his operation alone, but I don't know why. I know he has a major shipment going out soon from one of the piers, but I don't know exactly when or where. I know—"

"Shipment?"

"Drugs. Try to keep up, Marlin."

Another waggle of the Glock. *Go on.*

"I know he has a base of operations somewhere in Puerto Rico where he makes his transfers of goods, but I don't know where it is. And trust me, I've looked. His headquarters is invisible. *He* is invisible."

The Glock faltered for a moment as the man visibly rested his weight against the doorframe. This guy wasn't lasting upright much longer.

"Forgive my rudeness, but you look like shit, señor," he observed.

"What else," the man said.

Toño took a long look at the man and sighed. "You said, you saw me at the dock. For how long?"

"Long enough."

"Ah," he said again. "So, at this point you must be wondering, Am I looking to apprehend this drug lord? Or am I working for him myself?"

The two looked at each other for a long beat. The man squinted at him, and Toño had the distinctly uncomfortable sense of his thoughts being scrutinized. Like a psychic MRI.

"Not. Drugs," the man said.

"I don't follow. What are you—"

"La Empresa. El cargamento. El Rucco's big shipment. It's not drugs, Rivera. It's children. They're trafficking kids. That's their 'enterprise.'"

Toño stared at the man for a few long seconds more as his meaning sunk in. Then his knees buckled and he sank down into his chair.

"Dios mío," he murmured.

The man who wasn't really Marlin Pike nodded to himself, then stepped all the way into the room and collapsed into the empty chair across from him. Put the Glock on the desk and slid it over.

Evidently Toño had just passed the test. And without saying a thing.

"That's why the crime families won't have anything to do with La Empresa," the wounded man said. "There are lines they won't cross."

"*Children,*" Toño murmured. He looked down at the desk and carefully picked up the Glock. Looked it over. Then set it down again.

"Tell me now, Señor Pike. What else do you know?"

The man heaved a sigh, whether of capitulation or exhaustion he couldn't tell.

"I know who El Rucco is," he said. "And I know where she is right now."

Toño put both hands on the crappy desktop and leaned forward, his eyes narrowing.

"'*She*'?"

105

Despite the urge to chase after the wounded SEAL, Monica stayed where she was on the pier, going back and forth between the two shipping containers, doing her best to reassure the huddled masses of children that they were going to be okay, that they were safe, that she was there to help.

She put a call in to the number he'd given her. Lucy Santiago picked up on the second ring. Monica hurriedly introduced herself and stammered through a summary of the situation. She heard a sharp gasp on the other end when she explained that the containers were packed with what appeared to be shipments of kidnapped children, but otherwise Lucy was all business.

"Are you at pier nine right now?"

"I am. With maybe two hundred terrified kids. Starving, probably."

And, she hardly needed to add, traumatized beyond imagination.

"Stay there," said Lucy. "We need to get those kids somewhere safe before the storm hits."

They spent a few hurried minutes discussing details, and Lucy hung up with the promise that she would be there within fifteen minutes, with more help not far behind.

Monica disconnected from the call and went back to reassuring the children as best she could. But her mind was elsewhere.

Still wondering about the shot she'd taken.

The SEAL had been no more than five yards away when she squeezed the trigger. Yet she'd hit him in the shoulder blade.

She'd seen the Glock stuffed into his waistband. The scenario called for a kill shot, and she'd known it.

Did she simply miss?

Who was she kidding. Monica had grown up on a West Texas ranch and knew her way around guns before she was old enough for braces. She never missed.

As she spoke soothing words to the terrified children, she kept replaying the look on Finn's face as he emerged from the container. That map of horror and grief.

She tried to tell herself not to listen to her gut.

But right now it was screaming at her.

How could the man behind that face have possibly killed those kids in Mukalla?

106

He was bluffing, of course, when he said he knew where El Rucco was.

He had no idea.

All he knew was that he couldn't go after her by himself.

That last punishing trip across the Sound had nearly killed him. After taking a 9mm round in the back, he was now going into full-blown shock. He didn't know exactly where the bullet had struck him, or how much damage it had done, or whether he'd survive the next few hours.

But if he did, he'd need help.

They took Rivera's car, a vintage two-tone Crown Vic, island green over white. He told the other man to drive them east on the highway, toward the coast, and that he would say more when they got close.

The truth was, he just couldn't think of anywhere else to go.

The highway was nearly deserted. It was far too late to evacuate. Far too late for anything.

"You need medical attention, amigo," said Rivera.

"No time. Drive."

Rivera drove.

Finn collapsed into the death seat. Closed his eyes. And started with where it all began.

In the Sound.

What did they see?

Had to be some kind of drug-running operation, that had been his guess. But he'd been wrong. Those hoofbeats weren't horses, after all. They were zebras. Not drugs. Humans. They were kidnapping children, maybe from other countries, other islands, other possessions. Maybe snatched off cruise ships, like Nico Santiago's sister. And shipping them up to the United States to sell for wealthy Americanos' entertainment.

He'd seen the shipments himself. Three containers' worth.

Except one of the three was empty.

Why?

Because they were still waiting for one more large shipment from the Venezuelans. Who had been waiting for the Coast Guard to stop searching for two missing children—and now wanted to wait out the storm. Probably harbored somewhere on the southern coast of Haiti or the Dominican Republic.

If we can't resolve within 24 hrs I will go down and offload the cargo myself.

But what kind of lunatic commandeers a seagoing vessel straight into the path of a hurricane?

Or was that the right question?

Reframe.

Assuming you *were* commandeering a vessel straight through a hurricane, one that could collect as many as a hundred children or more and bring them back, what kind of vessel would it take?

He felt his consciousness starting to slip away.

Hold on. Bail, and hold on.

He pulled his thoughts back into focus.

What had Rivera said?

I know he has a base of operations somewhere . . . his headquarters is invisible.

Where was it?

Finn rolled back through his mental footage of the past week—the docks, Old San Juan, the abandoned farmhouse, Humacao, Fajardo, Esperanza, the beach—

Stop. Rewind.

Esperanza.

The Paper Mill.

Hugo's ancient grandmother sitting in her old rocker, muttering nonsense.

La Bestia.

The old woman who spent years up on her widow's walk, gazing out at the distant Caribbean.

The beast.

A man-eating whale, the priest told him. The Devil's Ride. Who lives deep in the Devil's Ditch. With an entourage of demons with pitchforks.

That could be a description of men in wet suits with spearguns.

And it all clicked.

Not a whale.

"A halibut," he mumbled.

Rivera threw him a worried glance.

"Not delirious," Finn said. "Just thinking out loud."

Hold on, just a little longer.

Rivera almost had it right. El Rucco's base of operations wasn't invisible.

It was just underwater.

—

It was called Project 877. A class of attack submarines, built by the Soviet Union back in the eighties, mainly for use in shallow coastal waters. NATO code-named Kilo, Soviet designation "Paltus." The Russian word for "halibut."

Finn knew about these. Every student of submarine warfare knew about them.

Of the thirty-one known units completed and put into operation, ten were sold to India, three to Iran, two each to China and Algeria, one each to Poland and Romania. The remaining twelve went to Russia. Most had long been decommissioned.

There was nothing remarkable about any of that. Any number of other models of submarine had been designed, built, and deployed by nations all over the world. What made Finn think of Project 877 in particular was one unique bit of their history.

One was missing.

Of the dozen sold to Russia, one had since been listed as "unaccounted for." There were lingering suspicions that it had gone to Cuba.

And Cuba could have sold it.

Say, to an ambitious politician with a booming business plan.

The Sound was shallow, compared to the two oceans it connected, but deep enough for a sub to transit without ever being observed.

Except that the Paltus was a diesel-electric hybrid. It ran on batteries, which allowed it to run in silent mode, making it practically undetectable—but recharging the battery required running its diesel generator. And that required oxygen.

Which meant that, periodically, it needed to surface. To breathe.

Just like a whale.

That was what Pedro and Miranda saw.

That's where they were now.

He opened his eyes.

"You're bleeding all over my car, mi amigo," said Rivera.

"Puerto Chico," said Finn. "The marina."

"El Rucco is in Puerto Chico? Right now?"

"No," said Finn. "But to get to her, we need a crew."

And he explained what he wanted them to do.

107

They pulled into the parking lot and walked through the downpour, down a paved path to the dockmaster's office. When they reached the door, Finn turned to Rivera.

"Let me talk to him for a moment. Alone."

"You want me to wait outside? In this?"

"Stay in the lee of the building. Five minutes."

He entered the cramped space, shut the door, and leaned his weight back against the jamb.

The dockmaster was sitting in a rolling chair at a creaky metal desk by the window, watching the harbor and waiting out the storm. He looked around when Finn entered. Didn't look surprised. Didn't look like he was ever surprised.

"Hola," said Finn.

"Hola yourself. You look like hell, brother."

"I've been worse." Finn nodded at the man's leg. "'Nam?"

"Patrol Boat, Riverine, Mekong Delta, June of '71. Should've swerved. Pass-in-review March of '69," he added. He nodded back at Finn. "Iraq?"

"BUD/S class 251, March '04, then straight into Fallujah that fall." He took a few steps and put out his hand. "Chief Finn."

"Derek Quinteros." The dockmaster shook his hand. Glanced out the window at Agent Rivera, standing in the driving rain. Back at Finn. Who had now taken his place back at the door again. "Was an officer in here looking for you, couple days ago. Emma Something. Told her I hadn't seen you, but I'd keep an eye out."

Finn nodded once. *Thanks for that.*

"What'd you do?"

"They say I wiped out a village of non-combatants. Also killed a few of my own teammates. And my lieutenant." Finn tipped his head toward Rivera, who looked like an unreasonably cheerful house cat drowning in a car wash. "He's from the cops. Taking me in."

"And what do you say?"

"I—" Finn swayed and nearly toppled over.

The old dockmaster lifted one foot and used it to shove an empty metal chair over toward the door.

"Sit your ass in the chair, son, and tell me what you're doing here."

Finn sat and put his head down for a moment. When the dizziness passed, he looked up again. "You heard about the two missing kids from Vieques. The guy they call El Rucco has them, out there"—he nodded out at the Sound—"on a Russian-made sub, heading south right now. Though he's not a guy, he's Graciela Dominguez. The mayor of Ceiba. And her business isn't drugs, it's trafficking children. My cop friend and I want to go get her."

The dockmaster took all this in without any change of expression. When Finn was finished, he took a long breath, then said, "That right there is some of the craziest shit I ever heard." He looked out the window, then back at Finn.

"Graciela Dominguez?"

Finn nodded.

The man shook his head. "Politicians." He paused, then said, "What do you need me to do?"

Five minutes later the three of them stood together out on the dock by a line of tightly moored boats. Finn nodded at the one with the orange radar tower.

The *Cuttyhunk,* poised to launch its rescue efforts in the aftermath.

If there was a boat anywhere on the entire coast of Puerto Rico that could chase down a sub in a hurricane, it was this one. Made to take a complete rollover. Virtually unsinkable.

"Captain Ahab?" Finn heard Rivera say to the dockmaster. "Meet your *Pequod.*"

The edges of his vision darkened.

"Can you pilot that thing?" Rivera's voice.

And that was the last thing he remembered before his face hit the concrete.

108

Thunder. Lightning, and more thunder.

Rain pelts the highway far below as it curls its way through the forests of broadleaf maples and Oregon evergreens.

He can see the lone car creeping along, going probably seventy or more, but from his perspective up in the clouds it resembles a black bug trundling along a seam in a worn bedroom carpet, its high beams stretched out like feelers, finding its way through the slow twists and turns.

Driving in the rain, driving in the rain . . .

At a distance, from the other direction, an eighteen-wheeler.

Driving in the rain, driving in the rain . . .

No! he cries out. *Stop! Look out!* But the cries make no sound in his airless space. He is looking through a plate-glass wall at a scene he can't touch. The collision is coming, and there's nothing he can do to stop it.

Driving in the rain, driving in the rain . . .

He cries and he screams and he begs, but the clouds swallow up his voice, and he is powerless to do anything but watch as the two vehicles draw closer and closer—

Driving in the—

There is a sudden brilliant flash of light, answered in the next instant by an earth-shattering clap of thunder.

As if someone hit a switch, the storm vanishes.

He blinks in disbelief, then blinks again, staring at the transformed scene below.

No rain. No thunder, no lightning. There is the car, trundling along, winding its way through the divots in the carpet of evergreens.

There is no truck.

click click click click

Finn feels himself descending, drifting down until he is in front of the car, level with its headlights as it drives on, heedless. There is a man behind the wheel, an old flip phone pressed to his ear. Finn sees him nodding, his mouth moving as he lowers the phone and speaks a few words to the figure sitting next to him

click click click click

he cannot see the two clearly but he can see their mouths, see their lips moving, and he reads the words

There's been an accident

the man is saying

Ray's been shot, we have to go back

click click click click

and the woman's lips move

keep going

but we have to—

no, just keep going . . .

The car and its two passengers fade to black, and now he's standing on a dark street corner, half hidden by a building, hearing the *click click click click* of heels echoing through the rain-soaked streets, watching the woman with the aquiline profile striding purposefully through her charade, luring him into her web of deception.

And he knows what it was about Graciela Dominguez's face that so struck him from the first, that captivated him and drew him in, that elusive quality, the sharpness of features, the glitter in the eyes . . . it was the look of a person convinced beyond any possibility of question that she is right, that her cause, her mission, justifies any course of action, no matter how cruel. The true believer.

It was the look of insanity.

It was evil.

And he recognizes it, because he has seen that look before.

He recognizes it, because all at once he remembers his mother's face.

Light switch.

He was lying flat, facedown.

Hospital bed?

No. He could smell the salt air, feel the familiar pitch and roll of the ocean beneath him. He hoisted himself over onto his right side, then pushed up on all fours, wincing. What had they done to his back? It was screaming with pain.

He remembered.

The shipping container. The children. *Freeze, Chief Finn!* Shot in the back by West Texas. Struggling through the sodden streets of Old San Juan. Snaking through the nearly deserted police precinct building. Finding the office that went with the single lighted window. Toño Rivera. Derek Quinteros, the dockmaster. The *Cuttyhunk*.

He looked up and saw an expanse of brilliant blue sky. The morning sun shone bright. A gentle breeze caressed his face.

The storm was *gone*?

He was still dreaming.

Had to be.

The hurricane had vanished.

He blinked, then blinked again. Staggered to his feet and grabbed onto the steel rail. Looked out at the horizon and saw a thick blanket of roiling crimson-black hurtling in their direction.

He wasn't dreaming.

They were in the eye of the hurricane.

109

"You're still with us."

He looked around and saw Agent Rivera standing in the door of the bridge.

"If that had been a high-speed round, I expect you'd be quite dead. As it was, it looks like the thing struck your scapula, then went oblique and lodged in the scapular ridge. I stopped the bleeding and patched the wound. That's about all I could do. We're probably better off just leaving the thing in there."

Finn stared at the red-black horizon.

"Whoever shot you," the agent added, "apparently they weren't using a sniper rifle."

"How long have we been in the eye?" Finn ignored the man's implicit question. Who shot him, at least for now, would remain Finn's business.

"Less than a minute. You slept through a Cat Three eyewall, mi amigo. Your buddy is a hell of a pilot."

Finn stared out at the sky and the sunny waves.

Rivera stared with him. "Strangest damn thing I ever saw. It was like someone flipped a light switch."

Like a light switch.

Yes, Finn had seen it, too.

"How long have we got?"

"The eye is tight, maybe ten miles across. Moving at twenty-two, twenty-three knots. And we're already a few minutes in."

Which meant they had no more than twenty minutes before the far side of the eyewall crashed into them and plunged them back into the hurricane's full force.

The eyewall, as they both knew, contained the storm's most furious winds.

"Yes, that's the bad part. Here's the good part," said Rivera. "We've got a blip on the radar, about four miles dead ahead."

Finn's breath caught in his chest.

This was amazing.

Rivera and the dockmaster had been shooting in the dark. The cutter's onboard radar was nearly useless when it came to locating vessels underwater. The only way the sub would show up on their screen was if it had surfaced to recharge its batteries.

Which maybe, possibly, gave them a shot.

Rivera pointed at a spot on the horizon and handed Finn a set of binoculars, then brought up a pair of his own. "No visual fix yet."

No, there wouldn't be. The curvature of the earth would cut off their view at about three miles. The radar gave them a general fix, but not specific enough to get close. And certainly not before the eye closed on them. The field of possibilities was too vast. They needed a visual.

Give us a visual, thought Finn. *Something. Anything.*

110

The place stank of cooked cabbage, diesel fuel, and sweat. Especially sweat. They had been brought in through the top, down a narrow ladder, and through a maze of tight little metal corridors leading to the room where they were now being held, a tiny barracks-type chamber filled with triple bunk beds barely deep enough for them to fit into, and they were kids.

On their way in they'd passed by shelves and compartments crammed with all kinds of equipment, some of it baffling and most of it terrifying. An axe (*an axe on a submarine?*); a flare gun; half a dozen spearguns (*the same ones he and Miranda had seen that day, in the Sound?*); what looked like inflatable rafts and oxygen tanks. He knew it was probably all emergency supplies, designed to save lives, but somehow it all just made him feel more certain that the two of them were going to die here.

They weren't alone in their prison cell. Their captors had put a man in there with them, who was now sitting in one of the room's two metal chairs, reading a magazine and muttering curses under his breath in a language Pedro didn't understand.

Suddenly there was a commotion. Chatter in the corridor outside their room, loud and urgent.

Their guard got up and opened the door to ask what was going on. Pedro caught a single Spanish word: "guardacostas." Somewhere out there in the storm, they must have seen a Coast Guard ship, and they didn't sound happy about it.

Pedro sat up and looked over at Miranda. She was sitting up, too. She looked fierce. The truck driver's cousin may have betrayed them to the police, but whatever medicine she'd given his sister, it had worked. She looked strong again. Like herself.

He heard receding footsteps. It sounded like the person their guard was talking to had left. The guard stood there by himself, just outside the open door, swearing under his breath.

This was it. The moment. Their chance. And the only one they'd get, Pedro was sure of it.

He had to *do* something.

But what?

What would Mimo do, if he were here?

He tried to think, but no brilliant ideas came. He was terrified. The harder he tried to think, the more his mind was a blank.

And then, through the stink of sweat and unwashed bedclothes and diesel fumes, he caught the scent of something that couldn't be real, something impossible.

Mangoes.

Woodsmoke.

Cinnamon.

As real as the skin on his fingertips.

And he heard a voice whisper, right in his ear.

Be brave, tesoro.

Be brave.

I can't! he thought, and then answered himself: *You have to.*

He looked at the guard, still standing at the open door and muttering his strange curses, then at Miranda. He gave a nod toward the open door.

She looked at the door, then stared back at Pedro, her eyes wide.

Pedro nodded.

They both stood—silently, like Mimo—and took a few soundless steps toward the guard—

And then Pedro bolted out the door, Miranda a flicker behind him.

The guard shouted and grabbed at them—

But they were already darting through the corridors, the guard after them, and as they came to the ladder leading up to the top deck Pedro grabbed the flare gun he'd seen and they both scrambled up the ladder and out through the open hatch.

Three men and a woman stood on the deck.

As the two kids burst out onto the deck they turned in unison—

The woman shouted—

Pedro pointed the gun straight up into the air and fired—

And then, holding hands, they both turned, ran to the very end of the flat deck—

And jumped off into the ocean.

111

"There!"

They both saw it—the red rocket trail of a flare shooting up from the horizon about ten degrees to their left and cutting a high arc before plummeting into the ocean again.

He swung his binoculars toward the spot where the flare had emerged—and now the beast itself came into view.

The cutter was traveling at near its top speed of thirty knots, nearly twice that of the sub. They were gaining fast.

He saw two figures running along the deck.

Pedro and Miranda.

They reached the end of the deck and leaped into the waves.

"*Dios mío*," Rivera whispered, his own binos also trained on the sub.

In the hurricane's eye, the sky had abruptly cleared, the air gone eerily calm—but not the water. Freed from the cyclonic shackles of the wind, the waves still leapt and tumbled and crashed into one another.

The children had jumped off into a watery mayhem.

"Tell Captain Ahab to hold us on station about two hundred meters off, and don't take your eye off that sub," Finn said as he stripped down to his boxers.

Rivera stared at him.

"I know," said Finn. *But if I don't do this, they're gone.*

He grabbed a coil of line, cut off a ten-foot length, and tied it once around his waist, leaving both ends trailing a good three feet. Then tied off a quick knot at either end for handgrips.

He knew these two, knew their capacity. They were both exceptional swimmers. But who knew what they'd been through in the past five days, or what condition they were in?

He climbed onto the outer railing of the bridge, got a visual on the kids, and dove.

His right arm was useless, incapacitated by the gunshot wound. He stroked as best as he could with his left, relying on powerful kicks to drive him forward.

The kids were a good 150 meters away.

After about a minute he had covered eighty meters. The children had made at least fifty.

It took the three of them only seconds to close the gap.

"Grab the rope!" he shouted as he made a fast turn.

They both grabbed an end, now all three of them kicking and one-arming it, shooting through the water together like a trio of Blue Angels in an air show being reflected on the ocean's surface.

The big Coast Guard cutter was seventy meters off. Sixty. Fifty.

And then Finn heard it.

Sssssnap! CRACK. *Sssssnap!* CRACK.

High-speed rounds, the *crack* of the report reaching their ears only after the *snap!* of the bullet breaking the sound barrier as it hurtled past.

Chinese-made AK-47s, from the sound of it. Not the most accurate weapons in the world, but plenty good at killing when they hit you.

"Dive!"

They dove in unison.

Not that that would save them. Water wouldn't do much to slow the trajectory of a steel-jacketed bullet traveling at the speed of a fighter jet and more than twice the speed of sound.

Still, it would make them harder to aim at.

Cords of white zipped past about ten meters to his right—the traces of missed bullets.

Ten meters was not far off.

Pedro and Miranda had let go of the rope once they submerged. They all swam hard.

They had to be close to the boat, but Finn couldn't see it. They were all running out of air. He streamed upward, knowing they would follow.

He broke the surface and looked dead ahead, then frantically right and left.

The patrol boat was gone.

Impossible! Where could—

"Here!" Agent Rivera's shout came from directly behind him.

Smart. He'd had the dockmaster swing the cutter around and put its metal hull between them and the bullets.

Rivera threw down a big rope ladder over the side rail and first Miranda, then Pedro scrambled up and over the steel rail and onto the boat's deck.

Finn grabbed hold of the ladder with his left hand

and hung there, too whipped to climb all the way up and over.

The dockmaster had now veered them left, passing the sub on its port side and breaking off to follow the Vieques coastline.

The sub attempted to follow, but the faster patrol boat had pulled away to the point where the AKs had become next to useless.

Home free.

BOOM!

A sound like a cannon. Which was exactly what it was. Finn knew the sound. He'd fired one of these monsters himself in training, dozens of times.

Carl Gustaf 84mm shoulder-fired recoilless antitank rifle.

A second later he heard the high-explosive round detonate at the water's surface about forty meters off starboard. Way too close.

"Get them below!" he shouted—but Rivera had already disappeared below with the two children, leaving their Ahab at the helm and Finn hanging on to his ladder.

Their cutter was outfitted with a Bushmaster autocannon and two big .50-cal guns, but there was no way Rivera could get one of those weapons in play soon enough. The dockmaster was piloting the boat. Finn was barely hanging on.

They were sitting mallards in a duck hunter's dream.

The Carl Gustaf had an effective fire-reload rate of six shells per minute. Ten seconds apiece. Finn counted off, and sure enough, right at ten seconds—BOOM!—there came the next explosion.

This one landed twenty-five meters to port—a correction shot. The next one would land center mass, and the *Cuttyhunk* would be nothing but a memory.

Finn counted down the seconds. Five.

Four.

Three.

Two—

And then the sun went dark and all hell broke loose.

They had hit the eyewall.

112

The cutter flew straight up in the air, perched on its stern like a tail-walking dolphin, then pitched back into the brine. The next second it was thrown to the port, then rolled to the starboard, the great currents of water and wind tossing it back and forth, a game of Wiffle ball played by a team of demented giants.

In a momentary space between the crash of waves Finn caught a glimpse of Derek the dockmaster at the helm. From what he could see through the rain-soaked darkness, the man had strapped himself securely down to the seat and wasn't going anywhere—at least nowhere the boat didn't drag him.

A saddle bronc rider on the world's roughest roughstock.

Finn briefly spotted the sub, some two hundred meters off, and then it disappeared, and then reappeared again, this time farther off as the cutter sped away from it. In a fleeting lull between waves Finn saw two long crests of water surging away from each side of the sub as the Paltus initiated a frantic dive—

Where La Bestia goes, the waters boil.

And then there was a flash of lighting and clap of

thunder, answered by an enormous roar of wind blasting at 120 miles per hour, maybe more.

It seemed to Finn then that the wind spoke with ten thousand voices—massive groans from the depths of the Muertos Trough, blinding screams from the Sahara carried through three thousand miles of Atlantic sky, howls rising up from centuries of subjugation, wailing generations of indignities and pain—

The voice of Juracán, calling out for retribution—

And as if in answer, the sea stood up.

As Finn watched, still clinging to the boat's ladder, a massive swell surged in from behind the great gray metal whale, shoving it off its course and straight toward the coast of Little Sister Island, slamming it into what almost looked like a rocky outcropping but was in fact a freshly exposed mass of far deadlier materials—

The cache of unexploded ordnance detonated in a colossal explosion, sending up a great plume of fire that tore through the hurricane's eyewall and illuminated the sky for miles around.

Apocalipsis, thought Finn.

The harlot rides the beast into the apocalypse.

113

They brought the children in first, wrapped in blankets, Agent Rivera carrying Pedro and the old dockmaster hoisting Miranda.

The place was intact, its interior lit by the soft glow of multiple Colemans, as if he'd been anticipating their arrival.

Finn brought up the rear, mounting the three little steps to the front porch, feeling each step in every bone. He noted that the mournful little bell was gone, torn away by the wind, no doubt, and transported to some faraway place. Perhaps out to sea.

When he stepped inside the two little ones flew to him, clutching on to him for dear life, Pedro's arms around his ribs, Miranda's around his middle, their faces buried in his side, both of them sobbing their hearts out. Miranda's hug was so fierce he thought it might leave bruise marks on his skin.

He hoped so.

I got them back, he thought. *And now I'm going to lose them again.*

Could you miss someone when they were right there with you?

He felt an ache, not from the bullet wound or the insults to his body of the past hours, but something deeper. It ached and at the same time felt strangely comforting. Like it grounded him. Like it told him who he was.

The two finally pulled away and ran to their grandfather, enveloping him in the same fierce clutch.

Finn watched.

And in that moment, he finally knew what the feeling was, what it was he'd felt in the hospital bed, what he'd felt about the lives he'd failed to save, what the identification of Frank Dugan evoked in him.

Loss.

That was the feeling.

Loss.

His parents hadn't abandoned him in the hospital; they'd abandoned him long before that. He'd never had parents. The distant cabin in the Oregon woods was never home. He'd had Ray. They'd had each other, and that was all the home there ever was.

He thought about Carol's email.

Come home.

And in the next breath—the next painful breath—he identified a second feeling. He'd had it with Ray, and with Kennedy. He had it with Carol. And with these two brave little warriors.

He couldn't put a name to it, not yet, but whatever it was called, it was the opposite of loneliness.

Zacharias stood listening to the two hugging Mimo, watching with the eyes in his heart, with the senses that surpassed explanation, tears running down his old face.

He heard his wife's voice in his ear, as clear as the

little bell at his front door. *Thank you,* she whispered. *Thank you for holding a place for them.*

And then they rushed into his arms, crying and trembling but mostly hugging.

He was grateful to have them back; grateful, but not surprised.

He'd known they would come.

He murmured words of love and reassurance, rubbing their backs with his hands, telling them again and again that they were safe, they were with him, they would always be with him, he would never leave their side. And he thought about the one who'd brought them back and who, in ways he was sure he would never know, risked everything in the process.

When the old man turned to thank him, he was gone.

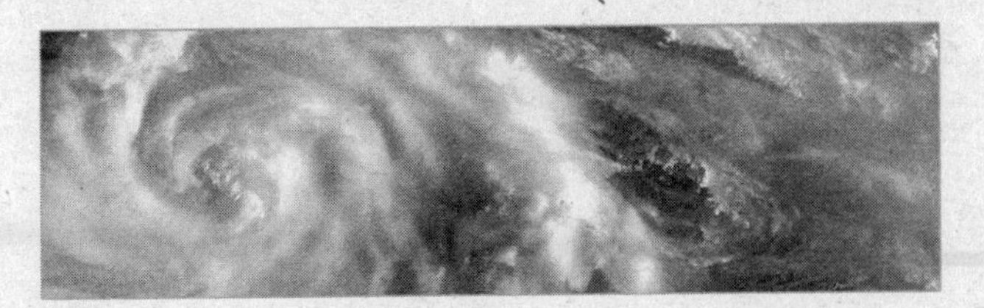

Epilogue

T plus 1

As the eye of the storm passed through Vieques Sound it rapidly lost power. By the time it made landfall at Roosevelt Roads in Ceiba, it had already been downgraded to Category 2, and soon thereafter to Category 1. The winds diminished further as the storm passed over Fajardo and out into the Atlantic, where it dissipated its remaining energy. Within twelve hours the sky had cleared.

The death toll in Puerto Rico, projected only yesterday to climb into the hundreds if not thousands, has barely reached double digits.

If not for the debris and minor flooding left behind, you would never guess that a massive storm had passed this way.

114

Lieutenant Monica Halsey took a long sip of the off-brand Scotch the refreshment cart had on offer. It was a four-hour flight from San Juan to DC, and she fully expected every one of those two-hundred-plus minutes to be some degree of torture.

The SEAL had been right about Dar: They found his body, or what was left of it, inside the ruins of a wooden farmhouse near the end of PR Route 731. Forensic techs on the scene estimated the shooters had expended over six hundred rounds. Then doused the place in accelerant and lit it on fire.

How many of those six-hundred-plus rounds actually hit their intended target was difficult to determine; a forensic analysis two days later would put the number as high as seventy-three. The work of one of Puerto Rico's crime families, they believed, though which one no one could say, any more than they could offer any explanation as to what made a band of cartel soldiers open fire on a visiting FBI agent in the middle of a hurricane.

That much, she would report.

The part she wouldn't report was Dar's unrelenting insistence that they keep local law enforcement completely in the dark about their mission and "contain" it themselves.

Now that she had a sense of his motives.

Though on that score, she had more questions than answers.

She lay back against the airplane seat and closed her eyes, then immediately opened them again. The seats in coach were always too short for her and her neck always got cranked. But that wasn't the real issue. In truth, even exhausted as she was, she just didn't dare drift off.

Didn't want to see what was there, waiting for her in the dark.

Monica was blessed, and cursed.

The blessing was that she was no longer plagued by the photos of the dead children in Mukalla. Somehow the process of pulling those 238 children from their dockside hellholes and, with Lucy Santiago's help, getting them safe, dry, fed, and on the long road to reuniting with their families had changed the footage in her brain.

That photograph of the slaughtered farm children had, blessedly, released its grip on her.

Except that it had been replaced by a new image—not a photo, but a freeze-frame from her own memory.

The look on Finn's face as he stepped out of that cargo container.

The look on his face the moment before she shot him.

"Oh, Lord," she murmured. "What have I done?"

115

Karachi Marriott, Pakistan

Commander Frank Dugan retreated to the hotel room he was using as his temporary base of operations and sat at the desk they'd supplied him with. An aide set down a steaming-hot cup of coffee on a cork-and-pewter US Navy coaster and withdrew to leave him to his business.

Commander Dugan had been here for less than a week, part of an ad hoc diplomatic effort to shore up US-Pakistan relations and put a chill in growing Chinese influence. He would be leaving again in a few days.

That he was here at all was remarkable, some would say a minor miracle. Only a year earlier his career had appeared to be heading for rough waters, when that business in Yemen went so completely off the rails. But in addition to being an outstanding officer, Frank Dugan was a skillful politician. Not as rare a combination as the untutored masses might think, but rare enough.

In just a year he had managed to put substantial daylight between himself and that former business, even among those who actually knew it had happened, whose number could be counted on the fingers of two hands.

Strings were pulled.

Egos were stroked.

And now he was just weeks from being frocked as captain, with admiral on the visible horizon. Leading seamlessly into a life in the real corridors of power.

He added a generous pour of cream—fresh, Pakistan was one of the largest dairy producers in the world, a fact he had only just learned—and took a sip of the hot coffee.

Perfection.

An aide had left the day's stack of mail for his attention. As was his custom, he took the entire stack and turned it over. He'd read somewhere that King George VI used to do this, because members of the government who wanted to bury certain papers from His Majesty's attention would slip those on the bottom. Or maybe he'd seen it on a television show. *The Crown*, probably. No matter. He liked it. The sequence of mail had been established, conspiratorially or not, by someone else, and Frank Dugan liked to set his own priorities.

On the very bottom—now the top—was what appeared to be a birthday card. No postmark. Evidently hand-delivered to his admin staff.

This displeased him. No one here was supposed to know the significance of today's date, and he had instructed his own staff to strictly avoid any sort of celebration, or even acknowledgment.

The commander didn't like to call attention to himself. It wasn't how leaders operated.

He held the envelope in one hand, as if weighing

it. Who would have done this? Not his wife. Not any of his staff. And no one else knew.

Though clearly, someone did.

Dugan felt a frisson of irritation as he slit open the envelope and tipped out the card.

The card was unsigned.

At the top was printed the predictable "Happy Birthday."

Underneath that, four hand-printed words, nothing else.

I'M COMING FOR YOU

Note from the Authors

Every good story starts with the collision of a handful of unrelated ideas.

When we started work on this third Finn book, all we knew was that it would take place in Puerto Rico, beginning in Vieques. One winter day, soon after the writing of *Cold Fear* was completed, Brandon mentioned to John that an advanced scuba dive he had taken with his kids to the bottom of the Atlantic off Puerto Rico had sparked a thought about opening the book with two kids, brother and sister, swimming in the Caribbean, and seeing something they weren't supposed to see.

The hair on the back of John's neck stood up—because just a few weeks prior to that phone call, he and his wife, Ana, had purchased this piece of art for their home, a breathtaking oil-on-wood by Argentinian artist Marco Ortolan:

Talk about synchronicity.

So we had our two swimming children. But who were they? What did they see, and what happened to them? And how were they connected to Finn?

We were also interested in exploring what happened to Finn thirty years earlier, when he was the age of the children in the painting. In *Steel Fear,* we focused on the terrible events that took place in that gun closet in the isolated eastern Oregon cabin. We wanted to follow what happened next, when Finn woke up screaming, strapped to a hospital bed, and the impact those traumatic days and weeks have had on him ever since. In *Blind Fear,* Finn goes looking for two missing children—and for his own missing childhood, too.

One more element rounded out the picture. On a SOFREP.com podcast we told Sean Spoonts, our host, that we were setting the next book in Puerto Rico. "You're going to have a hurricane, right?" he said.

Of course we were. Great idea.

Now we had a story: frame, quest, and ticking clock.

Like any good character, the hurricane in *Blind Fear* draws on inspiration from sources both fictional and non. In 1985 an Atlantic hurricane named Elena completely flummoxed all the forecasters when it suddenly reversed direction in the Gulf, then sat still for nearly forty-eight hours gathering strength, then reversed direction yet *again* and plowed up through Mississippi, Louisiana, and Arkansas, causing havoc everywhere it went—because nobody was prepared for it. Elena triggered what was then the largest peacetime evacuation in US history.

Finn's hurricane does not produce that kind of havoc, but like Elena it clearly has a mind of its own. Hurricane Will almost seems to have sprung up for a specific purpose—much like Prospero's storm in Shakespeare's *The Tempest*—and once it fulfills that singular aim, it dissipates relatively harmlessly.

Blind Fear is, of course, fiction, but like all the Finn books it is set against a real-world background. While we've fudged a bit on a few details (there is no Route 731), the facts of Puerto Rico's geography and history are largely accurate, from the decades of US bombing on Vieques to the prospect of abundant Puerto Rican gold being the prize that first caught European interest. (That lieutenant Graciela talks about who led the subjugation of native residents was Ponce de León.)

The Puerto Rico Trench really is the deepest spot on the Atlantic floor, and the Muertos Trough is real, too, though we invented the nickname "Devil's Ditch." While there is indeed a legend about a Caribbean sea monster, the name "La Bestia" and the details the priest describes to Finn are mostly fictional.

Human trafficking, and specifically the trafficking

of children, is unfortunately all too real; there is even a practice the experts refer to as "child sex tourism," a horrific term that no doubt gave El Rucco dark inspiration. If we could blow up the entire thing with a boat full of explosives, we would; as it is, we can at least do so on paper.

There are a lot of good people doing great work in the face of this gruesome reality. To learn more about what you can do to have an impact, one good place to start might be Thorn.org, the organization created by Ashton Kutcher and Demi Moore.

Turning an eleven-word idea ("A fugitive Navy SEAL risks everything to find two missing kids") into a novel and taking it out to the big wide world is something like taking to sea during a hurricane in a twelve-foot fishing skiff. The only reason we keep making it to the other side is that we have a crew of the generous, the stalwart, and the enormously skilled. Our thanks go out:

To Alyssa Rueben at William Morris Endeavor, captain of the good ship Finn; without Alyssa, this boat would never have left the harbor.

To Anne Speyer, our ace navigator (more prosaically referred to as "editor"), our own Derek the dockmaster; Anne is the one who steers every voyage of the USS *Finn* safely to shore.

To Jennifer Hershey, Kim Hovey, Kara Welsh, Kathleen Quinlan, Sarah C. Breivogel, and the rest of the crew at Bantam, for believing in Finn and his story and helping us tell it.

To Carlos Beltrán for yet another dazzling cover, and to Virginia Norrey for her always steady hand on the tiller of all the Finn books' interior design.

To Michael Baskhar at Canelo and Ivan Mulcahy at Mulcahy Association Literary Agency, for taking Finn's story across the Atlantic.

To insanely talented Johnathan McClain, for his remarkable incarnation of Finn's story through the audiobook series. (If you haven't already seen his electrifying feature-film thriller *The Outfit*, do yourself the favor!)

To Hilary Zaitz Michael and Jack Beloff at William Morris Endeavor, Ben Smith and Adam Docksey at Captivate Entertainment, and Jim Danger Gray, for their tireless efforts to bring Finn's story to the screen.

To David Krueger, MD, George Pratt, PhD, and J. T. Swick, MD, as always, for lending their psychiatric, psychological, and medical expertise in places where we couldn't have done without.

To Jorge Melendez Maysonet, who patiently answered roughly a million Puerto Rico–related questions and gave us the name "El Rucco." And to Carlos Alberto for pinch-hitting on additional questions on Puerto Rico and Vieques.

To Clint Emerson, whose *100 Deadly Skills: The SEAL Operative's Guide to Eluding Pursuers, Evading Capture, and Surviving Any Dangerous Situation* and other writings have helped us bring out Finn's inner MacGyver; Clint was our source for the disposable-camera tasers in *Cold Fear* and a whole lot more in all three Finn books.

To Hunter Webb, for sharing his expertise on things intel- and internet-related and for taking us on a tour of TOR and the "dark web."

To Sean Spoonts, for nudging us to build our story around a hurricane, and for everything he does at SOFREP.com to help take Finn's story out to the world.

To Marco Ortolan for the inspiration, and for permission to reproduce his evocative artwork (albeit in grayscale) here in this afterword.

To Erik Larson for *Isaac's Storm,* his electrifying account of the deadliest natural disaster in US history. There is a vast canon of great writings about storms and hurricanes; *Isaac's Storm* was the one that we leaned on most. If you haven't already read it, go grab a copy; when it comes to turning real-life events into a spine-tingling read, no one does it better than Erik.

To Marina Keegan for the unbearably poignant phrase "the opposite of loneliness," from her collection of writings of the same name (Scribner 2014). The book's title essay, "The Opposite of Loneliness," was Marina's final message to her Yale classmates upon her graduation in 2012. Much like Nico Santiago's sister, Marina was stolen from life far too early, abducted in Marina's case not by maritime criminals but by a tragic car accident, just five days after she graduated (magna cum laude).

To the esteemed Wm. Shakespeare—that other Will—and his final outing, *The Tempest,* for the inspiration.

To Matt Simon, for his illuminating piece on Saharan dust plumes in *Wired* ("Why Massive Saharan Dust Plumes Are Blowing into the US," June 25, 2020).

To Lou Berney, Steve Berry, Lee Child, Robert Crais, Jeffery Deaver, Philippa East, Michael Ledwidge, Jenny Milchman, Dan Pyne, and Brad Thor for your frankly flabbergasting level of support and encouragement; we'd always heard that "crime writers are the nicest people in the world," and whaddya know, it turns out to be entirely true!

To Jeff Popple at *Murder, Mayhem and Long Dogs*, Kashif Hussain and Steve Netter at *The Best Thriller Books*, Ryan Steck at *The Real Book Spy*, and the folks at *Booklist* and *Publishers Weekly* for your articulate generosity in review.

To all the independent bookstores in the land and the people who manage and run them: You are every author's heroes. In particular our thanks to Nat Herrold at Amherst Books (Amherst, MA), Rachael Bourque at Barnes & Noble (Holyoke, MA), Elizabeth Barnhill at Fabled Bookshop (Waco, TX), Carrie Jones at Interabang Books (Dallas, TX), John McDougall at Murder by the Book (Houston, TX), Deborah Goodrich Royce at the Ocean House (Watch Hill, RI), Jeremy Garber at Powell's Books (Beaverton, OR), Olivia Dodds and Julie Gordon at Savoy Bookshop (Westerly, RI), Ryan Lee Gilbert and Otto Penzler at The Mysterious Bookshop (New York, NY), and Julie Slavinsky at Warwick's (La Jolla, CA) for supporting our 2022 *Cold Fear* book tour.

To all the podcasters and interviewers who have talked with us about Finn and his journey and helped us spread the word, and especially to James Altucher (*The James Altucher Show*), Girish Bali (*Back2Basics*), Josh Cary (*The Hidden Entrepreneur*), Doug Crowe (*Author Your Brand*), Jed Diamond, PhD, Phil Gerbyshak (*GerbyCasts*), David Gutierrez and Stu Grazier (*Filling the Storehouse*), Bruce Van Horn (*Life Is a Marathon*), Mike Houtz and Sean Cameron (*The Crew Reviews*), Nick Hutchison (*BookThinkers*), Barney Levantino (*Turn the Page*), Annalisa Summea (*The Writing Gym*), Matthew

Harms and Nico Pengin (*PenPodcast*), Marianne Pestana (*Moments with Marianne*), Kent Sanders (*The Daily Writer*), Paula Shepherd (*The Confidence Sessions*), Laura Steward (*It's All About the Questions*), Chris Story (*On Top of the World Radio*), Ken Walls (*Breakthrough Walls*), and Lisa Wilber (*Monday Morning Madness*).

To the Friends of Finn, those fans and followers who've joined our website at WebbandMann.com—Finn feels the support and thanks you for it!

To our faithful crew of beta readers, Dan Clements, Deb and Charlie Austin, Abbie McClung, and George Easter; couldn't do this without you.

From Brandon: To my incredible kids, Hunter, Olivia, and Grayson, for motivating me to explore fiction and be the best version of myself.

From John: To Ana, my best friend, sweet companion, and first reader of everything I write; without your belief in me I'd never have dared attempt the insanity of writing a novel in the first place, let alone a series of them.

And finally to you, faithful reader, for traveling with us on Finn's journey wherever it leads. It's a daunting world sometimes, teeming with troubles and heartache, but there are good people in it trying their damnedest to do the right thing by others. We think Finn is one of them, and we're grateful you do, too.

About the Authors

Brandon Webb and John David Mann have been writing together for a decade, starting with their 2012 *New York Times* bestselling memoir *The Red Circle*. Their debut novel, *Steel Fear,* was nominated for a Barry Award and named "one of the best books of 2021" by *Publishers Weekly*. To stay informed on the next Finn thriller, join their website:

WebbandMann.com

After leaving home at sixteen, Brandon Webb joined the US Navy to become a Navy SEAL. His first assignment was as a helicopter search-and-rescue (SAR) swimmer and Aviation Warfare Systems Operator with HS-6. In 1997 his SEAL training package was approved; he joined more than two hundred students in BUD/S class 215 and went on to complete the training as one of twenty-three originals.

He served with SEAL Team 3, Naval Special Warfare Group One Training Detachment (sniper cell), and the Naval Special Warfare Center (sniper course) as the Naval Special Warfare West Coast sniper course manager. Over his navy career he completed four deployments to the Middle East and one to Afghanistan, and redeployed to Iraq in 2006–2007 as a contractor in support of the US Intelligence Community. His proudest accomplishment in the military was working as the SEAL sniper course manager, a schoolhouse that has produced some of the best snipers in military history.

An accomplished and proven leader, Brandon was meritoriously promoted to Petty Officer First Class, ranked first in the command, while assigned to Training Detachment sniper cell. Shortly thereafter he was promoted again, to the rank of Chief Petty Officer (E-7). He has received numerous distinguished service awards, including Top Frog at Team 3 (best combat diver), the Presidential Unit Citation (awarded by President George W. Bush), and the Navy and Marine Corps Commendation Medal with "V" device for valor in combat. Webb ended his navy career early to spend more time with his children and focus on business.

As an entrepreneur and creator, Webb founded two brands, SOFREP.com and CrateClub.com, and bootstrapped them to an eight-figure revenue before successfully exiting the Crate Club in 2020. He continues to run SOFREP Media, his military-themed digital media company, and as its CEO has created several hit online TV shows, books, and podcasts, including the series *Inside the Team Room* and the award-winning documentary *Big Mountain Heroes*.

Webb is a multiple *New York Times* bestselling author of nonfiction and is now focused on his new thriller series with his creative writing partner, John David Mann. The first in the series, *Steel Fear,* is a high-seas thriller that follows the US Navy's first serial killer. Brandon pursued his undergrad studies at Embry-Riddle Aeronautical University and Harvard

Business School's two-year OPM program. He is a member of the Young Presidents' Organization and has served as an appointed member on the veterans advisory committee to the US Small Business Administration.

He enjoys spending time with his tight circle of amazing family and friends, traveling the world, and flying his planes upside down or on floats.

brandontylerwebb.com
Facebook: /brandonwebbseal
X: @brandontwebb
Instagram: /brandontwebb

JOHN DAVID MANN has been creating careers since he was a teenager. At age seventeen, he and a few friends started their own high school in New Jersey, called "Changes, Inc." Before turning to business and writing, he forged a successful career as a concert cellist and prizewinning composer. At fifteen he was recipient of the 1969 BMI Awards to Student Composers and several New Jersey state grants for composition; his musical compositions were performed throughout the US, and his musical score for Aeschylus's *Prometheus Bound* (written at age thirteen) was performed at the amphitheater in Epidaurus, Greece, where the play was originally premiered.

John's diverse career has made him a thought leader in several different industries. In 1986 he founded *Solstice*, a journal on health and environmental issues; his series on the climate crisis (yes, he was writing about this back in the eighties) was selected for national reprint in *Utne Reader*. In 1992 John helped write and produce the underground bestseller *The Greatest Networker in the World*, by John Milton Fogg, which became the defining book in its field. During the nineties John built a multimillion-dollar sales/distribution organization of over a hundred thousand people. He was cofounder and senior editor of the legendary *Upline* journal and editor in chief of *Networking Times*.

John is the coauthor of more than thirty books, including four *New York Times* bestsellers and five national bestsellers. His books are published in thirty-eight languages, have sold over three million copies, and have earned the Axiom Business Book Award (Gold Medal), the Nautilus Award, Book-Pal's "Outstanding Works of Literature (OWL)" award, and Taiwan's Golden Book Award for Innovation. His bestselling classic *The Go-Giver* (with Bob Burg) received the Living Now Book Awards "Evergreen Medal" for its "contributions to positive global change." His books have been cited on *Inc.*'s "Most Motivational Books Ever Written," HubSpot's "20 Most Highly Rated Sales Books of All Time," *Entrepreneur*'s "10 Books Every Leader Should Read," *Forbes*'s "8 Books Every Young Leader Should Read," CNBC's "10 Books That Boost Money IQ," NPR's "Great Reads," and the *New York Post*'s "Best Books of the Week." His 2012 *Take the Lead* (with Betsy Myers) was named Best Leadership Book of the Year by Tom Peters and *The Washington Post*.

Over his decade of writing with Brandon, John has logged hundreds of hours of interviews with US military service members, along with their spouses, parents, children, and friends, to gain an intimate understanding of the military life and Special Operations community. In preparation for writing *Steel*

Fear he spent time on the aircraft carrier USS *Abraham Lincoln,* where the novel is set.

John is married to Ana Gabriel Mann and considers himself the luckiest mann in the world.

johndavidmann.com
Facebook: /johndavidmann
X: @johndavidmann
Instagram: /johndavidmann